PENGUIN CLASSICS

HOPE LESLIE

Catharine Maria Sedgwick was one of the leading figures of early American literary culture. Born in Stockbridge, Massachusetts, in 1789, she was the sixth child in a family whose federalist politics and Calvinist sentiments influenced her views and writing, even as she criticized them. Along with her contemporaries, including Washington Irving and James Fenimore Cooper, she helped to create a national literature shaped by those elements unique to the United States—its landscape, history, regional differences, variety of racial and ethnic groups, and democratic social structure—but she did so by focusing on the lives of women and on their foremothers' roles in building the republic. Popular among readers and critics alike, Sedgwick published six novels: *A New England Tale* (1822), *Redwood* (1824), *Hope Leslie* (1827), *Clarence* (1830), *The Linwoods* (1835), and *Married or Single?* (1857), as well as short stories and essays. She died in 1867.

Carolyn L. Karcher is a professor of English, American Studies, and Women's Studies at Temple University. She has edited the works of Lydia Maria Child, including *Hobomok and Other Writings on Indians* and *A Lydia Maria Child Reader*, and is the author of *The First Woman in the Republic: A Cultural Biography of Lydia Maria Child*.

HOPE LESLIE;
or
EARLY TIMES IN THE MASSACHUSETTS

―――――――

CATHARINE MARIA SEDGWICK

EDITED WITH AN
INTRODUCTION AND NOTES BY
CAROLYN L. KARCHER

PENGUIN BOOKS

PENGUIN BOOKS
Published by the Penguin Group
Penguin Putnam Inc., 375 Hudson Street,
New York, New York 10014, U.S.A.
Penguin Books Ltd, 27 Wrights Lane, London W8 5TZ, England
Penguin Books Australia Ltd, Ringwood, Victoria, Australia
Penguin Books Canada Ltd, 10 Alcorn Avenue,
Toronto, Ontario, Canada M4V 3B2
Penguin Books (N.Z.) Ltd, 182–190 Wairau Road,
Auckland 10, New Zealand
Penguin India, 210 Chiranjiv Tower, 43 Nehru Place,
New Delhi 11009, India

Penguin Books Ltd, Registered Offices:
Harmondsworth, Middlesex, England

First published in the United States of America 1827
This edition with an introduction and notes by
Carolyn L. Karcher published in Penguin Books 1998

5   7   9   10   8   6   4

LIBRARY OF CONGRESS CATALOGING IN PUBLICATION DATA
Sedgwick, Catharine Maria, 1789–1867.
Hope Leslie, or, Early times in the Massachusetts / Catharine
Maria Sedgwick; edited with an introduction and notes by
Carolyn L. Karcher.
p.   cm. — (Penguin classics)
ISBN 0 14 04.3676 6
1. Massachusetts—History—Colonial period, ca. 1600–1775—
Fiction.   2. Indians of North America—Massachusetts—Fiction.
3. Women—Massachusetts—Fiction.   I. Karcher, Carolyn L., 1945–
II. Title.   III. Series.
PS2798.H63   1998
813'.2—dc21   98–15385

Printed in the United States of America
Set in Stempel Garamond

ACKNOWLEDGMENTS

The introduction to this edition has benefited incalculably from the incisive criticisms, valuable suggestions, and stimulating insights offered by Andrea Kerr, Carla L. Peterson, Jean Pfaelzer, and Thorell Tsomondo, members of my writers group, and by H. Bruce Franklin, Carolyn Sorisio, and Etsuko Taketani, who also took the time to read and comment on it. For expert research assistance on the annotations, I am indebted to Clare Cotugno, who identified many hitherto unrecognized quotations and references. For a professional translation of a song in old French, I wish to thank William MacBain. To all of them I am deeply grateful.

In addition, I would like to acknowledge the pioneering scholarship of Edward Halsey Foster and especially of Mary Kelley, whose splendid editions of *Hope Leslie* and *The Power of Her Sympathy* have laid the basis for further study of Sedgwick. I have drawn heavily on her annotations to *Hope Leslie* in my own.

Finally, I wish to thank the Massachusetts Historical Society for facilitating my research there and for granting permission to quote from the following letters in the Catharine Maria Sedgwick Papers: Lydia Maria Francis [Child] to CMS, Aug. 28, n.d. [1827, misfiled under 1826], CMS Papers III; CMS to Charles Sedgwick, Feb. 24, 1826, CMS Papers I; Judge Samuel Howe to CMS, July 1, 1827, CMS Papers II; Charles Sismondi to CMS, Nov. 6, 1827 (enclosed in CMS to Henry D. Sedgwick, Dec. 19, 1827, CMS Papers III; CMS to Charles Sismondi, Mar. 15, 1828, CMS Papers I; Basil Hall to CMS, Oct. 2, 1827, CMS Papers II; Louisa Minot to CMS, July 4, 1827, CMS Papers II; Lydia Maria Francis [Child] to CMS, June 5, 1828, CMS Papers III.

This edition of *Hope Leslie* is dedicated to my students at Temple University, the imagined readers I have kept in mind while preparing the introduction and annotations.

CONTENTS

Acknowledgments
v

Introduction by Carolyn L. Karcher
ix

Suggestions for Further Readings
xxxix

A Note on the Text
xlv

HOPE LESLIE; OR EARLY TIMES IN
THE MASSACHUSETTS
xlvi

Explanatory Notes
373

INTRODUCTION

"[H]er fame is destined to be far more durable than that of any other female writer among us. In America, she deserves the rank accorded to Miss [Maria] Edgeworth in England; and an hundred years hence, when other and gifted competitors have crowded into the field, our country will still be as proud of her name." This accolade to Catharine Maria Sedgwick, then at the peak of her literary achievement, appeared in the May 1829 number of the *Ladies' Magazine*, a journal that specialized in promoting the work of American women writers. Introducing an omnibus review of the three novels Sedgwick had published to date—*A New-England Tale* (1822), *Redwood* (1824), and *Hope Leslie* (1827)—the tribute testified to the stature Sedgwick had by then attained. It also reflected the pride she kindled in those of her own sex who hoped to show that the United States, like England, could produce major women writers—and who aspired to follow in Sedgwick's footsteps. As one critic puts it, Sedgwick "provided a role model, an image, and a name for her successors to invoke. . . . [W]ith her example before them, American women could legitimately feel American literature was a field open to them" (Fetterley 44).

A prime case in point: the author of the review, Lydia Maria Child (identifiable through her quotations from Sedgwick's letters to her), had greeted Sedgwick as proof that publishing a novel need no longer disqualify a woman from being "regarded as a *lady*" (*LMC Reader* 403). The recognition Sedgwick had won for *A New-England Tale*—which Child read aloud to her class at the school she was running—apparently helped embolden her to publish her own first novel, *Hobomok, A Tale of Early Times* (1824). Eagerly cultivating Sedgwick's acquaintance, she confessed wishing "to *think*, and *write*, and *be*, like" her idol, and she assured Sedgwick: "I am but one among a large number whose minds you are enlarging, and whose hearts you are purifying" (CMS III, Aug. 21, 1826; Aug. 28, [1827], MHS).

Sedgwick's influence on the domestic novelists of the 1850s, notably Harriet Beecher Stowe and Maria Cummins, extended beyond serving as a role model, legitimating authorship as a career for a "lady," or supplying moral inspiration, as she did for Child. Sedgwick's realistic portrayal of regional manners, speech, and character types and her use of fiction as a vehicle for converting readers to a tolerant and heartfelt Christianity furnished Stowe with prototypes for such works as "A New England Sketch" (1834) and *The Minister's Wooing* (1859). Furthermore, by setting the pattern in *A New-England Tale* of what Nina Baym has called "woman's fiction"—the narrative of a young girl's maturation into adulthood—and by relocating this narrative in the city and expanding it into a critique of urban elites in *Clarence* (1830), Sedgwick anticipated Cummins's popular hit, *The Lamplighter* (1854); indeed Cummins, who attended the school run by Sedgwick's sister-in-law, Elizabeth Dwight Sedgwick, could hardly have avoided learning from her eminent predecessor (Baym 164).

Sedgwick won not only the adulation of her female successors but the respect of her male peers. Hawthorne praised her as "our most truthful novelist" (qtd. in Foster 137). William Cullen Bryant paid homage to her "fertile invention" and "skill in the drawing of characters" (*NAR* 20 [April 1825]:271). Poe acknowledged her as "one of our most celebrated and most meritorious writers." (*Works* 8:142). And Rufus Griswold's landmark anthology, *The Prose Writers of America*, pronounced her "delineations of New England manners . . . decidedly the best that have appeared" (1847:358). Nineteenth-century anthologies continued to feature Sedgwick's works as late as the 1880s, and critics of the day often set her on a par with Irving and Cooper. A Paris newspaper even misattributed *Redwood* (which Sedgwick had published anonymously) to Cooper—a tidbit Sedgwick relished. "It is to be hoped that Mr. C.'s self-complacency will not be wounded by this mortifying news," she quipped (*Life and Letters* 172). Cooper himself favorably reviewed *A New-England Tale* (Foster 50), and he took Sedgwick seriously enough as a rival to counter *Hope Leslie* with a New England-based historical novel of his own, *The Wept of Wish-ton-Wish* (1829).

Despite the honorable place Sedgwick occupies in U.S. literary history, she was not the first American woman to earn fame as a novelist. A generation before, women had produced two of America's earliest bestsellers: Susanna Rowson's *Charlotte Temple* (1791) and Hannah Webster Foster's *The Coquette* (1797). These novels, however, had centered around seduction plots—a genre originating in eighteenth-century England and expressing the middle class's revolt against the domination of a decadent, exploitative aristocracy. Though readers continued to relish stories of a pitiable heroine's pursuit by an evil rake, which Sedgwick would retain as subplots in her novels, by the 1820s American conditions required a new kind of fiction.

The main imperative of Sedgwick's era was to create a national literature that differentiated itself from British and European precedents by capitalizing on what made America unique: its landscape, history, folk heroes, regional idiosyncracies, potpourri of races and ethnic groups, and democratic social structure. Washington Irving and James Fenimore Cooper had begun that process—Irving in "Rip Van Winkle" and "The Legend of Sleepy Hollow" (1819–20), which memorialized the Dutch settlers of New York and caricatured their Yankee rivals, and Cooper in *The Spy* (1821) and *The Pioneers* (1823), which introduced the Yankee peddler and the frontiersman into American fiction. Sedgwick's contribution was to refocus the emergent national literature on the lives, domestic mores, and values of American women, as well as on their foremothers' roles in building the republic—the theme of *Hope Leslie*. In striking contrast to the works of Sedgwick's male contemporaries, *Hope Leslie* presents "early times in the Massachusetts" through the eyes of Puritan and Indian women and awards them the most heroic actions in the novel—actions that modify the course of history and herald the dawn of a more liberal America.

Sedgwick's own family history positioned her exceptionally well to perform the mission of commemorating the New England past. Born in Stockbridge, Massachusetts, on December 28, 1789, the sixth child of Pamela and Theodore Sedgwick, Catharine Maria Sedgwick descended from a long line of Connecticut Valley "River Gods," as the area's leading families were called. Pamela's paternal ancestors, the Dwights, were allied by marriage to Jonathan Edwards, the Connecticut Valley's most illustrious preacher, and Pamela's father, Joseph Dwight, had served as a General in the French and Indian War. Her maternal ancestors, the Williamses, gave their name to Williamstown and Williams College. They had figured conspicuously in the Puritan-Indian hostilities on which *Hope Leslie* pivots. Captured by Indians during King Philip's War, the Reverend John Williams had authored a famous account of his ordeal, *The Redeemed Captive, Returning to Zion* (1707). His daughter, Eunice, on whom Sedgwick based the story of Faith Leslie, had refused to be "redeemed," choosing rather to marry into her captors' people and convert, like them, to Catholicism. Though of humbler origins than the Williamses and Dwights, Theodore Sedgwick's roots likewise stretched back to the founding of colonial Massachusetts, where his great-great-grandfather had arrived in 1635. Theodore himself rose from State Legislator to Speaker of the U.S. House of Representatives and later U.S. Senator, becoming one of the country's most prominent Federalist politicians and presiding over the "Mountain Gods" of his native Berkshires (Foster 25). Catharine Maria Sedgwick ultimately repudiated her Puritan forebears' bigotry, along with her parents' Calvinist religion and Federalist politics, yet her elite heritage continued to shape her view of American society, past and present.

Sedgwick's parents molded her consciousness in other ways besides reinforcing a sense of class privilege. Her mother, whom Sedgwick characterized in her posthumously published autobiography as "essentially modest and humble," bequeathed to her a model of feminine deportment that she would often criticize in her novels, but never entirely reject in life. The path of "submission" that Pamela embraced as her "duty, . . . however hard," drove her into crippling depression, and eventually insanity (*Power of Her Sympathy* 59). Sedgwick's unconventional choices of spinsterhood and authorship saved her from her mother's fate, while her fiction allowed her to explore alternatives to it. Still, "an excessive love of approbation" (*Power* 75) kept Sedgwick submissive to the dictates of social convention.

From her father Sedgwick derived a more positive legacy: "that love of reading which has been to me 'education.' " During the Congressional recesses he spent at home in Stockbridge, she fondly remembered, he "kept me up and at his side till nine o'clock in the evening, to listen to him while he read aloud to the family Hume, or Shakespeare, or Don Quixote, or Hudibras!"—a regime that compensated for the thinness of the curriculum at the female academies she attended (*Power* 74). Sedgwick also took great pride in her father's contribution to ending slavery in Massachusetts, for in 1781, at the request of the slave Elizabeth Freeman, he had successfully challenged the constitutionality of slavery in Berkshire County, leading to the state's abolition of the institution two years later. The grateful Freeman promptly joined his household as a hired servant—and as a surrogate mother to Catharine when Pamela succumbed to insanity. In the long run, however, Theodore Sedgwick subordinated his antislavery principles to his reverence for the Union. For the sake of maintaining harmony between a South committed to slavery and a North moving toward emancipation, he defended the 1793 Fugitive Slave Law, which mandated returning escaped bondspersons to their masters. The same clashing loyalties haunted his daughter, epitomized in her ambivalent tribute to Elizabeth "Mumbet" Freeman as simultaneously a black female Washington and "a remarkable exception to the general character of her race" (*Power* 70). Sedgwick never resolved the conflict between allegiance and resistance to her father's values and to the patriarchal authority he represented, as her characterization of the Puritan fathers in *Hope Leslie* reveals.

Of Sedgwick's family members, her brothers Theodore, Harry, Robert, and Charles played the greatest part in fostering her intellectual development and advancing her literary career. They read her work in manuscript, offered penetrating critiques, bolstered her self-confidence, helped her deal with publishers and booksellers, and sent copies of her novels to kingmakers in the world of letters, at home and abroad. It was Theodore who first suggested to Sedgwick that she turn to account the flair for writing he discerned in her letters by trying her hand at a book, and Harry who persuaded her not only to "give . . . a larger form and scope" to the "tract" she had initially undertaken, but to publish it as a novel—the origin of *A New-England Tale* (*Life and Letters* 150–51). The nurturing, egalitarian relationships Sedgwick enjoyed with her brothers—contrasting markedly with the oppressive marriages of her mother and sisters—stood her in lieu of the romantic love that might have cost her the independence she needed to write. She described her favorite sibling, Robert, as "father, lover as well as brother to me" (quoted in *Power* 27). And to her younger brother, Charles, she wrote: "When I think of the possibility of living in the world without you . . . my soul loses all its courage. . . . your wife . . . [has] been to me a most faithful and affectionate Sister—and your children Charles you know I love as if they were part of my own body and soul" (CMS I, Feb. 24, 1826, MHS). Thus, it is not surprising that Sedgwick models the ideal marriage portended for her protagonists, Hope Leslie and Everell Fletcher, on a brother-sister bond and that she casts Hope as an "affectionate Sister" rather than a rival of the two women who share her love for Everell: the Pequot Magawisca and the Puritan Esther Downing.

Although her brothers provided Sedgwick with vital encouragement, her own psychic needs impelled her to set about writing the "tract" that grew into her first novel. "I wanted some pursuit, and felt spiritless and sad," she explained to her friend Susan Channing. By producing a work that might "lend a helping hand" to other sufferers and promote "some of the humbler and unnoticed virtues," she hoped to infuse her life with meaning (*Life and Letters* 153).

Until shortly before she began writing, Sedgwick had struggled in vain to accept the Calvinist creed preached in her parents' Congregationalist church, where ministers still thundered warnings that a righteous God could send sinners to hell at any moment. Calvinist theology held that all human beings since Adam were born with hearts utterly corrupted by sin; hence, they could do nothing to save themselves except cast themselves on

God's mercy and pray that they would be among the tiny group he had elected to let Christ redeem. Sedgwick found such teachings "unscriptural and very unprofitable, and . . . very demoralizing," as well as "a gross violation of the religion of the Redeemer, and an insult to a large body of Christians entitled to respect and affection" (*Life and Letters* 119). Yet so strong was the hold of Calvinism's "gloomy polemics" in the Connecticut Valley and so painful was the prospect of losing cherished friends who could not acknowledge "any religion beyond the pale of orthodoxy" that it took her many years to break away from the church of her youth (*Life and Letters* 144, 120). Finally in 1821 Sedgwick followed her brothers' example by converting to Unitarianism. Her new faith portrayed God as a benevolent father, not as a wrathful sovereign, and taught believers to cultivate the divinity within them, imitate the model of Jesus, and do good to others. Because it downplayed doctrine, Unitarianism also facilitated tolerance. To Sedgwick her adopted religion promised "liberty" to "captive" souls and liberalization to a bigoted society (*Life and Letters* 144). She entered on her literary career with the aim of diffusing the blessings of Unitarianism, and she interwove her religious beliefs into virtually all her fiction.

Written on the heels of Sedgwick's conversion, *A New-England Tale* clears the path toward a similar conversion for readers who have not yet "escaped from the thraldom of orthodox despotism" (*Life and Letters* 144). The novel presents a blistering exposé of the evils Calvinist theology begets: an obsession with "sound doctrine" at the expense of "benevolent practice"; a mean-spiritedness masked by ostentatious contributions to Tract Societies, Foreign Missions, and programs for evangelizing "the Cherokees, or Osages"; and a ban on "appropriate pleasures" that drives church members into "sins of a much deeper die" (*NET* 13, 23, 47). In the words of a character perverted by his Calvinist upbringing, the dogma that human beings can do "nothing acceptable" to God because they are by nature "totally depraved" actually licenses crime by convincing believers that there is "no difference between doing right and doing wrong" (*NET* 155). Rejecting the sectarianism she deplores among Calvinists, however, Sedgwick refrains from proffering Unitarianism as the answer. Instead, a Methodist and a Quaker—practitioners of religions likewise emphasizing ethical behavior and reliance on a loving God who guides believers toward right action through an inner monitor—articulate the spirit of true religion for the heroine.

A New-England Tale sold rapidly and brought Sedgwick instant celebrity. "I think, dear Kate, that your destiny is now fixed," exulted her brother Harry, adding, "I don't know of any thing which now gives me so much excitement as the certain prospect of your future eminence." At the same time, cautioning her that some readers had complained about the "unfavorable representation of the New England character," he endorsed her publisher's advice that she correct this "mistake" in her next book (*Life and Letters* 152–53). He did not have to repeat the caveat, for as Sedgwick confessed, "I could not endure the idea that I had written myself out of the affections of my own people" (*Life and Letters* 157).

To some extent, Sedgwick's second novel, *Redwood*, does concede to New England sensibilities. Replacing Calvinists, Shakers—a minority sect generally regarded as a laughingstock —now embody the religious dogmatism, hypocrisy, and fanaticism Sedgwick targets. Additionally, the "New England character" indeed appears in a more flattering light, personified by plain, openhanded farmers rather than by tightfisted merchants, and contrasted with the degeneracy of the South's slaveholding aristocracy. Yet far more complex and ambitious than *A New-England Tale, Redwood* depicts a cross-section of American classes and regional cultures. While seeking to cement national unity, it also upholds the democratic values best suited to a republic. The novel's denouement invites a political interpretation, as northern and southern branches of the Redwood family reconcile and the principled New England heroine inherits the family fortune, wins over her southern sister by her forbearance, and gives her sister's child a New England education. Sedgwick leaves no doubt that this projected solution to the conflict between North and South includes abolishing slavery, for she intervenes in the penultimate chapter to applaud the escape of a slave to Massachusetts, where "the white inhabitants would be very backward to enforce her master's rights" (2:271).

Redwood anticipates Sedgwick's third and best novel, *Hope Leslie*, not only in its broad political scope and panoply of cultural types but in its narrative method. Here Sedgwick experiments for the first time with the technique she would exploit so successfully in *Hope Leslie*—permitting her characters to speak for themselves and to share in narrating the story through interpolated letters. In subject matter, however, only one episode in *Redwood* gives any hint that Sedgwick would next turn her attention to pondering the fate of the Indian—the question that dominates *Hope Leslie*. That episode—a minor character's abduction by a seducer who hands her over to a drunken Indian savage—reinforces the very stereotypes Sedgwick would seek to counteract in *Hope Leslie*.

Set in the aftermath of the Pequot War, *Hope Leslie* interrogates Puritan historians' accounts of how and why the outbreak occurred, allowing her Pequot protagonists to present their own version of the facts. Through the relationships that develop between its Puritan and Indian characters, the novel also considers whether history might not have taken a less tragic course, and by implication, whether the two races can resolve their differences in the future.

What led Sedgwick to take up an issue she had hitherto ignored and to challenge the popular view of the Indian to which she had previously subscribed? One factor, surely, was the consensus among literary critics, reiterated in almost every number of the prestigious *North American Review*, that the history of Indian-white relations constituted a peculiarly appropriate field for American writers to explore in their quest for the elements of an indigenous national literature. The *North American*'s otherwise eulogistic review of *Redwood*, for example, written by William Cullen Bryant, had reproached Sedgwick with having "passed by" the most "obvious" subject for an American novel: "She has not gone back to the infancy of our country, to set before us the fearless and hardy men, who made the first lodgment in its vast forests . . . and the savage tribes by whom they were surrounded, to whose kindness they owed so much, and from whose enmity they suffered so severely" (*NAR* 20 [April 1825]:245–46; Welsh 25). As she had shown in her earlier response to her publisher's advice, Sedgwick was too canny to disregard such promptings.

The proliferation of frontier romances about Indians inspired by the arbiters of literary fashion would have provided further reason for Sedgwick to redirect herself toward this topic. James Fenimore Cooper's *The Pioneers*, Eliza Lanesford Cushing's *Saratoga*, Harriet Vaughan Cheney's *A Peep at the Pilgrims*, and Lydia Maria Child's *Hobomok* all appeared in 1823–24, as Sedgwick was preparing *Redwood* for the market, with Cooper's *The Last of the Mohicans* following in 1826. Keenly aware of her literary competitors, Sedgwick referred specifically in *Hope Leslie* to her "sister labourer" Cheney's account of two English women captives befriended by the wife of the Pequot chief, Mononotto, and to Cooper's descriptions in "a recent popular work" of the Indians' "sagacity in traversing their native forests" (*HL* 59, 84). Her acquaintance with Child would also have given her a special interest in *Hobomok*, which had scandalized reviewers by depicting a Puritan woman's marriage with an Indian. *Hobomok* may well have suggested to Sedgwick the idea of retelling the story of her ancestor Eunice Williams's Indian marriage—a story she had transcribed in her journal after meeting Eunice's descendant on a trip to Canada in 1821 (*Life and Letters* 129–30). The publication the same year as *Hobomok* of *A Narrative of the Life of Mrs. Mary Jemison* (1824), an as-told-to autobiographical account of a white captive who, like Eunice, had embraced native ways and remained loyal to her Indian husband, could have furnished an added inducement to tackle the theme of interracial marriage (Kolodny 81).

The vogue of Indian fiction itself reflected still another factor that must have influenced Sedgwick: the impending controversy over what policy to adopt toward the remaining Indian nations east of the Mississippi. After a 1791 treaty, the U.S. government had undertaken a program to "civilize" the Indians with the aid of Christian missionaries, and thus save them from extinction. Meanwhile, land-hungry settlers pressured the government to purchase—or simply seize—the vast tracts owned by the Cherokees and other southern nations and to "remove" their native inhabitants further west, across the Mississippi. As debates raged over whether Indians could be "civilized" and granted a place in the expanding United States, or were doomed to "vanish" before the advance of the white man, politicians inched toward the verdict that culminated in the Indian Removal Act of 1830 and the brutal expatriation of 1838–39 that the Cherokees called the "Trail of Tears."

Although writing before the Indian Removal controversy came to a head, frontier romancers of the 1820s realized that they were participating in a dialogue about the nation's destiny. As a medium for drawing lessons from the past, imagining the future, and forging a nationalist consciousness, they resorted to the historical novel, a genre created by Sir Walter Scott. Scott's novels typically honored the heroic struggles waged by the vanquished peoples of the British isles against their conquerors—highland Scots against lowland Scots, Scots against Britons, Anglo-Saxons against Normans—yet celebrated the fusion of these warring groups into a single nation, Great Britain. American frontier romancers adapted Scott's model to their own history and nationalist agenda. By restaging such events as the Pequot War and the French and Indian War and by letting their fictional characters test possibilities that might have arisen had history made them available, these novelists raised vital questions about the ongoing westward drive and its consequences for Indians: Was conflict between whites and Indians inevitable? Should America be a white man's country or a multiracial society? Could Indians be integrated into the nation through intermarriage, cultural assimilation, or political accommodation? Would they want to be, even if whites could accept them on those terms? If not, how else might the "Indian problem" be solved?

The "Indian problem," however central to this dialogue about the nation's destiny, was not its exclusive focus, either in the frontier romance or in other cultural forums. Of equally pressing concern to many was the transformation in women's roles that had been occurring since the American Revolution. Having supported the Revolution in crucial ways, women had begun asserting new claims as citizens and insisting "On the Equality of the Sexes" (the title of a 1790 essay by Judith Sargent Murray). In response, ideologues of the Revolution had awarded women the post of Republican Mothers, charged with teaching their sons to be virtuous citizens—a responsibility that carried with it a rationale for educating women.

As increasing numbers of women gained access to literacy and took up the pen, fiction became a vehicle for debating women's proper place in both the family and the republic. Should women cultivate helpless dependency and subordinate themselves meekly to patriarchal authority (as Cooper urges in *The Last of the Mohicans*)? Should they try to influence wrongheaded or politically misguided fathers, but obey them in the interim (as Cheney and Cushing intimate in *A Peep at the Pilgrims* and *Saratoga*?) Would granting women a voice in civic affairs result in "petticoat government" (as Irving warns in "Rip Van Winkle")? Would society benefit from a marriage of the woman's and Indian's causes that defies male tyranny and violates the ban against interracial unions (as Child suggests in *Hobomok*)?

In *Hope Leslie* Sedgwick offers her answers to such questions about whose bodies and voices should be included in the nation and empowered to determine its future. In the process, she comments on the scenarios of race and gender relations that earlier novelists had conjured up, articulates her vision of the model American republic, and devises a literary form consonant with her political ideals.

Unlike Cooper's *The Last of the Mohicans* and Cheney's *A Peep at the Pilgrims*, *Hope Leslie* refuses to dwell on Indian violence or to accept warfare as the unavoidable outcome of white colonists' encounters with Indians. Her depiction of the massacre that decimates the Fletcher family, for example, is remarkable at once for its restraint—Mrs. Fletcher faints before feeling the knife of her assailant and never sees the murder of her baby—and for its portrayal of an Indian warrior as "melted" by the "piteous supplication" of an infant (67). By contrast, Cooper's depiction of the massacre at Fort William Henry represents Indians as casting the "quivering remains" of an infant at its mother's feet, driving a tomahawk into her brain, and then "hellishly" drinking the blood of their enemies (*Mohicans* chap. 17).

Instead of accentuating Indian savagery, Sedgwick's narrative strategy works to foster recognition of the two peoples' common humanity—the prerequisite to preventing racial strife. Throughout the novel, parallels between Indian and white characters invite readers to view the two races in the same light. Accordingly, the old Indian medicine woman Nelema, the Pequot chief Mononotto, and the Puritan William Fletcher all lose their families in wanton massacres, and the Pequot mother Monoco and the Puritan mother Martha Fletcher share a protective maternal instinct that alerts each to the threat looming over her home (35, 48–49). In each instance, Sedgwick presents the tragedies through the eyes of their principal victims, women and children.

Sedgwick similarly prods readers to compare the "conflicting duties" that rend her twinned heroines, Magawisca and Hope Leslie, as they struggle to decide between loyalty to their respective families and peoples and to their friends on the opposite side of the racial divide (57, 214). In both cases, Sedgwick implicitly asks whether duty to the family of humanity ought not to take precedence over duty to one's "blood" kin.

Though she treats her Indian and Puritan male characters less sympathetically, Sedgwick once again suggests that analogous motives govern them. Thus, the Pequot chief Mononotto and the Puritan leader John Winthrop alike believe themselves required to sacrifice innocent victims in the name of religious principles and to suppress the humanitarian feelings that revolt against such cruelty. In her authorial comments on the two scenes, Sedgwick underscores the parallels between the Indian and Puritan onlookers' responses to situations that set their religious creeds against their innate human sympathies:

> There might have been among the [Indian] spectators, some . . . whose hearts moved them to interpose to save the selected victim; but they were restrained by their interpretation of natural justice, as controlling to them as our artifical codes of laws to us. (95)

[I]n the breasts of a great majority of the [Puritan] audience, a strange contrariety of opinion and feelings [persisted]. Their reason, guided by the best lights they possessed, deciding against [Magawisca]—the voice of nature crying out for her. (307)

Not until all learn to obey their hearts rather than their "artificial codes," Sedgwick implies, will such crimes against humanity cease.

Besides teaching her readers to regard Indians as fellow human beings, Sedgwick considers a wide range of solutions to the "Indian problem." Exemplifying the first solution—peaceful coexistence and mutually beneficial exchanges of goods and services—is the relationship Nelema establishes with Martha Fletcher, whom she is "in the habit of supplying . . . with wild berries and herbs," in return for blankets and occasional meals (36–38). Nelema's knowledge of herbal medicine—historically a field in which Indians outstripped Europeans—proves particularly helpful. When Hope Leslie's tutor, Cradock, is bitten by a snake, Hope turns to Nelema for an antidote to the venom. The result demonstrates, however, that Puritans cannot tolerate any contact with a race labeled as satanic—any reciprocity that might expose Christians to "heathen" practices. Spying on Nelema's shamanistic healing ritual, the Puritan servant woman, Jennet, becomes convinced that she is a witch, and the Puritan authorities therefore arrest and sentence Nelema to death. Hope succeeds in saving her by helping her to escape from prison, but Nelema's death from exhaustion soon after reaching Indian territory indicates the futility of that gesture. Puritan hostility, this episode suggests, makes cross-racial exchanges too hazardous, desirable though they might be.

Less desirable to Sedgwick is the second solution she considers to the "Indian problem": the path of interracial marriage chosen by Hope's sister, Faith. True, Sedgwick deserves credit for exploring an alternative most other novelists had shunned— and for depicting her interracial couple's relationship more fully than had her predecessor, Child. Yet she can hardly be said to uphold Faith and Oneco as a model to emulate. On the contrary, she portrays both as infantile and weak. Faith is a "wayward" and "spoiled child," whose name, seemingly out of keeping with "that most potent of the christian graces," betokens her mindless embrace of Catholicism (29, 34). Oneco, unlike his dead warrior brother and heroic sister, is "gay and volatile, giving scarcely one thought to the past, and not one care to the future" (34). Their attraction to each other, fated from the beginning, seems to betoken something unnatural in their characters. Reinforcing that unnatural bent, Faith's sojourn among Indians leaves her looking almost mentally retarded: "pale and spiritless," her face is "only redeemed from absolute vacancy by an expression of gentleness and modesty" (237). This description of Faith links her to another character who "stare[s] vacantly about, as if her reason were annihilated" and who describes herself as having "lost my way" (174, 304): the fallen woman, Rosa, likewise a Catholic. Seduced by the hypocritical knight, Sir Philip Gardiner, Rosa has accompanied him to Massachusetts disguised as his page, "Roslin." The similarities between Rosa and Faith suggest that Faith, too, despite her expression of "modesty," is in some sense a fallen woman and that she, too, is wearing a disguise (her Indian costume) that marks her as transgressive. As if these insinuations did not sufficiently undercut the marriage of Faith and Oneco, Sedgwick departs from her historical source, the story of Eunice Williams (and from her fictional precedent, *Hobomok*) in portraying the couple as childless. The possibility that Faith and Oneco incarnate, she intimates, is barren for America's future.

In the novel's first seven chapters, Sedgwick seems to point toward a more promising example of interracial marriage—that of Magawisca and Everell, who embody the best traits of their respective peoples. Their relationship heralds the cultural enrichment both whites and Indians might derive from intermingling —Everell teaching Magawisca to read and acquainting her with the epic literature of Europe, and she in turn "describing to him the customs of her people, and relating their traditionary tales" (32). Nevertheless, Sedgwick's plot violently blocks such an outcome. Before the Fletchers can nip the two teenagers' romance in the bud by sending Everell back to England (as Martha Fletcher urges), Mononotto disrupts it by killing off Everell's family and preparing to sacrifice the boy. Ultimately it is Magawisca's rescue of Everell that most decisively bars her from marrying him.

The famous scene in which Magawisca shields Everell with her body against her father's tomahawk unmistakably evokes the legend of Pocahontas and John Smith, as nineteenth-century readers recognized and as Sedgwick herself hints in her preface (*NAR* 68 [Jan. 1849]:205; *Life and Letters* 187; *HL* 4). Yet it just as unmistakably revises that legend. Pocahontas had survived her exploit physically unscathed and had gone on to convert to Christianity, rename herself Rebecca, and marry another Virginia settler, John Rolfe. Soon after the birth of their child, she had died during a visit to England, a victim of exposure to an alien disease environment. Unlike Pocahontas, Magawisca undergoes a shocking mutilation when "the stroke aimed at Everell's neck" severs her arm (96). What is the meaning of Sedgwick's dramatic departure from her source? Does it underscore the price the Indian woman pays for assuming the role of Pocahontas? Does it reinterpret Pocahontas's fate as a cultural mutilation, thereby honoring Magawisca's refusal to convert to Christianity or turn her back on her people?

Whatever else Sedgwick's revision of the Pocahontas saga signifies, it functions to exclude intermarriage as a mode of reconciling the races. By disfiguring Magawisca, her sacrificial gesture defeminizes and removes her as a potential sexual partner. Significantly, when Everell throws his arms around her bleeding torso, he "presse[s] her to his heart, as he would a *sister* that had redeemed his life with her own" (97; italics added). Having effectively aborted the romance of her second interracial couple, Sedgwick spells out her reasons for opposing such unions. "I might have loved [Magawisca]—might have forgotten that *nature had put barriers between us*," Everell later admits (222; italics added). Arrogating to herself the role of "nature," Sedgwick literally alters Magawisca's body to make the "barriers" against interracial marriage impassable. She then redirects Everell's romantic inclinations toward an appropriate sexual partner, Magawisca's white double, Hope. "[T]hings would *nat-

urally have taken another course after Miss Hope came among us. . . . Now all is as it should be," comments the Puritan soldier Digby (222; italics added). With this twist, Sedgwick exchanges the Pocahontas legend for another literary model, Sir Walter Scott's *Ivanhoe,* whose title character represses his attraction to the Jewish Rebecca and marries his fellow Saxon, Rowena.

Magawisca's ineligibility as a marriage partner need not be read solely in negative terms, however. It can also be read as liberating her to assume masculine prerogatives that would otherwise be closed to her. If the dismemberment she undergoes makes her less than a woman, it simultaneously makes her more than a woman. Hence the phallic overtones of the "lopped quivering member" severed from her body (97). By interposing herself between Everell and her father, Magawisca has received the symbolic castration intended for Everell. At the same time, she has divested her father of his masculine power. The heroic act that elevates her to the status of a "superior being" in her people's eyes "disorder[s]" her father's "reason" (97, 201). From this point on, he must speak through Magawisca, who serves as "priestess of the oracle" (201).

Indeed, Magawisca not only speaks for her father, but she publicly speaks out against white injustice, confronting the Puritan magistrates at their own tribunal. It would be Magawisca's bold exercise of the right to speak in a public forum—not her tragic displacement as a marriage partner—that would most catch the imaginations of Sedgwick's female readers; for the decade after the publication of *Hope Leslie* saw the emergence of the first women to address "promiscuous" (sexually mixed) audiences: the Scottish feminist Frances Wright (1828–29), the African American abolitionist Maria W. Stewart (1832–33), and the white abolitionists Sarah and Angelina Grimké (1837–38) and Abby Kelley Foster (1838–87). Working together in a movement to end slavery and racism, some of these women, like Magawisca and Hope, discovered the potential of cross-racial friendships.

Cross-racial friendship is the solution to the "Indian problem" that Sedgwick develops with most conviction, among the various possibilities she explores. It replaces romantic love be-

tween Magawisca and Everell, and it unfolds into a sisterhood
with Hope that transcends the biological sisterhood of Hope and
Faith.

Sedgwick's treatment of Indian-white friendship inevitably
invites comparison with Cooper's in *The Last of the Mohicans*.
Unlike the male bond between the white frontiersman, Hawkeye, and his Mohican comrades, Chingachgook and Uncas, the
brotherly-sisterly friendship that links Magawisca to Everell and
Hope does not isolate either party; both remain connected to
their families and communities. Although Magawisca's Pequot
nation, like the Mohican nation of Chingachgook and Uncas,
has been wiped out, the surviving remnant have taken refuge
with the Mohawks—the "Maquas" or "Mingoes" against whom
Chingachgook, Uncas, and Hawkeye do battle. Rather than ally
herself with whites against hostile Indian nations, as do Chingachgook and Uncas, Magawisca expresses her friendship for
Hope primarily by enabling her to renew contact with her sister.
Hope and Everell, on the other hand, express their friendship
for Magawisca by rescuing her not from enemy Indians, as
Hawkeye does Uncas, but from their own civil authorities, who
perpetually betray Indian benefactors. This pattern of betrayal
reverses the structure of Cooper's plot, revealing whites, not Indians, to be treacherous foes ready to turn against their unsus-
pecting victims at any moment. Just as the Puritans arrest
Nelema for witchcraft when she cures Hope's tutor of a snake-
bite, so they capture Magawisca at the rendezvous she arranges
between Hope and Faith. It is precisely because Magawisca
needs Hope and Everell to rescue her that friendship between
them proves doomed.

Whether intentionally or inadvertently, these episodes also
hint at a more somber verdict. "Friendly" whites like Hope and
Everell, they intimate, threaten Indian survival as much as do
outright persecutors, and perhaps even more so, because they
naively counsel trust in white good faith. In this sense, Magawisca's suspicion that Hope has served as a "decoy bird" (243)
to ensnare her may not be unwarranted. Hope after all, has not
only urged Magawisca to "come openly among us" but has offered to procure a guarantee of safety from Governor Winthrop.

"No one ever feared to trust his word," she claims (196)—an assertion ironically belied by Winthrop's words justifying his violation of his promise to Magawisca's mother to treat her children kindly. How little Magawisca can rely on the white man's "word"—or on the advocacy of white friends—becomes patent at her trial. Neither the prayer for mercy offered by the revered missionary John Eliot, nor the protests against ingratitude and injustice earlier voiced by Everell and his father sway the Puritan magistrates. Even when Magawisca succeeds in unmasking the main witness against her, Sir Philip Gardiner, as a liar, rake, and papist, all she gains is a month's adjournment of the trial, during which she must remain in prison. Hope and Everell draw the obvious inference: that to count on the white man's law as an instrument of justice to the Indian is to sign the Indian's death warrant—that extralegal action alone can rescue the Indian from white captivity. Thus, they help Magawisca escape from prison. Still, they cling to the illusions that indeed make the Indian's white friends "decoy bird[s]." "[T]he present difference of the English with the Indians, is but a vapour that has, even now, nearly passed away," Everell assures Magawisca, advising her not to flee forever "from those who are not yet prepared to do you justice." Soon, he insists, "I will answer for it—every heart and every voice will unite to recall you" (346).

Magawisca's rejection of this plea—eminently realistic in view of her past experience—amounts to an acknowledgment that friendship has turned out to be no more viable than the other alternatives to Indian-white conflict Sedgwick has entertained, despite the emotional intensity the novel has invested in it. The reasons Magawisca gives for refusing, however, and the solution she elects instead demand careful analysis:

> "It cannot be—it cannot be," replied Magawisca, the persuasions of those she loved, not, for a moment, overcoming her deep invincible sense of the wrongs her injured race had sustained. "My people have been spoiled—we cannot take as a gift that which is our own—the law of vengeance is written on our hearts—you say you have a written rule of forgiveness—it may be better—if ye would be guided by it—it is not for us—the Indian and the

white man can no more mingle, and become one, than day and night." (346)

What does Sedgwick mean by an "*invincible* sense" of past wrongs? Does she imply that even if whites were to cease violating Indian rights and to offer reparations, Indians would never be able to forgive former injuries? If so, is Indian implacability due to the unforgivable nature of white crimes or to the "law of vengeance . . . written on [Indian] hearts"? While passionately decrying the failure of Christians to be Christian, is Sedgwick also subtly reaffirming the superiority of the Christian "rule of forgiveness" to the (alleged) Indian "law of vengeance"? Is she invoking the Biblical precept: "Vengeance is mine; I will repay, saith the Lord" (Rom. 12. 19)? And what are we to make of the metaphor supporting the claim that "the Indian and the white man can no more mingle, and become one, than day and night"? Does it suggest that racial differences and antipathies are rooted in nature? Finally, when Sedgwick advocates racial separatism through Magawisca's mouth, is she speaking as a representative of the colonized or of the colonizer? Does the meaning of the doctrine change accordingly? Regardless of how we may answer these questions, we need to consider the significance of Magawisca's decision to opt for the very solution that the Indian Removal Act of 1830 would shortly ratify.

Ultimately, *Hope Leslie* seems to arrive at an impasse, having tested and found wanting three modes of accommodation between Indians and whites: peaceful coexistence, interracial marriage, and friendship. Nevertheless, Sedgwick refuses to concede that race war and Indian genocide are inevitable, as Cooper's *The Last of the Mohicans* would have it. What, then, remains? Does Sedgwick conclude that only by voluntarily emigrating beyond the bounds of white civilization can Indians save themselves from extinction? Some readers will find it difficult not to interpret the ending of *Hope Leslie* as regretfully endorsing the Indian removal policy that triumphed in the 1830s. Others, moved by the power of Magawisca's language and the depth of Sedgwick's sympathy for an "injured race," will prefer to read *Hope Leslie* rather as an indictment of white bad faith and perhaps, by extension, as a call for change. The novel allows room for both responses.

So far, we have been concentrating on the nineteenth-century context of *Hope Leslie*. Like most historical novels, however, *Hope Leslie* approaches the present by way of the past. Thus, we must attend to the ways Sedgwick rewrites Puritan history before we can fully understand how she intervenes in the politics of her own era. Yet shifting the focus from Sedgwick's dialogue with her fellow frontier romancers to her dialogue with her Puritan forefathers does not resolve *Hope Leslie*'s ambiguities, as Dana Nelson has shown.

On the one hand, the novel's narrative strategy undermines the authority of Puritan historians by allowing Indians to give their own accounts of their bloody confrontations with the English. First Nelema and then Magawisca describe the massacres of their families before readers are permitted to see the massacre of the Fletcher family, thus reenforcing Magawisca's caveat: "when the hour of vengeance comes, if it should come, remember it was provoked" (48). Meanwhile, although the Puritan soldier Digby, who characterizes the Pequots as treacherous and cunning savages, appeals to his superior authority—"Was not I in the Pequod War? I ought to know, I think" (44)—readers never hear his narrative of the war. By the time Sedgwick quotes the famous seventeenth-century chronicles of William Bradford and William Hubbard—after Magawisca has finished sharing her memories of the Pequot War with Everell—readers, like Everell, have concluded that the "enemies and conquerors of the Pequods" have "distorted" the historical record (55–56).

On the other hand, Sedgwick's authorial voice intrudes at key moments to validate the myth of an "exiled and suffering people" who braved attacks by "ruthless, vengeful savage[s]" for the sake of planting "religious and civil liberty, and equal rights" in the wilderness (75). That voice also reiterates one of the colonists' prime justifications for occupying Indian land—the allegation that the Indians did not practice agriculture and that European farmers consequently made better economic use of the land (86). True, Sedgwick explicitly condemns both the genocidal wars through which the Puritans won control of the land

and the bigotry they displayed toward the native peoples they vilified as "surly dogs" (3, 56). All the same, *Hope Leslie* deflects its censure of the Puritans onto a safe target: the old servant woman, Jennet, whose class, gender, and fictional status triply distance her from the true perpetrators of Puritan violence—the leaders. It is Jennet who calls Indians Tawneys, emissaries of Satan, witches, and vipers (24, 69, 109–111), Jennet who engineers the arrest of Nelema and attempts to thwart the rescue of Magawisca, Jennet who remains impervious throughout to any arguments in the Indians' favor, Jennet whom the novel consigns to a fitting punishment for her blind obduracy: to be blown up in an explosion with her head and face inextricably muffled in a shawl.

By contrast, Governor Winthrop appears almost benevolent. Even when he denies Magawisca's plea for "death or liberty," he shows that "his heart was touched with the general emotion, and [that] he was fain to turn away to hide tears more becoming to the man, than the magistrate" (306). He also manifests his "dispositions to clemency" in the mild sentences he metes out to Hope and Everell for liberating Magawisca from prison (360). Pointing toward the transformation of seventeenth-century Puritanism into nineteenth-century Unitarianism, Winthrop's gradual mellowing is "beautifully illustrated by one of the last circumstances of his life," when he refuses to "sign an order of banishment of an heterodox person, . . . saying,—'*I have done too much of that work already*'" (360). In short, while condemning the Puritans' systematic demonization of Indians, Sedgwick salvages them as founding fathers of a utopian society.

What Sedgwick seeks to articulate in *Hope Leslie* is above all her own utopian vision—a vision that includes, but extends beyond, a satisfactory resolution of the "Indian problem." As might be expected from her conflicted assessment of her Puritan forebears, the ideal America projected in *Hope Leslie* reveals traces of their intolerance. Puritan society's outcasts find no place in this brave new world. Not only do Magawisca, Mononotto, Oneco, and Faith opt for exile, but Sir Philip Gardiner and Rosa are blown up along with Jennet on the ship that is supposed to carry them back to England. Indians, Catholics, and fallen women, apparently, do not belong in a regenerated nation. Indeed Sedgwick brands religious and sexual deviants as menaces to public safety, for she associates Rosa—who causes the explosion by throwing a lantern into a barrel of gunpowder—with the Catholic conspirator, Guy Fawkes, accused of masterminding the 1605 Gunpowder Plot to blow up the king, his ministers, and both houses of Parliament.

Despite these obvious limitations, Sedgwick's America does promise far greater personal freedom, especially for white women. The character who best embodies the new nation's potential is, of course, Hope, as her name indicates. Her arrival on the scene in Chapter 6, in the wake of Magawisca's departure, immediately signals the role she will play as Magawisca's stand-in. Borne in a litter by two Indians singing the "chorus of a native song," she accompanies them "with the English words,— 'The home!—the home!—the chieftain's home!' " (71). Hope is a feminine version of the "white Indian," a fantasy figure who, like Cooper's frontiersman, Hawkeye, acquires the traits Anglo-Americans most admire in the Indian, yet remains racially "pure." Transplanted in Indian soil, she develops a "love for exploring hill and dale, ravine and precipice" that marks her as "unladylike" by English standards and an "elastic step and ductile grace which belong to all agile animals" (101, 125). Even her proto-Unitarian religious beliefs have "Indian" overtones: "like the bird that spreads his wings and soars above the limits by which each man fences in his own narrow domain, she enjoyed the capacities of her nature, and permitted her mind to expand beyond the contracted boundaries of sectarian faith" (127).

Throughout the novel, as we have seen, Hope represents the liberatory spirit of the future, defying the Puritan patriarchy to obtain freedom, if not justice, for her Indian sisters. She also represents the liberated woman of the future, as Governor Winthrop recognizes when he complains that she lacks "that passiveness, that, next to godliness, is a woman's best virtue" (159). Hence, he advises subjecting her to "the modest authority of a husband" and recommends a husband "old enough to be [her] father" (160). Instead, Hope's marriage with her adopted brother Everell at the end of the novel, which Winthrop has opposed

precisely because it departs from the patriarchal model, heralds
one of nineteenth-century women's major gains—the freedom
to choose their own husbands—and portends an equal partner-
ship of the sexes in guiding the nation's course.

Albeit less overtly, Hope's foil in the second half of the novel,
the "perpendicular" Puritan, Esther Downing (117–118), whom
Winthrop prefers as a bride for Everell, likewise embodies new
possibilities for women in Sedgwick's ideal America. If, unlike
Hope, she maintains that "we owe implicit deference to our elders and superiors" and "ought to be guided by their advice,
and governed by their authority" (187), she nonetheless shows
real courage in adhering to her convictions, whatever the cost:
"[N]o earthly consideration could have tempted her to waver
from the strictest letter of her religious duty, as that duty was
interpreted by her conscience" (289). Accordingly, Esther refuses to collaborate with Everell in helping Magawisca escape
from prison, though she knows she must forfeit his love. Sedgwick in fact gives Esther agency not only in determining her
own fate but in arranging the denouement of the novel, for it is
Esther who reunites Hope with Everell in a letter renouncing
her own ill-judged engagement with him. Like Sedgwick herself
(who would reject her latest suitor shortly after completing *Hope
Leslie*), Esther opts to remain single despite many attractive pro-
posals, thereby proving that "marriage is not *essential* to the
contentment, the dignity, or the happiness of woman" (367).
That choice, too, heralds a new privilege enjoyed by nineteenth-
century women. The novel's concluding sentence underscores
Esther's significance as an alternative role model: "[T]hose who
saw on how wide a sphere her kindness shone, how many were
made better and happier by her disinterested devotion, might
have rejoiced that she did not 'Give to a party what was meant
for mankind'" (367).

In addition to offering white women greater personal freedom
and wider opportunities for self-fulfillment, the utopian America
Sedgwick envisions in *Hope Leslie* grants many more of its citizens a voice in their future and promotes democratic dialogue
among contending parties. Sedgwick translates this ideal into the
novel's very form. From the first to the last chapters, she shares

narrative authority with her characters, allowing them to provide their distinct perspectives on the plot, and sometimes to alter it, as does Esther Downing, through interpolated letters. Even characters marginal to the novel or inimical to its ideals, like the frivolous Episcopalian Bertha Grafton and the villainous Sir Philip Gardiner, participate in narrating the action. Sedgwick extends the privilege of self-representation to the nonliterate Magawisca as well, who appropriately orates rather than writes. Significantly, Magawisca does not simply retell past events in her people's history or protest against present injustice; she *elects* a solution to their conflict with whites (though a solution whites themselves have elected).

Hope Leslie, in sum, *enacts* its vision of American democracy. The most multivocal and technically innovative of nineteenth-century frontier romances, it succeeds better than any other in involving readers in a continuing dialogue about the nation's destiny—a dialogue that addresses still unresolved questions as to the place Native Americans, religious dissenters, sexual transgressors, and women (among others) ought to occupy in a utopian America.

"I hear from all quarters what honestly seems to me very extravagant praise of 'Hope Leslie,' " Sedgwick wrote to her brother Robert shortly after the novel came off the press. "I trust I shall not be elated by it" (*Life and Letters* 187). Elated she certainly should have been, for she had reached the apex of her literary fame. "The most decided favourite of all her novels," *Hope Leslie* "became firmly associated in the public mind with the rising glories of a native literature" and was "familiarly quoted and applauded as a source of national pride," noted the nineteenth-century anthologist, John S. Hart, in *The Female Prose Writers of America* (1855: 18). It would go through nine printings—five in the United States and four in England—the last in 1872, five years after Sedgwick's death.

The reception of *Hope Leslie* by Sedgwick's nineteenth-century readers reflects the tensions so well captured by the novel's dialogic form—tensions between questioning and reenforcing America's dominant creed. Many patriotic spokesmen hailed *Hope Leslie* as the first work to do complete "justice" to the Puritans. In a glowing seven-page letter to Sedgwick, for example, Judge Samuel Howe of Northampton wrote:

> Ignorance enthusiasm & bigotry have been considered as almost the only peculiar characteristics by which they were distinguished while very little credit has been given them for their learning[,] for their ardent & unconquerable love of civil & religious liberty & for the noble liberality & prophetic foresight with which they provided for the religious & moral education of their posterity. As one of their descendants I feel very grateful to you for the manner in which you have illustrated their noble character. (CMS II, July 1, 1827, MHS)

Other "descendants of the pilgrims" paid Sedgwick similar tributes, with which she professed herself "very much gratified" (CMS I, July 6, 1827, MHS; *Life and Letters* 188).

In contrast to Sedgwick's fellow New Englanders, the Swiss historian, Charles Sismondi, focused on the negative side of what *Hope Leslie* revealed about the Puritan character. The novel had "not confirmed" the "predilection for the puritans" that he had hitherto cherished, he told Sedgwick; on the contrary, it had awakened him to the "tyranny" they had exhibited in the application of their "hard" and "pitiless" dogmas (CMS III, Dec. 19, 1827, MHS). Nothing more eloquently bespeaks the authorial ambivalence registered by these contradictory responses to *Hope Leslie* than the haste with which Sedgwick sought to "redeem" the "fault" she had "unintentionally committed in so delineating the pilgrims as to degrade them in [Sismondi's] estimation." Far from wishing to pillory her ancestors, she had "meant to touch their characters with filial reverence," she assured him. "Their bigotry—their superstition & above all their intolerance were . . . the vices of their age. . . . They had a most generous & self-devoting zeal to the cause of liberty, so far as they understood it, but they were still in the thraldom of Judaic superstition" (CMS I, Mar. 15, 1828, MHS; *Life and Letters* 192).

No less conflicted, Sedgwick's portrayal of Indians generated similarly conflicting responses from nineteenth-century reviewers. The *Western Monthly Review* accused Sedgwick, like Cooper, of romanticizing Indians: "From our knowledge of her race, we should have looked in any place for such a character [as Magawisca], rather than in an Indian wigwam," pontificated the reviewer. Driving the point home, he went on to imagine "one of these red men, with his shaggy black hair, high cheek bones, deep set and cunning eye, his dirty blanket around him," opening a novel by Sedgwick or Cooper with greasy hands and greeting the "grand speeches" attributed to noble savages with an incredulous "ugh!" (*WMR* 1 [Sept. 1827]:294–95). The *North American Review*, on the contrary, denied that Magawisca was "too noble, too delicate, too spiritual for an Indian." She might not be a "fair sample of the Indian character," conceded this Eastern organ, but "the best features of her character have had a real existence in savage life" (*NAR* 26 [April 1828]:418).

The same polarities reappear in nineteenth-century reactions to Sedgwick's heroines. The British historian Lucy Aikin found the submissive Martha Fletcher to be the best delineated of the novel's female protagonists (CMS II, Sept. 15, 1827, MHS). At the other extreme, male critics objected vociferously to the immoral Rosa. "[I]t would be more agreeable to every class of your readers—to women as well as to men—to avoid the introduction of persons, or of scenes, or of circumstances which would not bear to be introduced into conversation in good company, without raising a blush—or exciting horror," the English travel writer, Basil Hall, lectured Sedgwick (CMS II, Oct. 2, 1827, MHS). Sedgwick defended her inclusion of Rosa as vehemently as she proclaimed her fealty to her Puritan ancestors. Distinguishing between treatments of illicit sexuality that "excite" and "subdue" the passions, she retorted to Hall: "who but a prude would shun the contemplation of the *penitent* Magdalen!" (CMS I, Nov. 6, 1827, MHS).

The *North American Review* caught a whiff of feminist heresy in the depiction not only of Rosa, who, this journal agreed, "might be left out with advantage," but of Magawisca, Hope, and Esther as well (*NAR* 26 [April 1828]: 418). While hailing Magawisca as a creation of "genius," Hope as "a finely drawn character . . . sparkling with gaiety and wit," and Esther as

"lovely, too, in her way," the *North American* deemed it un-
realistic for the "three ladies . . . to love and admire each other
as much as they do Everell Fletcher." "Is this, or is it not, a
greater improbability than the character of the Indian heroine?"
demanded the reviewer, chiding: "Our authoress . . . appears to
entertain a decided partiality for her own sex" (*NAR* 26 [Apr.
1828]:418, 420).

Sedgwick's most fervent champion among "her own sex,"
Lydia Maria Francis (Child), sought to prove the *North American* wrong. Demonstrating toward Sedgwick the very freedom
from jealousy that the *North American* had considered so im-
plausible in the novel's heroines, Child refused to let her patrons
play her off against Sedgwick. "Miss Francis considers herself as
no rival & has a truly noble mind in all things, & an unadulter-
ated admiration of you," a mutual friend reported (CMS II,
July 4, 1827, MHS). For her part, Child objected that the tempered praise of the *North American* was "not half worthy" of
the novel. "If I were not too young and too ignorant to be
writing about my betters, I should just let the world know what
I [triple underlined] think upon the subject!" she fumed in a
letter to Sedgwick (CMS III, June 5, 1828, MHS). She acted on
that impulse, as we have seen, by publishing a review of "Miss
Sedgwick's Novels" in the *Ladies' Magazine*. Praising Sedgwick's close observation of "all the shadings of human character," she ranked *Hope Leslie* as her finest achievement, with
"more of the glow and vitality of genius" than any of her preceding works. "The celebrated Sismondi said, 'Magawisca is the
noblest conception imagination ever formed'—and his praise
was just," Child asserted (2 [May 1829]:234, 237–38). To Sedgwick she confided that Sismondi had "read 'Hope Leslie' as I
like to have it read" (CMS III, June 5, 1828, MHS). Child's letter
detailing precisely how she "read" *Hope Leslie* has not been
located, but the portion Sedgwick quoted to her brother Robert
indicates that Child recognized Magawisca as an unsurpassed rei-
magining of Pocahontas:

Miss Francis writes me that she had nearly completed a tale,
founded on the fortunes of Captain Smith. 'Alas for my Poca-

hontas!' she says. . . . 'However I give her up with less reluctance than the artist whose labors of fifteen years were destroyed by the French troops in their invasion of Italy, for I love my conqueror'—Is not this beautiful? (*Life and Letters* 187)

Like Sedgwick's women friends, modern feminist readers have responded powerfully to Magawisca and found the sisterly relations of *Hope Leslie*'s three heroines among the more attractive aspects of the novel. Most have identified Sedgwick herself with her title character, who often seems to speak and act for the author. If in fiction Sedgwick aligns herself with the rebellious Hope Leslie, however, in real life she showed a greater affinity with the orthodox Esther Downing. Unlike Child, who went on to campaign against Indian Removal, Sedgwick never translated the sympathy for Indians expressed in her novel into political activism on their behalf. Indeed, except for two stories in annual gift books—"The Catholic Iroquois" (1826) and "Amy Cranstoun" (1836)—and two brief episodes in her children's book, *The Travellers* (1825), she wrote no other fiction about Indians.

Sedgwick's later works no longer strike a balance between radical and conservative tendencies, but follow out the conservative implications of *Hope Leslie*. Her fourth novel, *Clarence* (1830), repeats the maneuver of projecting a critique of American society onto safe targets. Although it exposes the lives of wealthy socialites as frivolous, empty, and corrupt, *Clarence* scapegoats Irish immigrants as easy dupes of political demagogues—the only glimpse it provides of the class whose exploitation generates the fortunes of the rich—and makes the chief villain a pseudo-Spanish grandee.

Compensating for having censured the Puritan fathers in *Hope Leslie*, Sedgwick's fifth novel, *The Linwoods* (1835), presents a celebratory picture of the Revolutionary fathers. Sedgwick does address the contradiction of slavery, yet she proves unable to accord the black characters in *The Linwoods* the same dignity that she does the Indian characters in *Hope Leslie*, let alone to envision a friendship of equals between black and white on the model of Magawisca's friendship with Hope. Politically,

Sedgwick would keep herself as aloof from the abolitionist cause as from the crusade against Indian removal. She persistently rejected efforts by Child and other abolitionists to secure her support. As late as 1860, she refused to attend an antislavery fundraising fair because abolitionists spoke so "intemperately" that she did not want to "appear among them as one of them" (*Life and Letters* 378).

After *The Linwoods*, Sedgwick turned from novels to the kinds of tracts she had originally envisaged when she had set out to write *A New England Tale*. Fulfilling her desire to "do good" and winning her the approbation she had always craved, *Home* (1835), *The Poor Rich Man and the Rich Poor Man* (1836), *Live and Let Live; or, Domestic Service Illustrated* (1837), and *Means and Ends, or Self-Training* (1839) sought to promote better relations between haves and have nots without challenging the class system, and to expand the limits of woman's sphere without challenging the ideology of domesticity. Neither in these works nor in her last novel, *Married or Single?* (1857), did Sedgwick rise again to the heights she had reached in *Hope Leslie*. Nor did she ever again probe her country's history as deeply.

It would be left for other women of Sedgwick's generation to develop the possibilities she had opened up through her heroines. While Sedgwick herself remained an Esther Downing, she nevertheless made the roles of Hope Leslie and Magawisca imaginatively available to women who dared to embrace them. No one testified more eloquently to the influence Sedgwick's masterpiece exerted than Sarah Louisa Forten, an African-American contributor to the abolitionist newspaper, *The Liberator* (Mar. 26, 1831). Denouncing "the pale faces" for "The Abuse of Liberty" in "this boasted land of Philanthropy" and invoking "that Great Spirit, who created all men free and equal— . . . who made the sun to shine on the black man as well as on the white," this militant young activist signed her arraignment of white America "MAGAWISCA."

Carolyn L. Karcher

SUGGESTIONS FOR FURTHER READING

Selected Works by Catharine Maria Sedgwick

A New-England Tale; or, Sketches of New-England Character and Manners. 1822. Edited by Victoria Clements. New York: Oxford University Press, 1995.

Redwood: A Tale. 2 vols. 1824. New York: Garrett Press, 1969.

Hope Leslie; or Early Times in the Massachusetts. 2 vols. 1827. Edited by Mary Kelley. New Brunswick, N.J.: Rutgers University Press, 1987.

"Cacoethes Scribendi." 1830. In *Provisions: A Reader form 19th-Century American Women.* Edited by Judith Fetterley. Bloomington: Indiana University Press, 1985. 49–59.

Clarence: or, A Tale of Our Own Times. 2 vols. Philadelphia: Carey & Lea, 1830.

"Old Maids." 1834. In *Old Maids: Short Stories by Nineteenth-Century U.S. Women Writers.* Edited by Susan Koppelman. Boston: Pandora Press, 1984. 11–26.

The Linwoods; or, "Sixty Years Since" in America. 2 vols. New York: Harper & Brothers, 1835.

Home. Boston: J. Munroe, 1835.

Tales and Sketches. Philadelphia: Carey, Lea, and Blanchard, 1835.

The Poor Rich Man, and the Rich Poor Man. New York: Harper & Brothers, 1836.

Live and Let Live; or, Domestic Service Illustrated. New York: Harper & Brothers, 1837.

Means and Ends, or Self-Training. Boston: Marsh, Capen, Lyon & Webb, 1839.

Letters from Abroad to Kindred at Home. 2 vols. New York: Harper & Brothers, 1841.

Tales and Sketches. Second Series. New York: Harper & Brothers, 1844.

"Fanny McDermot." 1845. *Rediscoveries: American Short Stories by Women, 1832–1916.* Edited by Barbara H. Solomon. New York: Penguin-Mentor, 1994. 113–54.

Married or Single? 2 vols. New York: Harper & Brothers, 1857.

Life and Letters of Catharine M. Sedgwick. Edited by Mary E. Dewey. New York: Harper & Brothers, 1871.

The Power of Her Sympathy: The Autobiography and Journal of Catharine Maria Sedgwick. Edited by Mary Kelley. Boston: Massachusetts Historical Society and Northeastern University Press, 1993.

Catharine Maria Sedgwick Papers I, II, III. Massachusetts Historical Society.

Works Cited in the Introduction

Baym, Nina. *Woman's Fiction: A Guide to Novels by and about Women in America, 1820–1870.* Ithaca: Cornell University Press, 1978.

[Bryant, William Cullen]. Review of *Redwood. North American Review* 20 (April 1825): 245–72.

Child, Lydia Maria. *A Lydia Maria Child Reader.* Edited by Carolyn L. Karcher. Durham, N.C.: Duke University Press, 1997.

[————]. "Miss Sedgwick's Novels. REDWOOD, A NEW-ENGLAND TALE, HOPE LESLIE, &c." *Ladies' Magazine* 2 (May 1829): 234–38.

Fetterley, Judith. *Provisions: A Reader from 19th-Century American Women.* Bloomington: Indiana University Press, 1985.

[Forten, Sarah Louisa] "Magawisca." "The Abuse of Liberty." *Liberator* 26 Mar. 1831: 50.

Foster, Edward Halsey. *Catharine Maria Sedgwick.* New York: Twayne, 1974.

Griswold, Rufus Wilmot. *The Prose Writers of America. With a Survey of the History, Condition, and Prospects of American Literature.* Philadelphia: Carey and Hart, 1847.

Hart, John S. *The Female Prose Writers of America. With Por-*

traits, Biographical Notices, and Specimens of Their Writings. Rev. ed. Philadelphia: E. H. Butler, 1855.

Kolodny, Annette. *The Land Before Her: Fantasy and Experience of the American Frontiers, 1630–1860.* Chapel Hill, N.C.: University of North Carolina Press, 1984.

Nelson, Dana D. *The Word in Black and White: Reading "Race" in American Literature, 1638–1867.* New York: Oxford University Press, 1992.

Poe, Edgar Allan. *The Works of Edgar Allan Poe. Vol. 8: The Literati—Minor Contemporaries, Etc.* Edited by Edmund Clarence Stedman and George Edward Woodberry. 1895. Freeport, N.Y.: Books for Libraries Press, 1971.

Review of *Hope Leslie. North American Review* 26 (April 1828): 403–20.

Review of *Hope Leslie. Western Monthly Review* 1 (Sept. 1827): 289–95.

Review of *Merrymount. North American Review* 68 (Jan. 1849): 203–20.

Welsh, Sister Mary Michael. *Catharine Maria Sedgwick: Her Position in the Literature and Thought of Her Time Up to 1860.* Washington, D.C.: Catholic University, 1937.

Other Sources

Arch, Stephen Carl. "Romancing the Puritans: American Historical Fiction in the 1820s." *ESQ: Journal of the American Renaissance* 39 (2nd/3rd Quarter 1993): 107–32.

Bardes, Barbara, and Suzanne Gossett. *Declarations of Independence: Women and Political Power in Nineteenth-Century American Fiction.* New Brunswick, N.J.: Rutgers University Press, 1990.

Barnett, Louise K. *The Ignoble Savage: American Literary Racism, 1790–1890.* Westport, Conn.: Greenwood Press, 1975.

Bauermeister, Erica R. "*The Lamplighter, The Wide, Wide World,* and *Hope Leslie*: Reconsidering the Recipes for Nineteenth-Century American Women's Novels." *Legacy* 8 (Spring 1991): 17–28.

Baym, Nina. *American Women Writers and the Work of History, 1790–1860.* New Brunswick, N.J.: Rutgers University Press, 1995.

———. *Feminism and American Literary History: Essays.* New Brunswick, N.J.: Rutgers University Press, 1992. 19–35.

Bell, Michael Davitt. *Hawthorne and the Historical Romance of New England.* Princeton: Princeton University Press, 1971.

———. "History and Romance Convention in Catharine Sedgwick's *Hope Leslie.*" *American Quarterly* 22 (Summer 1970): 213–21.

Bradford, William. *Of Plymouth Plantation, 1620–1647.* 1647/1856. Edited by Samuel Eliot Morison. New York: Random-Modern Library, 1952.

Cagidemetrio, Alide. "A Plea for Fictional Histories and Old-Time 'Jewesses.'" In *The Invention of Ethnicity.* Edited by Werner Sollors. New York: Oxford University Press, 1989. 14–43.

Castiglia, Christopher. "In Praise of Extra-vagant Women: *Hope Leslie* and the Captivity Romance." *Legacy* 6 (Fall 1989): 3–16.

Child, Lydia Maria. *HOBOMOK and Other Writings on Indians.* Edited by Carolyn L. Karcher. Rev. ed. New Brunswick, N.J.: Rutgers University Press, 1995.

Cowie, Alexander. *The Rise of the American Novel.* New York: American Book Company, 1948.

Dippie, Brian W. *The Vanishing American: White Attitudes and U.S. Indian Policy.* Middletown, Conn.: Wesleyan University Press, 1982.

Drinnon, Richard. *Facing West: The Metaphysics of Indian-Hating and Empire-Building.* New York: New American Library, 1980.

Garvey, T. Gregory. "Risking Reprisal: Catharine Sedgwick's *Hope Leslie* and the Legitimation of Public Action by Women." *ATQ* 8 (Dec. 1994): 287–98.

Gould, Philip. *Covenant and Republic: Historical Romance and the Politics of Puritanism.* New York: Cambridge University Press, 1996.

Heckewelder, John Gottlieb Ernestus. *An Account of the His-

tory, Manners, and Customs of the Indian Nations, Who Once Inhabited Pennsylvania and the Neighbouring States. 1819. Rev. Ed. Philadelphia: Historical Society of Pennsylvania, 1876.

Hubbard, William. *A Narrative of the Indian Wars in New-England, from the First Planting Thereof in the Year 1607, to the Year 1677: Containing a Relation of the Occasions, Rise and Progress of the War with the Indians, in the Southern, Western, Eastern, and Northern Parts of Said Country.* 1677. Brattleborough, Vt.: William Fessenden, 1814.

Jennings, Francis. *The Invasion of America: Indians, Colonialism, and the Cant of Conquest.* 1975. New York: Norton, 1976.

Kelley, Mary. *Private Woman, Public Stage: Literary Domesticity in Nineteenth-Century America.* New York: Oxford University Press, 1984.

———. "A Woman Alone: Catharine Maria Sedgwick's Spinsterhood in Nineteenth-Century America." *New England Quarterly* 51 (June 1978): 209–25.

Maddox, Lucy. *Removals: Nineteenth-Century American Literature and the Politics of Indian Affairs.* New York: Oxford University Press, 1991.

Mitchell, Domhnall. "Acts of Intercourse: 'Miscegenation' in Three 19th-Century American Novels." *American Studies in Scandinavia* 27 (2, 1995): 126–41.

Pearce, Roy Harvey. *The Savages of America: A Study of the Indian and the Idea of Civilization.* Rev. ed. Baltimore: Johns Hopkins University Press, 1965.

Person, Leland S., Jr. "The American Eve: Miscegenation and a Feminist Frontier Fiction." *American Quarterly* 37 (Winter 1985): 668–85.

Ross, Cheri Louise. "(Re)Writing the Frontier Romance: Catharine Maria Sedgwick's *Hope Leslie*." *College Language Association Journal* 39 (March 1996): 320–40.

Salisbury, Neal. *Manitou and Providence: Indians, Europeans, and the Making of New England, 1500–1643.* New York: Oxford University Press, 1982.

Singley, Carol J. "Catharine Maria Sedgwick's *Hope Leslie*: Radical Frontier Romance." In *The (Other) American Traditions: Ninetenth-Century Women Writers*. Edited by Joyce W. Warren. New Brunswick, N.J.: Rutgers University Press, 1993. 39–53.

Slotkin, Richard. *The Fatal Environment: The Myth of the Frontier in the Age of Industrialization, 1800–1890*. Middletown, Conn.: Wesleyan University Press, 1985.

———. *Regeneration through Violence: The Mythology of the American Frontier, 1600–1860*. Middletown, Conn.: Wesleyan University Press, 1973.

Sullivan, Sherry. "The Literary Debate over 'The Indian' in the Nineteenth Century." *American Indian Culture and Research Journal* 9 (1, 1985): 13–31.

Trumbull, Benjamin. *A Complete History of Connecticut, Civil and Ecclesiastical, from the Emigration of Its First Planters from England, in MDCXXX, to MDCCXIII*. Hartford: Hudson & Goodwin, 1797.

Williams, Roger. *A Key into the Language of America*. 1643. Menston, U.K.: Scolar Press, 1971.

Winthrop, John. *The History of New England from 1630 to 1649*. Edited by James Savage. 2 vols. Boston: Phelps and Farnham, 1825–26.

Zagarell, Sandra A. "Expanding 'America': Lydia Sigourney's *Sketch of Connecticut*, Catharine Sedgwick's *Hope Leslie*." *Tulsa Studies in Women's Literature* 6 (Fall 1987): 225–45.

A NOTE ON THE TEXT

The present text has been reset from the first edition of *Hope Leslie* (White, Gallaher, and White, 1827) and preserves the division of the original into two volumes. Sedgwick's endnotes and footnotes have been incorporated into the annotations at the back of the volume. Nineteenth-century spellings, hyphenations, and punctuation have been retained, except for such typographical features as the use of periods after titles. Misprints have been silently emended.

HOPE LESLIE;

or

EARLY TIMES IN THE MASSACHUSETTS

Here stood the Indian chieftain, rejoicing in his glory!
How deep the shade of sadness that rests upon his story:
For the white man came with power—like brethren they met—
But the Indian fires went out, and the Indian sun has set!

And the chieftain has departed—gone is his hunting ground,
And the twanging of his bow-string is a forgotten sound:—
Where dwelleth yeserday? and where is Echo's cell?
Where has the rainbow vanished?——there does the Indian dwell.

E.

VOLUME I

Preface

The following volumes are not offered to the public as being in any degree an historical narrative, or a relation of real events. Real characters and real events are, however, alluded to; and this course, if not strictly necessary, was found very convenient in the execution of the author's design, which was to illustrate not the history, but the character of the times.

The antiquarian reader will perceive that some liberties have been taken with the received accounts of Sir Philip (or Sir Christopher) Gardiner;[1] and a slight variation has been allowed in the chronology of the Pequod war.[2]

The first settlers of New-England were not illiterate, but learned and industrious men. They seem to have understood the importance of their station. The Massachusetts colony, and some of the other establishments sparsely scattered on the coast, were illuminated spots, clear and bright lights, set on the borders of a dark and turbulent wilderness. Those who have not paid much attention to the history or character of these early settlements, if they choose to turn their attention to this interesting subject, will be surprised to find how clear, copious, and authentic are the accounts which our ancestors left behind them. The only merit claimed by the present writer, is that of a patient investigation of all the materials that could be obtained. A full delineation of these times was not even attempted; but the main solicitude has been, to exclude every thing decidedly inconsistent with them.

The Indians of North America are, perhaps, the only race of men of whom it may be said, that though conquered, they were never enslaved. They could not submit, and live.[3] When made captives, they courted death, and exulted in torture. These traits of their character will be viewed by an impartial observer, in a light very different from that in which they were regarded by our ancestors. In our histories, it was perhaps natural that they should be represented as "surly dogs," who preferred to die

rather than live, from no other motives than a stupid or malignant obstinacy. Their own historians or poets, if they had such,
would as naturally, and with more justice, have extolled their
high-souled courage and patriotism.

The writer is aware that it may be thought that the character
of Magawisca has no prototype among the aborigines of this
country. Without citing Pocohontas, or any other individual, as
authority, it may be sufficient to remark, that in such delineations, we are confined not to the actual, but the possible.

The liberal philanthropist will not be offended by a representation which supposes that the elements of virtue and intellect
are not withheld from any branch of the human family; and the
enlightened and accurate observer of human nature, will admit
that the difference of character among the various races of the
earth, arises mainly from difference of condition.

These volumes are so far from being intended as a substitute
for genuine history, that the ambition of the writer would be
fully gratified if, by this work, any of our young countrymen
should be stimulated to investigate the early history of their native land.

CHAPTER I

"Virtue may be assail'd, but never hurt,
Surpris'd by unjust force, but not inthrall'd;
Yea, even that which mischief meant most harm
Shall in the happy trial prove most glory."

COMUS[1]

William Fletcher was the son of a respectable country gentleman of Suffolk, in England; and the destined heir of his uncle Sir William Fletcher, an eminent lawyer, who had employed his talents with such effective zeal and pliant principle, that he had won his way to courtly favour and secured a courtly fortune.

Sir William had only one child—a daughter; and possessing the common ambition of transmitting his name with his wealth, he selected his nephew as the future husband of his daughter Alice.

"Take good heed," Sir William thus expressed himself in a letter to his brother, "take good heed that the boy be taught unquestioning and unqualified loyalty to his sovereign—the Alpha and Omega of political duty. These are times when every true subject has his price. Divers of the leaders of the Commons are secret friends of the seditious mischief-brewing puritans; and Buckingham himself is suspected of favouring their cabals—but this sub rosa—I burn not my fingers with these matters. 'He who meddleth with another man's strifes, taketh a dog by the ear,' said the wisest man that ever lived;[2] and he—thank God—was a king. Caution Will against all vain speculation and idle

5

inquiries—there are those that are for ever inquiring and inquiring, and never coming to the truth. One inquiry should suffice for a loyal subject. 'What is established?' and nat being well
ascertained, the line of duty is so plain, that he who runs may
read.³

"I would that all our youths had inscribed on their hearts that
golden rule of political religion, framed and well maintained by
our good Queen Elizabeth. 'No man should be suffered to de-
cline either on the left or on the right hand, from the drawn line
limited by authority, and by the sovereign's laws and injunctions.'

"Instead of such healthy maxims, our lads' heads are crammed
with the philosophy and rhetoric and history of those liberty-
loving Greeks and Romans. This is the pernicious lore that has
poisoned our academical fountains. Liberty, what is it! Daughter
of disloyalty and mother of all misrule—who, from the hour
that she tempted our first parents to forfeit paradise, hath ever
worked mischief to our race.

"But above all, brother, as you value the temporal salvation
of your boy, restrain him from all confederacy, association, or
even acquaintance with the puritans. If my master took counsel of me, he would ship these mad canting fools to our New-
England colonies, where their tender consciences would be no
more offended because, forsooth, a prelate saith his prayers in
white vestments, and where they might enjoy with the savages
that primitive equality, about which they make such a pother.
God forefend that our good lad William should company with
these misdoers! He must be narrowly watched; for, as I hear,
there is a neighbour of yours, one Winthrop,⁴ (a notable gentleman too, as they say, but he doth grievously scandalize his birth
and breeding) who hath embraced these scurvy principles, and
doth magnify them with the authority of his birth and condition,
and hath much weight with the country. There is in Suffolk too,
as I am told, one Eliot,⁵ a young zealot—a fanatical incendiary,
who doth find ample combustibles in the gossiping matrons, idle
maidens, and lawless youth who flock about him.

"These are dangerous neighbours—rouse yourself, brother—
give over your idle sporting with hawk and hound, and watch

over this goodly scion of ours—ours, I say, but I forewarn you, no daughter or guinea of mine shall ever go to one who is infected with this spreading plague."

This letter was too explicit to be misunderstood; but so far from having the intended effect of awakening the caution of the expectant of fortune, it rather stimulated the pride of the independent country gentleman. He permitted his son to follow the bent of accident, or the natural course of a serious, reflecting, and enthusiastic temper. Winthrop, the future governor of Massachusetts, was the counsellor of young Fletcher; and Eliot, the "apostle of New-England," his most intimate friend. These were men selected of Heaven to achieve a great work. In the quaint language of the time, "the Lord sifted three nations for precious seed to sow the wilderness."

There were interested persons who were not slow in conveying to Sir William unfavourable reports of his nephew, and the young man received a summons from his uncle, who hoped, by removing him from the infected region, to rescue him from danger.

Sir William's pride was gratified by the elegant appearance and graceful deportment of his nephew, whom he had expected to see with the "slovenly and lawyerlike carriage" that marked the scholars of the times. The pliant courtier was struck with the lofty independence of the youth who, from the first, shewed that neither frowns nor favour would induce him to bow the knee to the idols Sir William had served. There was something in this independence that awed the inferior mind of the uncle. To him it was an unknown mysterious power, which he knew not how to approach, and almost despaired of subduing. However, he was experienced in life, and had observed enough of human infirmity to convince him, that there was no human virtue that had not some weak—some assailable point. Time and circumstances were not long in developing the vulnerability of the nephew. Alice Fletcher had been the companion of his childhood. They now met without any of the reserve that often prevents an intimate intercourse between young persons, and proceeds from the consciousness of a susceptibility which it would seem to deny.

The intercourse of the cousins was renewed with all the frankness and artlessness of the sunny season of childish love and confidence. Alice had been educated in retirement, by her mother, whom she had recently attended through a long and fatal illness. She had been almost the exclusive object of her love, for there was little congeniality between the father and daughter. The ties of nature may command all dutiful observances, but they cannot control the affections. Alice was deeply afflicted by her bereavement. Her cousin's serious temper harmonized with her sorrow, and nature and opportunity soon indissolubly linked their hearts together.

Sir William perceived their growing attachment and exulted in it; for, as he fancied, it reduced his nephew to dependence on his will and whims. He had never himself experienced the full strength of any generous sentiment; but he had learned from observation, that love was a controlling passion, and he now most anxiously watched and promoted the kindling of the flame, in the expectation that the fire would subdue the principles of civil and religious liberty, with which he had but too well ascertained the mind of his nephew to be imbued.

He silently favoured the constant and exclusive intercourse of the young people: he secretly contrived various modes of increasing their mutual dependence; and, when he was certain their happiness was staked, he cast the die. He told his nephew that he perceived and rejoiced in the mutual affection that had so naturally sprung up between him and his daughter, and he confessed their union had been the favourite object of his life; and said, that he now heartily accorded his consent to it, prescribing one condition only—but that condition was unalterable. "You must abjure, William, in the presence of witnesses," he said, "the fanatical notions of liberty and religion with which you have been infected—you must pledge yourself, by a solemn oath, to unqualified obedience to the king, and adherence to the established church: you shall have time enough for the effervescence of your young blood. God send this fermentation may work off all impurities. Nay, answer me not now. Take a day—a week—a month for consideration; for on your decision depends fortune and love—or the alternative, beggary and exile."

If a pit had yawned beneath his feet, and swallowed Alice from his view, William Fletcher could not have been more shocked. He was soul-stricken, as one who listens to a sentence of death. To his eye the earth was shrouded in darkness; not an object of hope or pursuit remained.

He had believed his uncle was aware of what he must deem his political and religious delinquency; but he had never spoken to him on the subject: he had treated him with marked favour, and he had so evidently encouraged his attachment to his cousin, that he had already plighted his love to her, and received her vows without fearing that he had passed even the limit of strict prudence.

There was no accommodating flexibility in his principles; his fidelity to what he deemed his duty could not have been subdued by the fires of martyrdom, and he did not hesitate to sacrifice what was dearer than life to it. He took the resolution at once to fly from the temptation that, present, he dared not trust himself to resist.

"I shall not again see my Alice," he said. "I have not courage to meet her smiles; I have not strength to endure her tears."

In aid of his resolution there came, most opportunely, a messenger from his father, requiring his immediate presence. This afforded him a pretext for his sudden departure from London. He left a few brief lines for Alice, that expressed without explaining the sadness of his heart.

His father died a few hours before he arrived at the paternal mansion. He was thus released from his strongest natural tie. His mother had been long dead; and he had neither brother nor sister. He inherited a decent patrimony, sufficient at least to secure the independence of a gentleman. He immediately repaired to Groton, to his friend Winthrop; not that he should dictate his duty to him, but as one leans on the arm of a friend when he finds his own strength scarcely sufficient to support him.

Mr. Winthrop is well known to have been a man of the most tender domestic affections and sympathies; but he had then been long married—and *twice* married—and probably a little dimness had come over his recollection of the enthusiasm of a first passion. When Fletcher spoke of Alice's unequalled loveliness, and of his own unconquerable love, his friend listened as one listens to a tale he has heard a hundred times, and seemed to regard the cruel circumstances in which the ardent lover was placed only in the light of a fit and fine opportunity of making a sacrifice to the great and good cause to which this future statesman had even then begun to devote himself, as the sole object of his life. He treated his friend's sufferings as in their nature transient and curable; and concluded by saying, "the Lord hath prepared this fire, my friend, to temper your faith, and you will come out of it the better prepared for your spiritual warfare."

Fletcher listened to him with stern resolution, like him who permits a surgeon to probe a wound which he is himself certain is incurable.

Mr. Winthrop knew that a ship was appointed to sail from Southampton in a few days for New-England. With that characteristic zeal which then made all the intentions of Providence so obvious to the eye of faith, and the interpretation of all the events of life so easy, Mr. Winthrop assured his friend that the designs of Heaven, in relation to him, were plain. He said, "there was a great call for such services as he could render in the expedition just about to sail, and which was like to fail for the want of them; and that now, like a faithful servant to the cause he had confessed, he must not look behind, but press on to the things that were before."

Fletcher obeyed the voice of Heaven. This is no romantic fiction. Hundreds in that day resisted all that solicits earthly passions, and sacrificed all that gratifies them, to the cause of God and of man—the cause of liberty and religion. This cause was not to their eyes invested with any romantic attractions. It was not assisted by the illusions of chivalry, nor magnified by the spiritual power and renown of crusades. Our fathers neither had, nor expected their reward on earth.

One severe duty remained to be performed. Fletcher must announce their fate to Alice. He honoured her too much to believe she would have permitted the sacrifice of his integrity, if he would have made it. He, therefore, had nothing to excuse; nothing but to tell the terrible truth—to try to reconcile her to her father—to express, for the last time, his love, and to pray that he might receive, at Southampton, one farewell line from her. Accompanying his letter to Alice was one to Sir William, announcing the decision to resign his favour and exile himself for ever from England.

He arranged his affairs, and in a few days received notice that the vessel was ready to sail. He repaired to Southampton, and as he was quitting the inn to embark in the small boat that was to convey him to the vessel, already in the offing, a voice from an inner apartment pronounced his name—and at the next moment Alice was in his arms. She gently reproved him for having estimated her affection at so low a rate as not to have anticipated that she should follow him, and share his destiny. It was more than could have been expected from man, that Fletcher should have opposed such a resolution. He had but a moment for deliberation. Most of the passengers had already embarked; some still lingered on the strand protracting their last farewell to their country and their friends. In the language of one of the most honoured of these pilgrims—"truly doleful was the sight of that sad and mournful parting, to hear what sighs, and sobs, and prayers, did sound amongst them; what tears did gush from every eye, and pithy speeches pierced each other's hearts."[6]

With the weeping groupe Fletcher left Alice and her attendants, while he went to the vessel to prepare for her suitable reception. He there found a clergyman, and bespoke his holy offices to unite him to his cousin immediately after their embarcation.

All the necessary arrangements were made, and he was returning to the shore, his eye fixed on the lovely being whom he believed Heaven had interposed to give to him, when he descried Sir William's carriage guarded by a cavalcade of armed men, in the uniform of the King's guards, approaching the spot where she stood.

He comprehended at once their cruel purpose. He exhorted the boatmen to put forth all their strength; he seized the oars himself—despair gave him supernatural power—the boat shot forward with the velocity of light; but all in vain!—he only approached near enough to the shore to hear Alice's last impotent cries to him—to see her beautiful face convulsed with agony, and her arms outstretched towards him—when she was forced to the carriage by her father, and driven from his sight.

He leaped on the strand; he followed the troop with cries and entreaties; but he was only answered by the coarse jeering and profane jests of the soldiery.

Notice was soon given that the boat was ready to return to the ship for the last time, and Fletcher in a state of agitation and despair, almost amounting to insanity, permitted it to return without him.

He went to London and requested an interview with his uncle. The request was granted, and a long and secret conference ensued. It was known by the servants of the household, that their mistress, Alice, had been summoned by her father to this meeting; but what was said or done, did not transpire. Immediately after, Fletcher returned to Mr. Winthrop's in Suffolk. The fixedness of despair was on his countenance; but he said nothing, even to this confidential friend, of the interview with his uncle. The particulars of the affair at Southampton, which had already reached Suffolk, seemed sufficiently to explain his misery.

In less than a fortnight he there received despatches from his uncle, informing him that he had taken effectual measures to save himself from a second conspiracy against the honour of his family—that his daughter, Alice, had that day been led to the altar by Charles Leslie; and concluding with a polite hope, that though his voyage had been interrupted, it might not be long deferred.

Alice had, indeed, in the imbecility of utter despair, submitted to her father's commands. It was intimated at the time, and reported for many years after, that she had suffered a total alienation of mind. To the world this was never contradicted, for she lived in absolute retirement; but those who best knew could have attested, that if her mind had departed from its beautiful temple, an angelic spirit had entered in and possessed it.

William Fletcher was, in a few months, persuaded to unite himself with an orphan girl, a ward of Mr. Winthrop, who had, in the eyes of the elders, all the meek graces that befitted a godly maiden and dutiful helpmate. Fletcher remained constant to his purpose of emigrating to New-England, but he did not effect it till the year 1630, when he embarked with his family and effects in the ship Arabella, with Governor Winthrop, who then, for the first time, went to that land where his name will ever be held in affectionate and honourable remembrance.

"For the temper of the brain in quick apprehensions and acute judgments, to say no more, the most High and Sovereign God hath not made the Indian inferior to the European."
—ROGER WILLIAMS.[1]

The magnitude of the enterprise in which the first settlers of New-England were engaged, the terrific obstacles they encountered, and the hardships they endured, gave to their characters a seriousness and solemnity, heightened, it may be, by the severity of their religious faith.

Where all were serious the melancholy of an individual was not conspicuous; and Mr. Fletcher's sadness would probably have passed unnoticed, but for the reserve of his manners, which piqued the pride of his equals, and provoked the curiosity of his inferiors.

The first probably thought that the apostolic principle of community of goods at least extended to opinions and feelings; and the second always fancy when a man shuts the door of his lips that there must be some secret worth knowing within.

Like many other men of an ardent temperament and disinterested love of his species, Mr. Fletcher was disappointed at the slow operation of principles, which, however efficient and excellent in the abstract, were to be applied to various and discordant subjects. Such men, inexperienced in the business of life, are like children, who, setting out on a journey, are impatient

after the few first paces to be at the end of it. They cannot endure
the rebuffs and delays that retard them in their course. These are
the men of genius—the men of feeling—the men that the world
calls visionaries; and it is because they are visionaries—because
they have a beau-ideal in their own minds, to which they can
see but a faint resemblance in the actual state of things, that they
become impatient of detail, and cannot brook the slow progress
to perfection. They are too rapid in their anticipations. The character of man, and the institutions of society, are yet very far from
their possible and destined perfection. Still, how far is the present
age in advance of that which drove reformers to a dreary
wilderness!—of that which hanged quakers!—of that which
condemned to death, as witches, innocent, unoffending old
women! But it is unnecessary to heighten the glory of our risen
day by comparing it with the preceding twilight.

To return to Mr. Fletcher. He was mortified at seeing power,
which had been earned at so dear a rate, and which he had fondly
hoped was to be applied to the advancement of man's happiness,
sometimes perverted to purposes of oppression and personal ag-
grandizement. He was shocked when a religious republic, which
he fancied to be founded on the basis of established truth, was
disturbed by the out-break of heresies; and his heart sickened
when he saw those, who had sacrificed whatever man holds dearest to religious freedom, imposing those shackles on others from
which they had just released themselves at such a price. Partly
influenced by these disgusts, and partly by that love of contemplation and retirement that belongs to a character of his cast,
especially when depressed by some early disappointment, he refused the offices of honour and trust that were, from time to
time, offered to him; and finally, in 1636, when Pynchon, Holioke, and Chapin,[2] formed their settlement at Springfield, on
Connecticut river, he determined to retire from the growing
community of Boston to this frontier settlement.

Mrs. Fletcher received his decision as all wives of that age of
undisputed masculine supremacy (or most of those of our less
passive age) would do, with meek submission. The inconvenien-
cies and dangers of that outpost were not unknown to her, nor
did she underrate them; but Abraham would as soon have re-

monstrated against the command that bade him go forth from his father's house into the land of the Chaldees,³ as she would have failed in passive obedience to the resolve of her husband.

The removal was effected early in the summer of 1636. Springfield assumed, at once, under the auspices of its wealthy and enterprising proprietors, the aspect of a village. The first settlers followed the course of the Indians, and planted themselves on the borders of rivers—the natural gardens of the earth, where the soil is mellowed and enriched by the annual overflowing of the streams, and prepared by the unassisted processes of nature to yield to the indolent Indian his scanty supply of maize and other esculents. The wigwams which constituted the village, or, to use the graphic aboriginal designation, the 'smoke' of the natives gave place to the clumsy, but more convenient dwellings of the pilgrims.

Where there are now contiguous rows of shops, filled with the merchandise of the east, the manufactures of Europe, the rival fabrics of our own country, and the fruits of the tropics; where now stands the stately hall of justice—the academy—the bank—churches, orthodox and heretic, and all the symbols of a rich and populous community—were, at the early period of our history, a few log-houses, planted around a fort, defended by a slight embankment and palisade.

The mansions of the proprietors were rather more spacious and artificial than those of their more humble associates, and were built on the well-known model of the modest dwelling illustrated by the birth of Milton—a form still abounding in the eastern parts of Massachusetts, and presenting to the eye of a New-Englander the familiar aspect of an awkward friendly country cousin.

The first clearing was limited to the plain. The beautiful hill that is now the residence of the gentry (for there yet lives such a class in the heart of our democratic community) and is embellished with stately edifices and expensive pleasure-grounds, was then the border of a dense forest, and so richly fringed with the original growth of trees, that scarce a sun-beam had penetrated to the parent earth.

Mr. Fletcher was at first welcomed as an important acquisition to the infant establishment; but he soon proved that he purposed to take no part in its concerns, and, in spite of the remonstrances of the proprietors, he fixed his residence a mile from the village, deeming exposure to the incursions of the savages very slight, and the surveillance of an inquiring neighbourhood a certain evil. His domain extended from a gentle eminence, that commanded an extensive view of the bountiful Connecticut to the shore, where the river indented the meadow by one of those sweeping graceful curves by which it seems to delight to beautify the land it nourishes.

The border of the river was fringed with all the water-loving trees; but the broad meadows were quite cleared, excepting that a few elms and sycamores had been spared by the Indians, and consecrated, by tradition, as the scene of revels or councils. The house of our pilgrim was a low-roofed modest structure, containing ample accommodation for a patriarchal family; where children, dependants, and servants were all to be sheltered under one roof-tree. On one side, as we have described, lay an open and extensive plain; within view was the curling smoke from the little cluster of houses about the fort—the habitation of civilized man; but all else was a savage howling wilderness.

Never was a name more befitting the condition of a people, than 'Pilgrim' that of our forefathers. It should be redeemed from the puritanical and ludicrous associations which have degraded it, in most men's minds, and be hallowed by the sacrifices made by these voluntary exiles. They were pilgrims, for they had resigned, for ever, what the good hold most dear—their homes. Home can never be transferred; never repeated in the experience of an individual. The place consecrated by parental love, by the innocence and sports of childhood, by the first acquaintance with nature; by the linking of the heart to the visible creation, is the only home. There there is a living and breathing spirit infused into nature: every familiar object has a history—the trees have tongues, and the very air is vocal. There the vesture of decay doth not close in and control the noble functions of the soul. It sees and hears and enjoys without the ministry of gross material substance.

Mr. Fletcher had resided a few months in Springfield when

he one day entered with an open letter in his hand, that apartment of his humble dwelling styled, by courtesy, the parlour.
His wife was sitting there with her eldest son, a stripling of
fourteen, busily assisting him in twisting a cord for his cross-
bow. She perceived that her husband looked disturbed; but he
said nothing, and her habitual deference prevented her inquiring
into the cause of his discomposure.

After taking two or three turns about the room, he said to
his son, "Everell, my boy—go to the door, and await there the
arrival of an Indian girl; she is, as you may see, yonder by the
river-side, and will be here shortly. I would not that Jennet
should, at the very first, shock the child with her discourteous
ways."

"Child! coming here!" exclaimed the boy, dropping his bow
and gazing through the window—"Who is she?—that tall girl,
father—she is no more a child than I am!"

His mother smiled at an exclamation that betrayed a common
juvenile jealousy of the honour of dawning manhood, and bade
the boy obey his father's directions. When Everell had left the
apartment, Mr. Fletcher said, "I have just received letters from
Boston—from Governor Winthrop"—he paused.

"Our friends are all well, I hope," said Mrs. Fletcher.

"Yes, Martha, our friends are all well—but these letters contain something of more importance than aught that concerns the
health of the perishing body."

Mr. Fletcher again hesitated, and his wife, perplexed by his
embarrassment, inquired, "Has poor deluded Mrs. Hutchinson[4]
again presumed to disturb the peace of God's people?"

"Martha, you aim wide of the mark. My present emotions are
not those of a mourner for Zion. A ship has arrived from England, and in it came"—

"My brother Stretton!" exclaimed Mrs. Fletcher.

"No—no, Martha. It will be long ere Stretton quits his paradise to join a suffering people in the wilderness."

He paused for a moment, and when he again spoke, the softened tone of his voice evinced that he was touched by the expression of disappointment, slightly tinged by displeasure that
shaded his wife's gentle countenance. "Forgive me, my dear

wife," he said. "I should not have spoken aught that implied censure of your brother; for I know he hath ever been most precious in your eyes—albeit, not the less so, that he is yet without the fold——That which I have to tell you—and it were best that it were quickly told—is, that my cousin Alice was a passenger in this newly arrived ship.—Martha, your blushes wrong you. The mean jealousies that degrade some women have, I am sure, never been harboured in your heart."

"If I deserve your praise, it is because the Lord has been pleased to purify my heart and make it his sanctuary. But, if I have not the jealousies, I have the feelings of a woman, and I cannot forget that you was once affianced to your cousin Alice —and"—

"And that I once told you, Martha, frankly, that the affection I gave to her, could not be transferred to another. That love grew with my growth—strengthened with my strength. Of its beginning, I had no more consciousness than of the commencement of my existence. It was sunshine and flowers in all the paths of my childhood. It inspired every hope—modified every project —such was the love I bore to Alice—love immortal as the soul!—

"You know how cruelly we were severed at Southampton— how she was torn from the strand by the king's guards—within my view, almost within my grasp. How Sir William tempted me with the offer of pardon—my cousin's hand—and,—poor temptation indeed after that!—honours, fortune. You know that even Alice, my precious beautiful Alice, knelt to me. That smitten of God and man, and for the moment, bereft of the right use of reason, she would have persuaded me to yield my integrity. You know that her cruel father reproached me with virtually breaking my plighted troth. That many of my friends urged my present conformity; and you know, Martha, that there was a principle in my bosom that triumphed over all these temptations. And think you not that principle has preserved me faithful in my friendship to you? Think you not that your obedience——; your careful conformity to my wishes; your steady love, which hath kept far more than even measure with my deserts, is undervalued—can be lightly estimated?"

"Oh, I know," said the humble wife, "that your goodness to me does far surpass my merit; but bethink you, it is the nature of a woman to crave the first place."

"It is the right of a wife, Martha; and there is none now to contest it with you. This is but the second time I have spoken to you on a subject that has been much in our thoughts: that has made me wayward, and would have made my sojourning on earth miserable, but that you have been my support and comforter. These letters contain tidings that have opened a long sealed fountain. My uncle, Sir William, died last January. Leslie perished in a foreign service. Alice, thus released from all bonds, and sole mistress of her fortunes, determined to cast her lot in the heritage of God's people. She embarked with her two girls —her only children—a tempestuous voyage proved too much for a constitution already broken by repeated shocks. She was fully aware of her approaching death, and died as befits a child of faith, in sweet peace. Would to God I could have seen her once more—but," he added, raising his eyes devoutly, "not my will but thine be done! The sister of Leslie, a Mistress Grafton, attended Alice, and with her she left a will committing her children to my guardianship. It will be necessary for me to go to Boston to assume this trust. I shall leave home tomorrow, after making suitable provision for your safety and comfort in my absence. These children will bring additional labour to your household; and in good time hath our thoughtful friend Governor Winthrop procured for us two Indian servants. The girl has arrived. The boy is retained about the little Leslies; the youngest of whom, it seems, is a petted child; and is particularly pleased by his activity in ministering to her amusement."

"I am glad if any use can be made of an Indian servant," said Mrs. Fletcher, who, oppressed with conflicting emotions, expressed the lightest of them—a concern at a sudden increase of domestic cares where there were no facilities to lighten them.

"How any use! You surely do not doubt, Martha, that these Indians possess the same faculties that we do. The girl, just arrived, our friend writes me, hath rare gifts of mind—such as few of God's creatures are endowed with. She is just fifteen; she

understands and speaks English perfectly well,[5] having been
taught it by an English captive, who for a long time dwelt with
her tribe. On that account she was much noticed by the English
who traded with the Pequods; and young as she was, she acted
as their interpreter.

"She is the daughter of one of their chiefs, and when this
wolfish tribe were killed, or dislodged from their dens, she, her
brother, and their mother, were brought with a few other captives to Boston. They were given for a spoil to the soldiers.
Some, by a christian use of money, were redeemed; and others,
I blush to say it, for 'it is God's gift that every man should enjoy
the good of his own labour,'[6] were sent into slavery in the West
Indies. Monoca, the mother of these children, was noted for the
singular dignity and modesty of her demeanor.[7] Many notable
instances of her kindness to the white traders are recorded; and
when she was taken to Boston, our worthy governor, ever mindful of his duties, assured her that her good deeds were held in
remembrance, and that he would testify the gratitude of his people in any way she should direct. 'I have nothing to ask,' she
said, 'but that I and my children may receive no personal dishonour.'

"The governor redeemed her children, and assured her they
should be cared for. For herself, misery and sorrow had so
wrought on her, that she was fast sinking into the grave. Many
christian men and women laboured for her conversion but she
would not even consent that the holy word should be interpreted to her; insisting, in the pride of her soul, that all the
children of the Great Spirit were equal objects of His favour;
and that He had not deemed the book he had withheld, needful
to them."

"And did she," inquired Mrs. Fletcher, "thus perish in her
sins?"

"She died," replied her husband, "immoveably fixed in those
sentiments. But, Martha, we should not suit God's mercy to the
narrow frame of our thoughts. This poor savage's life, as far as
it has come to our knowledge, was marked with innocence and
good deeds; and I would gladly believe that we may hope for

her, on that broad foundation laid by the Apostle Peter—'In every nation, he that feareth God and worketh righteousness, is accepted of Him.' "[8]

"That text," answered Mrs. Fletcher, her heart easily kindling with the flame of charity, "is a light behind many a dark scripture, like the sun shining all around the edges of a cloud that would fain hide its beams."

"Such thoughts, my dear wife, naturally spring from thy kind heart, and are sweet morsels for private meditation; but it were well to keep them in thine own bosom lest, taking breath, they should lighten the fears of unstable souls. But here comes the girl, Magawisca, clothed in her Indian garb, which the governor has permitted her to retain, not caring, as he wisely says, to interfere with their innocent peculiarities; and she, in particular, having shewn a loathing of the English dress."

Everell Fletcher now threw wide open the parlour door, inviting the Indian girl, by a motion of his hand and a kind smile, to follow. She did so, and remained standing beside him, with her eyes rivetted to the floor, while every other eye was turned towards her. She and her conductor were no unfit representatives of the people from whom they sprung. Everell Fletcher was a fair ruddy boy of fourteen; his smooth brow and bright curling hair, bore the stamp of the morning of life; hope and confidence and gladness beamed in the falcon glance of his keen blue eye; and love and frolic played about his lips. The active hardy habits of life, in a new country, had already knit his frame, and given him the muscle of manhood; while his quick elastic step truly expressed the untamed spirit of childhood—the only spirit without fear and without reproach. His dress was of blue cloth, closely fitting his person; the sleeves reached midway between the elbow and wrist, and the naked, and as it would seem to a modern eye, awkward space, was garnished with deep-pointed lace ruffles of a coarse texture; a ruff, or collar of the same material, was worn about the neck.

The Indian stranger was tall for her years, which did not exceed fifteen. Her form was slender, flexible, and graceful; and there was a freedom and loftiness in her movement which, though tempered with modesty, expressed a consciousness of high birth. Her face, although marked by the peculiarities of her race, was beautiful even to an European eye. Her features were regular, and her teeth white as pearls; but there must be something beyond symmetry of feature to fix the attention, and it was an expression of dignity, thoughtfulness, and deep dejection that made the eye linger on Magawisca's face, as if it were perusing there the legible record of her birth and wrongs. Her hair, contrary to the fashion of the Massachusetts Indians, was parted on her forehead, braided, and confined to her head by a band of small feathers, jet black, and interwoven, and attached at equal distances by rings of polished bone. She wore a waistcoat of deer-skin, fastened at the throat by a richly wrought collar. Her arms, a model for sculpture, were bare. A mantle of purple cloth hung gracefully from her shoulders, and was confined at the waist by a broad band, ornamented with rude hieroglyphics. The mantle and her strait short petticoat or kilt of the same rare and costly material, had been obtained, probably, from the English traders. Stockings were an unknown luxury; but leggins, similar to those worn by the ladies of Queen Elizabeth's court, were no bad substitute. The moccasin, neatly fitted to a delicate foot and ankle, and tastefully ornamented with bead-work, completed the apparel of this daughter of a chieftain, which altogether, had an air of wild and fantastic grace, that harmonized well with the noble demeanor and peculiar beauty of the young savage.

Mr. Fletcher surveyed her for a moment with a mingled feeling of compassion and curiosity, and then turning away and leaning his head on the mantelpiece, his thoughts reverted to the subject that had affected him far more deeply than he had ventured to confess, even to the wife of his bosom.

Mrs. Fletcher's first feeling was rather that of a housewife than a tender woman. 'My husband,' she thought, 'might as well have brought a wild doe from the forest to plough his fields, as to give me this Indian girl for household labour; but the wisest men have no sense in these matters.' This natural domestic reflection was soon succeeded by a sentiment of compassion, which scarcely needed to be stimulated by Everell's whisper of "do, mother, speak to her."

"Magawisca," she said in a friendly tone, "you are welcome

among us, girl." Magawisca bowed her head. Mrs. Fletcher continued: "you should receive it as a signal mercy, child, that you
have been taken from the midst of a savage people, and set in a
christian family." Mrs. Fletcher paused for her auditor's assent,
but the proposition was either unintelligible or unacceptable to
Magawisca.

"Mistress Fletcher means," said a middle-aged serving woman
who had just entered the room, "that you should be mightily
thankful, Tawney, that you are snatched as a brand from the
burning."

"Hush, Jennet!" said Everell Fletcher, touching the speaker
with the point of an arrow which he held in his hand.

Magawisca's eyes had turned on Jennet, flashing like a sun-
beam through an opening cloud. Everell's interposition touched
a tender chord, and when she again cast them down, a tear trembled on their lids.

"You will have no hard service to do," said Mrs. Fletcher,
resuming her address. "I cannot explain all to you now; but you
will soon perceive that our civilized life is far easier—far better
and happier than your wild wandering ways, which are indeed,
as you will presently see, but little superior to those of the
wolves and foxes."

Magawisca suppressed a reply that her heart sent to her quivering lips; and Everell said, "hunted, as the Indians are, to their
own dens, I am sure, mother, they need the fierceness of the
wolf, and the cunning of the fox."

"True—true, my son," replied Mrs. Fletcher, who really
meant no unkindness in expressing what she deemed a self-
evident truth; and then turning again to Magawisca, she said, in
a gentle tone, "you have had a long and fatiguing journey—was
it not, girl?"

"My foot," replied Magawisca, "is used to the wild-wood
path. The deer tires not of his way on the mountain, nor the
bird of its flight in the air."

She uttered her natural feeling in so plaintive a tone that it
touched the heart like a strain of sad music; and when Jennet
again officiously interposed in the conversation, by saying, that
"truly these savages have their house in the wilderness, and their

way no man knows," her mistress cut short her outpouring by
directing her to go to the outer door and learn who it was that
Digby was conducting to the house.

A moment after Digby, Mr. Fletcher's confidential domestic,
entered with the air of one who has important intelligence to
communicate. He was followed by a tall gaunt Indian, who held
in his hand a deer-skin pouch. "Ha! Digby," said Mr. Fletcher,
"have you returned? What say the Commissioners? Can they
furnish me a guide and attendants for my journey?"

"Yes, an' please you, sir. I was in the nick of time, for they
were just despatching a messenger to the Governor."

"On what account?"

"Why, it's rather an odd errand," replied Digby, scratching
his head with an awkward hesitation. "I would not wish to
shock my gentle mistress, who will never bring her feelings to
the queer fashions of the new world; but Lord's mercy, sir, you
know we think no more of taking off a scalp here, than we did
of shaving our beards at home."

"Scalp!" exclaimed Mr. Fletcher. "Explain yourself, Digby."

The Indian, as if to assist Digby's communication, untied his
pouch and drew from it a piece of dried and shrivelled skin, to
which hair, matted together with blood, still adhered. There was
an expression of fierce triumph on the countenance of the savage
as he surveyed the trophy with a grim smile. A murmur of indignation burst from all present.

"Why did you bring that wretch here?" demanded Mr.
Fletcher of his servant, in an angry tone.

"I did but obey Mr. Pynchon, sir. The thing is an abomina-
tion to the soul and eye of a christian, but it has to be taken to
Boston for the reward."

"What reward, Digby?"

"The reward, sir, that is in reason expected for the scalp of
the Pequod chief."

As Digby uttered these last words Magawisca shrieked as if
a dagger had pierced her heart. She darted forward and grasped
the arm that upheld the trophy. "My father!—Mononotto!" she
screamed in a voice of agony.

"Give it to her—by Heaven, you shall give it to her," cried

Everell, springing on the Indian and losing all other thought in his instinctive sympathy for Magawisca.

"Softly, softly, Mr. Everell," said Digby, "that is the scalp of Sassacus, not Mononotto. The Pequods had two chiefs you know."[9]

Magawisca now released her hold; and as soon as she could again command her voice, she said, in her own language to the Indian, "my father—my father—does he live?"

"He does," answered the Indian in the same dialect; "he lives in the wigwam of the chief of the Mohawks."

Magawisca was silent for a moment, and knit her brows as if agitated with an important deliberation. She then undid a bracelet from her arm and gave it to the Indian: "I charge ye," she said, "as ye hope for game in your hunting-grounds, for the sun on your wigwam, and the presence of the Great Spirit in your death-hour—I charge ye to convey this token to my father. Tell him his children are servants in the house of his enemies; but," she added, after a moment's pause, "to whom am I trusting?—to the murderer of Sassacus!—my father's friend!"

"Fear not," replied the Indian; "your errand shall be done. Sassacus was a strange tree in our forests; but he struck his root deep, and lifted his tall head above our loftiest branches, and cast his shadow over us; and I cut him down. I may not return to my people, for they called Sassacus brother, and they would fain avenge him. But fear not, maiden, your errand shall be done."

Mr. Fletcher observed this conference, which he could not understand, with some anxiety and displeasure, and he broke it off by directing Jennet to conduct Magawisca to another apartment.

Jennet obeyed, muttering, as she went, "a notable providence this concerning the Pequod caitiff. Even like Adonibezek, as he has done to others the Lord hath requited him."[10]

Mr. Fletcher then most reluctantly took into his possession the savage trophy, and dismissed the Indian, deeply lamenting that motives of mistaken policy should tempt his brethren to depart from the plainest principles of their religion.

CHAPTER III

"But ah, who can deceive his destiny,
Or ween, by Warning, to avoid his Fate?"
FAIRY QUEEN[1]

On the following morning Mr. Fletcher set out for Boston, and escaping all perils by flood and field, he arrived there at the expiration of nine days, having accomplished the journey, now the affair of a single day, with unusual expedition.

His wards were accompanied by two individuals who were now, with them, to become permanent members of his family. Mrs. Grafton, the sister of their father, and one Master Cradock, a scholar "skilled in the tongues," who attended them as their tutor. Mrs. Grafton was a widow, far on the shady side of fifty; though, as that was a subject to which she never alluded, she probably regarded age with the feelings ascribed to her sex, that being the last quality for which womankind would wish to be honoured, as is said by one whose satire is so good-humoured that even its truth may be endured. She was, unhappily for herself as her lot was cast, a zealous adherent to the church of England. Good people, who take upon themselves the supervisorship of their neighbours' consciences, abounded in that age; and from them Mrs. Grafton received frequent exhortations and remonstrances. To these she uniformly replied, 'that a faith and mode of religion that had saved so many was good

27

enough to save her'—'that she had received her belief, just as it was, from her father, and that he, not she, was responsible for it.' Offensive such opinions must needs be in a community of professed reformers, but the good lady did not make them more so by the obtrusiveness of over-wrought zeal. To confess the truth, her mind was far more intent on the forms of head-pieces, than modes of faith; and she was far more ambitious of being the leader of fashion, than the leader of a sect. She would have contended more earnestly for a favourite recipe, than a favourite dogma; and though she undoubtedly believed "a saint in crape" to be "twice a saint in lawn," and fearlessly maintained that "no man could suitably administer the offices of religion without 'gown, surplice, and wig,'" yet she chiefly directed her hostilities against the puritanical attire of the ladies of the colony, who, she insisted, 'did most unnaturally belie their nature as women, and their birth and bringing-up as gentlewomen, by their ill-fashioned, ill-sorted, and unbecoming apparel.' To this heresy she was fast gaining proselytes; for, if we may believe the "simple cobbler of Agawam," there were, even in those early and pure days, "nugiperous gentle dames who inquired what dress the Queen is in this week." The contagion spread rapidly; and when some of the most vigilant and zealous sentinels proposed that the preachers should make it the subject of public and personal reproof, it was whispered that the scandal was not limited to idle maidens, but that certain of the deacons' wives were in it, and it was deemed more prudent to adopt gentle and private measures to eradicate the evil; an evil so deeply felt as to be bewailed by the merciless 'cobbler,' above quoted, in the following affecting terms: "Methinks it would break the hearts of Englishmen to see so many goodly English women imprisoned in French cages, peeping out of their hood-holes for some men of mercy to help them with a little wit, and nobody relieves them. We have about five or six of them in our colony. If I see any of them accidentally, I cannot cleanse my phansie of them for a month after."[2]

It would seem marvellous that a woman like Mrs. Grafton, apparently engrossed with the world, living on the foam and froth of life, should become a voluntary exile to the colonies;

but, to do her justice, she was kind-hearted and affectionate—susceptible of strong and controlling attachment, and the infant children of a brother on whom she had doated, outweighed her love of frivolous pleasures and personal indulgence.

She certainly believed that the resolution of her sister to go to the wilderness, had no parallel in the history of human folly and madness; but the resolution once taken, and, as she perceived, unconquerable, she made her own destiny conformable, not without some restiveness, but without serious repining. It was an unexpected shock to her to be compelled to leave Boston for a condition of life not only more rude and inconvenient, but really dangerous. Necessity, however, is more potent than philosophy, and Mrs. Grafton, like most people, submitted with patience to an inevitable evil.

As 'good Master Cradock' was a man rather acted upon than acting, we shall leave him to be discovered by our readers as the light of others falls on him.

Mr. Fletcher received the children—the relicts and gifts of a woman whom he had loved as few men can love, with an intense interest. The youngest, Mary, was a pretty petted child, wayward and bashful. She repelled Mr. Fletcher's caresses, and ran away from him to shelter herself in her aunt's arms—but Alice, the eldest, seemed instinctively to return the love that beamed in the first glance that Mr. Fletcher cast on her—in that brief eager glance he saw the living and beautiful image of her mother. So much was he impressed with the resemblance, that he said, in a letter to his wife, that it reminded him of the heathen doctrine of metempsychosis[3]—and he could almost believe the spirit of the mother was transferred to the bosom of the child. The arrangement Mr. Fletcher made, for the transportation of his charge to Springfield, might probably be traced to the preference inspired by this resemblance.

He dispatched the little Mary with her aunt and the brother of Magawisca, the Indian boy Oneco, and such attendants as were necessary for their safe conduct—and he retained Alice and the tutor to be the companions of his journey. Before the children were separated, they were baptised by the Reverend Mr.

Cotton,[4] and in commemoration of the christian graces of their mother, their names were changed to the puritanical appellations of Hope and Faith.

Mr. Fletcher was detained, at first by business, and afterwards by ill-health, much longer than he had expected, and the fall, winter, and earliest months of spring wore away before he was able to set his face homeward. In the mean time, his little community at Bethel proceeded more harmoniously than could have been hoped from the discordant materials of which it was composed. This was owing, in great part, to the wise and gentle Mrs. Fletcher, the sun of her little system—all were obedient to the silent influence that controlled, without being perceived. But a letter which she wrote to Mr. Fletcher, just before his return, containing some important domestic details, may be deemed worth the perusal of our readers.

SPRINGFIELD, 1636

"To my good and honoured husband!

"Thy kind letter was duly received fourteen days after date, and was most welcome to me, containing, as it does, a portion of that stream of kindness that is ever flowing out from thy bountiful nature towards me. Sweet and refreshing was it, as these gentle days of spring after our sullen winter. Winter! ever disconsolate in these parts, but made tenfold more dreary by the absence of that precious light by which I have ever been cheered and guided.

"I thank thee heartily, my dear life, that thou dost so warmly commend my poor endeavours to do well in thy absence. I have truly tried to be faithful to my little nestlings, and to cheer them with notes of gladness when I have drooped inwardly for the voice of my mate. Yet my anxious thoughts have been more with thee than with myself; nor have I been unmindful of any of thy perplexities by sickness and otherwise, but in all thy troubles I have been troubled, and have ever prayed, that whatever might betide me, thou mightest return, in safety, to thy desiring family.

"I have had many difficulties to contend with in thy absence, of which I have forborne to inform thee, deeming it the duty of a wife never to disquiet her husband with her household cares;

but now that, with the Lord's permission, thou art so soon to be with us, I would fain render unto thee an account of my stewardship, knowing that thou art not an hard master, and wilt consider the will and not the weakness of thy loving wife.

"This Dame Grafton is strangely out of place here—fitter for a parlour bird, than a flight into the wilderness; and but that she cometh commended to us as a widow, a name that is a draft from the Lord upon every Christian heart, we might find it hard to brook her light and wordly ways. She raileth, and yet I think not with an evil mind, but rather ignorantly, at our most precious faith, and hath even ventured to read aloud from her book of Common Prayer—an offence that she hath been prevented from repeating by the somewhat profane jest of our son Everell; whose love of mischief, proceeding from the gay temper of youth, I trust you will overlook. It was a few nights ago, when a storm was raging, that the poor lady's fears were greatly excited. My womanish apprehensions had a hard struggle with my duty, so terrific was the hideous howling of the wolves, mingling with the blasts that swept through the forest; but I stilled my beating heart with the thought, that my children leant on me, and I must not betray my weakness. But Dame Grafton was beside herself. At one moment she fancied we should be the prey of the wild beast, and at the next, that she heard the alarm yell of the savages. Everell brought her, her prayer-book, and affecting a well-beeseeming gravity, he begged her to look out the prayer for distressed women, in imminent danger of being scalped by North American Indians. The poor lady, distracted with terror, seized the book, and turned over leaf after leaf, Everell meanwhile affecting to aid her search. In vain I shook my head, reprovingly, at the boy—in vain I assured Mistress Grafton that I trusted we were in no danger; she was beyond the influence of reason; nothing allayed her fears, till chancing to catch a glance of Everell's eye, she detected the lurking laughter, and rapping him soundly over the ears with her book, she left the room greatly enraged. I grieve to add, that Everell evinced small sorrow for his levity, though I admonished him thereupon. At the same time I thought it a fit occasion to commend the sagacity whereby he had detected the short-comings of written prayers, and to express my hope, that unpromising as his beginnings are, he may prove a son of Jacob that shall wrestle and prevail.

"I have something farther to say of Everell, who is, in the main, a most devoted son, and as I believe, an apt scholar; as his master telleth me that he readeth Latin like his mother tongue, and is well grounded in the Greek. The boy doth greatly affect the company of the Pequod girl, Magawisca. If, in his studies, he meets with any trait of heroism, (and with such, truly, her mind doth seem naturally to assimilate) he straightway calleth for her and rendereth it into English, in which she hath made such marvellous progress, that I am sometimes startled with the beautiful forms in which she clothes her simple thoughts. She, in her turn, doth take much delight in describing to him the customs of her people, and relating their traditionary tales, which are like pictures, captivating to a youthful imagination. He hath taught her to read, and reads to her Spenser's rhymes, and many other books of the like kind; of which, I am sorry to say, Dame Grafton hath brought hither stores. I have not forbidden him to read them, well knowing that the appetite of youth is often whetted by denial; and fearing that the boy might be tempted, secretly, to evade my authority; and I would rather expose him to all the mischief of this unprofitable lore, than to tempt him to a deceit that might corrupt the sweet fountain of truth—the well-spring of all that is good and noble.

"I have gone far from my subject. When my boy comes before my mind's eye, I can see no other object. But to return. I have not been unmindful of my duty to the Indian girl, but have endeavoured to instil into her mind the first principles of our religion, as contained in Mr. Cotton's Catechism, and elsewhere. But, alas! to these her eye is shut and her ear is closed, not only with that blindness and deafness common to the natural man, but she entertaineth an aversion, which has the fixedness of principle, and doth continually remind me of Hannibal's hatred to Rome, and is like that inwrought with her filial piety. I have, in vain, attempted to subdue her to the drudgery of domestic service, and make her take part with Jennet; but as hopefully might you yoke a deer with an ox. It is not that she lacks obedience to me—so far as it seems she can command her duty, she is ever complying; but it appeareth impossible to her to clip the wings of her soaring thoughts, and keep them down to household matters.

"I have, sometimes, marvelled at the providence of God, in bestowing on this child of the forest, such rare gifts of mind, and other and outward beauties. Her voice hath a natural deep and most sweet melody in it, far beyond any stringed instrument. She hath too, (think not that I, like Everell, am, as Jennet saith, a charmed bird to her) she hath, though yet a child in years, that in her mien that doth bring to mind the lofty Judith, and the gracious Esther. When I once said this to Everell, he replied, "Oh, mother! is she not more like the gentle and tender Ruth?"[5] To him she may be, and therefore it is, that innocent and safe as the intercourse of these children now is, it is for thee to decide whether it be not most wise to remove the maiden from our dwelling. Two young plants that have sprung up in close neighbourhood, may be separated while young; but if disjoined after their fibres are all intertwined, one, or perchance both, may perish.

"Think not that this anxiety springs from the mistaken fancy of a woman, that love is the natural channel for all the purposes, and thoughts, and hopes, and feelings of human life. Neither think, I beseech thee, that doating with a foolish fondness upon my noble boy, I magnify into importance whatsoever concerneth him. No—my heart yearneth towards this poor heathen orphan-girl; and when I see her, in his absence, starting at every sound, and her restless eye turning an asking glance at every opening of the door; every movement betokening a disquieted spirit, and then the sweet contentment that stealeth over her face when he appeareth;—oh, my honoured husband! all my woman's nature feeleth for her—not for any present evil, but for what may betide.

"Having commended this subject to thy better wisdom, I will leave caring for it to speak to thee of others of thy household. Your three little girls are thriving mightily, and as to the baby, you will not be ashamed to own him; though you will not recognise, in the bouncing boy that plays bo-peep and creeps quite over the room, the little creature who had scarcely opened his eyes on the world, when you went away. He is by far the largest child I ever had, and the most knowing; he has cut his front upper teeth, and sheweth signs of two more. He is surprisingly fond of Oneco, and clappeth his hands with joy whenever he sees him. Indeed, the boy is a favourite with all the young ones, and greatly aideth me by continually pleasuring them. He is far different from his sister—gay and volatile, giving scarcely one thought to the past, and not one care to the future. His sister often taketh him apart to discourse with him, and sometimes doth produce a cast of seriousness over his countenance, but at the next presented object, it vanisheth as speedily as a shadow before a sunbeam. He hath commended himself greatly to the favour of Dame Grafton, by his devotion to her little favourite: a spoiled child is she, and it seemeth a pity that the name of Faith was given to her, since her shrinking timid character doth not promise, in any manner, to resemble that most potent of the christian graces. Oneco hath always some charm to lure her way- wardness. He bringeth home the treasures of the woods to please her—berries, and wild flowers, and the beautiful plumage of birds that are brought down by his unerring aim. Everell hath much advantage from the wood-craft of Oneco: the two boys daily enrich our table, which, in truth, hath need of such helps, with the spoils of the air and water.

"I am grieved to tell thee that some misrule hath crept in among thy servants in thy absence. Alas, what are sheep without their shepherd! Digby is, as ever, faithful—not serving with eye- service; but Hutton hath consorted much with some evil-doers, who have been violating the law of God and the law of our land, by meeting together in merry companies, playing cards, dancing, and the like. For these offences, they were brought before Mr. Pynchon, and sentenced to receive, each, "twenty stripes well laid on." Hutton furthermore, having been overtaken with drink, was condemned to wear suspended around his neck for one month, a bit of wood on which Toper is legibly written:— and Darby, who is ever a dawdler, having gone, last Saturday, with the cart to the village, dilly-dallied about there, and did not set out on his return till the sun was quite down, both to the eye and by the kalender. Accordingly, early on the following Monday, he was summoned before Mr. Pynchon, and ordered to receive ten stripes, but by reason of his youth and my intercession, which, being by a private letter, doubtless had some effect, the punishment was remitted; whereupon he heartily promised amendment and a better carriage.

"There hath been some alarm here within the last few days, on account of certain Indians who have been seen lurking in the woods around us. They are reported not to have a friendly appearance. We have been advised to remove, for the present, to the Fort; but as I feel no apprehension, I shall not disarrange my family by taking a step that would savour more of fear than prudence. I say I feel no apprehension—yet I must confess it— I have a cowardly womanish spirit, and fear is set in motion by the very mention of danger. There are vague forebodings hanging about me, and I cannot drive them away even by the thought that your presence, my honoured husband, will soon relieve me from all agitating apprehensions, and repair all the faults of my poor judgment. Fearful thoughts press on me—untoward accidents have prolonged thy absence—our re-union may yet be far distant, and if it should never chance in this world, oh remember that if I have fallen far short in duty, the measure of my love hath been full. I have ever known that mine was Leah's portion—that I was not the chosen and the loved one; and this has sometimes made me fearful—often joyless—but remember, it is only the perfect love of the husband that casteth out the fear of the wife.

"I have one request to prefer to thee which I have lacked courage to make by word of mouth, and therefore now commend it by letter to thy kindness. Be gracious unto me, my dear husband, and deem not that I overstep the modest bound of a woman's right in meddling with that which is thy prerogative— the ordering of our eldest son's education. Everell here hath few except spiritual privileges. God, who seeth my heart, knoweth I do not undervalue these—the manna of the wilderness. Yet to them might be added worldly helps, to aid the growth of the boy's noble gifts, a kind Providence having opened a wide door therefor in the generous offer of my brother Stretton. True, he hath not attained to our light whereby manifold errors of church and state are made visible; yet he hath ever borne himself uprightly, and to us, most lovingly, and as I remember there was a good Samaritan, and a faithful centurion, I think we are permitted to enlarge the bounds of our charity to those who work righteousness, albeit not of our communion."

"Thou hast already sown the good seed in our boy's heart, and it hath been (I say it not presumingly) nurtured with a mother's tears and prayers. Trust then to the promised blessing, and fear not to permit him to pass a few years in England, whence he will return to be a crown of glory to thee, my husband, and a blessing and honour to our chosen country. Importunity, I know, is not beseeming in a wife—it is the instrument of weakness, whereby, like the mouse in the fable, she would gnaw away what she cannot break. I will not, therefore, urge thee farther, but leave the decision to thy wisdom and thy love. And now, my dear husband, I kiss and embrace thee, and may God company with thee, and restore thee, if it be his good pleasure, to thy ever faithful and loving and obedient wife,

Martha Fletcher.

"To her honoured husband
these be delivered."

The above letter may indicate, but it feebly expresses, the character and state of mind of the writer. She never magnified her love by words, but expressed it by that self-devoting, self-sacrificing conduct to her husband and children, which characterizes, in all ages and circumstances, faithful and devoted woman. She was too generous to communicate all her fears, (about which a woman is usually least reserved) to her husband.

Some occurrences of the preceding day had given her just cause of alarm. At a short distance from Bethel, (the name that Mr. Fletcher had given his residence) there lived an old Indian woman, one of the few survivors of a tribe who had been faithful allies of the Pequods. After the destruction of her people, she had strayed up the banks of the Connecticut, and remained in Springfield. She was in the habit of supplying Mrs. Fletcher with wild berries and herbs, and receiving favours in return, and on that day went thither, as it appeared, on her customary errand. —She had made her usual barter, and had drawn her blanket around her as if to depart, but still she lingered standing before Mrs. Fletcher and looking fixedly at her. Mrs. Fletcher did not at first observe her; her head was bent over her infant sleeping on her lap, in the attitude of listening to its soft breathing. As she perused its innocent face a mother's beautiful visions floated before her; but, as she raised her eye and met the piercing glance of the old woman, a dark cloud came over the clear heaven of her thoughts. Nelema's brow was contracted, her lips drawn in, and her little sunken eye gleamed like a diamond from its dark recess.

"Why do you look at my baby thus?" asked Mrs. Fletcher.

The old woman replied in her own dialect, in a hurried inarticulate manner. "What says she, Magawisca?" asked Mrs. Fletcher of the Indian girl who stood beside her, and seemed to listen with unwonted interest.

"She says, madam, the baby is like a flower just opened to the sun, with no stain upon it—that he better pass now to the Great Spirit. She says this world is all a rough place—all sharp stones, and deep waters, and black clouds."

"Oh, she is old, Magawisca, and the days have come to her that have no pleasure in them. Look there," she said, "Nelema, at my son Everell;" the boy was at the moment passing the window, flushed with exercise and triumphantly displaying a string of game that he had just brought from the forest—"Is there not sunshine in my boy's face! To him every day is bright, and every path is smooth."

"Ah!" replied the old woman with a heavy groan, "I had sons too—and grandsons; but where are they? They trod the earth as lightly as that boy; but they have fallen like our forest trees, before the stroke of the English axe. Of all my race, there is not one, now, in whose veins my blood runs. Sometimes, when the spirits of the storm are howling about my wigwam, I hear the voices of my children crying for vengeance, and then I could myself deal the death-blow." Nelema spoke with vehemence and wild gesture; and her language, though interpreted by Magawisca's soft voice, had little tendency to allay the feeling her manner inspired. Mrs. Fletcher recoiled from her, and instinctively drew her baby closer to her breast.

"Nay," said the old woman, "fear me not, I have had kindness from thee, thy blankets have warmed me, I have been fed from thy table, and drank of thy cup, and what is this arm," and she threw back her blanket and stretched out her naked, shrivelled, trembling arm, "what is this to do the work of vengeance?"

She paused for an instant, glanced her eye wildly around the room, and then again fixed it on Mrs. Fletcher and her infant. "They spared not our homes," she said; "there where our old men spoke, where was heard the song of the maiden, and the laugh of our children; there now all is silence, dust, and ashes. I can neither harm thee, nor help thee. When the stream of vengeance rolls over the land, the tender shoot must be broken, and the goodly tree uprooted, that gave its pleasant shade and fruits to all."

"It is a shame and a sin," said Jennet who entered the room just as Magawisca was conveying Nelema's speech to Mrs. Fletcher; "a crying shame, for this heathen hag to be pouring forth here as if she were gifted like the prophets of old; she that can only see into the future by reading the devil's book, and if that be the case, as more than one has mistrusted, it were best, forthwith, to deliver her to the judges and cast her into prison."

"Peace, Jennet," said Mrs. Fletcher, alarmed lest Nelema should hear her, and her feelings, which were then at an exalted pitch, should be wrought to frenzy; but her apprehensions were groundless; the old woman saw nothing but the visions of her imagination; heard nothing but the fancied voices of the spirits of her race. She continued for a few moments to utter her thoughts in low inarticulate murmurs, and then, without again addressing Mrs. Fletcher, or raising her eyes, she left the house.

A few moments after her departure, Mrs. Fletcher perceived that she had dropped at her feet a little roll, which she found on examination, to be an arrow, and the rattle of a rattle-snake enveloped in a skin of the same reptile. She knew it was the custom of the savages to express much meaning by these symbols, and she turned to demand an explanation of Magawisca, who was deeply skilled in all the ways of her people.

Magawisca had disappeared, and Jennet, who had ever looked on the poor girl with a jealous and an evil eye, took this occasion to give vent to her feelings. "It is a pity," she said, "the child is out of the way the first time she was like to do a service; she may be skilled in snake's rattles, and bloody arrows, for I make no doubt she is as used to them, as I am to my broom and scrubbing-cloth."

"Will you call Magawisca to me," said Mrs. Fletcher, in a voice that from her would have been a silencing reproof to a more sensitive ear than Jennet's; but she, no ways daunted, replied, "Ah! that will I, madam, if I can find her; but where to look for her no mere mortal can tell; for she does not stay longer on a perch than a butterfly, unless indeed, it be when she is working on Mr. Everell's moccasins, or filling his ears with wild fables about those rampaging Indians. Ah, there she is!" she exclaimed, looking through the window, "talking with Nelema, just a little way in the wood—there, I see their heads above those scrub-oaks—see their wild motions—see Magawisca starts homeward—now the old woman pulls her back—now she seems entreating Nelema—the old hag shakes her head—Magawisca covers her eyes—what can all this mean? no good, I am sure. The girl is ever going to Nelema's hut, and of moonlight nights too, when they say witches work their will—birds of a feather flock together. Well, I know one thing, that if Master Everell was mine, I would sooner, in faith, cast him into the lion's den, or the fiery furnace, than leave him to this crafty offspring of a race that are the children and heirs of the evil one."

"Jennet," said Mrs. Fletcher, "thy tongue far outruns thy discretion. Restrain thy foolish thoughts, and bid Magawisca come to me."

Jennet sullenly obeyed, and soon after Magawisca entered. Mrs. Fletcher was struck with her changed aspect. She turned away, as one conscious of possessing a secret, and fearful that the eye, the herald of the soul, will speak unbidden. Her air was troubled and anxious, and instead of her usual light and lofty step, she moved timidly and dejectedly.

"Come to me, Magawisca," said Mrs. Fletcher, "and deal truly by me, as I have ever dealt by thee."

She obeyed, and as she stood by Mrs. Fletcher the poor girl's tears dropped on her benefactor's lap. "Thou hast been more than true," she said, "thou hast been kind to me as the mother-bird that shelters the wanderer in her nest."

"Then, Magawisca, if it concerneth me to know it, thou wilt explain the meaning of this roll which Nelema dropped at my feet."

The girl started and became very pale—to an observing eye, the changes of the olive skin are as apparent as those of a fairer complexion. She took the roll from Mrs. Fletcher and shut her eyes fast. Her bosom heaved convulsively; but after a short struggle with conflicting feelings, she said, deliberately, in a low voice—"That which I may speak without bringing down on me the curse of my father's race, I will speak. This," she added, unfolding the snake's skin, "this betokeneth the unseen and silent approach of an enemy. This, you know," and she held up the rattle, "is the warning voice that speaketh of danger near. And this," she concluded, taking the arrow in her trembling hand, "this is the symbol of death."

"And why, Magawisca, are these fearful tokens given to me? Dost thou know, girl, aught of a threatening enemy—of an ambushed foe?"

"I have said all that I may say," she replied.

Mrs. Fletcher questioned further, but could obtain no satisfaction. Magawisca's lips were sealed; and it was certain that if her resolution did not yield to the entreaties of her own heart, it would resist every other influence.

Mrs. Fletcher summoned Everell, and bade him urge Magawisca to disclose whatever Nelema had communicated. He did so, but sportively, for, he said, "the old woman was cracked, and Magawisca's head was turned. If there were indeed danger," he continued, "and Magawisca was apprised of it, think you, mother, she would permit us to remain in ignorance?" He turned an appealing glance to Magawisca, but her face was averted. Without suspecting this was intentional, he continued, "you ought to do penance, Magawisca, for the alarm you have given mother. You and I will act as her patrole to-night."

Magawisca assented, and appeared relieved by the proposition, though her gloom was not lightened by Everell's gaiety. Mrs. Fletcher did not, of course, acquiesce in this arrangement, but she deemed it prudent to communicate her apprehensions to her trusty Digby. After a short consultation, it was agreed that Digby should remain on guard during the night, and that the two other men-servants should have their muskets in order, and be ready at a moment's warning. Such precautions were not infrequent, and caused no unusual excitement in the household. Mrs. Fletcher had it, as she expressed herself, 'borne in upon her mind, after the evening exercise, to make some remarks upon the uncertainty of life.' She then dismissed the family to their several apartments, and herself retired to indite the epistle given above.

Everell observed Magawisca closely through the evening, and he was convinced, from the abstraction of her manner and from the efforts she made, (which were now apparent to him) to maintain a calm demeanor, that there was more ground for his mother's apprehensions than he, at first, supposed. He determined to be the companion of Digby's watch, and standing high in that good fellow's confidence, he made a private arrangement with him, which he easily effected without his mother's knowledge, for his youthful zeal did not render him regardless of the impropriety of heightening her fears.

CHAPTER IV

"It would have been happy if they had converted some before they had killed any."

—ROBINSON[1]

The house at Bethel had, both in front and in rear, a portico, or, as it was more humbly, and therefore more appropriately named, a shed; that in the rear, was a sort of adjunct to the kitchen, and one end of it was enclosed for the purpose of a bed-room, and occupied by Magawisca. Everell found Digby sitting at the other extremity of this portico; his position was prudently chosen. The moon was high, and the heavens clear, and there concealed and sheltered by the shadow of the roof, he could, without being seen, command the whole extent of cleared ground that bordered on the forest, whence the foe would come, if he came at all.

Everell, like a good knight, had carefully inspected his arms and just taken, his position beside Digby, when they heard Magawisca's window cautiously opened, and saw her spring through it. Everell would have spoken to her, but Digby made a signal of silence, and she, without observing them, hastened with a quick and light step towards the wood, and entered it, taking the path that led to Nelema's hut.

"Confound her!" exclaimed Digby; "she is in a plot with the old woman."

"No—no. On my life she is not, Digby."

42

"Some mischief—some mischief," said Digby, shaking his head. "They are a treacherous race. Let's follow her. No, we had best keep clear of the wood. Do you call after her; she will hearken to you."

Everell hesitated. "Speak quickly, Mr. Everell," urged Digby; "she will be beyond the reach of your voice. It is no light matter that could take her to Nelema's hut at this time of the night."

"She has good reason for going, Digby. I am sure of it; and I will not call her back."

"Reason," muttered Digby; "reason is but a jack-o'-lantern light in most people's minds. You trust her too far, Mr. Everell; but there, she is returning! See how she looks all around her, like a frightened bird that hears an enemy in every rustling leaf. Stand close—observe her—see, she lays her ear to the earth—it is their crafty way of listening—there, she is gone again!" he exclaimed, as Magawisca darted away into the wood. "It is past doubt she holds communication with some one. God send us a safe deliverance. I had rather meet a legion of Frenchmen than a company of these savages. They are a kind of beast we don't comprehend—out of the range of God's creatures—neither angel, man, nor yet quite devil. I would have sent to the fort for a guard to-night, but I liked not being driven hither and yon by that old hag's tokens; nor yet quite to take counsel from your good mother's fears, she being but a woman."

"I think you have caught the fear, Digby, without taking it's counsel," said Everell, "which does little credit to your wisdom; the only use of fear, being to provide against danger."

"That is true, Mr. Everell; but don't think I am afraid. It is one thing to know what danger is, and wish to shun it; and another thing to feel like you, fear-nought lads, that have never felt a twinge of pain, and have scarce a sense of your own mortality. You would be the boldest at an attack, Mr. Everell, and I should stand a siege best. A boy's courage is a keen weapon that wants temper."

"Apt to break at the first stroke from the enemy, you mean, Digby?" Digby nodded assent. "Well, I should like, at any rate, to prove it," added Everell.

"Time enough this half-dozen years yet, my young master. I

should be loath to see that fair skin of thine stained with blood; and, besides, you have yet to get a little more worldly prudence than to trust a young Indian girl, just because she takes your fancy."

"And why does she take my fancy, Digby? because she is true and noble-minded. I am certain, that if she knows of any danger approaching us, she is seeking to avert it."

"I don't know that, Mr. Everell; she'll be first true to her own people. The old proverb holds fast with these savages, as well as with the rest of the world—'hawks won't pick out hawks' eyes.' Like to like, throughout all nature. I grant you, she hath truly a fair seeming."

"And all that's foul is our own suspicion, is it not, Digby?"

"Not exactly; there's plainly some mystery between Maga-wisca and the old woman, and we know these Pequods were famed above all the Indian tribes for their cunning."

"And what is superior cunning among savages but superior sense?"

"You may out-talk me, Mr. Everell," replied Digby, with the impatience that a man feels when he is sure he is right, without being able to make it appear. "You may out-talk me, but you will never convince me. Was not I in the Pequod war? I ought to know, I think."

"Yes, and I think you have told me they shewed more reso-lution than cunning there; in particular, that the brother of Magawisca, whom she so piteously bemoans to this day, fought like a young lion."

"Yes, he did, poor dog!—and he was afterwards cruelly cut off; and it is this that makes me think they will take some terrible revenge for his death. I often hear Magawisca talking to Oneco of her brother, and I think it is to stir his spirit; but this boy is no more like to him than a spaniel to a bloodhound."

Nothing Digby said had any tendency to weaken Everell's confidence in Magawisca.

The subject of the Pequod war once started, Digby and Ev-erell were in no danger of sleeping at their post. Digby loved, as well as another man, and particularly those who have had brief military experience, to fight his battles o'er again; and Everell was at an age to listen with delight to tales of adventure, and danger. They thus wore away the time till the imaginations of both relater and listener were at that pitch, when every shadow is embodied, and every passing sound bears a voice to the quickened sense. "Hark!" said Digby, "did you not hear footsteps?"

"I hear them now," replied Everell; "they seem not very near. Is it not Magawisca returning?"

"No; there is more than one; and it is the heavy, though cautious, tread of men. Ha! Argus scents them." The old house-dog now sprang from his rest on a mat at the door-stone, and gave one of those loud inquiring barks, by which this animal first hails the approach of a strange footstep. "Hush, Argus, hush," cried Everell; and the old dog, having obeyed his instinct, seemed satisfied to submit to his master's voice, and crept lazily back to his place of repose.

"You have hushed Argus, and the footsteps too," said Digby; but it is well, perhaps, if there really is an enemy near, that he should know we are on guard."

"If there really is, Digby!" said Everell, who, terrific as the apprehended danger was, felt the irrepressible thirst of youth for adventure; "do you think we could both have been deceived?"

"Nothing easier, Mr. Everell, than to deceive senses on the watch for alarm. We heard something, but it might have been the wolves that even now prowl about the very clearing here at night. Ha!" he exclaimed, "there they are"—and starting forward he levelled his musket towards the wood.

"You are mad," said Everell, striking down Digby's musket with the butt end of his own. "It is Magawisca." Magawisca at that moment emerged from the wood.

Digby appeared confounded. "Could I have been so deceived?" he said; "could it have been her shadow—I thought I saw an Indian beyond that birch tree; you see the white bark? well, just beyond in the shade. It could not have been Magawisca, nor her shadow, for you see there are trees between the foot-path and that place; and yet, how should he have vanished without motion or sound?"

"Our senses deceive us, Digby," said Everell, reciprocating Digby's own argument.

"In this tormenting moonlight they do; but my senses have been well schooled in their time, and should have learned to know a man from a woman, and a shadow from a substance."

Digby had not a very strong conviction of the actual presence of an enemy, as was evident from his giving no alarm to his auxiliaries in the house; and he believed that if there were hostile Indians prowling about them, they were few in number, and fearful; still he deemed it prudent to persevere in their precautionary measures. "I will remain here," he said, "Mr. Everell, and do you follow Magawisca; sift what you can from her. Depend on't, there's something wrong. Why should she have turned away on seeing us? and did you not observe her hide something beneath her mantle?"

Everell acceded to Digby's proposition; not with the expectation of confirming his suspicions, but in the hope that Magawisca would shew they were groundless. He followed her to the front of the house, to which she seemed involuntarily to have bent her steps on perceiving him.

"You have taken the most difficult part of our duty on yourself, Magawisca," he said, on coming up to her. "You have acted as vidette,[2] while I have been quiet at my post."

Perhaps Magawisca did not understand him, at any rate she made no reply.

"Have you met an enemy in your reconnoitring? Digby and I fancied that we both heard and saw the foe."

"When and where?" exclaimed Magawisca, in a hurried, alarmed tone.

"Not many minutes since, and just at the very edge of the wood."

"What! when Digby raised his gun? I thought that had been in sport to startle me."

"No—Magawisca. Sporting does not suit our present case. My mother and her little ones are in peril, and Digby is a faithful servant."

"Faithful!" echoed Magawisca, as if there were more in Everell's expression than met the ear; "he surely may walk straight who hath nothing to draw him aside. Digby hath but one path, and that is plain before him—but one voice from his heart, and why should he not obey it?" The girl's voice faltered as she spoke, and as she concluded she burst into tears. Everell had never before witnessed this expression of feeling from her. She had an habitual self-command that hid the motions of her heart from common observers, and veiled them even from those who most narrowly watched her. Everell's confidence in Magawisca had not been in the least degree weakened by all the appearances against her. He did not mean to imply suspicion by his commendation of Digby, but merely to throw out a leading observation which she might follow if she would.

He felt reproached and touched by her distress, but struck by the clew, which, as he thought, her language afforded to the mystery of her conduct, and confident that she would in no way aid or abet any mischief that her own people might be contriving against them, he followed the natural bent of his generous temper, and assured her again, and again, of his entire trust in her. This seemed rather to aggravate than abate her distress. She threw herself on the ground, drew her mantle over her face, and wept convulsively. He found he could not allay the storm he had raised, and he seated himself beside her. After a little while, either exhausted by the violence of her emotion, or comforted by Everell's silent sympathy, she became composed; and raised her face from her mantle, and as she did so, something fell from beneath its folds. She hastily recovered and replaced it, but not till Everell had perceived it was an eagle's feather. He knew this was the badge of her tribe, and he had heard her say, that "a tuft from the wing of the monarch-bird was her father's crest." A suspicion flashed through his mind, and was conveyed to Magawisca's, by one bright glance of inquiry. She said nothing, but her responding look was rather sorrowful than confused, and Everell, anxious to believe what he wished to be true, came, after a little consideration, to the conclusion, that the feather had been dropped in her path by a passing bird. He did not scrutinise her motive in concealing it; he could not think her capable of evil, and anxious to efface from her mind the distrust his countenance might have expressed—"This beautiful moon and her train of stars," he said, "look as if they were keeping their watch over our dwelling. There are those, Magawisca, who believe the stars

have a mysterious influence on human destiny. I know nothing
of the grounds of their faith, and my imagination is none of the
brightest, but I can almost fancy they are stationed there as
guardian angels, and I feel quite sure that nothing evil could walk
abroad in their light."

"They do look peaceful," she replied mournfully; "but ah!
Everell, man is ever breaking the peace of nature. It was such a
night as this—so bright and still, when your English came upon
our quiet homes."

"You have never spoken to me of that night Magawisca."

"No—Everell, for our hands have taken hold of the chain of
friendship, and I feared to break it by speaking of the wrongs
your people laid on mine."

"You need not fear it; I can honour noble deeds though done
by our enemies, and see that cruelty is cruelty, though inflicted
by our friends."

"Then listen to me; and when the hour of vengeance comes,
if it should come, remember it was provoked."

She paused for a few moments, sighed deeply, and then began
the recital of the last acts in the tragedy of her people; the principal circumstances of which are detailed in the chronicles of the
times, by the witnesses of the bloody scenes. "You know," she
said, "our fortress-homes were on the level summit of a hill.
Thence we could see as far as the eye could stretch, our hunting-
grounds, and our gardens, which lay beneath us on the borders
of a stream that glided around our hill, and so near to it, that in
the still nights we could hear its gentle voice. Our fort and wigwams were encompassed with a palisade, formed of young trees,
and branches interwoven and sharply pointed. No enemy's foot
had ever approached this nest, which the eagles of the tribe had
built for their mates and their young. Sassacus and my father
were both away on that dreadful night. They had called a council
of our chiefs, and old men; our young men had been out in their
canoes, and when they returned they had danced and feasted,
and were now in deep sleep. My mother was in her hut with
her children, not sleeping, for my brother Samoset had lingered
behind his companions, and had not yet returned from the
water-sport. The warning spirit, that ever keeps its station at a

mother's pillow, whispered that some evil was near; and my mother, bidding me lie still with the little ones, went forth in quest of my brother. All the servants of the Great Spirit spoke to my mother's ear and eye of danger and death. The moon, as she sunk behind the hills, appeared a ball of fire; strange lights darted through the air; to my mother's eye they seemed fiery arrows; to her ear the air was filled with death-sighs.

"She had passed the palisade, and was descending the hill, when she met old Cushmakin. "Do you know aught of my boy?" she asked.

"Your boy is safe, and sleeps with his companions; he returned by the Sassafras knoll; that way can only be trodden by the strong-limbed, and light-footed." "My boy is safe," said my mother; "then tell me, for thou art wise, and canst see quite through the dark future, tell me, what evil is coming to our tribe?" She then described the omens she had seen. "I know not," said Cushmakin, "of late darkness hath spread over my soul, and all is black there, as before these eyes, that the arrows of death have pierced; but tell me, Monoco, what see you now in the fields of heaven?"

"Oh, now," said my mother, "I see nothing but the blue depths, and the watching stars. The spirits of the air have ceased their moaning, and steal over my cheek like an infant's breath. The water-spirits are rising, and will soon spread their soft wings around the nest of our tribe."

"The boy sleeps safely," muttered the old man, "and I have listened to the idle fear of a doating mother."

"I come not of a fearful race," said my mother.

"Nay, that I did not mean," replied Cushmakin, "but the panther watching her young is fearful as a doe." The night was far spent, and my mother bade him go home with her, for our powwows have always a mat in the wigwam of their chief. "Nay," he said, "the day is near, and I am always abroad at the rising of the sun." It seemed that the first warm touch of the sun opened the eye of the old man's soul, and he saw again the flushed hills, and the shaded vallies, the sparkling waters, the green maize, and the gray old rocks of our home. They were just passing the little gate of the palisade, when the old man's dog sprang from him with a fearful bark. A rushing sound was heard. "Owanox! Owanox! (the English! the English!") cried Cushmakin. My mother joined her voice to his, and in an instant the cry of alarm spread through the wigwams. The enemy were indeed upon us. They had surrounded the palisade, and opened their fire.

"Was it so sudden? Did they so rush on sleeping women and children?" asked Everell, who was unconsciously lending all his interest to the party of the narrator.

"Even so; they were guided to us by the traitor Wequash; he from whose bloody hand my mother had shielded the captive English maidens—he who had eaten from my father's dish, and slept on his mat. They were flanked by the cowardly Narragansetts, who shrunk from the sight of our tribe—who were pale as white men at the thought of Sassacus, and so feared him, that when his name was spoken, they were like an unstrung bow, and they said, 'He is all one God—no man can kill him.' These cowardly allies waited for the prey they dared not attack."[3]

"Then," said Everell, "as I have heard, our people had all the honour of the fight."

"Honour! was it, Everell—ye shall hear. Our warriors rushed forth to meet the foe; they surrounded the huts of their mothers, wives, sisters, children; they fought as if each man had a hundred lives, and would give each, and all, to redeem their homes. Oh! the dreadful fray, even now, rings in my ears! Those fearful guns that we had never heard before—the shouts of your people—our own battle yell—the piteous cries of the little children—the groans of our mothers, and, oh! worse—worse than all—the silence of those that could not speak——The English fell back; they were driven to the palisade; some beyond it, when their leader gave the cry to fire our huts, and led the way to my mother's. Samoset, the noble boy, defended the entrance with a prince-like courage, till they struck him down; prostrate and bleeding he again bent his bow, and had taken deadly aim at the English leader, when a sabre-blow severed his bowstring. Then was taken from our hearth-stone, where the English had been so often warmed and cherished, the brand to consume our dwellings. They were covered with mats, and burnt like dried straw.

The enemy retreated without the palisade. In vain did our warriors fight for a path by which we might escape from the consuming fire; they were beaten back; the fierce element gained on us; the Narragansetts pressed on the English, howling like wolves for their prey. Some of our people threw themselves into the midst of the crackling flames, and their courageous souls parted with one shout of triumph; others mounted the palisade, but they were shot and dropped like a flock of birds smitten by the hunter's arrows. Thus did the strangers destroy, in our own homes, hundreds of our tribe."

"And how did you escape in that dreadful hour, Magawisca —you were not then taken prisoners?"

"No; there was a rock at one extremity of our hut, and beneath it a cavity into which my mother crept, with Oneco, myself, and the two little ones that afterwards perished. Our simple habitations were soon consumed; we heard the foe retiring, and when the last sound had died away, we came forth to a sight that made us lament to be among the living. The sun was scarce an hour from his rising, and yet in this brief space our homes had vanished. The bodies of our people were strewn about the smouldering ruin; and all around the palisade lay the strong and valiant warriors—cold—silent—powerless as the unformed clay."

Magawisca paused; she was overcome with the recollection of this scene of desolation. She looked upward with an intent gaze, as if she held communion with an invisible being. "Spirit of my mother!" burst from her lips. "Oh! that I could follow thee to that blessed land where I should no more dread the war-cry, nor the death-knife." Everell dashed the gathering tears from his eyes, and Magawisca proceeded in her narrative.

"While we all stood silent and motionless, we heard footsteps and cheerful voices. They came from my father and Sassacus, and their band, returning from the friendly council. They approached on the side of the hill that was covered with a thicket of oaks, and their ruined homes at once burst upon their view. Oh! what horrid sounds then pealed on the air! shouts of wailing, and cries for vengeance. Every eye was turned with suspicion and hatred on my father. *He* had been the friend of the

English; *he* had counselled peace and alliance with them; *he* had protected their traders; delivered the captives taken from them, and restored them to their people: now *his* wife and children alone were living, and they called him traitor. I heard an angry murmur, and many hands were lifted to strike the death-blow. He moved not—'Nay, nay,' cried Sassacus, beating them off. 'Touch him not; his soul is bright as the sun; sooner shall you darken that, than find treason in his breast. If he hath shown the dove's heart to the English when he believed them friends, he will show himself the fierce eagle now he knows them enemies. Touch him not, warriors; remember my blood runneth in his veins.'

"From that moment my father was a changed man. He neither spoke nor looked at his wife, or children; but placing himself at the head of one band of the young men he shouted his war-cry, and then silently pursued the enemy. Sassacus went forth to assemble the tribe, and we followed my mother to one of our villages."

"You did not tell me, Magawisca," said Everell, "how Samoset perished; was he consumed in the flames, or shot from the palisade?"

"Neither—neither. He was reserved to whet my father's revenge to a still keener edge. He had forced a passage through the English, and hastily collecting a few warriors, they pursued the enemy, sprung upon them from a covert, and did so annoy them that the English turned and gave them battle. All fled save my brother, and him they took prisoner. They told him they would spare his life if he would guide them to our strong holds; he refused.[4] He had, Everell, lived but sixteen summers; he loved the light of the sun even as we love it; his manly spirit was tamed by wounds and weariness; his limbs were like a bending reed, and his heart beat like a woman's; but the fire of his soul burnt clear. Again they pressed him with offers of life and reward; he faithfully refused, and with one sabre-stroke they severed his head from his body."

Magawisca paused—she looked at Everell and said with a bitter smile—"You English tell us, Everell, that the book of your law is better than that written on our hearts,[5] for ye say it teaches mercy, compassion, forgiveness—if ye had such a law and believed it, would ye thus have treated a captive boy?"

Magawisca's reflecting mind suggested the most serious obstacle to the progress of the christian religion, in all ages and under all circumstances; the contrariety between its divine principles and the conduct of its professors; which, instead of always being a medium for the light that emanates from our holy law, is too often the darkest cloud that obstructs the passage of its rays to the hearts of heathen men. Everell had been carefully instructed in the principles of his religion, and he felt Magawisca's relation to be an awkward comment on them, and her inquiry natural; but though he knew not what answer to make, he was sure there must be a good one, and mentally resolving to refer the case to his mother, he begged Magawisca to proceed with her narrative.

"The fragments of our broken tribe," she said, "were collected, and some other small dependent tribes persuaded to join us. We were obliged to flee from the open grounds, and shelter ourselves in a dismal swamp. The English surrounded us; they sent in to us a messenger and offered life and pardon to all who had not shed the blood of Englishmen. Our allies listened, and fled from us, as frightened birds fly from a falling tree. My father looked upon his warriors; they answered that look with their battle-shout. 'Tell your people,' said my father to the messenger, 'that we have shed and drank English blood, and that we will take nothing from them but death.'

"The messenger departed and again returned with offers of pardon, if we would come forth and lay our arrows and our tomahawks at the feet of the English. 'What say you, warriors,' cried my father—'shall we take *pardon* from those who have burned your wives and children, and given your homes to the beasts of prey—who have robbed you of your hunting-grounds, and driven your canoes from their waters?' A hundred arrows were pointed to the messenger. 'Enough—you have your answer,' said my father, and the messenger returned to announce the fate we had chosen."

"Where was Sassacus?—had he abandoned his people?" asked Everell.

"Abandoned them! No—his life was in theirs; but accustomed to attack and victory, he could not bear to be thus driven, like a fox to his hole. His soul was sick within him, and he was silent and left all to my father. All day we heard the strokes of the English axes felling the trees that defended us, and when night came, they had approached so near that we could see the glimmering of their watch-lights through the branches of the trees. All night they were pouring in their bullets, alike on warriors, women, and children. Old Cushmakin was lying at my mother's feet, when he received a death-wound. Gasping for breath he called on Sassacus and my father—'Stay not here,' he said; 'look not on your wives and children, but burst your prison bound; sound through the nations the cry of revenge! Linked together, ye shall drive the English into the sea. I speak the word of the Great Spirit—obey it!' While he was yet speaking he stiffened in death. 'Obey him, warriors,' cried my mother; 'see,' she said, pointing to the mist that was now wrapping itself around the wood like a thick curtain—'see, our friends have come from the spirit-land to shelter you. Nay, look not on us—our hearts have been tender in the wigwam, but we can die before our enemies without a groan. Go forth and avenge us.'

" 'Have we come to the counsel of old men and old women!' said Sassacus, in the bitterness of his spirit.

" 'When women put down their womanish thoughts and counsel like men, they should be obeyed,' said my father. 'Follow me, warriors.'

"They burst through the enclosure. We saw nothing more, but we heard the shout from the foe, as they issued from the wood—the momentary fierce encounter—and the cry, 'they have escaped!' Then it was that my mother, who had listened with breathless silence, threw herself down on the mossy stones, and laying her hot cheek to mine—'Oh, my children—my children!' she said, 'would that I could die for you! But fear not death—the blood of a hundred chieftains, that never knew fear, runneth in your veins. Hark, the enemy comes nearer and nearer. Now lift up your heads, my children, and show them that even the weak ones of our tribe are strong in soul.'

"We rose from the ground—all about sat women and children

in family clusters, awaiting unmoved their fate. The English had penetrated the forest-screen, and were already on the little rising-ground where we had been entrenched. Death was dealt freely. None resisted—not a movement was made—not a voice lifted —not a sound escaped, save the wailings of the dying children.

"One of your soldiers knew my mother, and a command was given that her life and that of her children should be spared. A guard was stationed round us.

"You know that, after our tribe was thus cut off, we were taken, with a few other captives, to Boston. Some were sent to the Islands of the Sun, to bend their free limbs to bondage like your beasts of burden. There are among your people those who have not put out the light of the Great Spirit; they can remember a kindness, albeit done by an Indian; and when it was known to your Sachems that the wife of Mononotto, once the protector and friend of your people, was a prisoner, they treated her with honour and gentleness. But her people were extinguished—her husband driven to distant forests—forced on earth to the misery of wicked souls—to wander without a home; her children were captives—and her heart was broken. You know the rest."

This war, so fatal to the Pequods, had transpired the preceding year. It was an important event to the infant colonies, and its magnitude probably somewhat heightened to the imaginations of the English, by the terror this resolute tribe had inspired. All the circumstances attending it were still fresh in men's minds, and Everell had heard them detailed with the interest and particularity that belongs to recent adventures; but he had heard them in the language of the enemies and conquerors of the Pequods; and from Magawisca's lips they took a new form and hue; she seemed, to him, to embody nature's best gifts, and her feelings to be the inspiration of heaven. This new version of an old story reminded him of the man and the lion in the fable. But here it was not merely changing sculptors to give the advantage to one or the other of the artist's subjects; but it was putting the chisel into the hands of truth, and giving it to whom it belonged.

He had heard this destruction of the original possessors of the soil described, as we find it in the history of the times, where, we are told, "the number destroyed was about four hundred;" and "it was a fearful sight to see them thus frying in the fire, and the streams of blood quenching the same, and the horrible scent thereof; but the victory seemed a sweet sacrifice, and they gave the praise thereof to God."[6]

In the relations of their enemies, the courage of the Pequods was distorted into ferocity, and their fortitude, in their last extremity, thus set forth: "many were killed in the swamp, like sullen dogs, that would rather, in their self-willedness and madness, sit still to be shot or cut in pieces, than receive their lives for asking, at the hands of those into whose power they had now fallen."[7]

Everell's imagination, touched by the wand of feeling, presented a very different picture of those defenceless families of savages, pent in the recesses of their native forests, and there exterminated, not by superior natural force, but by the adventitious circumstances of arms, skill, and knowledge; from that offered by those who "then living and worthy of credit did affirm, that in the morning entering into the swamp, they saw several heaps of them [the Pequods] sitting close together, upon whom they discharged their pieces, laden with ten or twelve pistol bullets at a time, putting the muzzles of their pieces under the boughs, within a few yards of them."[8]

Everell did not fail to express to Magawisca, with all the eloquence of a heated imagination, his sympathy and admiration of her heroic and suffering people. She listened with a mournful pleasure, as one listens to the praise of a departed friend. Both seemed to have forgotten the purpose of their vigil, which they had marvellously kept without apprehension, or heaviness, when they were roused from their romantic abstraction by Digby's voice: "Now to your beds, children," he said; "the family is stirring, and the day is at hand. See the morning star hanging just over those trees, like a single watch-light in all the wide canopy. As you have not to look in a prayer-book for it, master Everell, don't forget to thank the Lord for keeping us safe, as your mother, God bless her, would say, through the night-watches. Stop one moment," added Digby, lowering his voice to Everell as he rose to follow Magawisca, "did she tell you?"

"Tell me! what?"

"What! Heaven's mercy! what ails the boy! Why, did she tell you what brought her out to-night? Did she explain all the mysterious actions we have seen? Are you crazy? Did not you ask her?"

Everell hesitated—fortunately for him the light was too dim to expose to Digby's eye the blushes that betrayed his consciousness that he had forgotten his duty. "Magawisca did not tell me," he said, "but I am sure Digby that"——

"That she can do no wrong—hey, Master Everell, well, that may be very satisfactory to you—but it does not content me. I like not her secret ways—'it's bad ware that needs a dark store.'"

Everell had tried the force of his own convictions on Digby, and knew it to be unavailing, therefore having no reply to make, he very discreetly retreated without attempting any.

Magawisca crept to her bed, but not to repose—neither watching nor weariness procured sleep for her. Her mind was racked with apprehensions, and conflicting duties, the cruellest rack to an honourable mind.

Nelema had communicated to her the preceding day, the fact which she had darkly intimated to Mrs. Fletcher, that Monotnotto, with one or two associates was lurking in the forest, and watching an opportunity to make an attack on Bethel. How far his purpose extended, whether simply to the recovery of his children, or to the destruction of the family, she knew not. The latter was most probable, for hostile Indians always left blood on their trail. In reply to Magawisca's eager inquiries, Nelema said she had again, and again, assured her father of the kind treatment his children had received at the hands of Mrs. Fletcher; but he seemed scarcely to hear what she said, and precipitately left her, telling her that she would not again see him, till his work was done.

Magawisca's first impulse had been to reveal all to Mrs. Fletcher; but by doing this, she would jeopard her father's life. Her natural sympathies—her strong affections—her pride, were all enlisted on the side of her people; but she shrunk, as if her own life were menaced, from the blow that was about to fall on her friends. She would have done or suffered any thing to avert it—any thing but betray her father. The hope of meeting him, explains all that seemed mysterious to Digby. She did go to Nelema's hut—but all was quiet there. In returning she found an eagle's feather in the path,—she believed it must have just been dropped there by her father, and this circumstance determined her to remain watching through the night, that if her father should appear, she might avert his vengeance.

She did not doubt that Digby had really seen and heard him; and believing that her father would not shrink from a single armed man, she hoped against hope, that his sole object was to recover his children; hoped against hope, we say, for her reason told her, that if that were his only purpose, it might easily have been accomplished by the intervention of Nelema.

Magawisca had said truly to Everell, that her father's nature had been changed by the wrongs he received. When the Pequods were proud and prosperous, he was more noted for his humane virtues, than his warlike spirit. The supremacy of his tribe was acknowledged, and it seemed to be his noble nature, as it is sometimes the instinct of the most powerful animals, to protect and defend, rather than attack and oppress. The ambitious spirit of his brother chieftain Sassacus, had ever aspired to dominion over the allied tribes; and immediately after the appearance of the English, the same temper was manifest in a jealousy of their encroachments. He employed all his art and influence and authority, to unite the tribes for the extirpation of the dangerous invaders. Mononotto, on the contrary, averse to all hostility, and foreseeing no danger from them, was the advocate of a hospitable reception, and pacific conduct.

This difference of feeling between the two chiefs, may account for the apparent treachery of the Pequods, who, as the influence of one or the other prevailed, received the English traders with favour and hospitality, or, violating their treaties of friendship, inflicted on them cruelties and death.

The stories of the murders of Stone, Norton, and Oldham, are familiar to every reader of our early annals;[9] and the anecdote of the two English girls, who were captured at Wethersfield, and protected and restored to their friends by the wife of Mononotto, has already been illustrated by a sister labourer;[10] and is precious to all those who would accumulate proofs, that the image of God is never quite effaced from the souls of his creatures; and that in their darkest ignorance, and deepest degradation, there are still to be found traits of mercy and benevolence. These will be gathered and treasured in the memory, with that fond feeling with which Mungo Park describes himself to have culled and cherished in his bosom, the single flower that bloomed in his melancholy track over the African desert.[11]

The chieftain of a savage race, is the depository of the honour of his tribe; and their defeat is a disgrace to him, that can only be effaced by the blood of his conquerors. It is a common case with the unfortunate, to be compelled to endure the reproach of inevitable evils; and Mononotto was often reminded by the remnant of his tribe, in the bitterness of their spirit, of his former kindness for the English. This reproach sharpened too keenly the edge of his adversity.

He had seen his people slaughtered, or driven from their homes and hunting-grounds, into shameful exile; his wife had died in captivity, and his children lived in servile dependence in the house of his enemies.

Sassacus perished by treachery, and Mononotto alone remained to endure this accumulated misery. In this extremity, he determined on the rescue of his children, and the infliction of some signal deed of vengeance, by which he hoped to revive the spirit of the natives, and reinstate himself as the head of his broken and dispersed people: in his most sanguine moments, he meditated a unity and combination that should eventually expel the invaders.

CHAPTER V

"There have been sweet singing voices
  In your walks that now are still;
There are seats left void in your earthly homes,
Which none again may fill."

MRS. HEMANS[1]

Magawisca rose from her sleepless pillow to join the family at prayers, her mind distracted with opposing fears, which her face, the mirror of her soul, too truly reflected.

Mrs. Fletcher observed her narrowly, and confirmed in her forebodings by the girl's apprehensive countenance, and still farther by Digby's report of her behaviour during the night, she resolved to dispatch him to Mr. Pynchon for his advice and assistance, touching her removal to the fort, or the appointment of a guard for Bethel. Her servant, (who prudently kept his alarm to himself, knowing, as he said, that a woman's fears were always ahead of danger) applauded her decision, and was on the point of proceeding to act upon it, when a messenger arrived with the joyful tidings, that Mr. Fletcher was within a few hours ride of Bethel. And the intelligence, no less joyful to Dame Grafton, that with his luggage, already arrived at the village, was a small box of millinery, which she had ordered from London.

Mrs. Fletcher feeling, as good wives do, a sense of safety from the proximity of her husband, bade Digby defer any new arrangement till he had the benefit of his master's counsel. The whole house was thrown into the commotion so common in a retired family, when an arrival is about to interrupt the equable current of life. Whatever unexpressed and superior happiness some others might have felt, no individual made such bustling demonstrations as Mrs. Grafton. It was difficult to say which excited her most, the anticipation of seeing her niece, Hope Leslie, or of inspecting the box of millinery.

Immediately after dinner, two of the men-servants were despatched to the village to transport their master's luggage. They had hardly gone when Mrs. Grafton recollected that her box contained a present for Madam Holioke, which it would be a thousand pities to have brought to Bethel, and lie there, perhaps a week before it would be sent to her, and 'she would like of all things, if Mrs. Fletcher saw no objection, to have the pony saddled and ride to the village herself, where the present could be made forthwith.'

Mrs. Fletcher was too happy to throw a shadow across any one's path, and wearied too, perhaps, with Mrs. Grafton's fidgetting, (for the good dame had all day been wondering whether her confidential agent had matched her orange satin; how she had trimmed her cap, &c. &c. &c.) she ordered a horse to be saddled and brought to the door. The animal proved a little restive, and Mrs. Grafton, not excelling in horsemanship, became alarmed and begged that Digby might be allowed to attend her.

Digby's cleverness was felt by all the household, and his talents were always in requisition for the miscellaneous wants of the family; but Digby, like good servants in every age, was aware of his importance, and was not more willing than a domestic of the present day, to be worked like a machine. He muttered something of "old women's making fools of themselves with new topknots," and saying aloud, that "Mistress Grafton knew it was his master's order, that all the men-servants should not be away from the place at the same time," he was turning off, when Mrs. Fletcher, who was standing at the door observing him, requested him with more authority than was usual in her manner, to comply with Mrs. Grafton's request.

"I would not wish," said Digby, still hesitating, "to disoblige Mistress Grafton—if it were a matter of life and death," he added, lowering his voice; "but to get more furbelows for the old lady when with what she has already, she makes such a fool of herself, that our young witlings, Master Everell and Oneco, garnish out our old Yorkshire hen with peacock's feathers and dandalions, and then call her, 'Dame Grafton in a flurry.' "

"Hush, Digby!" said Mrs. Fletcher, "it ill fits you to laugh at such fooleries in the boys—they shall be corrected, and do you learn to treat your master's friend with respect."

"Come—come, Digby," screamed Mrs. Grafton.

"Shall I go and break my master's orders?" asked Digby, still bent on having his own way.

"For this once you shall, Digby," answered Mrs. Fletcher, "and if you need an apology to your master, I shall not fail to make it."

"But if any thing should happen to you, Mistress Fletcher"—

"Nothing will happen, my good Digby. Is not your master at hand? and an hour or two will be the extent of your absence. So, get thee along without more ado."

Digby could not resist any farther the authority of his gentle mistress, and he walked by the side of Mrs. Grafton's pony, with slow unwilling steps.

All was joy in Mrs. Fletcher's dwelling. "My dear mother," said Everell, "it is now quite time to look out for father and Hope Leslie. I have turned the hour-glass three times since dinner, and counted all the sands I think. Let us all go on the front portico where we can catch the first glimpse of them, as they come past the elm-trees. Here, Oneco," he continued, as he saw assent in his mother's smile, "help me out with mother's rocking-chair—rather rough rocking," he added as he adjusted the rockers lengthwise with the logs that served for the flooring—"but mother wont mind trifles just now. Ah! blessed baby brother," he continued, taking in his arms the beautiful infant—"you shall come too, even though you cheat me out of my birthright, and get the first embrace from father." Thus saying, he placed the laughing infant in his go-cart, beside his mother. He then aided his little sisters in their arrangement of the playthings they had brought forth to welcome and astonish Hope; and finally he made an elevated position for Faith Leslie, where she might, he said, as she ought, catch the very first glimpse of her sister.

"Thank, thank you, Everell," said the little girl as she mounted her pinnacle; "if you knew Hope, you would want to see her first too—every body loves Hope. We shall always have pleasant times when Hope gets here."

It was one of the most beautiful afternoons at the close of the month of May. The lagging spring had at last come forth in all her power; her "work of gladness" was finished, and forests, fields, and meadows were bright with renovated life. The full Connecticut swept triumphantly on, as if still exulting in its release from the fetters of winter. Every gushing rill had the spring-note of joy. The meadows were, for the first time, enriched with patches of English grain, which the new settlers had sown, scantily, by way of experiment, prudently occupying the greatest portion of the rich mould, with the native Indian corn. This product of our soil is beautiful in all its progress, from the moment, when as now it studded the meadow with hillocks, shooting its bright-pointed spear from its mother earth, to its maturity, when the long golden ear bursts from the rustling leaf.

The grounds about Mrs. Fletcher's house had been prepared with the neatness of English taste; and a rich bed of clover that overspread the lawn immediately before the portico, already rewarded the industry of the cultivators. Over this delicate carpet, the domestic fowls, the first civilized inhabitants of the country, of their tribe, were now treading, picking their food here and there like dainty little epicures.

The scene had also its minstrels; the birds, those ministers and worshippers of nature, were on the wing, filling the air with melody; while, like diligent little housewifes, they ransacked forest and field for materials for their house-keeping.

A mother, encircled by healthful sporting children, is always a beautiful spectacle—a spectacle that appeals to nature in every human breast. Mrs. Fletcher, in obedience to matrimonial duty, or, it may be, from some lingering of female vanity, had, on this occasion, attired herself with extraordinary care. What woman does not wish to look handsome?—in the eyes of her husband.

"Mother," said Everell, putting aside the exquisitely fine lace that shaded her cheek, "I do not believe you looked more beautiful than you do to-day when, as I have heard, they called you 'the rose of the wilderness'—our little Mary's cheek is as round and as bright as a peach, but it is not so handsome as yours, mother. 'Your heart has sent this colour here," he continued, kissing her tenderly—"it seems to have come forth to tell us that our father is near."

"It would shame me, Everell," replied his mother, embracing him with a feeling that the proudest drawing-room belle might have envied, "to take such flattery from any lips but thine."

"Oh do not call it flattery, mother—look, Magawisca—for heaven's sake cheer up—look, would you know mother's eye? just turn it, mother, one minute from that road—and her pale cheek too—with this rich colour on it?"

"Alas! alas!" replied Magawisca, glancing her eyes at Mrs. Fletcher, and then as if heart-struck, withdrawing them, "how soon the flush of the setting sun fades from the evening cloud."

"Oh Magawisca," said Everell impatiently, "why are you so dismal? your voice is too sweet for a bird of ill-omen. I shall begin to think as Jennet says—though Jennet is no text-book for me—I shall begin to think old Nelema has really bewitched you."

"You call me a bird of ill-omen," replied Magawisca, half proud, half sorrowful, "and you call the owl a bird of ill-omen, but we hold him sacred—he is our sentinel, and when danger is near he cries, awake! awake!"

"Magawisca, you are positively unkind—Jeremiah's lamentations on a holiday would not be more out of time than your croaking is now—the very skies, earth, and air seem to partake our joy at father's return, and you only make a discord. Do you think if your father was near I would not share your joy?"

Tears fell fast from Magawisca's eye, but she made no reply, and Mrs. Fletcher observing and compassionating her emotion, and thinking it probably arose from comparing her orphan state to that of the merry children about her, called her and said, "Magawisca, you are neither a stranger, nor a servant, will you not share our joy? Do you not love us?"

"Love you!" she exclaimed, clasping her hands, "love you! I would give my life for you."

"We do not ask your life, my good girl," replied Mrs. Fletcher, kindly smiling on her, "but a light heart and a cheerful look. A sad countenance doth not become this joyful hour. Go and help Oneco—he is quite out of breath, blowing those soap bubbles for the children."

Oneco smiled, and shook his head, and continued to send off one after another of the prismatic globes, and as they rose and floated on the air and brightened with the many-coloured ray, the little girls clapped their hands, and the baby stretched his to grasp the brilliant vapour.

"Oh!" said Magawisca, impetuously covering her eyes, "I do not like to see any thing so beautiful, pass so quickly away."

Scarcely had she uttered these words, when suddenly, as if the earth had opened on them, three Indian warriors darted from the forest and pealed on the air their horrible yells.

"My father! my father!" burst from the lips of Magawisca, and Oneco.

Faith Leslie sprang towards the Indian boy, and clung fast to him—and the children clustered about their mother—she instinctively caught her infant and held it close within her arms as if their ineffectual shelter were a rampart.

Magawisca uttered a cry of agony, and springing forward with her arms uplifted, as if deprecating his approach, she sunk down at her father's feet, and clasping her hands, "save them—save them," she cried, "the mother—the children—oh they are all good—take vengeance on your enemies—but spare—spare our friends—our benefactors—I bleed when they are struck—oh command them to stop!" she screamed, looking to the companions of her father, who unchecked by her cries, were pressing on to their deadly work.

Mononotto was silent and motionless, his eye glanced wildly from Magawisca to Oneco. Magawisca replied to the glance of fire—"yes, they have sheltered us—they have spread the wing of love over us—save them—save them—oh it will be too late," she cried, springing from her father, whose silence and fixedness showed that if his better nature rebelled against the work of revenge, there was no relenting of purpose. Magawisca darted before the Indian who was advancing towards Mrs. Fletcher with an uplifted hatchet. "You shall hew me to pieces ere you touch her," she said, and planted herself as a shield before her bene-factress.

The warrior's obdurate heart untouched by the sight of the helpless mother and her little ones, was thrilled by the courage of the heroic girl—he paused and grimly smiled on her when his companion, crying, "hasten, the dogs will be on us!" levelled a deadly blow at Mrs. Fletcher—but his uplifted arm was pen-etrated by a musket shot and the hatchet fell harmless to the floor.

"Courage, mother!" cried Everell, reloading the piece, but neither courage nor celerity could avail—the second Indian sprang upon him, threw him on the floor, wrested his musket from him, and brandishing his tomahawk over his head, he would have aimed the fatal stroke, when a cry from Mononotto arrested his arm.

Everell extricated himself from his grasp, and one hope flash-ing into his mind, he seized a bugle-horn which hung beside the door, and winded it. This was the conventional signal of alarm —and he sent forth a blast—long and loud—a death-cry.

Mrs. Grafton and her attendants were just mounting their horses to return home. Digby listened for a moment—then ex-claiming, "it comes from our master's dwelling! ride for your life, Hutton!" he tossed away a bandbox that encumbered him, and spurred his horse to its utmost speed.

The alarm was spread through the village, and in a brief space Mr. Pynchon with six armed men were pressing towards the fatal scene.

In the mean time the tragedy was proceeding at Bethel. Mrs. Fletcher's senses had been stunned with terror. She had neither spoken nor moved after she grasped her infant. Everell's gallant interposition, restored a momentary consciousness; she screamed to him—"Fly, Everell, my son, fly; for your father's sake, fly."

"Never," he replied, springing to his mother's side.

The savages, always rapid in their movements, were now aware that their safety depended on despatch. "Finish your work, warriors," cried Mononotto. Obedient to the command, and infuriated by his bleeding wound, the Indian, who on receiving the shot, had staggered back, and leant against the wall, now sprang forward, and tore the infant from its mother's breast. She shrieked, and in that shriek, passed the agony of death. She was unconscious that her son, putting forth a strength beyond nature, for a moment kept the Indian at bay; she neither saw nor felt the knife struck at her own heart. She felt not the arms of her defenders, Everell and Magawisca, as they met around her neck. She fainted, and fell to the floor, dragging her impotent protectors with her.

The savage, in his struggle with Everell, had tossed the infant boy to the ground; he fell quite unharmed on the turf at Mononotto's feet. There raising his head, and looking up into the chieftain's face, he probably perceived a gleam of mercy, for with the quick instinct of infancy, that with unerring sagacity directs its appeal, he clasped the naked leg of the savage with one arm, and stretched the other towards him with a piteous supplication, that no words could have expressed.

Mononotto's heart melted within him; he stooped to raise the sweet suppliant, when one of the Mohawks fiercely seized him, tossed him wildly around his head, and dashed him on the doorstone. But the silent prayer—perhaps the celestial inspiration of the innocent creature, was not lost. "We have had blood enough," cried Mononotto, "you have well avenged me, brothers."

Then looking at Oneco, who had remained in one corner of the portico, clasping Faith Leslie in his arms, he commanded him to follow him with the child. Everell was torn from the lifeless bodies of his mother and sisters, and dragged into the forest. Magawisca uttered one cry of agony and despair, as she looked, for the last time, on the bloody scene, and then followed her father.

As they passed the boundary of the cleared ground, Mononotto tore from Oneco his English dress, and casting it from him—"Thus perish," he said, "every mark of the captivity of my children. Thou shalt return to our forests," he continued, wrapping a skin around him, "with the badge of thy people."

CHAPTER VI

"It is but a shadow vanished—a bubble broke, a dreame finish't—
Eternitie will pay for all."

ROGER WILLIAMS[1]

Scarcely had the invaders disappeared, and the sound of their
footsteps died away, when Digby and Hutton came in view of
the dwelling. "Ah!" said Hutton, reining in his horse, "I thought
all this fluster was for nothing—the blast a boy's prank. A pretty
piece of work we've made of it; you'll have Mistress Grafton
about your ears for tossing away her Lon'on gimcracks. All is
as quiet here as a Saturday night; nothing to be seen but the
smoke from the kitchen-chimney, and that's a pleasant sight to
me, for I went off without my dinner, and methinks it will now
taste as savoury as Jacob's pottage."

Digby lent no attention to his companion's chattering, but
pressed on; his fears were allayed, but not removed. As he approached the house, he felt that the silence which pervaded it,
boded no good; but the horrors of the reality far surpassed the
worst suggestions of his vague apprehensions. "Oh, my mistress!
my mistress!" he screamed, when the havoc of death burst upon
his sight. "My good mistress—and her girls!—and the baby too!
Oh, God—have mercy on my master!" and he bent over the
bodies and wrung his hands: "not one—not one spared!"

"Yes, one," spoke a trembling whining voice, which proved

to be Jennet's, who had just emerged from her hiding-place covered with soot; "by the blessing of a kind Providence, I have been preserved for some wise end, but," she continued, panting, "the fright has taken my breath away, besides being squeezed as flat as a pancake in the bed-room chimney."

"Stop—for Heaven's sake, stop, Jennet, and tell me, if you can, if Mr. Everell was here."

Jennet did not know; she remembered having seen the family in general assembled, just before she heard the yell of the savages.

"How long," Digby inquired, "have they been gone? how long since you heard the last sound?"

"That's more than mortal man, or woman either, in my case, could tell, Mr. Digby. Do you think, when a body seems to feel a scalping knife in their heads, they can reckon time? No; hours are minutes, and minutes hours, in such a case."

"Oh fool! fool!" cried Digby, and turning disgusted away, his eye fell on his musket. "Thank the Lord!" he exclaimed, "Mr. Everell has poured one shot into the fiends; he alone knew where the gun was, bless the boy—bless him; he has a strong arm, and a stout soul—bless him. They have taken him off— we'll after him, Hutton. Jennet, bring my hunting pouch. Look to your fire-lock, Hutton. Magawisca!—Oneco! Faith Leslie, all gone!" he continued, his first amazement dissipating, and thought after thought flashing the truth on his mind. "I remember last night—Oh, Mr. Everell, how the girl deceived you— she knew it all."

"Ah, Magawisca! so I thought," said Jennet. "She knows every thing evil that happens in earth, sea, or air; she and that mother-witch, Nelema. I always told Mrs. Fletcher she was warming a viper in her bosom, poor dear lady; but I suppose it was for wise ends she was left to her blindness."

"Are you ready, Hutton?" asked Digby, impatiently.

"Ready!—yes, I am ready, but what is the use, Digby? what are we two against a host? and, besides, you know not how long they have been gone."

"Not very long," said Digby, shuddering and pointing to blood that was trickling, drop by drop, from the edge of the flooring to the step. How long the faithful fellow might have urged, we know not, for cowardice hath ever ready and abundant arguments, and Hutton was not a man to be persuaded into danger; but the arrival of Mr. Pynchon and his men, put an end to the debate.

Mr. Pynchon was the faithful, paternal guardian of his little colony. He saw in this scene of violent death, not only the present overwhelming misery of the family at Bethel, but the fearful fate to which all were exposed who had perilled their lives in the wilderness; but he could give but brief space to bitter reflections, and the lamentings of nature. Instant care and service were necessary for the dead and the living. The bodies of the mother and children were removed to one of the apartments, and decently disposed, and then, after a fervent prayer, a duty never omitted in any emergency by the pilgrims, whose faith in the minute superintendence of Providence was practical, he directed the necessary arrangements for the pursuit of the enemy.

Little could be gathered from Jennet. She was mainly occupied with her own remarkable preservation, not doubting that Providence had specially interposed to save the only life utterly insignificant in any eyes but her own. She recollected to have heard Magawisca exclaim, 'My father!' at the first onset of the savages. The necessary conclusion was, that the party had been led by the Pequod chief. It was obviously probable that he would return, with his children and captives, to the Mohawks, where, it was well known, he had found refuge; of course the pursuers were to take a westerly direction. Jennet was of opinion that the party was not numerous; and encumbered as they must be with their prisoners, the one a child whom it would be necessary, in a rapid flight to carry, Mr. Pynchon had sanguine expectations that they might be overtaken.

The fugitives, obliged to avoid the cleared meadows, had, as Mr. Pynchon believed, taken an indirect path through the forest to the Connecticut; which, in pursuance of their probable route, they would, of course cross, as soon as they could, with safety. He selected five of his men, whom he deemed fittest for the expedition, and recommending it to them to be guided by the counsel of Digby, whose impatient zeal was apparent, he directed them to take a direct course to the river. He was to return to the village, and despatch a boat to them, with which they were to ply up the river, in the hope of intercepting the passage of the Indians.

The men departed, led by Digby, to whose agitated spirit every moment's delay had appeared unnecessary and fatal; and Mr. Pynchon was mounting his horse, when he saw Mr. Fletcher, who had avoided the circuitous road through the village, emerge from the forest, and come in full view of his dwelling. Mr. Pynchon called to Jennet, "yonder is your master—he must not come hither while this precious blood is on the threshold—I shall take him to my house, and assistance shall be sent to you. In the mean time, watch those bodies faithfully."

"Oh! I can't stay here alone," whimpered Jennet, running after Mr. Pynchon—"I would not stay for all the promised land."

"Back, woman," cried Mr. Pynchon, in a voice of thunder; and Jennet retreated, the danger of advancing appearing, for the moment, the greater of the two.

Mr. Fletcher was attended by two Indians, who followed him, bearing on a litter, his favourite, Hope Leslie. When they came within sight of Bethel, they shouted the chorus of a native song. Hope inquired its meaning. They told her, and raising herself, and tossing back the bright curls that shaded her eyes, she clapped her hands, and accompanied them with the English words,—'The home!—the home!—the chieftain's home!'— "And my home too, is it not?" she said.

Mr. Fletcher was touched with the joy with which this bright little creature, who had left a palace in England, hailed his rustic dwelling in the wilderness. He turned on her a smile of delight —he could not speak; the sight of his home had opened the flood-gates of his heart. "Oh now," she continued, with growing animation, "I shall see my sister. But why does not she come to meet us?—Where is your Everell? and the girls? There is no one looking out for us."

The stillness of the place, and the absence of all living objects, struck Mr. Fletcher with fearful apprehensions, heightened by the sight of his friend, who was coming, at full gallop, towards him. To an accurate observer, the effects of joy and sorrow, on the human figure, are easily discriminated—misery depresses, contracts, and paralyses the body, as it does the spirit.

"Remain here for a few moments," said Mr. Fletcher to his attendants, and he put spurs to his horse, and galloped forward.

"Put down the litter," said Hope Leslie to her bearers. "I cannot stand stock-still, here, in sight of the house where my sister is." The Indians knew their duty, and determined to abide by the letter of their employer's orders, did not depress the litter.

"There, take that for your sulkiness," she said, giving each a tap on his ear, and half impatient, half sportive, she leaped from the litter, and bounded forward.

The friends met. Mr. Pynchon covered his face, and groaned aloud. "What has happened to my family?" demanded Mr. Fletcher. "My wife?—my son?—my little ones?——Oh! speak —God give me grace to hear thee!"

In vain Mr. Pynchon essayed to speak—he could find no words to soften the frightful truth. Mr. Fletcher turned his horse's head towards Bethel, and was proceeding to end, himself, the insupportable suspense, when his friend, seizing his arm, cried—"Stop, stop—go not thither—thy house is desolate"— and then, half-choked with groans and sobs, he unfolded the dismal story.

Not a sound, nor a sigh, escaped the blasted man. He seemed to be turned into stone, till he was roused by the wild shrieks of the little girl, who, unobserved, had listened to the communication of Mr. Pynchon.

"Take the child with you," he said—"I shall go to my house. If—if my boy returns, send a messenger instantly; otherwise, suffer me to remain alone till to-morrow."

He passed on, without appearing to hear the cries and entreaties of Hope Leslie, who, forcibly detained by Mr. Pynchon, screamed, "Oh! take me—take me with you——there are but us two left—I will not go away from you!" but at last, finding resistance useless, she yielded, and was conveyed to the village, where she was received by her aunt Grafton, whose grief was as noisy and communicative, as Mr. Fletcher's had been silent, and unexpressed by any of the forms of sorrow.

Early on the following morning, Mr. Pynchon, attended by

several others, men and women, went to Bethel to offer their
sympathy and service. They met Jennet at the door, who, greatly
relieved by the sight of human faces, and ears willing to listen,
informed them, that immediately after her master's arrival, he
had retired to the apartment that contained the bodies of the
deceased, charging her not to intrude on him.

A murmur of apprehension ran around the circle. "It was
misjudged to leave him here alone," whispered one. "It is not
every man, though his faith stand as a mountain in his prosperity, that can bear to have the Lord put forth his hand, and touch
his bone and his flesh."

"Ah!" said another, "my heart misgave me when Mr. Pynchon told us how calm he took it; such a calm as that is like the
still dead waters that cover the lost cities—quiet is not the nature
of the creature, and you may be sure that unseen havoc and ruin
are underneath."

"The poor dear gentleman should have taken something to
eat or drink," said a little plump, full-fed lady; "there is nothing
so feeding to grief as an empty stomach. Madam Holioke, do
not you think it would be prudent for us to guard with a little
cordial and a bit of spiced cake—if this good girl can give it to
us," looking at Jennet. "The dear lady that's gone was ever
thrifty in her housewifery, and I doubt not she hath left such
witnesses behind."

Mrs. Holioke shook her head, and a man of a most solemn and
owl aspect, who sat between the ladies, turned to the last speaker
and said, in a deep guttural tone, "Judy, thou shouldst not bring
thy carnal propensities to this house of mourning—and perchance of sin. Where the Lord works, Satan worketh also, tempt-
ing the wounded. I doubt our brother Fletcher hath done violence
to himself. He was ever of a proud—that is to say, a peculiar and
silent make—and what won't bend, will break."

The suggestion in this speech communicated alarm to all present. Several persons gathered about Mr. Pynchon. Some advised
him to knock at the door of the adjoining apartment; others
counselled forcing it if necessary. While each one was proffering
his opinion, the door opened from within, and Mr. Fletcher
came among them.

"Do you bring me any news of my son?" he asked Mr. Pynchon.

"None, my friend—the scouts have not yet returned."

Till this question was put and answered, there was a tremulousness of voice, a knitting of the brow, and a variation of colour, that indicated the agitation of the sufferer's soul; but then a sublime composure overspread his countenance and figure. He noticed every one present with more than his usual attention, and to a superficial observer, one who knew not how to interpret his mortal paleness, the wild melancholy of his glazed eye and his rigid muscles, which had the inflexibility and fixedness of marble, he might have appeared to be suffering less than any person present. Some cried outright—some stared with undisguised and irrepressible curiosity—some were voluble in the expression of their sympathy, while a few were pale, silent, and awe-struck. All these many coloured feelings fell on Mr. Fletcher like light on a black surface—producing no change—meeting no return. He stood leaning on the mantel-piece, till the first burst of feeling was over—till all, insensibly yielding to his example, became quiet, and the apartment was as still as that in which death held his silent dominion.

Mr. Pynchon then whispered to him. "My friend, bear your testimony now—edify us with a seasonable word, showing that you are not amazed at your calamity—that you counted the cost before you undertook to build the Lord's building in the wilderness. It is suitable that you should turn your affliction to the profit of the Lord's people."

Mr. Fletcher felt himself stretched on a rack, that he must endure with a martyr's patience; he lifted up his head and with much effort spoke one brief sentence—a sentence which contains all that a christian could feel, or the stores of language could express—he uttered, "God's will be done!" and then hurried away, to hide his struggles in solitude.

Relieved from the restraint of his presence, the company poured forth such moral, consoling, and pious reflections as usually flow spontaneously from the lips of the spectators of suffering; and which would seem to indicate that each individual has a spare stock of wisdom and patience for his neighbour's occasions, though, through some strange fatality, they are never applied to his own use.

We hope our readers will not think we have wantonly sported with their feelings, by drawing a picture of calamity that only exists in the fictitious tale. No—such events, as we have feebly related, were common in our early annals, and attended by horrors that it would be impossible for the imagination to exaggerate. Not only families but villages, were cut off by the most dreaded of all foes—the ruthless, vengeful savage.

In the quiet possession of the blessings transmitted, we are, perhaps, in danger of forgetting, or undervaluing the sufferings by which they were obtained. We forget that the noble pilgrims lived and endured for us—that when they came to the wilderness, they said truly, though it may be somewhat quaintly, that they turned their backs on Egypt—they did virtually renounce all dependence on earthly supports—they left the land of their birth—of their homes—of their father's sepulchres—they sacrificed ease and preferment, and all the delights of sense—and for what?—to open for themselves an earthly paradise?—to dress their bowers of pleasure and rejoice with their wives and children? No—they came not for themselves—they lived not to themselves. An exiled and suffering people, they came forth in the dignity of the chosen servants of the Lord, to open the forests to the sun-beam, and to the light of the Sun of Righteousness—to restore man—man oppressed and trampled on by his fellow; to religious and civil liberty, and equal rights —to replace the creatures of God on their natural level—to bring down the hills, and make smooth the rough places, which the pride and cruelty of man had wrought on the fair creation of the Father of all.

What was their reward? Fortune?—distinctions?—the sweet charities of home? No—but their feet were planted on the mount of vision, and they saw, with sublime joy, a multitude of people where the solitary savage roamed the forest—the forest vanished, and pleasant villages and busy cities appeared—the tangled foot-path expanded to the thronged high-way—the consecrated church planted on the rock of heathen sacrifice.

And that we might realize this vision—enter into this promised land of faith—they endured hardship, and braved death—deeming, as said one of their company, that "he is not worthy to live at all, who, for fear or danger of death, shunneth his country's service, or his own honour—since death is inevitable and the fame of virtue immortal."

If these were the fervors of enthusiasm, it was an enthusiasm kindled and fed by the holy flame that glows on the altar of God—an enthusiasm that never abates, but gathers life and strength as the immortal soul expands in the image of its Creator.

We shall now leave the little community, assembled at Bethel, to perform the last offices for one who had been among them an example of all the most attractive virtues of woman. The funeral ceremony was then, as it still is, among the descendants of the pilgrims, a simple affectionate service; a gathering of the people—men, women, and children, as one family, to the house of mourning.

Mononotto and his party in their flight had less than an hour's advantage of their pursuers; and, retarded by their captives, they would have been compelled to despatch them, or have been overtaken, but for their sagacity in traversing the forest; they knew how to wind around morasses, to shape their course to the margin of the rivulets, and to penetrate defiles, while their pursuers, unpractised in that accurate observation of nature, by which the savage was guided, were clambering over mountains, arrested by precipices, or half buried in swamps.

After an hour's silent and rapid flight, the Indians halted to make such arrangements as would best accelerate their retreat. They placed the little Leslie on the back of one of the Mohawks, and attached her there by a *happis,* or strong wide band, passed several times over her, and around the body of her bearer. She screamed at her separation from Oneco, but being permitted to stretch out her hand and place it in his, she became quiet and satisfied.

The Mohawk auxiliaries, who so lately had seemed two insatiate bloodhounds, now appeared to regard the reciprocal devotion of the children with complacency; but their amity was not extended to Everell; and Saco in particular, the Indian whom he had wounded, and whose arm was irritated and smarting, eyed him with glances of brooding malignity. Magawisca perceived this, and dreading lest the savage should give way to a sudden impulse of revenge, she placed herself between him, and Everell. This movement awakened Mononotto from a sullen reverie, and striking his hands together, angrily, he bade Magawisca remove from the English boy.

She obeyed, and mournfully resumed her place beside her father, saying, as she did so, in a low thrilling tone, "my father —my father!—where is my father's look, and voice?——Mononotto has found his daughter, but I have not found my father."

Mononotto felt her reproach—his features relaxed, and he laid his hand on her head.

"My father's soul awakes!" she cried, exultingly. "Oh, listen to me—listen to me!"—she waived her hand to the Mohawks to stop, and they obeyed. "Why," she continued in an impassioned voice—"why hath my father's soul stooped from its ever upward flight? Till this day his knife was never stained with innocent blood. Yonder roof," and she pointed towards Bethel, "has sheltered thy children—the wing of the mother-bird was spread over us—we ate of the children's bread; then, why hast thou shed their blood?—why art thou leading the son into captivity? Oh, spare him!—send him back—leave one light in the darkened habitation!"

"One," echoed Mononotto; "did they leave me one? No;— my people, my children, were swept away like withered leaves before the wind—and there where our pleasant homes were clustered, is silence and darkness—thistles have sprung up around our hearth-stones, and grass has overgrown our path-ways. Magawisca, has thy brother vanished from thy memory? I tell thee, that as Samoset died, that boy shall die. My soul rejoiced when he fought at his mother's side, to see him thus make himself a worthy victim to offer to thy lion-hearted brother—even so fought Samoset."

Magawisca felt that her father's purpose was not to be shaken. She looked at Everell, and already felt the horrors of the captive's fate—the scorching fires, and the torturing knives; and when her father commanded the party to move onward, she uttered a piercing shriek.

"Be silent, girl," said Mononotto, sternly; "cries and screams are for children and cowards."

"And I am a coward," replied Magawisca, reverting to her habitually calm tone, "if to fear my father should do a wrong, even to an enemy, is cowardice." Again her father's brow soft-ened, and she ventured to add, "send back the boy, and our path will be all smooth before us—and light will be upon it, for my mother often said, 'the sun never sets on the soul of the man that doeth good.' "

Magawisca had unwittingly touched the spring of her father's vindictive passions. "Dost thou use thy mother's words," he said, "to plead for one of the race of her murderers? Is not her grave among my enemies? Say no more, I command you, and speak not to the boy; thy kindness but sharpens my revenge."

There was no alternative. Magawisca must feel, or feign sub-mission; and she laid her hand on her heart, and bowed her head, in token of obedience. Everell had observed, and understood her intercession, for, though her words were uttered in her own tongue, there was no mistaking her significant manner; but he was indifferent to the success of her appeal. He still felt the dying grasp of his mother—still heard his slaughtered sisters cry to him for help—and, in the agony of his mind, he was incapable of an emotion of hope, or fear.

The party resumed their march, and suddenly changing their direction, they came to the shore of the Connecticut. They had chosen a point for their passage where the windings of the river prevented their being exposed to view for any distance; but still they cautiously lingered till the twilight had faded into night. While they were taking their bark canoe from the thicket of underwood, in which they had hidden it, Magawisca said, unob-served, to Everell, "keep an eagle-eye on our path-way—our journey is always towards the setting sun—every turn we make is marked by a dead tree, a lopped branch, or an arrow's head carved in the bark of a tree; be watchful—the hour of escape may come." She spoke in the lowest audible tone, and without

changing her posture or raising her eyes; and though her last
accents caught her father's ear, when he turned to chide her he
suppressed his rebuke, for she sat motionless, and silent as a
statue.

The party were swiftly conveyed to the opposite shore. The
canoe was then again taken from the river and plunged into the
wood; and believing they had eluded pursuit, they prepared to
encamp for the night. They selected for this purpose a smooth
grassy area, where they were screened and defended on the river-
side by a natural rampart, formed of intersecting branches of
willows, sycamores, and elms.

Oneco collected dead leaves from the little hollows, into
which they had been swept by eddies of wind, and, with the
addition of some soft ferns, he made a bed and pillow for his
little favourite, fit for the repose of a wood nymph. The Mohawks regarded this labour of love with favour, and one of them
took from his hollow girdle some pounded corn, and mixing
grains of maple-sugar with it, gave it to Oneco, and the little girl
received it from him as passively as the young bird takes food
from its mother. He then made a sylvan cup of broad leaves,
threaded together with delicate twigs, and brought her a draught
of water from a fountain that swelled over the green turf and
trickled into the river, drop by drop, as clear and bright as crys-
tal. When she had finished her primitive repast, he laid her on
her leafy bed, covered her with skins, and sang her to sleep.

The Indians refreshed themselves with pounded maize, and
dried fish. A boyish appetite is not fastidious, and, with a mind
at ease, Everell might have relished this coarse fare; but now,
though repeatedly solicited, he would not even rise from the
ground where he had thrown himself in listless despair. No excess of misery can enable a boy of fifteen for any length of time
to resist the cravings of nature for sleep. Everell, it may be remembered, had watched the previous night, and he soon sunk
into oblivion of his griefs. One after another, the whole party
fell asleep, with the exception of Magawisca, who sat apart from
the rest, her mantle wrapped closely around her, her head leaning
against a tree, and apparently lost in deep meditation. The Mohawks, by way of precaution, had taken a position on each side

of Everell, so as to render it next to impossible for their prisoner to move without awakening them. But love, mercy, and hope, count nothing impossible, and all were at work in the breast of Magawisca. She warily waited till the depth of the night, when sleep is most profound, and then, with a step as noiseless as the falling dew, she moved round to Everell's head, stooped down, and putting her lips close to his ear, pronounced his name distinctly. Most persons have experienced the power of a name thus pronounced. Everell awakened instantly and perfectly—and at once understood from Magawisca's gestures, for speak again she dared not, that she urged his departure.

The love of life and safety is too strong to be paralyzed for any length of time. Hope was kindled; extrication and escape seemed possible; quickening thoughts rushed through his mind. He might be restored to his father; Springfield could not be far distant; his captors would not dare to remain in that vicinity after the dawn of day; one half hour and he was beyond their pursuit. He rose slowly and cautiously to his feet. All was yet profoundly still. He glanced his eye on Faith Leslie, whom he would gladly have rescued; but Magawisca shook her head, and he felt that to attempt it, would be to ensure his own failure.

The moon shone through the branches of the trees, and shed a faint and quivering light on the wild groupe. Everell looked cautiously about him, to see where he should plant his first footstep. 'If I should tread on those skins,' he thought, 'that are about them; or on those dead rustling leaves, it were a gone case with me.'—During this instant of deliberation, one of the Indians murmured something of his dreaming thoughts, turned himself over, and grasped Everell's ankle. The boy bit his quivering lip, and suppressed an instinctive cry, for he perceived it was but the movement of sleep, and he felt the hold gradually relaxing. He exchanged a glance of joy with Magawisca, when a new source of alarm startled them—they heard the dashing of oars. Breathless—immoveable—they listened. The strokes were quickly repeated, and the sound rapidly approached, and a voice spoke—"not there boys—not there, a little higher up."

Joy and hope shot through Everell's heart as he sprang, like a startled deer, but the Mohawk, awakened too by the noise, grasped his leg with one hand, and with the other drawing his knife from his girdle, he pointed it at Everell's heart, in the act to strike if he should make the least movement, or sound.

Caution is the instinct of the weaker animals; the Indian cannot be surprised out of his wariness. Mononotto and his companions, thus suddenly awakened, remained as fixed and silent as the trees about them.

The men in the canoes suspended their oars for a moment, and seemed at a loss how to proceed, or whether to proceed at all. "It is a risky business, I can tell you, Digby," said one of them, "to plunge into those woods—'it is ill fighting with wild beasts in their own den'—they may start out upon us from their holes when we are least looking for them."

"And if they should," replied Digby, in the voice of one who would fain enforce reason with persuasion, "if they should, Lawrence, are we not six stout christian men, with bold hearts, and the Lord on our side, to boot?"

"I grant ye, that's fighting at odds; but I mistrust we have no command from the Lord to come out on this wild-goose chase."

"I take a known duty," replied Digby, "always to be a command from the Lord, and you, Lawrence, I am sure, will be as ready as another man to serve under such an order."

Lawrence was silenced for a moment, and another voice spoke—"Yes, so should we all, Master Digby, if you could make out the order; but I can't see the sense of risking all our lives, and getting but a 'thank ye for nothing' when we get back, if, indeed, we ever get out of the bowels of the forest again, into a clearing. To be sure, we've tracked them thus far, but now, on the river, we lose scent. You know they thread the forest as handily as my good woman threads her needle; and for us to pursue them, is as vain a thing as for my old chimney-corner cat to chase a catamount through the woods. Come, come—let's head about, and give it up for a bad job."

"Stop, stop, my friends," cried Digby, as they were about to put the boat around; "ye surely have not all faint hearts. Fearenaught, you will not so belie your christian-name, as to turn your back on danger. And you, John Wilkin, who cut down the Pequods, as you were wont to mow the swarth in Suffolk, will you have it thrown up to you, that you wanted courage to pursue the caitiffs? Go home, Lawrence, and take your curly-pated boy on your knee, and thank God with what heart you may, for his spared life; and all, all of you go to that childless man, at Bethel, and say, 'we could not brave the terrors of the forest to save your child, for we have pleasant homes and wives and children.' For myself, the Lord helping, while I've life, I'll not turn back without the boy; and if there's one among you, that hopes for God's pity, let him go with me."

"Why, I'm sure it was not I that proposed going back," said Lawrence.

"And I'm sure," said the second speaker, "that I'm willing, if the rest are, to try our luck further."

"Now, God above reward ye, my good fellows," cried Digby, with renewed life; "I knew it was but trying your metal, to find it true. It is not reasonable that you should feel as I do, who have seen my master's home looking like a slaughter-house. My mistress—the gentlest and the best!——Oh! it's too much to think of. And then that boy, that's worth a legion of such men as we are—of such as I, I mean. But come, let's pull away; a little further up the stream—there's no landing here, where the bank is so steep."

"Stay—row a little closer," cried one of the men; "I see something like a track on the very edge of the bank; its being seemingly impossible, is the very reason why the savages would have chosen it."

They now approached so near the shore that Everell knew they might hear a whisper, and yet to move his lips was certain death. Those who have experienced the agony of a night-mare, when life seemed to depend on a single word, and that word could not be pronounced, may conceive his emotions at this trying moment. Friends and rescue so near, and so unavailing!

"Ye are mistaken," said another of the pursuing party, after a moment's investigation, "it's but a heron's track," which it truly was; for the savages had been careful not to leave the slightest trace of their footsteps where they landed. "There's a cove a little higher up," continued the speaker; "we'll put in there, and then if we dont get on their trail, Master Digby must tell us what to do."

"It's plain what we must do then," said Digby, "go strait on westerly. I have a compass, you know; there is not, as the hunters tell us, a single smoke between this and the vallies of the Housatonick. There the tribes are friendly, and if we reach them without falling in with our enemy, we will not pursue them further."

"Agreed, agreed," cried all the men, and they again dashed in their oars and made for the cove. Everell's heart sunk within him as the sounds receded; but hope once admitted, will not be again excluded, and with the sanguine temperament of youth, he was already mentally calculating the chances of escape. Not so Magawisca; she knew the dangers that beset him; she was aware of her father's determined purpose. Her heart had again been rent by a divided duty; one word from her would have rescued Everell, but that word would have condemned her father; and when the boat retired, she sunk to the ground, quite spent with the conflict of her feelings.

It may seem strange that the Indians did not avail themselves of the advantage of their ambush to attack their pursuers; but it will be remembered, the latter were double their number, and besides, Mononotto's object now was, to make good his retreat with his children; and to effect this, it was essential he should avoid any encounter with his pursuers. After a short consultation with his associates, they determined to remain in their present position till the morning. They were confident they should be able to detect and avoid the track of the enemy, and soon to get in advance of them.

CHAPTER VII

"—— —— ——But the scene
Is lovely round; a beautiful river there
Wanders amid the fresh and fertile meads,
The paradise he made unto himself,
Mining the soil for ages. On each side
The fields swell upwards to the hills; beyond,
Above the hills, in the blue distance, rise
The mighty columns with which earth props heaven.
    There is a tale about these gray old rocks,
A sad tradition"——

BRYANT[1]

It is not our purpose to describe, step by step, the progress of the Indian fugitives. Their sagacity in traversing their native forests; their skill in following and eluding an enemy, and all their politic devices, have been so well described in a recent popular work,[2] that their usages have become familiar as household words, and nothing remains but to shelter defects of skill and knowledge under the veil of silence; since we hold it to be an immutable maxim, that a thing had better not be done, than be ill-done.

Suffice it to say, then, that the savages, after crossing the track of their pursuers, threaded the forest with as little apparent uncertainty as to their path, as is now felt by travellers who pass through the same still romantic country, in a stage-coach and on a broad turnpike. As they receded from the Connecticut, the pine levels disappeared; the country was broken into hills, and rose into high mountains.

They traversed the precipitous sides of a river that, swoln by the vernal rains, wound its way among the hills, foaming and raging like an angry monarch. The river, as they traced its course, dwindled to a mountain rill, but still retaining its impetuous character, leaping and tumbling for miles through a descending defile, between high mountains, whose stillness, grandeur, and immobility, contrasted with the noisy reckless little stream, as stern manhood with infancy. In one place, which the Indians called the throat of the mountain, they were obliged to betake themselves to the channel of the brook, there not being room on its margin for a footpath. The branches of the trees that grew from the rocky and precipitous declivities on each side, met and interlaced, forming a sylvan canopy over the imprisoned stream. To Magawisca, whose imagination breathed a living spirit into all the objects of nature, it seemed as if the spirits of the wood had stooped to listen to its sweet music.

After tracing this little sociable rill to its source, they again plunged into the silent forest—waded through marshy ravines, and mounted to the summits of sterile hills; till at length, at the close of the third day, after having gradually descended for several miles, the hills on one side receded, and left a little interval of meadow, through which they wound into the lower valley of the Housatonick.

This continued and difficult march had been sustained by Everell with a spirit and fortitude that evidently won the favour of the savages, who always render homage to superiority over physical evil. There was something more than this common feeling, in the joy with which Mononotto noted the boy's silent endurance, and even contempt of pain. One noble victim seemed to him better than a "human hecatomb." In proportion to his exultation in possessing an object worthy to avenge his son, was his fear that his victim would escape from him. During the march, Everell had twice, aided by Magawisca, nearly achieved his liberty. These detected conspiracies, though defeated, rendered the chief impatient to execute his vengeance; and he secretly resolved that it should not be delayed longer than the morrow.

As the fugitives emerged from the narrow defile, a new scene opened upon them; a scene of valley and hill, river and meadow, surrounded by mountains, whose encircling embrace, expressed protection and love to the gentle spirits of the valley. A light summer shower had just fallen, and the clouds, "in thousand liveries dight," had risen from the western horizon, and hung their rich draperies about the clear sun. The horizontal rays passed over the valley, and flushed the upper branches of the trees, the summits of the hills, and the mountains, with a flood of light, whilst the low grounds reposing in deep shadow, presented one of those striking and accidental contrasts in nature, that a painter would have selected to give effect to his art.

The gentle Housatonick wound through the depths of the valley, in some parts contracted to a narrow channel, and murmuring over the rocks that rippled its surface; and in others, spreading wide its clear mirror, and lingering like a lover amidst the vines, trees, and flowers, that fringed its banks. Thus it flows now—but not as then in the sylvan freedom of nature, when no clattering mills and bustling factories, threw their prosaic shadows over the silver waters—when not even a bridge spanned their bosom—when not a trace of man's art was seen save the little bark canoe that glided over them, or lay idly moored along the shore. The savage was rather the vassal, than the master of nature; obeying her laws, but never usurping her dominion. He only used the land she prepared, and cast in his corn but where she seemed to invite him by mellowing and upheaving the rich mould. He did not presume to hew down her trees, the proud crest of her uplands, and convert them into "russet lawns and fallows grey." The axman's stroke, that music to the *settler's* ear, never then violated the peace of nature, or made discord in her music.

Imagination may be indulged in lingering for a moment in those dusky regions of the past; but it is not permitted to reasonable instructed man, to admire or regret tribes of human beings, who lived and died, leaving scarcely a more enduring memorial, than the forsaken nest that vanishes before one winter's storms.

But to return to our wanderers. They had entered the expanded vale, by following the windings of the Housatonick around a hill, conical and easy of ascent, excepting on that side which overlooked the river, where, half-way from the base to the summit, rose a perpendicular rock, bearing on its beetling

front the age of centuries. On every other side, the hill was gar-
landed with laurels, now in full and profuse bloom; here and
there surmounted by an intervening pine, spruce, or hemlock,
whose seared winter foliage was fringed with the bright tender
sprouts of spring. We believe there is a chord, even in the heart
of savage man, that responds to the voice of nature. Certain it
is, the party paused, as it appeared from a common instinct, at
a little grassy nook, formed by the curve of the hill, to gaze on
this singularly beautiful spot. Everell looked on the smoke that
curled from the huts of the village, embosomed in pine trees, on
the adjacent plain. The scene, to him, breathed peace and happiness, and gushing thoughts of home filled his eyes with tears.
Oneco plucked clusters of laurels, and decked his little favourite,
and the old chief fixed his melancholy eye on a solitary pine,
scathed and blasted by tempests, that rooted in the ground where
he stood, lifted its topmost branches to the bare rock, where
they seemed, in their wild desolation, to brave the elemental fury
that had stripped them of beauty and life.

The leafless tree was truly, as it appeared to the eye of Mononotto, a fit emblem of the chieftain of a ruined tribe. "See you,
child," he said, addressing Magawisca, "those unearthed roots?
the tree must fall—hear you the death-song that wails through
those blasted branches?"

"Nay, father, listen not to the sad strain; it is but the spirit
of the tree mourning over its decay; rather turn thine ear to the
glad song of this bright stream, image of the good. She nourishes
the aged trees, and cherishes the tender flowrets, and her song
is ever of happiness, till she reaches the great sea—image of our
eternity."

"Speak not to me of happiness, Magawisca; it has vanished
with the smoke of our homes. I tell ye, the spirits of our race
are gathered about this blasted tree. Samoset points to that
rock—that sacrifice-rock." His keen glance turned from the rock
to Everell.

Magawisca understood its portentous meaning, and she
clasped her hands in mute and agonizing supplication. He answered to the silent entreaty. "It is in vain—my purpose is fixed,
and here it shall be accomplished. Why hast thou linked thy

heart, foolish girl, to this English boy? I have sworn, kneeling on the ashes of our hut, that I would never spare a son of our enemy's race. The lights of heaven witnessed my vow, and think you, that now this boy is given into my hands to avenge thy brother, I will spare him for thy prayer? No—though thou lookest on me with thy mother's eye, and speakest with her voice, I will not break my vow."

. Mononotto had indeed taken a final and fatal resolution; and prompted, as he fancied, by supernatural intimations, and, perhaps, dreading the relentings of his own heart, he determined on its immediate execution. He announced his decision to the Mohawks. A brief and animated consultation followed, during which they brandished their tomahawks, and cast wild and threatening glances at Everell, who at once comprehended the meaning of these menacing looks and gestures. He turned an appealing glance to Magawisca. She did not speak. "Am I to die now?" he asked; she turned shuddering from him.

Everell had expected death from his savage captors, but while it was comparatively distant, he thought he was indifferent to it, or rather, he believed he should welcome it as a release from the horrible recollection of the massacre at Bethel, which haunted him day and night. But now that his fate seemed inevitable, nature was appalled, and shrunk from it; and the impassive spirit, for a moment, endured a pang that there cannot be in any "corp'ral sufferance." The avenues of sense were closed, and past and future were present to the mind, as if it were already invested with the attributes of its eternity. From this agonizing excitement, Everell was roused by a command from the savages to move onward. "It is then deferred," thought Magawisca, and heaving a deep sigh, as if for a moment relieved from a pressure on her over-burthened heart, she looked to her father for an explanation; he said nothing, but proceeded in silence towards the village.

The lower valley of the Housatonick, at the period to which our history refers, was inhabited by a peaceful, and, as far as that epithet could ever be applied to our savages, an agricultural tribe, whose territory, situate midway between the Hudson and the Connecticut, was bounded and defended on each side by mountains, then deemed impracticable to a foe. These inland people had heard from the hunters of distant tribes, who occasionally visited them, of the aggressions and hostility of the English strangers, but regarding it as no concern of theirs, they listened, much as we listen to news of the Burmese war—Captain Symmes' theory—or lectures on phrenology. One of their hunters, it is true, had penetrated to Springfield, and another had passed over the hills to the Dutch fort at Albany, and returned with the report that the strangers' skin was the colour of cowardice—that they served their women, and spoke an unintelligible language. There was little in this account to interest those who were so ignorant as to be scarcely susceptible of curiosity, and they hardly thought of the dangerous strangers at all, or only thought of them as a people from whom they had nothing to hope or fear, when the appearance of the ruined Pequod chief, with his English captives, roused them from their apathy.

The village was on a level, sandy plain, extending for about half a mile, and raised by a natural and almost perpendicular bank fifty feet above the level of the meadows. At one extremity of the plain, was the hill we have described; the other was terminated by a broad green, appropriated to sports and councils.

The huts of the savages were irregularly scattered over the plain—some on cleared ground, and others just peeping out of copses of pine trees—some on the very verge of the plain, overlooking the meadows—and others under the shelter of a high hill that formed the northern boundary of the valley, and seemed stationed there to defend the inhabitants from their natural enemies—cold, and wind.

The huts were the simplest structures of human art; but, as in no natural condition of society a perfect equality obtains, some were more spacious and commodious than others. All were made with flexible poles, firmly set in the ground, and drawn and attached together at the top. Those of the more indolent, or least skilful, were filled in with branches of trees and hung over with coarse mats; while those of the better order were neatly covered with bark, prepared with art, and considerable labour for the purpose. Little garden patches adjoined a few of the dwellings, and were planted with beans, pumpkins, and squashes; the seeds of these vegetables, according to an Indian tradition, (in which we may perceive the usual admixture of fable and truth,) having been sent to them, in the bill of a bird, from the south-west, by the Great Spirit.

The Pequod chief and his retinue passed, just at twilight, over the plain, by one of the many foot-paths that indented it. Many of the women were still at work with their stone-pointed hoes, in their gardens. Some of the men and children were at their sports on the green. Here a straggler was coming from the river with a string of fine trout; another fortunate sportsman appeared from the hill-side with wild turkeys and partridges; while two emerged from the forest with still more noble game, a fat antlered buck.

This village, as we have described it, and perhaps from the affection its natural beauty inspired, remained the residence of the savages long after they had vanished from the surrounding country. Within the memory of the present generation the remnant of the tribe migrated to the west; and even now some of their families make a summer pilgrimage to this, their Jerusalem, and are regarded with a melancholy interest by the present occupants of the soil.

Mononotto directed his steps to the wigwam of the Housatonick chief, which stood on one side of the green. The chief advanced from his hut to receive him, and by the most animated gestures expressed to Mononotto his pleasure in the success of his incursion, from which it seemed that Mononotto had communicated with him on his way to the Connecticut.

A brief and secret consultation succeeded, which appeared to consist of propositions from the Pequod, and assent on the part of the Housatonick chief, and was immediately followed by a motion to separate the travellers. Mononotto and Everell were to remain with the chief, and the rest of the party to be conducted to the hut of his sister.

Magawisca's prophetic spirit too truly interpreted this arrangement; and thinking or hoping there might be some saving power in her presence, since her father tacitly acknowledged it by the pains he took to remove her, she refused to leave him.

He insisted vehemently; but finding her unyielding, he commanded the Mohawks to force her away.

Resistance was vain, but resistance she would still have made, but for the interposition of Everell. "Go with them, Magawisca," he said, "and leave me to my fate.——We shall meet again."

"Never!" she shrieked; "your fate is death."

"And after death we shall meet again," replied Everell, with a calmness that evinced his mind was already in a great degree resigned to the event that now appeared inevitable. "Do not fear for me, Magawisca. Better thoughts have put down my fears. When it is over, think of me."

"And what am I to do with this scorching fire till then?" she asked, pressing both her hands on her head. "Oh, my father, has your heart become stone?"

Her father turned from her appeal, and motioned to Everell to enter the hut. Everell obeyed; and when the mat dropped over the entrance and separated him from the generous creature, whose heart had kept true time with his through all his griefs, who he knew would have redeemed his life with her own, he yielded to a burst of natural and not unmanly tears.

If this could be deemed a weakness, it was his last. Alone with his God, he realized the sufficiency of His presence and favour. He appealed to that mercy which is never refused, nor given in stinted measure to the humble suppliant. Every expression of pious confidence and resignation, which he had heard with the heedless ear of childhood, now flashed like an illumination upon his mind.

His mother's counsels and instructions, to which he had often lent a wearied attention—the passages from the sacred book he had been compelled to commit to memory, when his truant thoughts were ranging forest and field, now returned upon him as if a celestial spirit breathed them into his soul. Stillness and peace stole over him. He was amazed at his own tranquillity. 'It may be,' he thought, 'that my mother and sisters are permitted to minister to me.'

He might have been agitated by the admission of the least ray of hope; but hope was utterly excluded, and it was only when he thought of his bereft father, that his courage failed him.

But we must leave him to his solitude and silence, only interrupted by the distant hootings of the owl, and the heavy tread of the Pequod chief, who spent the night in slowly pacing before the door of the hut.

Magawisca and her companions were conducted to a wigwam standing on that part of the plain on which they had first entered. It was completely enclosed on three sides by dwarf oaks. In front there was a little plantation of the edible luxuries of the savages. On entering the hut, they perceived it had but one occupant, a sick emaciated old woman, who was stretched on her mat covered with skins. She raised her head, as the strangers entered, and at the sight of Faith Leslie, uttered a faint exclamation, deeming the fair creature a messenger from the spirit-land—but being informed who they were and whence they came, she made every sign and expression of courtesy to them, that her feeble strength permitted.

Her hut contained all that was essential to savage hospitality. A few brands were burning on a hearth-stone in the middle of the apartment. The smoke that found egress, passed out by a hole in the centre of the roof, over which a mat was skilfully adjusted, and turned to the windward-side by a cord that hung within. The old woman, in her long pilgrimage, had accumulated stores of Indian riches: piles of sleeping-mats laid in one corner; nicely dressed skins garnished the walls; baskets, of all shapes and sizes, gaily decorated with rude images of birds and flowers, contained dried fruits, medicinal herbs, Indian corn, nuts, and game. A covered pail, made of folds of birch-bark, was filled with a kind of beer—a decoction of various roots and aromatic shrubs. Neatly turned wooden spoons and bowls, and culinary utensils of clay supplied all the demands of the inartificial house-wifery of savage life.

The travellers, directed by their old hostess, prepared their evening repast, a short and simple process to an Indian; and having satisfied the cravings of hunger, they were all, with the exception of Magawisca and one of the Mohawks, in a very short time, stretched on their mats and fast asleep.

Magawisca seated herself at the feet of the old woman, and

had neither spoken nor moved since she entered the hut. She watched anxiously and impatiently the movements of the Indian, whose appointed duty it appeared to be, to guard her. He placed a wooden bench against the mat which served for a door, and stuffing his pipe with tobacco from the pouch slung over his shoulder, and then filling a gourd with the liquor in the pail and placing it beside him, he quietly sat himself down to his night-watch.

The old woman became restless, and her loud and repeated groans, at last, withdrew Magawisca from her own miserable thoughts. She inquired if she could do aught to allay her pain; the sufferer pointed to a jar that stood on the embers in which a medicinal preparation was simmering. She motioned to Magawisca to give her a spoonful of the liquor; she did so, and as she took it, "it is made," she said, "of all the plants on which the spirit of sleep has breathed," and so it seemed to be; for she had scarcely swallowed it, when she fell asleep.

Once or twice she waked and murmured something, and once Magawisca heard her say, "Hark to the wekolis!³—he is perched on the old oak, by the sacrifice-rock, and his cry is neither musical, nor merry—a bad sign in a bird."

But all signs and portents were alike to Magawisca—every sound rung a death-peal to her ear, and the hissing silence had in it the mystery and fearfulness of death. The night wore slowly and painfully away, as if, as in the fairy tale, the moments were counted by drops of heart's-blood. But the most wearisome nights will end; the morning approached; the familiar notes of the birds of earliest dawn were heard, and the twilight peeped through the crevices of the hut, when a new sound fell on Magawisca's startled ear. It was the slow measured tread of many feet. The poor girl now broke silence, and vehemently entreated the Mohawk to let her pass the door, or at least to raise the mat.

He shook his head with a look of unconcern, as if it were the petulant demand of a child, when the old woman, awakened by the noise, cried out that she was dying—that she must have light and air, and the Mohawk started up, impulsively, to raise the mat. It was held between two poles that formed the door-posts, and while he was disengaging it, Magawisca, as if inspired, and quick as thought, poured the liquor from the jar on the fire into the hollow of her hand, and dashed it into the gourd which the Mohawk had just replenished. The narcotic was boiling hot, but she did not cringe; she did not even feel it; and she could scarcely repress a cry of joy, when the savage turned round and swallowed, at one draught, the contents of the cup.

Magawisca looked eagerly through the aperture, but though the sound of the footsteps had approached nearer, she saw no one. She saw nothing but a gentle declivity that sloped to the plain, a few yards from the hut, and was covered with a grove of trees; beyond and peering above them, was the hill, and the sacrifice-rock: the morning star, its rays not yet dimmed in the light of day, shed a soft trembling beam on its summit. This beautiful star, alone in the heavens, when all other lights were quenched, spoke to the superstitious, or, rather, the imaginative spirit of Magawisca. 'Star of promise,' she thought, 'thou dost still linger with us when day is vanished, and now thou art there, alone, to proclaim the coming sun; thou dost send in upon my soul a ray of hope; and though it be but as the spider's slender pathway, it shall sustain my courage.' She had scarcely formed this resolution, when she needed all its efficacy, for the train, whose footsteps she had heard, appeared in full view.

First came her father, with the Housatonick chief; next, alone, and walking with a firm undaunted step, was Everell; his arms folded over his breast, and his head a little inclined upward, so that Magawisca fancied she saw his full eye turned heavenward; after him walked all the men of the tribe, ranged according to their age, and the rank assigned to each by his own exploits.

They were neither painted nor ornamented according to the common usage at festivals and sacrifices, but every thing had the air of hasty preparation. Magawisca gazed in speechless despair. The procession entered the wood, and for a few moments, disappeared from her sight—again they were visible, mounting the acclivity of the hill, by a winding narrow foot-path, shaded on either side by laurels. They now walked singly and slowly, but to Magawisca, their progress seemed rapid as a falling avalanche.

She felt that, if she were to remain pent in that prison-house, her heart would burst, and she sprang towards the door-way in the hope of clearing her passage, but the Mohawk caught her arm in his iron grasp, and putting her back, calmly retained his station. She threw herself on her knees to him—she entreated—she wept—but in vain: he looked on her with unmoved apathy. Already she saw the foremost of the party had reached the rock, and were forming a semicircle around it—again she appealed to her determined keeper, and again he denied her petition, but with a faltering tongue, and a drooping eye.

Magawisca, in the urgency of a necessity that could brook no delay, had forgotten, or regarded as useless, the sleeping potion she had infused into the Mohawk's draught; she now saw the powerful agent was at work for her, and with that quickness of apprehension that made the operations of her mind as rapid as the impulses of instinct, she perceived that every emotion she excited but hindered the effect of the potion, suddenly seeming to relinquish all purpose and hope of escape, she threw herself on a mat, and hid her face, burning with agonizing impatience, in her mantle. There we must leave her, and join that fearful company who were gathered together to witness what they believed to be the execution of exact and necessary justice.

Seated around their sacrifice-rock—their holy of holies—they listened to the sad story of the Pequod chief, with dejected countenances and downcast eyes, save when an involuntary glance turned on Everell, who stood awaiting his fate, cruelly aggravated by every moment's delay, with a quiet dignity and calm resignation, that would have become a hero, or a saint. Surrounded by this dark cloud of savages, his fair countenance kindled by holy inspiration, he looked scarcely like a creature of earth.

There might have been among the spectators, some who felt the silent appeal of the helpless courageous boy; some whose hearts moved them to interpose to save the selected victim; but they were restrained by their interpretation of natural justice, as controlling to them as our artificial codes of laws to us. Others of a more cruel, or more irritable disposition, when the Pequod described his wrongs, and depicted his sufferings, brandished their tomahawks, and would have hurled them at the boy, but the chief said—"Nay, brothers—the work is mine— he dies by my hand—for my first-born—life for life—he dies by a single stroke, for thus was my boy cut off. The blood of sachems is in his veins. He has the skin, but not the soul of that mixed race, whose gratitude is like that vanishing mist," and he pointed to the vapour that was melting from the mountain tops into the transparent ether; "and their promises are like this," and he snapped a dead branch from the pine beside which he stood, and broke it in fragments. "Boy, as he is, he fought for his mother, as the eagle fights for its young. I watched him in the mountain-path, when the blood gushed from his torn feet; not a word from his smooth lip, betrayed his pain."

Mononotto embellished his victim with praises, as the an-cients wreathed theirs with flowers. He brandished his hatchet over Everell's head, and cried, exultingly, "See, he flinches not. Thus stood my boy, when they flashed their sabres before his eyes, and bade him betray his father. Brothers—My people have told me I bore a woman's heart towards the enemy. Ye shall see. I will pour out this English boy's blood to the last drop, and give his flesh and bones to the dogs and wolves."

He then motioned to Everell to prostrate himself on the rock, his face downward. In this position the boy would not see the descending stroke. Even at this moment of dire vengeance, the instincts of a merciful nature asserted their rights.

Everell sunk calmly on his knees, not to supplicate life, but to commend his soul to God. He clasped his hands together. He did not—he could not speak; his soul was

> "Rapt in still communion that transcends
> The imperfect offices of prayer."[4]

At this moment a sun-beam penetrated the trees that enclosed the area, and fell athwart his brow and hair, kindling it with an almost supernatural brightness. To the savages, this was a token that the victim was accepted, and they sent forth a shout that rent the air. Everell bent forward, and pressed his forehead to the rock. The chief raised the deadly weapon, when Magawisca, springing from the precipitous side of the rock, screamed—"Forbear!" and interposed her arm. It was too late. The blow was levelled—force and direction given—the stroke aimed at Everell's neck, severed his defender's arm, and left him unharmed. The lopped quivering member dropped over the precipice. Mononotto staggered and fell senseless, and all the savages, uttering horrible yells, rushed toward the fatal spot.

"Stand back!" cried Magawisca. "I have bought his life with my own. Fly, Everell—nay, speak not, but fly—thither—to the east!" she cried, more vehemently.

Everell's faculties were paralyzed by a rapid succession of violent emotions. He was conscious only of a feeling of mingled gratitude and admiration for his preserver. He stood motionless, gazing on her. "I die in vain then," she cried, in an accent of such despair, that he was roused. He threw his arms around her, and pressed her to his heart, as he would a sister that had redeemed his life with her own, and then tearing himself from her, he disappeared. No one offered to follow him. The voice of nature rose from every heart, and responding to the justice of Magawisca's claim, bade him "God speed!" To all it seemed that his deliverance had been achieved by miraculous aid. All—the dullest and coldest, paid involuntary homage to the heroic girl, as if she were a superior being, guided and upheld by supernatural power.

Every thing short of miracle she had achieved. The moment the opiate dulled the senses of her keeper, she escaped from the hut; and aware that, if she attempted to penetrate to her father through the semicircular line of spectators that enclosed him, she should be repulsed, and probably borne off the ground, she had taken the desperate resolution of mounting the rock, where only her approach would be unperceived. She did not stop to ask herself if it were possible, but impelled by a determined spirit, or rather, we would believe, by that inspiration that teaches the bird its unknown path, and leads the goat, with its young, safely over the mountain crags, she ascended the rock. There were crevices in it, but they seemed scarcely sufficient to support the eagle with his grappling talon, and twigs issuing from the fissures, but so slender, that they waved like a blade of grass under the weight of the young birds that made a rest on them, and yet, such is the power of love, stronger than death, that with these inadequate helps, Magawisca scaled the rock, and achieved her generous purpose.

CHAPTER VIII

"Powwow—a priest. These do begin and order their service and invocation of their gods, and all the people follow, and join interchangeably in a laborious bodily service unto sweating, especially of the priest, who spends himself in strange antick gestures and actions, even unto fainting. Being once in their houses and beholding what their worship was, I never durst be an eye-witness, spectator, or looker-on, lest I should have been a partaker of Satan's inventions and worships."

—Roger Williams[1]

The following letter, written by Hope Leslie, and addressed to Everell Fletcher, then residing in England, will show, briefly, the state of affairs at Bethel, seven years subsequent to the date of the events already detailed. Little had occurred, save the changes of the seasons, in nature and human life, to mark the progress of time.

"Dear Everell,

"This is the fifth anniversary of the day you left us—your birth-day, too, you know; so we celebrate it, but with a blended joy and grief, which, as my dear guardian says, is suitable to the mixed condition of human life.

"I surprised him, this morning, with a painting, on which I had expended much time and laid out all my poor skill. The scene is a forest glade—a boy is sleeping under a birch tree, near a thicket of hazle bushes, and from their deepest shadow peeps a gaunt wolf in the act of springing on him, while just emerging from the depths of the wood, in the back ground, appears a man with a musket levelled at the animal. I had placed the painting on the mantel-piece, and it caught your father's eye as he entered to attend our morning exercise. He said nothing, for, you know, the order of our devotions is as strictly observed as were the services of the ancient temple. So we all took our accustomed places—I mine on the cushion beside your father; yours still stands on the other side of him, like the vacant seat of Banquo. Love can paint as well as fear; and though no form, palpable to common eyes, is seated there, yet, to our second sight, imagination produces from her shadowy regions the form of our dear Everell.

"I believe the picture had touched the hidden springs of memory, for your father, though he was reading the chapter of Exodus that speaks of the wise-hearted men who wrought for the sanctuary,[2] (a portion of scripture not particularly moving,) repeatedly wiped the gathering tears from his eyes. Jennet is never lagging in the demonstration of religious emotion, and I inferred, from her responsive hems! and hahs! that, as there was no obvious cause for tears, she fancied affecting types were lurking in the 'loops and selvedges, and tenons and sockets, and fine twined linen,' about which your father was reading. But when he came, in his prayer, to his customary mention of his absent child— when he touched upon the time when his habitation was made desolate—and then upon the deliverance of his son, his only son, from the savage foe, and the ravening beast—his voice faltered —every heart responded; Digby sobbed aloud—and even aunt Grafton, whose aversion to standing at her devotions has not diminished with her increasing years, stood a monument of patience till the clock twice told the hour; though it was but the other day when she thought your father was drawing to a close, and he started a new topic, that she broke out, after her way of thinking aloud, "well, if he is going on t'other tack, I'll sit down."

"When the exercise was finished, Digby gave vent to his pleasure. 'There, Jennet,' he said, rubbing his hands exultingly, 'you are always on the look-out for witchcraft. I wonder what you call that? It is a perfect picture of the place where I found Mr. Everell, as that fellow there, in the frieze jacket is of me; and any body would know that, though they would not expect to see John Digby painted in a picture. To be sure, Mr. Everell does not look quite so pale and famished as he did when I first saw him sleeping under that birch tree: as I live, she has put his name there, just as he had carved it. Well, it will be a kind of a history for Mr. Everell's children, when we, and the forest too, are laid low.'

"Your father permitted the honest fellow's volubility to flow unrepressed; he himself only said, as he drew me to him and kissed me, 'you have kept a faithful copy of our dear Everell in your memory.'

"My honest tutor Cradock and aunt Grafton contended for the honour of my excellence in the art—poor Cradock, my Apollo! He maintained that he had taught me the theory, while aunt Grafton boasted her knowledge of the practice: but, alas! the little honour my success reflected on them, was not worth their contest; and I did them no injustice in secretly ascribing all my skill to the source whence the Corinthian maid derived her power to trace, by the secret lamp, the shade of her lover. Affection for my dear Everell and for his father is my inspiration; but, I confess, it might never have appeared in the mimicry, of even this rude painting, if aunt Grafton had not taken lessons at the Convent of the Chartreux at Paris, and had daily access, as you know she has a thousand times repeated to us, to the paintings of Rossi and Albati in the palace of Fontainbleau.

"But into what egotism does this epistolary journalizing betray me? The day is yours, Everell, and I will not speak again of myself.

"Aunt Grafton, meaning to do it what honour she could, had our dinner-table set out with massive silver dishes, engraved with her family's armorial bearings. They have never before seen the light in America. Your father smiled at their contrast with our bare walls, pine tables, chairs, &c.—and said, 'we looked like Attila, in his rude hut, surrounded with the spoils of Rome;' and aunt Grafton, who has a decided taste for all the testimonials of her family grandeur, entered into a warm discussion with Master Cradock as to how far the new man might lawfully indulge in a vain show. By the way, their skirmishing on the debateable grounds of church and state, have of late almost ceased. When I remarked this to your father, he said, he believed I had brought about the present amicable state of affairs by affording them a kind of neutral ground, where their common affections and interests met. Whatever has produced this result, it is too happy not to be carefully cherished, so I have taken care that my poor tutor, who never would intentionally provoke a human being, should avoid, as far as possible, all those peculiarities, which, as some colours offend certain animals, were sure, every day, and thrice a day, to call forth aunt Grafton's animadversions. I have, too, entered into a secret confederacy with Digby—the effect of which is, that Master Cradock's little brown wig is brushed every morning, and is, at least once each day, straight on his head. The brush has invaded too, the hitherto unexplored regions of his broadcloth, and his black stock gives place, on every Lord's day at least, to a white collar. Aunt Grafton herself has more than once remarked, that 'for one of these scholar-folks, he goes quite decent.' As to aunt Grafton, I am afraid that if you were here, though we may both have gained with our years a little discretion—yet I am afraid we should laugh, as we were wont to do, at her innocent peculiarities. She spends many a weary hour in devising new head-gear, and doth daily, as Jennet says, break the law against costly apparel. Jennet is the same untired and tiresome railer. If there are anodynes for the tongue in England, pray send some for her.

"We are going, to-morrow, on an excursion to a new settlement on the river, called Northampton. Your father feared the toils and perils of the way for me, and has consented, reluctantly, to my being of the party. Aunt Grafton remonstrated, and expressed her natural and kind apprehensions, by alleging that it was 'very unladylike, and a thing quite unheard of in England,' for a young person, like me, to go out exploring a new country. I urged, that our new country developes faculties that young ladies, in England, were unconscious of possessing. She maintained, as usual, that whatever was not practised and known in England, was not worth possessing; but finally she concluded her opposition with her old customary phrase, 'Well, it's peculiar of you, Miss Hope,' which, you know, she always uses to characterize whatever opposes her opinions or inclinations.

"My good tutor, who would fain be my ægis-bearer, insists on attending me. You may laugh at him, Everell, and call him my knight-errant, or squire, or what you will; but I assure you, he is a right godly and suitable appendage to a pilgrim damsel. I will finish my letter when I return; a journey of twenty miles has put my thoughts, (which, you know, are ever ready to take wing,) to flight.

"25th October, Thursday,—or, as the injunction has come from Boston that we be more particular in avoiding these heathen designations, 10th month, 5th day.

"Dear Everell,—We followed the Indian foot-path that winds along the margin of the river, and reached Northampton without any accident. There is but a narrow opening there, scooped out of the forest, and Mr. Holioke, wishing to have an extensive view of the country, engaged an Indian guide to conduct your father and himself to the summit of a mountain, which rises precipitously from the meadows, and overlooks an ocean of forest.

"I had gazed on the beautiful summits of this mountain, that, in this transparent October atmosphere, were as blue and bright as the heavens themselves, till I had an irrepressible desire to go to them; and, like the child who cried for the horns of the silver moon, I should have cried too, if my wishes had been unattainable.

"Your father acquiesced (as my conscience tells me, Everell, he does too easily) in my wishes, and nobody objected but my tutor, who evidently thought it would be unmanly for him to shrink from toils that I braved, and who looked forward with dread and dismay to the painful ascent. However, we all reached the summit, without scath to life or limb, and then we looked down upon a scene that made me clap my hands, and my pious companions raise their eyes in silent devotion. I hope you have not forgotten the autumnal brilliancy of our woods. They say the foliage in England has a paler sickly hue, but for our western world—nature's youngest child—she has reserved her many-coloured robe, the brightest and most beautiful of her garments.

Last week the woods were as green as an emerald, and now they look as if all the summer-spirits had been wreathing them with flowers of the richest and most brilliant dyes.

"Philosophers may inquire into the process of nature, and find out, if they can, how such sudden changes are produced, though, after all, I fancy their inquiries will turn out like the experiment of the inquisitive boy, who cut open the drum to find the sound; but I love to lend my imagination to poets' dreams, and to fancy nature has her myriads of little spirits, who

> *"do wander every where,*
> *"Swifter than the moone's sphere."*

He must have a torpid imagination, and a cold heart, I think, who does not fancy these vast forests filled with invisible intelligences. Have these beautiful vallies of our Connecticut, which we saw from the mountain, looking like a smile on nature's rugged face, and stretching as far as our vision extended, till the broad river diminished in the shadowy distance, to a silver thread; have they been seen and enjoyed only by those savages, who have their summer home in them? While I was pondering on this thought, Mr. Holioke, who seldom indulges in a fanciful suggestion, said to your father, 'The Romans, you know, brother Fletcher, had their Cenotapha, empty sepulchres, in honour of those who died in their country's cause, and mouldered on a distant soil. Why may we not have ours? and surmise that the spirits of those who have died for liberty and religion, have come before us to this wilderness, and taken possession in the name of the Lord?'

"We lingered for an hour or two on the mountain. Mr. Holioke and your father were noting the sites for future villages, already marked out for them by clusters of Indian huts. The instinct of the children of the forest guides them to these rich intervals, which the sun and the river prepare and almost till for them. While the gentlemen were thus engaged, I observed that the highest rock of the mountain was crowned with a pyramidal pile of stones, and about them were strewn relicts of Indian sacrifices. It has, I believe, been the custom of people, in all ages, who were instructed only by nature, to worship on high places. I pointed to the rude altar, and ventured to ask Mr. Holioke if an acceptable service might not have been offered there?

"He shook his head at me, as if I were little better than a heathen, and said, 'it was all worship to an unknown God.'

" 'But,' said your father, 'the time is approaching, when through the vallies beneath, and on this mount, incense shall rise from christian hearts.'

" 'It were well,' replied Mr. Holioke, 'if we now, in the spirit, consecrated it to the Lord.'

" 'And let me stand sponsor for it,' said I, 'while you christen it Holioke.'

"I was gently rebuked for my levity, but my hint was not unkindly taken; for the good man has never since spoken of his name-sake, without calling it *Mount Holioke.*'

"My senses were enchanted on that high place. I listened to the mighty sound that rose from the forest depths of the abyss, like the roar of the distant ocean, and to the gentler voices of nature, borne on the invisible waves of air—the farewell notes of the few birds that still linger with us—the rustling of the leaves beneath the squirrel's joyous leap—the whizzing of the partridge startled from his perch; the tinkling of the cow-bell, and the barking of the Indian's dog. I was lying with my ear over the rock, when your father reminded me that it was time to return, and bade Digby, who had attended us, 'look well to Miss Leslie's descent, and lend a helping hand to Master Cradock.'

"My poor tutor's saffron skin changed to brick colour; and that he might not think I heard the imputation cast upon his serviceable powers, I stepped between him and Digby, and said, 'that with such wings on each side of me, I might fly down the mountain.'[3]

" 'Ah, Miss Hope Leslie,' said Cradock, restored to his self-complacency, 'you are a merry thought atween us.' He would fain have appeared young and agile; not from vanity, Everell, but to persuade me to accept his proffered assistance. Poor old man! he put me in mind, as he went after Digby, panting and leaping (or rather settling) from crag to crag, of an ancient horse, that almost cracks his bones to keep pace with a colt. His involuntary groans betrayed the pain of his stiffened muscles, and I lingered on every projecting cliff, on the pretence of taking a farewell look of the vallies, but really to allow him time to recover breath.

"In the mean time the gentlemen had got far in advance of us. We came to the last rock of difficult passage; Digby gave me his hand to assist me in springing from it, and asked Cradock to ascertain if the foot-hold below was sure; a necessary precaution, as the matted leaves had sometimes proved treacherous. Cradock in performing this office, startled a rattle-snake, that lay concealed under a mass of leaves and moss; the reptile coiled himself up, and darted his fangs into his hand. I heard the rattle of victory, and saw the poor man's deathly paleness, as he sunk to the ground, exclaiming, 'I am but a dead sinner!'

"Digby turned to pursue the snake, and I sprang from the rock. I begged Cradock to show me the wound; it was on the back of his hand. I assured him I could easily extract the venom, and would have applied my lips to the wound, but he withdrew his hand. Digby at that moment returned. 'She would suck the poison from my hand, Digby,' said Cradock; 'verily, she is but little lower than the angels.'

" 'What! Miss Hope!' exclaimed Digby, 'would you be guilty of self-murder, even if you could save the old gentleman from dying—and dying, as it were, by the will of the Lord?' I assured Digby that there was no danger whatever to me; that I had read of many cases of poison being extracted in that way, without the slightest injury to the person extracting it. He asked me where I had read such stories. I was obliged to refer to a book of aunt Grafton's, called 'The Wonders of the Crusades.' This seemed to Digby but apocryphal authority; he shook his head, and said, 'he would believe such fables no where out of the Bible.' I entreated, vehemently, for I well knew it could not harm me, and I believed it to be life or death to my poor tutor. He seemed half disposed to yield to me. 'Thou hast a marvellous persuasion, child,' he said; 'and now I remember me of a proverb they have in Italy—the lips extract venom from the heart, and poison from the wound.'

"Digby again shook his head. 'Nothing but one of those flourishes they put into verses,' he said. 'Come, come, Master Cradock, stir up a manly spirit, and let's on to the fort, where we may get help it's lawful for you to use; and don't ransack your memory for any more such scholar-rubbish to uphold you in consenting to our young lady's exposing her life, to save the fag end of yours.'

" 'Expose her life!' retorted Cradock, rising with a feeling of honest indignation, that for a moment overcame the terror of death. 'Digby, you know that if I had a hundred lives, I would rather lose them all, than expose her precious life.'

" 'I believe you, Master Cradock—I believe you; and whether you live, or die, I will always uphold you for a true-hearted man; and you must excuse me for my boldness in speaking, when I thought our young Mistress was putting herself in the jaws of death.'

"We now made all speed to reach the fort; but when we arrived there, no aid could be obtained, and poor Cradock's death was regarded as inevitable. I remembered to have heard Nelema say, that she knew a certain antidote to the poison of a rattle-snake; and when I told this to your father, he ordered our horses to be saddled, and we set out immediately for home, where we arrived in six hours. Even in that brief space the disease had made fearful progress. The wound was horribly inflamed, and the whole arm swoln and empurpled. I saw despair in every face that looked on Cradock. I went myself, attended by Jennet and Digby, to Nelema's hut, for I knew if the old woman was in one of her moody fits, she would not come for any bidding but mine.

"Jennet, as you know was always her wont, took up her testimony against 'the old heathen witch.' 'It were better,' she said, 'to die, than to live by the devil's help.' I assured her, that if the case were her own, I would not oppose her pious preference; but that now I must have my own way, and I believed the Giver of life would direct the means of its preservation.

"Though it was near midnight, we found Nelema sitting at the entrance of her hut. I told her my errand. 'Peace be with you, child,' she said. 'I knew you were coming, and have been

waiting for you.' She is superstitious, or loves to affect supernatural knowledge, and I should have thought nothing of her
harmless boast, had I not seen by the significant shake of Jennet's
head, that she set it down against her. The old woman filled a
deer-skin pouch from a repository of herbs in one corner of her
hut, and then returned to Bethel with us. We found Cradock in
a state of partial delirium, and nervous restlessness, which, your
father said, was the immediate precursor of death. Aunt Grafton
was kneeling at his bedside, reading the prayers for the dying.

Nelema ordered every one, with the exception of myself, to
leave the room, for she said her cures would not take effect,
unless there was perfect silence. Your father retired to his own
apartment, and gave orders that he should, in no case, be diverted
from his prayers. Aunt Grafton withdrew with evident reluctance, and Jennet, lingered till Nelema's patience was exhausted,
when she pushed her out of the room, and barred the door
against her.

"I confess, Everell, I would gladly have been excluded too,
for I recoiled from witnessing Cradock's mortal agony; but I
dared in no wise cross Nelema, so I quietly took the lamp, as
she bade me, and stood at the head of the bed. She first threw
aside her blanket, and discovered a kind of wand, which she had
concealed beneath it, wreathed with a snake's skin. She then
pointed to the figure of a snake delineated on her naked shoulder. 'It is the symbol of our tribe,' she said. 'Foolish child!' she
continued, for she saw me shudder; 'it is a sign of honour, won
for our race by him who first drew from the veins the poison
of the king of all creeping things. The tale was told by our fathers, and sung at our feasts; and now am I, the last of my race,
bidden to heal a servant in the house of our enemies.' She remained for a moment, silent, motionless, and perfectly abstracted. A loud groan from Cradock roused her. She bent over
him, and muttered an incantation in her own tongue. She then,
after many efforts, succeeded in making him swallow a strong
decoction, and bathed the wound and arm with the same liquor.
These applications were repeated at short intervals, during which
she brandished her wand, making quick and mysterious motions,
as if she were writing hieroglyphics on the invisible air. She

writhed her body into the most horrible contortions, and tossed her withered arms wildly about her, and, Everell, shall I confess to you, that I trembled lest she should assume the living form of the reptile whose image she bore? So violent was her exercise, that the sweat poured from her face like rain, and, ever and anon, she sank down in momentary exhaustion, and stupor; and then would spring to her feet, as a race horse starts on the course, fling back her long black locks that had fallen over her bony face, and repeat the strange process.

"After a while—how long I know not, for anxiety and terror prevented my taking any note of time—Cradock showed plain symptoms of amendment—his respiration became free—the colour in his face subsided—his brow, which had been drawn to a knot, relaxed, and his whole appearance became natural and tranquil. 'Now,' whispered Nelema to me, 'fear no more for him—he has turned his back on the grave. I will stay here and watch him; but go thou to thy bed—thy cheek is pale with weariness and fear.'

"I was too happy at that moment to feel weariness, and would have remained, but Nelema's gestures for me to withdraw were vehement, and I left her, mentally blessing her for her effectual aid. As I opened the door, I stumbled against Jennet. It was evident from her posture, that she had been peeping through the key-hole. Do not think me a vixen, Everell, if I confess that my first impulse was to box her ears; however, I suppressed my rage, and, for the first time in my life, was prudent and temporizing, and I stooped to beg her to go with me to my room—I am sure it was with the timid voice of one who asks a favour, for, the moment we were in the light, I saw by her mien that she felt the power was all in her own hands. 'It is enough,' she said, 'to make the hair of a saint stand on end to have such carryings-on in my master's house; and you, Miss Hope Leslie, that have been, as it were, exalted to heaven in point of privileges, that you should be nothing better than an aid and abetment of this emissary of Satan.'

" 'Hush,' said I, 'Jennet, and keep your breath to give thanks for good Mr. Cradock's recovery. Nelema has cured him—Satan does not send forth his emissaries with healing gifts.'

" 'Now, Miss Leslie,' retorted the provoking creature, 'you are in the very gall of bitterness and blindness of the flesh. Did not the magicians with their enchantments even as did Moses and Aaron? The sons of darkness always put on the form of the sons of light. I always said so. I knew what it would come to. I said she was a witch in Mistress Fletcher's time.'

" 'And you spoke falsely then, as you do now, Jennet, for Nelema is no witch.'

" 'No witch!' rejoined Jennet, screaming with her screech-owl voice, so loud that I was afraid your father would overhear her; 'try her then—see if she can read in the Bible—or Mr. Cotton's catechism—no, no; but give her your aunt Grafton's prayer book, and she will read as glib as a minister.'

" 'Jennet,' said I, 'you are mad outright—you seem to forget that Nelema cannot read any thing.'

" 'It is all the same as if she could,' persisted Jennet; 'her master makes short teaching—there are none so deaf as those that won't hear. I tell you again, Miss Hope Leslie—remember Mrs. Fletcher——remember what she got for shutting her ears to me.'

"You will forgive me, Everell, for losing my patience utterly at these profane allusions to your mother, and commanding Jennet to leave my room.

"She made me bitterly repent my want of self-command; for, self-willed as the fools of Solomon's time, she determined to have her own way, and went to your father's room, where she gained admittance, and gave such a description of Nelema's healing process, that, late as it was, I was summoned to his presence.

"As I followed Jennet along the passage, she whispered to me, 'now for the love of your own soul, don't use his blind partiality to pervert his judgment.'

"I made no reply, but mentally resolved that I would task my power and ingenuity to the utmost to justify Nelema. When we came into the study, Jennet, to my great joy, was dismissed. It is much easier for me to contend with my superiors, than my inferiors. Your father bade me sit down by him. I seated myself on the foot-stool at his feet, so that I could look straight into his eyes; for many a time, when my heart has quailed at his solemn address, the tender spirit stationed in that soft hazle eye of his—so like yours, Everell—has quieted all my apprehensions. I spoke first, and said, 'I was sure Jennet had spoiled the good news of my tutor's amendment, or he would not look so grave.'

"He replied, 'that it was time to look grave when a pow-wow dared to use her diabolical spells, mutterings, and exorcisms, beneath a christian roof, and in the presence of a christian maiden, and on a christian man; but,' he added, 'perhaps Jennet hath not told the matter rightly—her zeal is not always according to knowledge. I would gladly believe that my house has not been profaned. Tell me, Hope, all you witnessed—tell me truly.'

"I obeyed. Your father heard me through without any comment, but now and then a deep-drawn sigh; and when I had finished, he asked, 'what I understood by the strange proceedings I had described?'

" 'May I not answer,' I said, 'in the language of scripture, 'that this only I know, that whereas thy servant was sick, he is now whole.' '

" 'Do not, my dear child,' said your father, 'rashly misapply scripture—and thus add to your sin, in (as I trust ignorantly) dealing with this witch and her familiars.'

"I replied, 'I did not believe Nelema had used any witchcraft.'

"He asked me, 'if I had not been told, that some of our catechised Indians had confessed that when they were pagans they were pow-wows, devoted in their infancy to demons—that these pow-wows were factors for the devil—that they held actual conversation, and were in open and avowed confederacy with him?'

"I said, 'I had heard all this;' but asked, 'if it were right to take the confession of these poor children of ignorance and superstition against themselves?' I repeated what I had often heard you, Everell, say, that Magawisca believed the mountain, and the valley, the air, the trees, every little rivulet, had their present invisible spirit—and that the good might hold discourse with them. 'Why not believe the one,' I asked, 'as well as the other?'

"Your father looked at me sternly. 'Dost thou not believe in witchcraft, child?' he said. While I hesitated how to reply, lest I should, in some way, implicate Nelema, your father hastily turned the leaves of the Bible, that lay on his table, and opened to every text where familiar spirits, necromancers, sorcerers, wizards, witches, and witchcraft, are spoken of.

"I felt as if the windows of heaven were opened on my devoted head. As soon as I could collect my wits, I said something, confusedly, about not having thought much on the subject; but that I had supposed, as indeed I always did, that bad spirits were only permitted to appear on earth, when there were, also, good spirits and holy prophets to oppose them.

"Your father looked steadily at me, for a few moments, then closing the Bible, he said, 'I will not blame thee, my child, but myself, that I have left thee to the guidance of thy natural erring reason; I should have better instructed thee.' He then kissed me, bade me good night, and opened the door for me to depart. I ventured to ask, 'if I might not say to Jennet, that it was his order, she should be silent in regard to Nelema?'

" 'No, no,' he said, 'meddle no farther with that matter, but go to your own apartment, and remain there till the bell rings for morning prayers.'

"My heart rebelled, but I dared not disobey. I came to my room, and have been sitting by my open window, in the hope of hearing Nelema's parting footsteps; but I have listened in vain, and unable to sleep, I have tried to tranquillize my mind by writing to you. Poor old Nelema! if she is given up to the magistrates, it will go hard with her—Jennet is such an obstinate self-willed fool! I believe she will be willing to see Nelema hung for a witch, that she may have the pleasure of saying, 'I told you so.'

"Poor Nelema!—such a harmless, helpless, lonely being—my tears fall so fast on my paper, that I can scarcely write. I blame myself for bringing her into this hapless case—but it may be better than I fear. I will leave my letter and try to sleep.

"It is as I expected: Nelema was sent, early this morning, to the magistrates. She was tried before our triumvirate, Mr. Pynchon, Holioke, and Chapin. It was not enough to lay on her the crime of curing Cradock, but Jennet and some of her gossips imputed to her all the mischances that have happened for the last seven years. My testimony was extorted from me, for I could not disguise my reluctance to communicate any thing that could be made unfavourable to her. Our magistrates looked sternly on me, and Mr. Holioke said, 'Take care, Hope Leslie, that thou art not found in the folly of Balaam, who would have blessed, when the Lord commanded him to curse.'

"I said, 'It was better to mistake in blessing than in cursing, and that I was sure Nelema was as innocent as myself.' I know not whence I had my courage, but I think truth companies not with cowardice; however, what I would fain call courage, Mr. Pynchon thought necessary to rebuke as presumption:—'Thou art somewhat forward, maiden,' he said, 'in giving thy opinion; but thou must know, that we regard it but as the whistle of a bird; withdraw, and leave judgment to thy elders.'

"In leaving the room I passed close to Nelema. I gave her my hand in token of kindness; and though I heard a murmur of 'shame—shame!' I did not withdraw it till the poor old creature had bowed her wrinkled brow upon it, and dropped a tear which no suffering could have extorted.

"The trial went on, and she was pronounced worthy of death; but as the authority of our magistracy does not extend to life, limb, or banishment, her fate is referred to the court at Boston. In the mean time, she awaits her sentence in a cell, in Mr. Pynchon's cellar. We have, as yet, no jail.

"Digby has been summoned before the magistrates, and publickly reproved for expressing himself against their proceedings. Mr. Pynchon charged him to speak no more against godly governors and righteous government, for "to such scoffers heaven had sent divers plagues—some had been spirited away by Satan—some blown up in our harbours—and some, like poor Austin of Quinnepaig, taken into Turkish captivity!!" Digby's feelings are suppressed, but not subdued.

"How I wish you were here, dear Everell. Sometimes I wish your mother's letter had not been so persuasive. Nothing but that last request of hers, would have induced your father to send you to your uncle Stretton. If you were here, I am sure you would devise some way to save Nelema. When she is gone, you will never again hear of Magawisca. I shall never hear more of my sweet sister. They both, if we may believe Nelema, still dwell safely in the wigwam of Mononotto, among the Mohawks. These Mohawks are said to be a fierce race; and all those tribes who dwell near the coast, and have, in some measure, come under a christian jurisdiction, and are called 'praying and catechised Indians,' say, that the Mohawks are to them as wolves to sheep. I cannot bear to think of my gentle timid sister, a very dove in her nature, among these fierce tribes. I wonder that I am ever happy, and yet it is so natural to me to be happy! The commander of the fort at Albany, at Governor Winthrop's request, has made great efforts to obtain some information about my sister, but without any satisfactory result. Still Nelema insists to me, that her knowledge is certain; and when I have endeavoured to ascertain the source whence she derived it, she pointed upwards, indicating that she held mysterious intelligence with the spirits of the air; but I believe she employed this artifice to hide some intercourse she holds with distant and hostile tribes.

"What a tragi-comedy is life, Everell!—I am sure your favourite, Shakespear, has copied nature in dividing his scenes between mirth and sadness. I have laughed to-day, heartily, and for a few moments I quite forgot poor Nelema, and all my heart-rending anxieties about her. My tutor, for the first time since his most unlucky mishap, left his room, and made his appearance in the parlour. I was sitting there with aunt Grafton, and I rose to shake his hand, and express my unfeigned joy on his recovery. His little gray eyes were, for a moment, blinded with tears at what he was pleased to call the 'condescendency of my regard for him.' He then stood for a moment, as if he were lost, as you know is always his wont, when a blur comes over his mind, which is none of the clearest at best. I thought he looked pale and weak, and I offered him a chair and begged him to sit down, but he declined it with a wave, or rather a poke, of his hand, for he never in his life made a motion so graceful as a wave, and drawing a paper from his pocket, he said, 'I have here an address

to thee, sweet Miss Hope Leslie, wherein I have put in a body
of words the spirit of my late meditations, and I have endeavoured to express, in the best latinity with which many years of
daily and nightly study have possessed me, my humble sense of
that marvellous wit and kindness of thine, which made thee, as
it were, a ministering angel unto me, when I was brought nigh
unto the grave by the bite of that most cunning beast of the
field, with whom, I verily believe, the devil left a portion of his
spirit, in payment of the body he borrowed to beguile our first
parents.'

"This long preamble finished, Master Cradock began the
reading of his address, of which, being in the language of the
learned, I could not, as you know, understand one word; however, he did not perceive that my smiles were not those of intelligence, nor hear aunt Grafton's remark, that 'much learning
and little wit had made him as crazy as a loon.' He had not
proceeded far, when his knees began to shake under him, and
disdaining to sit, (an attitude, I suppose, proscribed in the ceremonies of the schools, the only ceremonies he observes) he contrived, with the aid of the chair I had placed for him, to kneel.
When he had finished his address, which, according to the rules
of art, had a beginning, a middle, and, thank heaven, an end, he
essayed to rise; but, alas! though, like Falstaff, he had an 'alacrity
in sinking,' to rise was impossible; for beside the usual impedi-
ments of his bulk and clumsiness, he was weakened and stiffened
by his late sickness; so I was fain to call Digby to his assistance,
and run away to my own apartment to write you, dear Everell,
who are ever patient with my Bethel chronicles, an account of
what aunt Grafton calls, 'this *scholar* foolery.'

"Yesterday was our lecture day, and I went to the village to
attend the meeting. A sudden storm of hail and wind came on
during the exercises, and continued after, and I was obliged to
accept Mrs. Pynchon's invitation to go home with her. After we
had taken our supper, I observed Mr. Pynchon fill a plate, boun-
tifully, with provisions from the table, and give it with a large
key, which he took from a little cupboard over the fireplace, to

a serving woman. She returned, in a short time, with the key, and, as I observed, restored it to its place. Digby came shortly after to attend me home. The family hospitably urged me to remain, and ascertaining from Digby that there was no especial reason for my return, I dismissed him.

"The next morning I was awakened from a deep sleep by one of Mr. Pynchon's daughters, who told me, with a look of terror, that a despatch had arrived early that morning from Boston, notifying the acquiescence of the Court there, in the opinion of our magistrates, and Nelema's sentence of condemnation to death—that her father had himself gone to the cell to announce her fate to her, when lo! she had vanished—the prison-door was fast—the key in its usual place—but the witch was spirited away. I hurried on my clothes, and trembling with surprise, pleasure, or whatever emotion you may please to ascribe to me, I descended to the parlor, where the family and neighbours had assembled to talk over the strange event. I only added exclamations to the various conjectures that were made. No one had any doubt as to who had been Nelema's deliverer, unless a suspicion was implied in the inquiring glances which Mr. Pynchon cast on me, but which, I believe, no one but myself observed. Some could smell sulphur from the outer kitchen door to the door of the cell; and there were others who fancied that, at a few yards distance from the house, there were on the ground marks of a slight scorching—a plain indication of a visitation from the enemy of mankind. One of the most sagacious of our neighbours remarked, that he had often heard of Satan getting his servants into trouble, but he never before heard of his getting them out. However, the singularity of the case only served to magnify their wonder, without, in the least, weakening their faith in the actual, and, as it appeared, friendly alliance between Nelema, and the evil one. Indeed, I was the only person present whose belief in her witchcraft was not, as it were, converted into sight.

"Everell, I had been visited by a strange dream that night, which I will venture to relate to you; for you, at least, will not think me confederate with Nelema's deliverer.

"Methought I stood, with the old woman, beneath the elm

tree, at the end of Mr. Pynchon's garden; the moon, through an opening of the branches, shone brightly on her face—it was wet with tears.

"'I shall not forget,' she said, 'who saved me from dying by the hand of an enemy. As surely as the sun will appear there again,' she added, pointing to the east—'so surely, Hope Leslie, you shall see your sister.'

"'But, Nelema,' said I, 'my poor little sister is in the far western forests—you can never reach there.'

"'I will reach there,' she replied—'if I crawl on my hands and knees, I will reach there.'

"Think you, dear Everell, my sister will ever expound this dream to me?

"I was the first to carry the news to Bethel. Your father was in one of his meditative humours, and heeded it no more than if I had told him a bird had flown from its cage. Jennet joined in the general opinion, that Satan, or at least one of his emissaries, had opened the prison door; and our good Digby, with his usual fearlessness, maintained, in the teeth of her exhortation and invective, that an angel had wrought for the innocent old woman.

"A week has elapsed. It is whispered that on the night Nelema vanished, Digby was missed by his bed-fellow!—strange depredations were committed on Jennet's larder!—and muffled oars were heard on the river!

"Our magistrates have made long and frequent visits to Bethel, and have held secret conferences with your father. The purport of them I leave you to conjecture from the result. Yesterday he sent for me to the study. He appeared deeply affected. It was some time before he could command his voice; at length he said, that he had determined to accept for me Madam Winthrop's invitation to Boston. I told him, and told him truly, that I did not wish to go to Boston—that I was perfectly contented—perfectly happy. 'And what,' I asked, 'will you and poor aunt Grafton do without me?'

"'Your aunt goes with you,' he said; 'and as for me, my dear child, I have too long permitted myself the indulgence of having you with me. I have a pilgrimage to accomplish through this wilderness, and I am sinful if I linger to watch the unfolding of even the single flower that has sprung up in my path.'

" 'But,' said I, 'does not He who appoints the path through the wilderness, set the flowers by the wayside? I will not—I will not be plucked up and cast away.' He kissed me, and said, 'I believe, my beloved child, thou wert sent in mercy to me; but it were indeed sinful to convert the staff vouchsafed to my pilgrimage into fetters. I should ever bear in mind that life is a race and a warfare, and nothing else: you have this yet to learn, Hope. I have proved myself not fit to teach, or to guide thee—nor is your aunt. Madam Winthrop will give you pious instruction and counsel, and her godly niece, Esther Downing, will, I trust, win you to the narrow path, which, as the elders say, she doth so steadily pursue.'

"The idea of this puritanical guardianship did not strike me agreeably, and besides, I love Bethel—I love your father—with my whole soul I love him; and, as you already know, Everell, therefore it is no confession, I love to have my own way, and I said, I would not go.

" 'You must go, my child,' said your father; 'I cannot find it in my heart to chide you for your reluctance, but you must go. Neither you, nor I, have any choice.'

" 'But why must I go?' I asked.

" 'Ask no questions,' he replied; 'it is fixed that you must go. Tell your aunt Grafton that she must be ready to leave Springfield next week. Mr. Pynchon and his servants attend you. Now leave me, my child, for when you are with me, you touch at will every chord in my heart, and I would fain keep it still now.'

"I left him, Everell, while I could command my tears; and after I had given them free course, I informed aunt Grafton of our destiny. She was so delighted with the prospect of a visit to Boston, that I, too, began to think it must be very pleasant; and my dread of this straight-laced Mrs. Winthrop and her perpendicular niece, gave place to indefinite anticipations of pleasure. I shall, at any rate, see you sooner than if I remained here. Thank heaven, the time of your return approaches; and now that it is so near, I rejoice that your father has not been persuaded, by those who seem to me to take a very superfluous care of his private affairs, to recall you sooner. On this subject he has stood firm: satisfied, as he has always said, that he could not err in complying with the last request of your sainted mother.

"Aunt Grafton charges me with divers messages to you, but I will not add a feather to this leaden letter, which you will now have to read, as I have written it, by instalments.

"Farewell, dear Everell, forget not thy loving friend and sister,
"Hope Leslie."

As Hope had declined her aunt's messages, the good lady affixed them herself—and here they follow.

"To Everell Fletcher.
"Valued sir—Being much hurried in point of time, I would fain have been myself excused from writing, but Miss Hope declines adding to her letter what I have indited.

In your last, you mention being visited with the great cold, which, I take from your account of it, to be the same as that with which we were all shaken soon after the coronation of his present Majesty. (God bless him!) I had then a recipe given me for an infallible remedy, by the Lady Penyvere, great aunt, by the mother's side, to la belle Rosette, maid of honour to the queen.

"I enclose it for you, believing it will greatly advantage you, though Hope insists that if the cold has not yet left you, it will be a chronic disease before this reaches you; in which case, I would advise you to apply to old Lady Lincoln, who hath in her family receipt-book, many renowned cures for chronics. I remember one in particular, somewhere about the middle of the book, which follows immediately after a rare recipe for an every-day plum-pudding.

"I doubt not that years have mended thee, and that thou wouldst now condemn the folly and ignorance of thy childhood, which made thee then deride the most sovereign remedies. Hope,

I am sorry to say, is as obstinate as ever; and it was but yesterday, when I wished her to take some diluents for a latent fever,
that she reminded me of the time when she, and you, in one of
your mischievous pranks, threw the pennyroyal tea out of the
window, and suffered me to believe that it had cured an incipient
pleurisy. Thus presumptuous is youth! Hope is, to be sure, notwithstanding her living entirely without medicine, in indifferent
good health; her form is rather more slender than when you left
us, as is becoming at seventeen; but her cheek is as round and
as ruddy as a peach. I should not care so much about her self-
will on the score of medicine, but that her stomach being in such
perfect order now, would bear every kind of preventive, and
medicines of this class are so simple, that they can do no harm.
I believe it is true, as old Doctor Panton used to say, 'your
healthy people are always prejudiced against medicine.' I wish
you would drop a hint on this subject in your next letter to
her, for the slightest hint from you goes further than a lecture
from me.

"It was very thoughtful in you, Mr. Everell, and what I once
should not have expected, to inquire so particularly after my
health. I am happy to say, that at this present I am better than
I have been for years, which is unaccountable to me, as, since
the hurry of our preparations for Boston, I have forgotten my
pills at night, and my tonics in the morning.

"I wish you to present many thanks to Lady Amy for assisting you in my commissions. The articles in general suited,
though the pinking of the flounces was too deep. My gown was
a trifle too dark—but do not mention that to Lady Amy, for I
make no doubt she took due pains, and only wanted a right
understanding of the real hue, called feuille morte, which, between you and I—sub rosa, mind—my gown would not be
called, by any person skilled in the colours of silk. Hope thought
to convince me I was wrong by matching it with a dead leaf
from the forest. Was not that peculiar of Hope?

"Now, Mr. Everell, I do not wish to be an old woman before
my time, therefore I will have another silk of a brighter cast.
Brown it must be, but lively—lively. I will enclose a lock of
Hope's hair, which is precisely the hue I mean. You will observe

it has a golden tinge, that makes it appear in all lights as if there were sunshine on it, and yet it is a decided brown; a difficult colour to hit, but by due inquiry, and I am sure, from the pains you were at to procure the articles I requested for Hope, you will spare no trouble, I think it may be obtained.

"I am greatly beholden to you for the pocket-glass you sent me; it is a mighty convenient article, and an uncommon pretty little attention, Mr. Everell.

"Your present to Hope was a real beauty. The only blue fillet, and the prettiest, of any colour, I ever saw; and such a marvellous match for her eyes—that is, when the light is full on them; but you know they always had a changeable trick with them. I remember Lady Amy's once saying to me before we left England, that my niece would yet do mischief with those laughing *black* eyes of hers. I liked her sister's (poor dear Mary—God help her the while!) better then, they were the true Leslie blue. But one word more of the fillet. Your taste in it cannot be too much commended; but then, as I tell Hope, one does not want always to see the same thing; and she doth continually wear it; —granted, it keeps the curls out of her eyes, and they do look lovely falling about it, but she wears it, week-days and Sundays, feast days and fast days, and she never yet has put on the Henriette; (do remember a thousand thanks to Lady Amy for the pattern) the Henriette, I made her, like that worn by the queen the first night she appeared in the royal box.

"I should like to have a little more chit-chat with you, Mr. Everell, now my pen has got, so to speak, warm in the harness; but business before pleasure. I beg you will remember me to all inquiring friends. Alas! few in number now, as most of my surviving contemporaries have died since I left England.

"Farewell, Mr. Everell, these few lines are from your friend and well-wisher,

"*Bertha Grafton.*

"N.B. It is a great pleasure to me to think you are living in a churchman's family, where you can't but steer clear of—you know what—peculiarities.

"N.B. Hope will have given you the particulars of poor Master Cradock's miscarriage; his mind was set a little *agee* by it, but he appears to be mending.

"N.B. The enclosed recipe hath marvellous virtues in fevers, as well as in colds."

CHAPTER IX

"A country lad is my degree,
    An' few there be that ken me, O;
But what care I how few they be,
    I'm welcome aye to Nannie, O."
                               BURNS[1]

There are hints in Miss Leslie's letter to Everell Fletcher, that require some amplification to be quite intelligible to our readers. She looked upon herself, as the unhappy, though innocent cause, of the old Indian woman's misfortune—and, rash as generous, she had resolved, if possible, to extricate her. With the inconsiderate warmth of youthful feeling, she had, before the grave and reverend magistrates, declared her belief in Nelema's innocence, and thereby implied a censure of their wisdom. This was, certainly, an almost unparalleled presumption, in those times, when youth was accounted inferiority; but the very circumstance that, in one light, aggravated her fault, in another, mitigated it; and her youth, being admitted in extenuation of her offence, she was allowed to escape with a reproof and admonition of moderate length—while her poor guardian was condemned to a long and private conference, on the urgency of reclaiming the spoiled child. Various modes of effecting so desirable an object were suggested, for, as the Scotchman said, in an analogous case, "Ilka man can manage a wife but him that has her."

This matter had passed over, and justice was proceeding in her stern course, when fortune, accident, or more truly, Providence, favoured the benevolent wishes of our heroine. She had, as has been seen, been carried by an unforeseen circumstance, to the house of one of the magistrates. There, mindful of the poor old prisoner, whose sentence, she knew, was daily expected from Boston; she had been watchful of every circumstance relating to her, and when she observed the key of her prison deposited in an accessible place, (no one dreaming of any interference in behalf of the condemned) she was inspired with a sudden resolution to set her free. This was a bold, dangerous, and unlawful interposition; but Hope Leslie took counsel only from her own heart, and that told her that the rights of innocence were paramount to all other rights, and as to danger to herself, she did not weigh it—she did not think of it.

Digby came to the village to attend her home, and this afforded her an opportunity of concert with him: in the depths of the night, when all the household were in profound sleep, she stole from her bed, found her way to the door of the dungeon, and leading out the prisoner, gave her into Digby's charge, who had a canoe in waiting, in which he ferried her to the opposite shore, where he left her, after having supplied her with provisions to sustain her to the vallies of the Housatonick, if, indeed, her wasted strength should enable her to reach there. The gratitude of the poor old creature for her unexpected deliverance from shameful death, is faintly touched on in Hope's letter. She could scarcely, without magnifying her own merit, have described the vehement emotion with which Nelema promised that she would devote the remnant of her miserable days to seeking and restoring her lost sister. Again and again, while Hope urged her departure, she reiterated this promise, and finally, when she parted from Digby, she repeated, as if it were a prophecy, 'She shall see her sister.'

Young persons are not apt to make a very exact adjustment of means and ends, and our heroine certainly placed an undue confidence in the power of the helpless old woman, to accomplish her promise; but she needed not this, to increase her present joy at her success. She crept to her bed, and was awakened in the morning, as she has herself related, with the information of Nelema's escape. She had now a part to play to which she was unused—to mask her feelings, affect ignorance, and take part in the consternation of the assembled village. As may be imagined, her assumed character was awkwardly enough performed, but all were occupied with their own surmises, and no one thought of her—no one, excepting Mr. Pynchon, who had scarcely fixed his eye on her, when a suspicion that had before flashed on his mind, was confirmed. He knew, from the simplicity of her nature, and from her habitual frankness, that she would not have hesitated to avow her pleasure in Nelema's escape, if she had not herself been accessory to it. He watched her averted eye—he observed her unbroken silence, and her lips that, in spite of all her efforts, played into an inevitable smile at the superstitious surmises of some of the wise people, whose philosophy had never dreamed of that every-day axiom of modern times—that supernatural aid should not be called in to interpret events which may be explained by natural causes.

However satisfactory Mr. Pynchon's conclusions were to himself, he confined them, for the present, to his own bosom. He was a merciful man, and probably felt an emotion of joy at the old woman's escape, that could not be suppressed by the stern justice that had pronounced her worthy of death. But while he easily reconciled himself to the loss of the prisoner, he felt the necessity of taking instant and efficient measures to subdue to becoming deference and obedience, the rash and lawless girl, who had dared to interpose between justice and its victim. His heart recoiled from punishing her openly, and he contented himself with insisting, in a private interview with Mr. Fletcher, on the necessity of her removal to a stricter control than his; and recommended, for a time, a temporary transfer of his neglected authority to less indulgent hands.

Mr. Fletcher complied so far as to consent that his favourite should be sent, for a few months, to Boston, to the care of Madam Winthrop, whose character being brought out by the light of her husband's official station, was held up as a sort of pattern throughout New-England. But we must, for the present, pass by state characters; gallery portraits, for the miniature picture that lies next our heart, and which it is full time should be formally presented to our readers, whose curiosity, we trust, has not been sated by occasional glimpses.

Nothing could be more unlike the authentic, 'thoroughly educated,' and thoroughly disciplined young ladies of the present day, than Hope Leslie; as unlike as a mountain rill to a canal— the one leaping over rocks and precipices, sportive, free, and beautiful, or stealing softly on, in unseen, unpraised loveliness; the other, formed by art, restrained within prescribed and formal limits, and devoted to utility. Neither could any thing in outward show, be more unlike a modern belle, arrayed in the mode de Paris of the last Courier des dames, than Hope Leslie, in her dress of silk or muslin, shaped with some deference to the fashion of the day, but more according to the dictates of her own skill and classic taste, which she followed, somewhat pertinaciously, in spite of the suggestions of her experienced aunt.

Fashion had no shrines among the pilgrims; but where she is most abjectly worshipped, it would be treason against the paramount rights of nature, to subject such a figure as Hope Leslie's to her tyranny. As well might the exquisite classic statue be arrayed in corsets, manches en gigot, garnitures en tulle, &c. Her height was not above the medium standard of her sex; she was delicately formed; the high health and the uniform habits of a country life, had endowed her with the beauty with which poetry has invested Hebe; while her love for exploring hill and dale, ravine and precipice, had given her that elastic step and ductile grace which belong to all agile animals, and which made every accidental attitude, such, as a painter would have selected to express the nymphlike beauty of Camilla.

It is in vain to attempt to describe a face, whose material beauty, though that beauty may be faultless, is but a medium for the irradiations of the soul. For the curious, we would, if we could, set down the colour of our heroine's eyes; but, alas! it was undefinable, and appeared gray, blue, hazle, or black, as the outward light touched them, or as they kindled by the light of her feelings.

Her rich brown hair, turned in light waves from her sunny brow, as if it would not hide the beauty it sheltered. Her mouth, at this early period of her life, had nothing of the seriousness and contemplation that events might afterwards have traced there. It rather seemed the station of all sportive, joyous, and kindly feeling, and at the slightest motion of her thoughts, curled into smiles, as if all the breathings of her young heart were happiness and innocence.

It may appear improbable that a girl of seventeen, educated among the strictest sect of the puritans, should have had the open, fearless, and gay character of Hope Leslie; but it must be remembered that she lived in an atmosphere of favour and indulgence, which permits the natural qualities to shoot forth in unrepressed luxuriance—an atmosphere of love, that like a tropical climate, brings forth the richest flowers and most flavorous fruits. She was transferred from the care of the gentlest and tenderest of mothers, to Mr. Fletcher, who, though stern in his principles, was indulgent in his practice; whose denying virtues were all self-denying; and who infused into the parental affection he felt for the daughter, something of the romantic tenderness of the lover of her mother. Her aunt Grafton doated on her; she was the depository of her vanity, as well as of her affection. To her simple tutor, she seemed to embody all that philosophers and poets had set down in their books, of virtue and beauty; and those of the old and rigid, who were above, or below, the influence of less substantial charms, regarded the young heiress with deference. In short, she was the petted lamb of the fold.

It has been seen that Hope Leslie was superior to some of the prejudices of the age. This may be explained, without attributing too much to her natural sagacity. Those persons she most loved, and with whom she had lived from her infancy, were of variant religious sentiments. Her father had belonged to the established church, and though he had much of the gay spirit that characterized the cavaliers of the day; he was serious and exact in his observance of the rites of the church. She had often been her mother's companion at the proscribed 'meeting,' and witnessed the fervor with which she joined in the worship of a persecuted and suffering people. Early impressions sometimes form moulds for subsequent opinions; and when at a more reflecting age, Hope heard her aunt Grafton rail with natural good sense, and with the freedom, if not the point, of mother wit, at some of the peculiarities of the puritans, she was led to doubt their infallibility; and like the bird that spreads his wings and soars above the limits by which each man fences in his own narrow domain, she enjoyed the capacities of her nature, and permitted her mind to expand beyond the contracted boundaries of sectarian faith. Her religion was pure and disinterested—no one, therefore, should doubt its intrinsic value, though it had not been coined into a particular form, or received the current impress.

Though the history of our heroine, like a treasured flower, has only left its sweetness on the manuscript page, from which we have amplified it; yet we have been compelled to infer, from some transactions which we shall faithfully record, that she had faults; but we leave our readers to discover them. Who has the resolution to point out a favourite's defects?

As our fair readers are not apt to be observant of dates, it may be useful to remind them that Miss Leslie's letter was written in October. In the following May, two ships, from the mother country, anchored at the same time in Boston-Bay. Some passengers, from each ship, availed themselves of the facility of the pilot-boat to go up to the town. Among others, were two gentlemen, who met now for the first time: the one, a youth in manhood's earliest prime, with a frank, intelligent, and benevolent countenance, over which, as he strained his eyes to the shore, joy and anxiety flitted with rapid vicissitude. The other had advanced further into life; he might not be more than five and thirty, possibly not so much; but his face was deeply marked by the ravages of the passions, or perhaps the stirring scenes of life. His eyes were black and piercing, set near together, and overhung by thick black brows, whose incessant motion indicated a restless mind. The concentration of thought, or the designing purpose, expressed by the upper part of his face, was contradicted by his loose, open flexible lips. His complexion had the same puzzling contrariety—it was dark and saturnine, but enlivened with the ruddy hue of a bon-vivant. His nose neither turned up nor down, was neither Grecian nor Roman. In short, the countenance of the stranger was a worthless dial-plate—a practical refutation of the *science* of physiognomy;[2] and as the infallible art of phrenology was unknown to our fathers, they were compelled to ascertain the character (as their unlearned descendants still are) by the slow developement of the conduct. The person of the stranger had a certain erect and gallant bearing that marks a man of the world, but his dress was strictly puritanical; and his hair, so far from being permitted the 'freedom of growing long,' then deemed 'a luxurious feminine prolixity,' or being covered with a wig, (one of the abominations that, according to Eliot, had brought on the country the infliction of the Pequod war,) was cropped with exemplary precision. But though the stranger's apparel was elaborately puritanical, still there was a certain elegance about it, which indicated that his taste had reluctantly yielded to his principles. His garments were of the finest materials, and exactly fitted to a form of striking manly symmetry. His hair, it is true, was scrupulously clipped, but being thick and jet black, it becomingly defined a forehead of uncommon whiteness and beauty. In one particular he had departed from the letter of the law, and instead of exposing his throat by the plain, open linen collar, usually worn, he sheltered its ugly protuberance with a fine cambric ruff, arranged in box-plaits. In short, though, with the last exception, a nice critic could not detect the most venial error in his apparel; yet, among the puritans, he looked much like a 'dandy quaker' of the present day, amidst his sober-suited brethren.

Whilst the boat, impelled by a favouring tide, and fair breeze, glided rapidly towards the metropolis of the now thriving colony, the gentlemen fell into conversation with the pilot. The elder stranger inquired if Governor Winthrop had been re-elected?

"Yes—God bless him," replied the sailor; "the worthy gentleman has taken the helm once more."

"Has he," asked the stranger, eagerly, "declared for King or Parliament?"

"Ho! I don't know much about their land-tackle," replied the seaman; "but, to my mind, the fastings we have had all along when the King won the day, and the rejoicings when the Parliament gained it, was what you might call a declaration. Since you speak of it, I do remember I heard the boys up in town saying, that our magistrates, at election, did scruple about the oath, and concluded to leave out that part which promises to bear true faith and allegiance to our sovereign lord King Charles."

"So, we have thrown his Majesty overboard, and are to sail under Parliament colours," said the young gentleman. "Well," he continued, "this might have been predicted some five or six years since, for, I remember, there were then disputes, whether the King's ensign should be spread there," and he pointed to the fortifications on Castle Island, past which the boat was, at that moment, gliding. "They scruple now about the oath. Then their consciences rebelled against the red cross in the ensign; which, I remember, was called, 'the Pope's gift,' 'a relique of papacy,' 'an idolatrous sign,' &c."

"Scruples of conscience are ever honourable," said the elder stranger; "and doubtless your Governor has good reason for not complying with the scripture rule—'render unto Cæsar, the things that are Cæsar's'."

"There is no doubt of it," replied the seaman. "The Governor—God bless him—knows the rules of the good book as well as I know the ropes of a ship; and there is no better pilot than he for all weathers, as he shows by not joining in the hue and cry against the good creature tobacco. Fair winds through life, and a pleasant harbour at last, do I wish him for this piece of christian love!"—at the same time he illustrated his benediction by putting a portion of the favourite luxury in his mouth.

"I am sorry," said the young gentleman, "that our magistrates have volunteered a public expression of their feelings—their sympathies, of course, are with the Parliament party—they virtually broke the yoke of royal authority, when they left their native land, and shewed what value they set on liberty by sacrificing for it every temporal good. Now they have a right to enjoy their liberty in peace."

"Peace!" said the elder gentleman, emphatically—"thus it ever is with the natural man, crying peace—peace—where there is no peace.—Think you, young man, that if the King were to recover his power, he would not resume all the privileges he has formerly granted to these people, who—thanks to Him whose

ark abideth with them!—shew themselves so ready to cast off
their allegiance?"

"The King, no doubt," replied the young gentleman, "would
like to resume both power and possession; but still, I think we
might retain our own, on the principle that he had no right to
give, and in truth could not give, what was not his, and what
we have acquired, either by purchase of the natives, or by lawful
conquest, which gives us the right to the vacuum domicilium."[3]

"I am happy to see, sir," said the elder gentleman, slightly
bowing and smiling, "that your principles, at least, are on the
side of the puritans."

"My feelings and principles both, sir; but that does not render
me insensible to the happiness of the adverse party, or the wisdom of all parties, which is peace; the peace which the generous
Falkland[4] so earnestly invokes, every patriot may ardently desire.
Peace, if I may borrow a figure from our friend the pilot here,
is a fair wind and a flood-tide—and war a storm, that must
wreck some, and may wreck both friend and foe."

The young gentleman seemed tired of the conversation, and
turned away, fixing his eager gaze on the shore, towards which
his heart bounded. His companion, however, was not disposed
to indulge him in silence. "This town, sir," he said, "appears to
be familiar to you. I, alas! am a stranger and a wanderer." This
was spoken in a tone of unaffected seriousness.

"Of such this country is the natural home," replied the young
man, regarding his companion for the first time with some interest, for he had been repelled by what seemed to him to savour
of cant, of which he had heard too much in the mother country.
"I should be happy, sir," he said, courteously, "to render my
acquaintance with the town of any service to you."

The stranger bowed in acknowledgment of the civility. "I
would gladly," he said, "find entertainment with some godly
family here. Is Mr. Wilson[5] still teacher of the congregation?"

"No, sir—if he were, you might securely count on his hospitality, as it was so notorious, that, 'come in, you are heartily
welcome,' was said to be the anagram of his name. But if he is
gone, the doors in Boston are always open to the stranger. Mr.
Cotton, I believe, is the present minister—is he not, pilot?"

"Yes—an please you, sir—but I'm thinking," he added, with a leer, "that that butterfly will be an odd fish to harbour with any of our right godly ones." The young gentleman followed the direction of the pilot's eye, and for the first time observed a lad, who sat on one side of the boat leaning over, and amusing himself with lashing the waves with a fanciful walking-stick. He overheard the pilot's remark, and raised his head, as it appeared involuntarily, for he immediately averted it again, but not till he had exposed a face of uncommon beauty. He looked about fifteen. He had the full melting dark eye, and rich complexion of southern climes; masses of jetty curls parted on his forehead, shaded his temples and neck, and "smooth as Hebe's was his unrazored lip." It was obvious that it was his dress which had called forth the sailor's sarcasm. The breast and sleeves of his jerkin were embroidered, a deep-pointed rich lace ruff embellished his neck, if a neck round and smooth as alabaster could be embellished, and his head was covered with a little fantastic Spanish hat, decorated with feathers.

"Does that youth appertain to you, sir?" asked the young gentleman of the elder stranger.

"Yes—he is a sort of dependant—a page of mine," he replied, with an embarrassed manner; but in a moment recovering his self-possession, he added, "I infer from the gratuitous remarks of our very frank pilot, and from the survey you have taken of the lad, that you think his apparel extraordinary."

"It might, possibly," replied the young man, with a smile, "offend against certain sumptuary laws of our colony, and thus prove inconvenient to you."

"Roslin, do you hear," said the master to the page, who nodded his head without raising it; "thy finery, boy, as I have told thee, must be retrenched;" then turning to his companion, and lowering his voice to a confidential tone, he added; "the lad hath lived on the continent, and hath there imbibed these vanities, of which I hope in good time to reform him; perhaps his youth hath overwrought, with my indulgence, in suffering them thus long."

The young gentleman courteously prevented any further, and as he thought, unnecessary exculpation, by saying, "that the offence was certainly a very trifling one, and if observed at all, would be, by the most scrupulous, considered as venial in so young a lad." He now again turned his ardent gaze to the shore. "Ah! there is the spire of the new meeting-house," he said; "when I went away the good people assembled under a thatched roof, and within mud walls."

"And I can remember," said the pilot, "for I was among the first comers to the wilderness, when for weeks the congregation met under an oak tree—and there was heart-worship there, gentlemen, if there ever was on the ball."

A church standing where *Joy's buildings* are now located, was the only one then in Boston. The greater part of the houses were built in its vicinity, just about the heart of the peninsula, on whose striking and singular form, its first possessors aver they saw written prophecies of its future greatness. Some of its most prominent features have been softened by time, and others changed by the busy art of man. Wharves, whole streets, and the noble granite market-house, (a prouder memorial to its founder than a triumphal arch) now stand where the deep "cove" stretched its peaceful harbour, between the two hills that stood like towers of defence at its extremities. That at the north rose to the height of fifty feet above the sea, and on its level summit stood a windmill; towards the sea it presented an abrupt declivity, and was fortified at its base by a strong battery. The eastern hill was higher than its sister by some thirty feet; it descended kindly towards the town, and was, on that side planted with corn. Towards the sea its steep and ragged cliffs announced that nature had formed it for defence; and accordingly our fathers soon fortified it with "store of great artillery," and changed the first pastoral name of Cornhill, which they had given it, to the more appropriate designation of Fort-hill. A third hill flanked the town, rising to the height of one hundred and thirty-eight feet. "All three," says Johnson,[6] "like over-topping towers, keepe a constant watch to foresee the approach of forrein dangers, being furnished with a beacon, and loud babbling guns, to give notice by their redoubled eccho, to all their sister townes."

Shawmut, a word expressing living fountains, was the Indian name of Boston. Tri-mountain, its first English name, and de-

scriptive of Beacon-hill, which, as we are told, rose in three ma-
jestic and lofty eminences; the most eastern of these summits
having on its brow three little hillocks. Its present, and, as we
fondly believe immortal name, was given with characteristic reverence in honour of one of its first pastors, Mr. Cotton, who
came from Boston, in England.

But we return from this digression to our pilot-boat, which
now had nearly reached its landing place. A throng had gathered
on the "town-dock" in expectation of friends, or news from
friends. In vain did the young stranger's eye explore the crowd
for some familiar face; he was obliged to check the greetings that
rose to his lips, and repress the throbbings of his heart. "Time,"
he said, "has wrought strange changes. I fancied that even the
stones in Boston would know me; but now, I see not one welcoming
look, unless it be in those barbary and rose bushes, that
appear just as they did the last time I scrambled over wind-mill
hill." They now landed at the foot of this hill, and the young
gentleman told his companion, that he should go to his old home
at Governor Winthrop's, where he was sure of finding friends
to welcome him. "And if you will accompany me thither," he
said, "I am certain our kind Governor will render you all the
courtesies, which, as a stranger, you may require."

This opportune offer was, of course accepted; and the gentlemen proceeded like old acquaintances, arm in arm together, after
a short consultation between the master and page, the amount
of which seemed to be that the boy should attend him, and await
without Governor Winthrop's door, further orders.

They had not gone far, when, as they turned a corner, two
young ladies issued from the door of a house a little in advance,
and walked on without observing them. The young gentleman
quickened his steps. "It must be she!" he exclaimed, in a most
animated tone. "There is but one person in the world that has
such tresses!" and his eye rested on the bright golden ringlets
that peeped from beneath a chip gipsy hat, worn by one of the
ladies.

"That is not a rational conclusion of yours," said his companion. "Women have cunning devices, by which to change the
order of nature in the colouring of the hair. I have seen many a

court dame arrayed in the purchased locks of her serving-maid; besides, you know it is the vain fashion of the day to make much use of coloured powders, fluids, and unguents."

"That may all be; but do you not see this nymph's locks are, as Rosalind⁷ says, of the colour God chooses?"

"It were better, my friend, if you explained your meaning without a profane quotation from a play; a practice to which our godless cavaliers are much addicted; but pardon my reproof— age has privileges."

"I do not know," replied the young gentleman, "what degree of seniority may confer this privilege—if some half dozen years, I submit to your right; and the more readily, as I am just now too happy to quarrel about any thing; but excuse me, I must quicken my pace to overtake this girl, who trips it along as if she had Mercury's wings on those pretty feet."

"Ah, that's a foot to leave its print in the memory," said the elder gentleman, in an animated and natural tone, that eagerly as his companion was pressing on, did not escape his observation.

They had now approached the parties they were pursuing, near enough to hear their voices, and catch a few words of their conversation. "You say it's edifying, and all that," said the shortest of the two young ladies, in reply to what seemed, from the tone in which it was concluded, to have been an expostulation; "and I dare say, dear Esther, you are quite right, for you are as wise as Solomon, and always in the right; but for my part, I confess, I had infinitely rather be at home drying marigolds, and matching embroidery silks for aunt Grafton."

"Hope Leslie! by Heaven!" exclaimed the young man, springing forward. The young lady turned at the sound of her name, uttered a scream of joy, and under the impulse of strong affection and sudden delight, threw her arms around the stranger's neck, and was folded in the embrace of Everell Fletcher.

The next instant, the consciousness that the street was an awkward place for such a demonstration of happiness, or, perhaps, the thought that the elegant young man before her was no longer the play-fellow of her childhood, suffused her neck and face with the deepest crimson; and a sort of exculpatory exclamation of, "I was so surprised!" burst from her lips, and extorted a smile even from Everell's new acquaintance, whose gravity had all the fixedness of premeditation.

For a moment, Everell's eyes were rivetted to Hope Leslie's face, which he seemed to compare with the image in his memory. "Yes," he said, as if thinking aloud, "the same face that I saw, for the first time, peeping through my curtains, the day Digby brought me home to Bethel—how is Digby?—my dear father? —Mrs. Grafton?—the Winthrops?—every body?"

"All, all well; but I must defer particulars till I have introduced you to my friend, Miss Downing."

"Miss Downing! is it possible!" exclaimed Everell, and a recognition followed, which shewed, that though he had not, before, observed the lady, who had turned aside, and was sheltered under the thick folds of a veil, the parties were not unknown to each other. Miss Leslie now drew her friend's arm within hers, and as she did so, she perceived she trembled excessively; but too considerate to remark an agitation, which it was obvious the lady did not mean to betray, she did not appear to notice it, and proceeded to give Everell such particulars of his friends, as he must be most impatient to hear. She told him that his father was in Boston, and that in compliance with his son's wishes, he had determined to fix his residence there. Everell was rejoiced at this decision, for gloomy recollections were, in his mind, always associated with Bethel, and he was never happy when he thought of the dangers to which Miss Leslie was exposed there.

"My last letters from America," he said, "informed me that you had as yet no tidings from your sister, or my friend Magawisca."

"Nor have we now—still I cling to my belief, that my poor sister will some day be restored to me; Nelema's promise is prophecy to me."

They had by this time reached Governor Winthrop's. Miss Downing withdrew her arm from her friend, with the intention of retiring to her own apartment; but her steps faltered, and she sunk down in the first chair she could reach, hoping to escape all observation in the bustle of joy occasioned by the unexpected arrival of Everell; and she did so, excepting that her aunt called the colour to her cheek, by saying, "My dear Esther, you have

sadly fatigued yourself—you are as pale as death!" and Hope
Leslie, noticing that Everell cast stolen glances of anxious inquiry
at her friend, made, with the usual activity of a romantic imagination, a thousand conjectures as to the nature of their acquaintance. But there was nothing said or done to assist her
speculations, and while the governor was looking over a letter
of introduction, presented to him by Everell's chance acquaintance, who had announced himself by the name of Sir Philip
Gardiner, the young ladies withdrew to their own apartment.

CHAPTER X

A "pensive Nun, devout and pure,
Sober, stedfast, and demure."

IL PENSEROSO[1]

When the two ladies were alone, there were a few moments of embarrassed and uninterrupted silence, a rare occurrence between two confidential young friends. Hope Leslie was the first to speak. "Come, my dear Esther," she said, "it is in vain for you to think of hiding your heart from me; if you do not fairly conduct me through its mazes, I shall make use of the clue you have dropped, and find my own way through the labyrinth."

"Hope Leslie—what clue do you mean? You should not trifle thus."

"Well then, I will be as serious as you please, and most solemnly demand why thou hast never hinted to the friend of thy bosom, that thou hadst seen, in thine own country, this youth, Everell Fletcher, of whom I have, at divers times and sundry places, most freely spoken to thee?"

"I never told you I had not seen him."

"Oh no! but methinks, for a godly, gracious maiden, as thou art, Esther; approved by our elders, the pattern of our deacons' wives; your actions, as well as your language, should be the gospel 'yea, yea, and nay, nay;' this 'paltering with a double sense,' as the poet has it, would better become a profane damsel, like myself."

"If I have lacked sincerity, I merit your reproach; but I meant to have told you. Mr. Fletcher's arrival now was unexpected"—

"And you were indisposed? your nerves deranged? your circulations disordered? I thought so, when I saw that burning blush, that looked, even through the folds of your veil, as if it would set it on fire; but now your surprise is over, why look so like the tragic muse? Raise up your eyes and look at me, dear Esther, and do not let those long eye-lashes droop over your pale cheek, like a weeping willow over the monumental marble."

"Oh, Hope Leslie! if it were not sinful, I could wish that monumental marble might press the clods on my cold bosom."

Hope was startled at the unaffected solemnity, and deep distress, of her friend: every pulsation of her heart was audible, and her lips, which before were as pale as death, became absolutely blue. She threw her arms around her, and kissed her tenderly. "Dear, dear Esther," she said, "forgive me for offending thee. I never will ask thee any thing again—never, so long as I live. You may look glad, or sorry—blush, or faint—do any thing you please, and I never will ask you for a reason."

"You are very kind, very generous, Hope; but have you not, already, guessed the secret I have striven to hide?——you hesitate—answer me truly."

"Why, then, if I must answer truly—perhaps, I have," replied Hope, looking, in spite of herself, as archly as the mischievous little god, when he sees one of his own arrows trembling in the heart; " 'set a thief to catch a thief,' dear Esther, is an old maxim; and though I have never felt this nervous malady, yet, you know, I am skilled in the books that describe the symptoms, thanks to aunt Grafton's plentiful stock of romances and plays."

"Oh most unprofitable skill! but I have no right to reproach thee, since what hath been but the sport of thy imagination, is my experience—degrading experience. Whatever it may cost me, you shall know all, Hope Leslie. You have justly reproached me with insincerity—I will, at least, lighten my conscience of the burden of that sin."

Hope's curiosity was on tiptoe; and notwithstanding her generous resolution, not voluntarily to penetrate her friend's mystery, she was delighted with the dawn of a disclosure, which, she believed, would amount to a simple confession of a tender sentiment. She sincerely pitied Miss Downing's sufferings; but it is, perhaps, impossible for a third person to sympathise fully with feelings of this nature. "Now, Esther," she said, sportively, "fancy me to be the priest, and yourself the penitent. Confess freely, daughter—our holy church, through me, her most unworthy servant, doth offer thee full absolution."

"Stop, stop, Hope Leslie—do not trifle with holy words, and most unholy rites; but listen, seriously, and compassionate a weakness that can never be forgotten."

Miss Downing then proceeded to relate some of the following particulars; but as her narrative was confused by her emotions, and as it is necessary our readers should, for the sake of its illustration, be possessed of some circumstances which were omitted by her, we here give it, more distinctly, in our own language.

Esther was the daughter of Emanuel Downing,[2] the husband of Governor Winthrop's sister, so often mentioned by that gentleman in his journal, as the faithful and useful friend of the pilgrims, whom he finally joined in New-England.

Esther Downing was of a reserved, tender, and timid cast of character, and being bred in the strictest school of the puritans, their doctrines and principles easily commingled with the natural qualities of her mind. She could not have disputed the nice points of faith, sanctification and justification, with certain celebrated contemporary female theologians,[3] but no one excelled her in the practical part of her religion. In the language of the times, justification was witnessed, both by word, and work.

That young ladies were then indulged in a moderate degree of personal embellishment, we learn from one of the severest pilgrim satirists, who avers, that he was 'no cynic to the due *bravery* of the true gentry,' and allows that "a good text always deserves a fair margent.' Miss Downing was certainly a pure and beautiful 'text,' but her attire never varied from the severest gospel simplicity. It is possible that she was fortified in this self-denying virtue, by that lively little spirit, (that ever hovers about a woman's toilette) whispering in her ear, that all the arts of the tyring-woman could not improve the becomingness of her Madonna style. She wore her hair, which was of a sober brown hue, parted on her forehead, and confined behind in a braid that was so adjusted, it may be accidentally, as to perfectly define the graceful contour of her head. Her complexion was rather pale, but so exquisitely fair and transparent, that it showed the faintest tinge of colour, and set off, to the greatest advantage, features, which, if not striking, had the admitted beauty of perfect symmetry. She was, at least, half a head taller than our heroine, or the Venus de Medicis; but as neither of these were standards with the pilgrims, no one who ventured to speak of the personal graces of Esther Downing, ever impeached their perfection. Spiritual graces were then, (as they should always be) in far higher estimation, than external charms, and Miss Downing, who would have been a reigning belle in our degenerate times, was always characterized by a religious epithet—she was the 'godly,' or the 'gracious maiden.' She attained the age of nineteen, without one truant wish straying beyond the narrow bound of domestic duty and religious exercises; but the course of youth and beauty 'never doth run smooth,' and the perils that commonly beset it, now assailed the tender Esther.

Everell Fletcher came to her father's, to pass two months. He had then, for some years, resided in the family of his uncle Stretton, a moderate churchman; who, though he had not seen fit to eradicate the religious and political principles that had been planted in the mind of the boy, had so tempered them, that, to confess the truth, the man fell far below the standard of puritanism. At first Esther was rather shocked, by the unsubdued gaiety, the unconstrained freedom, and the air of a man of society, that distinguished Everell from the few demure solemn young men of her acquaintance; but there is an irresistible charm in ease, simplicity, and frankness, when chastened by the refinements of education, and there is a natural affinity in youth, even when there is no resemblance in the character; and Esther Downing, who, at first, remained in Everell's presence but just as long as the duties of hospitality required, soon found herself lingering in the parlor, and strolling in the walks, that were his favourite resort. It seemed as if the sun had risen on her after a polar winter, and cheerfulness and her pleasant train sprung up in a mind that had been chilled and paralyzed by the absence of whatever cherishes the gay temper of youth; but it was, after all, but the stinted growth of a polar summer.

She felt a change stealing over her—new thoughts were in her heart—

"And love and happiness their theme."

She did not investigate the cause of this change, but suffered the current of her feelings to flow unchecked, till she was roused to reflection by her serving maid, who said to her mistress, one evening when she came in from a long moon-light walk with Everell, "our worthy minister has been here today, and he asked me, what kept you from the lecture-room, so oft, of late? I minded him it rained last night. He said, that in months past no tempest detained you from the place of worship. I made no answer to that—beside, that it was not for me to gainsay the minister. He stood, as if meditating a minute, and then he took up your psalm-book, and, as he did so, a paper dropped with some verses written on it, and he said, with almost a smile, 'ah, Judy, then your young lady tries her hand, sometimes, at versifying the words of the royal psalmist?'"

"Did he look at the lines, Judy?" asked Esther, blushing deeply with the consciousness that they were but a profane sentimental effusion.

"Yes, my lady—but he looked solemnized and said nothing more about them; but turning to me and speaking as if he would ask a question, he said, 'Judy, it was your mistress' wont to keep the wheel of prayer in perpetual motion. I doubt not her private duty is still faithfully done?' I answered to him, that your honoured parents had been absent the last week, and you had company to entertain, and you were not quite as long at closet-exercise as usual."

"Judy, you were very ready with your excuses for me," said her mistress, after a moment's thoughtfulness.

"It must be a dumb dog, indeed," replied the girl, "that cannot bark for such a kind mistress as thou art."

How often does an accident—a casual word even—serve as a key to unlock feelings of which the possessor has been unconscious. The conscientious girl was suddenly awakened from what appeared to her a sinful dream. Had she perceived, on investigation, a reciprocal sentiment in Everell Fletcher, she would probably have permitted her feelings to flow in their natural channel; but not mingling with his, they were, like a stream, that being dammed-up, flows back, and spreads desolation, where it should have produced life and beauty.

The severest religionists of the times did not require the extinction of the tenderest human affections. On the contrary, there was, perhaps, never a period when they were more frequently and perfectly illustrated. How many delicate women, whom the winds of heaven had never visited roughly, subscribed with their lives to that beautiful declaration of affection from a tender and devoted wife—"Whithersoever your fatall destinie," she said to her husband, "shall dryve you, eyther by the furious waves of the great ocean, or by the manifolde and horrible dangers of the lande, I will surely beare you company. There can be no peryll chaunce to me so terrible, nor any kynde of deathe so cruell, that shall not be much easier for me to abyde than to live so farre separate from you."

But though human affections were permitted, they were to be in manifest subservience to religious devotion—their encroachments were watched with a vigilance resembling the jealousy with which the Israelites defended, from every profane footstep, the holy circle around the ark of the living God. It was this jealousy that now alarmed the fearful superstitious girl; and after some days of the most unsparing self-condemnation, embittered by an indefinite feeling of disappointment, she fell into a dangerous illness; and in the paroxysms of her fever, she prayed fervently that her Creator would resume the spirit, which had been too weak, to maintain its fidelity. It seemed as if her prayer were soon to be granted—she felt herself, and was pronounced by her physician, to be on the verge of the grave. She then was inspired with a strong desire, proceeding, as she believed, from a divine intimation, but which might possibly have sprung from natural feeling, to open her heart to Everell. This disclosure, followed by her dying admonition, would, she hoped, rescue him from the vanities of youth. She accordingly requested her mother to conduct him to her bedside, and to leave them alone for a few moments; and when her request was complied with, she made, to the astonished youth, in the simplicity and sincerity of her heart, a confession, that in other circumstances the rack would not have extorted.

At first, Fletcher fancied her reason was touched. He soothed her, and attempted to withdraw, to call her attendants. She interpreted his thoughts, assured him he was mistaken, and begged that he would not waste one moment of her ebbing life. He then knelt at her bedside, took her burning hand in his, and bathed it with tears of deep commiseration, and tender regret. He promised to lay up her exhortations in his heart, and cherish them as the law of his life; but he did not intimate that he had ever felt a sentiment responding to hers. There was that in the solemnity of the death-bed, in her purity and truth, that would have rebuked the slightest insincerity, however benevolent the feeling that dictated it.

This strange interview lasted but a few moments. Miss Downing, in the energy of her feeling, raised herself on her elbow—the effort exhausted her, and she sunk back in a stupor which appeared to be the immediate precursor of death. Her friends flocked around her, and Fletcher retired to his own room, filled with sorrowful concern at the involuntary influence he had exercised on this sensitive being, who seemed to him far better fitted for heaven, than for earth.

But Miss Downing was not destined yet to be translated to a more congenial sphere. Her unburthened heart reposed, after its long struggles—the original cause of her disease was lightened, if not removed, and the elasticity of a youthful constitution rose victorious over her malady. She never mentioned Everell Fletcher; but she heard, incidentally, that he had remained at her father's, till she was pronounced out of danger, and had then gone to his uncle Stretton's, in Suffolk.

The following autumn, her father, in compliance with a request of Madam Winthrop, and in the hope that a voyage would benefit her health, which was still delicate, sent her to Boston.

There she met Hope Leslie—a bright gay spirit—an allegro to her penseroso. They were unlike in every thing that distinguished each; and it was therefore more probable, judging from experience, that they would become mutually attached. Whatever the theory of the affections may be, the fact was, that they soon became inseparable and confidential friends. Hope sometimes ventured to rally Esther on her over-scrupulousness, and Miss Downing often rebuked the laughing girl's gaiety; but, however variant their dispositions, they melted into each other, like light and shade, each enhancing the beauty and effect of the other.

Hope often spoke of Everell, for he was associated with all the most interesting recollections of her childhood, and probably with her visions of the future; for what girl of seventeen has not a lord for her air-built castles?

Miss Downing listened calmly to her description of the hero of her imagination, but never, by word or sign, gave token that she knew aught of him, other than was told her; and the secret might have died with her, had not her emotion, at Everell's unexpected appearance, half revealed the state of her heart to her quick-sighted friend. This revelation she finished by a full confession, interrupted by tears of bitter mortification.

"Oh!" she concluded, "had I but known how to watch and rule my own spirit, I should have been saved these pangs of remorse and shame."

"My dear Esther," said Hope, brushing away the tears of sympathy that suffused her eyes, "I assure you I am not crying because I consider it a crying case; you people that dwell in the clouds have always a mist before you; now I can see that your path is plain, and sure the end thereof; just give yourself up to my guidance, who, though not half so good and wise as you are, am far more sure-footed. I do not doubt in the least, Everell feels all he ought to feel. I defy any body to know you and not love you, Esther. And do you not see, that if he had made any declaration at the time, it might have seemed as if he were moved by pity, or gratitude. He knew you was coming to New-England, and that he was to follow you; and now he has anticipated his return by some weeks, and why, nobody knows, and it must be because you are here—don't you think so? You will not speak, but I know by your smile what you think, as well as if you did."

Arguments appear very sound that are fortified by our wishes, and Miss Downing's face was assuming a more cheerful expression, when Jennet (our old friend Jennet) came into the room to give the young ladies notice to prepare for dinner, and to inform them that Sir Philip Gardiner was to dine with them—"and a godly appearing man he is," said Jennet, "as ever I laid my eyes on; and it is a wonder to me, that our Mr. Everell should have fallen into such profitable company, for, I am sorry to see it, and loath to say it, he looks as gay as when he used to play his mad pranks at Bethel—when it was next to an impossibility to keep you and him, Miss Hope, from talking and laughing even on a Sabbath day. I think," she continued, glancing her eye at Miss Downing, "sober companions do neither of you any good; and it is so strange Mr. Everell should come home with his hair looking like one of those heathen pictures of your aunt's."

"Oh! hush Jennet! It would be a sin to crop those dark locks of Mr. Everell."

"A sin indeed, Miss Leslie! That is the way you always turn things wrong side out; a sin to have his hair cropped like his father's—or the honourable Governor's—or this Sir Philip Gardiner's—or any other christian man's."

"Well, Jennet, I wish it would come into your wise head, that christian tongues were not made for railing. As to my being serious to-day, that is entirely out of the question; therefore, you may spare yourself hint and exhortation, and go to my aunt, and ask her for my blue boddice and necklace. But no—" she said, stopping Jennet, for she recollected that she had directed the blue boddice because it matched her blue fillet, Everell's gift, and a secret voice told her she had best, under existing circumstances, lay that favourite badge aside. "No, Jennet, bring me my pink boddice, and my ruby locket." Jennet obeyed, but not without muttering as she left the room, a remonstrance against the vanities of dress.

Jennet was one of those persons, abounding in every class of life, whose virtues are most conspicuous in "damning sins they

are not inclined to." We ought, perhaps, to apologise for ob-
truding so humble and disagreeable a personage upon our readers. But the truth is, she figured too much on the family record
of the Fletchers, to be suppressed by their faithful historian.
Those personages, yclep'd bores in the copious vocabulary of
modern times, seem to be a necessary ingredient in life, and like
pinching shoes, and smoky rooms, constitute a portion of its
trials. Jennet had first found favour with Mrs. Fletcher from her
religious exterior. To employ none but godly servants was a rule
of the pilgrims; and there were certain set phrases and modes of
dress, which produced no slight impression upon the minds of
the credulous. To do Jennet justice, she had many temporal virtues; and though her religion was of the ritual order, and, therefore, particularly disagreeable to her spiritual Mistress, yet her
household faculties were invaluable, for then, as now, in the interior of New-England, a faithful servant was like the genius of
a fairy tale—no family could hope for more than one.

Long possession legalized Jennet's rights, and increased her
tyrannical humours, which were naturally most freely exercised
on those members of the family, who had grown from youth to
maturity under her eye. In nothing was the sweetness of Hope
Leslie's temper more conspicuous, than in the perfect good nature with which she bore the teasing impertinencies of this menial, who, like a cross cur, was ready to bark at every passer by.

Youth and beauty abridge the labours of the toilet, and our
young friends, though on this occasion unusually solicitous
about the impression they were to make, were not long in attir-
ing themselves; and when Mrs. Grafton presented herself to attend them to dinner, they were awaiting her. "Upon my word,"
she said, "young ladies, you have done honour to the occasion;
it is not every day we have two gentlemen fresh from Old England to dine with us; I am glad you have shown yourselves
sensible of the importance of the becomings. It is every woman's
duty, upon all occasions, to look as well as she can."

"And a duty so faithfully performed, my dear aunt," said
Hope, "that I fancy, like other duties, it becomes easy from
habit."

"Easy," replied Mrs. Grafton, with perfect naiveté; "second

nature, my dear—second nature. I was taught from a child, to determine the first thing in the morning, what I should wear that day; and now it is as natural to me as to open my eyes when I wake."

"I should think, madam," said Esther, "that other and higher thoughts were more fitting a rational creature, preserved through the night-watches."

Hope was exquisitely susceptible to her aunt's frailties, but she would fain have sheltered them from the observation of others. "Now, my gentle Esther," she whispered to Miss Downing, "lecturing is not your vocation, and this is not lecture day. On jubilee days slaves were set free, you know, and why should not follies be?

Miss Downing could not have failed to have made some sage reply to her friend's casuistry, but the ringing of a bell announced the dinner, and the young ladies, arm in arm, followed Mrs. Grafton to the dining-room. Just as they entered, Hope whispered, "remember, Esther, the festal day is sacred, and may not be violated by a sad countenance." This was a well-timed caution; it called a slight tinge to Miss Downing's cheeks, and relieved her too expressive paleness.

Everell Fletcher met them at the door. The light of his happiness seemed to gild every object. He complimented Mrs. Grafton on her appearance; told her she had not, in the least, changed since he saw her—an implied compliment, always, after a woman has passed a *certain age.* He congratulated Miss Downing upon the very apparent effect of the climate on her health, and then, breaking through the embarrassment that slightly constrained him in addressing her, he turned to Hope Leslie, and they talked of the past, the present, and the future, with spontaneous animation; their feelings according and harmonising, as naturally as the music of the stars when they sang together.

CHAPTER XI

"Our New-England shall tell and *boast* of her *Winthrop,* a *Law-giver* as patient as *Lycurgus,* but not admitting any of *his* criminal disorders; as devout as Numa, but not liable to any of *his* heathen-ish madnesses; a Governor in whom the excellencies of *christianity* made a most improving addition unto the *virtues,* wherein, even without *those,* he would have made a *parallel* for the great men of *Greece* or of *Rome,* which the pen of a *Plutarch* has eternized."

COTTON MATHER[1]

We hold ourselves bound by all the laws of decorum, to give our readers a formal introduction to the government-mansion, and its inmates. The house stood in the main street, (Washington-street) on the ground now occupied by 'Southrow.' There was a little court in front of it: on one side, a fine garden; on the other, a beautiful lawn, or, as it was called, 'green,' extending to the corner on which the 'Old South' (church) now stands, and an ample yard and offices in the rear.

The mighty master of fiction has but to wave the wand of his office, to present the past to his readers, with all the vividness and distinctness of the present;[2] but we, who follow him at an immeasurable distance—we who have no magician's enchant-ments, wherewith we can imitate the miracles wrought by the rod of the prophet; we must betake ourselves to the compass and the rule, and set forth our description as minutely and ex-actly, as if we were making out an inventory for a salesman. In obedience to this necessity, we offer the following detailed de-scription of the internal economy of a pilgrim mansion, not on any apocryphal authority, but quoted from an authentic record of the times.

"In the principal houses was a great hall, ornamented with pictures; a great lantern; velvet cushions in the window-seat to look into the garden: on either side, a great parlour, a little parlour or study, furnished with great looking-glasses, turkey carpets, window-curtains and valance, picture and a map, a brass clock, red leather back chairs, a great pair of brass andirons. The chambers well furnished with feather-beds, warming-pans, and every other elegance and comfort. The pantry well filled with substantial fare and dainties, Madeira wine, prunes, marmalade, silver-tankards and wine-cups, not uncommon."

If any are incredulous as to the correctness of the above extract, we assure them that its truth is confirmed by the spaciousness of the pilgrim habitations still standing in Boston, and occupied by their descendants. These pilgrims were not needy adventurers, nor ruined exiles. Mr. Winthrop himself, had an estate in England, worth seven hundred pounds per annum. Some of his associates came from lordly halls, and many of them brought wealth, as well as virtue, to the colony.

The rigour of the climate, and the embarrassments incident to their condition, often reduced the pilgrims, in their earliest period, to the wants of extreme poverty; but their sufferings had the dignity and merit of being voluntary, and are now, as the tattered garments of the saints are to the faithful, sacred in the eyes of their posterity.

Our humble history has little to do with the public life of Governor Winthrop, which is so well known to have been illustrated by the rare virtue of disinterested patriotism, and by such even and paternal goodness, that a contemporary witty satirist could not find it in his heart to give him a harsher name than 'Sir John Temperwell.'[3] His figure, (if we may believe the portrait that honourably decorates the wall of his lineal descendant) was tall and spare; his eye, dark blue, and mild in its expression: he had the upraised brow, which is said to be indicative of a religious disposition; his hair, and his beard which he wore long, were black. On the whole, we must confess, the external man presents the solemn and forbidding aspect of the times in which he flourished; though we know him to have been a model

of private virtue, gracious and gentle in his manners, and exact
in the observance of all gentlemanly courtesy.

His wife was admirably qualified for the station she occupied.
She recognised, and continually taught to matron and maiden,
the duty of unqualified obedience from the wife to the husband,
her appointed lord and master; a duty that it was left to modern
heresy to dispute; and which our pious fathers, or even mothers,
were so far from questioning, that the only divine right to govern, which they acknowledged, was that vested in the husband
over the wife. Madam Winthrop's matrimonial virtue never de-
generated into the slavishness of fear, or the obsequiousness of
servility. If authorised and approved by principle, it was
prompted by feeling; and, if we may be allowed a coarse comparison, like a horse easy on the bit, she was guided by the
slightest intimation from him who held the rein; indeed—to pursue our humble illustration still farther—it sometimes appeared
as if the reins were dropped, and the inferior animal were left to
the guidance of her own sagacity.

Without ever overstepping the limits of feminine propriety,
Madam Winthrop manifestly enjoyed the dignity of her official
station, and felt that if the governor were the greater, she was
the lesser light. There was a slight tinge of official importance in
her manner of conferring her hospitalities, and her counsel; but
she seemed rather to intend to heighten the value of the gift,
than the merit of the giver.

Governor Winthrop possessed the patriarchal blessing of a
numerous offspring; but as they were in no way associated with
the personages of our story, we have not thought fit to encumber
it with any details concerning them.

We return from our long digression to the party we left in
Governor Winthrop's parlour.

The tables were arranged for dinner. Tables, we say, for a
side-table was spread, but in a manner so inferior to the principal
board, which was garnished with silver tankards, *wine cups,* and
rich china, as to indicate that it was destined for inferior guests.
This indication was soon verified, for on a servant being sent to
announce dinner to Governor Winthrop, who was understood

to be occupied with some of the natives on state business; that gentleman appeared attended by four Indians—Miantunnomoh,[4] the young and noble chief of the Narragansetts, two of his counsellors, and an interpreter. Hope turned to Everell to remark on the graceful gestures by which they expressed their salutations to the company—"Good heavens!" she exclaimed, "Everell, what ails you?" for she saw he was as pale as death.

"Nothing, nothing," said Everell, wishing to avoid observation, and turning towards the window: he then added in explanation to Hope, who followed him, "these are the first Indians I have seen since my return, and they brought, too vividly to mind, my dear mother's death."

Governor Winthrop motioned to his Indian guests to take their seats at the side-table, and the rest of the company, including the elder Fletcher and Cradock, surrounded the dinner table, and serving-men and all, reverently folded their arms and bowed their heads, while the grace, or prefatory prayer, was pronouncing.

After all the rest had taken their seats, the Indians remained standing;[5] and although the governor politely signified to the interpreter that their delay wronged the smoking viands, they remained motionless, the chief drawn aside from the rest, his eye cast down, his brow lowering, and his whole aspect expressive of proud displeasure.

The governor rose and demanded of the interpreter the meaning of their too evident dissatisfaction.

"My chief bids me say," replied the savage, "that he expects such treatment from the English saggamore, as the English receive in the wigwam of the Narragansett chief. He says, that when the English stranger visits him, he sits on his mat, and eats from his dish."

"Tell your chief," replied the governor, who had urgent state reasons for conciliating Miantunnomoh, "that I pray him to overlook the wrong I have done him; he is right; he deserves the place of honour. I have heard of his hospitable deeds, and that he doth give more than even ground to his guests; for our friend, Roger Williams, informed us, that he hath known him, with his family, to sleep abroad to make room in his wigwam for English visitors."

Governor Winthrop added the last circumstance, partly as a full confession of his fault, and partly as an apology to his helpmate, who looked a good deal disconcerted by the disarrangement of her dinner. However, she proceeded to give the necessary orders; the table was remodelled—a sufficient addition made, and the haughty chief, his countenance relaxing to an expression of grave satisfaction, took his seat at the governor's right hand. His associates being properly accommodated at the table, the rest of the company resumed their stations.

Everell cast his eye around on the various viands which covered the hospitable board.—"Times have mended," he said to Madam Winthrop, "in my absence. I remember once sitting down with my father, to a good man's table, on which was nothing but a sorry dish of clams; but our host made up for the defect of his entertainment by the excess of his gratitude, for, as I remember, he gave thanks that 'we were permitted to eat of the abundance of the seas, and of treasures hid in the sand.' "

Hope Leslie understood so well the temper of the company she was in, that she instantly perceived a slight depression of their mercury at what appeared to them, a tone of levity in Everell. She interposed her shield. "What may we expect for the future," she said, "if now it seems strange to us, that ten years ago, the best in the colony were reduced to living upon muscles, acorns, and ground nuts; and that our bountiful governor, having shared his flour and meat with the poorest in the land, had his last batch of bread in the oven, when the ship with succours arrived? the Lion, or the Blessing of the Bay—which was it, Master Cradock? for it was you who told me the story," she added, bending towards Cradock, who sat opposite to her.

Cradock, who always felt, at the slightest notice from Hope, an emotion similar to that of a pious catholic, when he fancies the image of the saint he worships to bend propitiously towards him; Cradock dropped his knife and fork, and erecting his body with one of those sudden jerks characteristic of awkward men, he hit the elbow of a servant who was just placing a gravy-boat on the table, and brought the gravy down on his little brown wig, whence it found its way, in many a bubbling rill, over his face, neck, and shoulders.

A murmur of sympathy and suppressed laughter ran around the table; and while a servant, at his mistress' bidding, was applying napkins to Cradock, he seemed only intent on replying to Miss Leslie. "It was the Lion, Miss Hope—ha—indeed—a wonderful memory—yes, yes—it was the Lion. The Blessing of the Bay was the governor's own vessel."

"That name," said Sir Philip Gardiner, in a low tone to Hope Leslie, next whom he sat, "should, I think, have been reserved, where names are significant, for a more just appropriation."

He spoke in a tone of confidential gallantry so discordant with his demeanor, that the fair listener lost the matter in the manner, and turning to him with one of those looks so confounding to a man who means to speak but to one ear in the company—"What did you say, sir?" she asked.

"He said, my dear," said Mrs. Grafton, who sat at the knight's left hand, and who would have considered it worse to suppress a compliment, than to conceal treason; "he said, my dear, that you should have been named, the Blessing of the Bay."

Sir Philip recoiled a little at this flat version of his compliment; but he had other interests to sustain, more important than his knightly courtesy, and he was just contriving something to say, which might secure him a safe passage past Scylla and Charybdis, when Madam Winthrop, who was exclusively occupied with the duty of presiding, begged Sir Philip would change his plate, and take a piece of wild turkey, which she could recommend as savoury and tender; or, a piece of the venison—the venison, she said, was a present from the son of their good old friend and ally, Chicatabot,[6] and she was sure it was of the best.

The knight declined the proffered delicacies, alleging he had already been tempted to excess by the cod's-head and shoulders—a rarity to a European.

"But," said Miss Leslie, "you will not dine on fish alone, and on Friday too—why we shall suspect you of being a Romanist."

If there was any thing in the unwonted blush that deepened the knight's complexion, which might lead an observer to suspect that an aimless dart had touched a vulnerable point, he adroitly averted suspicion by saying, "that he trusted temperance and self-denial were not confined to a corrupt and superstitious church, and that for himself, he found much use in voluntary mortifications of appetite."

"Fastings oft," said Cradock, who had been playing the part of a valiant trencherman, taking liberally of all of the various feast, "fastings oft are an excellent thing for those who have grace for them; and yours, Sir Philip, if one may judge from the ruddiness of your complexion, are wonderfully prospered." The knight received the simple compliment with a silent bow.

Cradock turned to Miss Downing, who sat on his right— "Now, Miss Esther, you do wrong yourself; there is that pigeon's wing, just as I gave it to you."

Hope Leslie looked up with a deprecating glance, as if she would have said, 'Heaven help my tutor! he never moves without treading on somebody's toes.'

"Is not Miss Downing well?" asked the elder Fletcher, who now, for the first time, noticed that she looked unusually pale and pensive.

"Perfectly well," said Esther.

"Indifferently well, my dear, you mean," said Madam Winthrop. "Esther," she added, "always feeds like a Canary bird; but I never despair of a young lady—they have all the cameleon gift of living upon air."

"Will Miss Downing mend her appetite with wine," asked young Fletcher, "and allow me the honour of taking it with her?"

"Everell!" exclaimed Hope, touching his elbow, but not in time to check him.

"My son!" said his father, in a voice of rebuke.

"Mr. Fletcher!" exclaimed Governor Winthrop, in a tone of surprise.

"What have I done now?" asked Everell of Hope Leslie; but Hope was too much diverted with his mistake and honest consternation to reply.

"You have done nothing inexcusable, my young friend," said the governor; "for you probably did not know that the vain custom of drinking, one to another, has been disused, at my table, for ten years; and that our general court prohibited this 'employment of the creature out of its natural use,' by their order, in the year of our Lord, 1639, four years since; so that the custom hath become quite obsolete with us, though it may be still in practice among our laxer brethren of England."

"With due deference I speak," said Everell, "to my elders and superiors; but it really appears to me to border on the quixotism of fighting windmills, to make laws against so innocent a custom."

"No vanity is innocent, Mr. Everell Fletcher," replied the governor, "as you will, yourself, after proper consideration, confess. Tell me, when but now, you would have proffered wishes of health to my niece, Esther, was it not an empty compliment, and not meant by you for an argument of love, which should always be unfeigned?"

The governor's proposition appeared to himself to be merely an abstract metaphysical truth; but to the younger part of his audience, at least, it conveyed much more than met the ear.

Miss Downing blushed deeply, and Everell attempted, in vain, to stammer a reply. Hope Leslie perceived the pit, and essayed a safe passage over it. "Esther," she said, "Everell shall not be our knight at tilt or tournament, if he cannot use the lance your uncle has dropped at his feet. Are there not always, Everell, in your heart, arguments of love unfeigned, when you drink to the health of a fair lady?"

Before Everell had time to reply, except by a sparkling glance, the governor said, "This is somewhat too light a discussion of a serious topic."

This rebuke quenched, at once, the spark of gaiety Hope had kindled, and the dinner, never a prolonged meal in this pattern mansion, was finished without any other conversation than that exacted by the ordinary courtesies of the table.

After the repast was ended, the Indian chief took his leave with much fainter expressions of attachment than he had vouchsafed on a former visit, as the governor had afterwards occasion to remember.

The party dispersed in various directions, and the governor

withdrew, with the elder Fletcher, to his study. When there, Governor Winthrop lighted his pipe, a luxury in which he sparingly indulged; and then, looking over a packet of letters, he selected one, and handed it to Mr. Fletcher, saying, "There is an epistle from brother Downing which your son has brought to me. Read it, yourself; you will perceive that he has stated his views on a certain subject, interesting to you, and to us all; and stated them directly, without any of the circumlocution and ambiguity, which a worldly-minded man would have employed on a like occasion."

Mr. Downing introduced the important topic of his epistle, which Mr. Fletcher read with the deepest attention, by saying that "Fletcher, junior, returns to the colony, a fit instrument, as I trust, to promote its welfare and honour. He is gifted with divers and goodly talents, and graced with sufficient learning.

"I have often been sorely wounded at hearing the censures passed on our brother Fletcher, for having sent his son into the bosom of a prelatical family, but I confidently believe the youth returns to his own country with his puritan principles uncorrupted; although, it is too true, as our stricter brethren often remark, that he has little of the outward man of a 'pilgrim indeed.'

"He is, brother Winthrop, a high-metalled youth, and on this account I feel, as you doubtless will, the urgency of coupling him with a member of the congregation, and one who may, in all likelihood, accomplish for him that precious promise of the apostle, 'the believing wife shall sanctify the unbelieving husband.'

"I have already taken the first step towards bringing about so desirable an end, by inviting the young man to my house, where he spent two months of the summer. I then favoured his intimate intercourse with my well-beloved daughter Esther, whose outward form, I may say without boasting, is a fit temple for the spirit within."

Mr. Downing then proceeded to state some circumstances already known to the reader, and particularly dwelt on Everell's remaining at his house during his daughter's dangerous illness; touched lightly on their having had an interview, very affecting to both parties, and in regard to the particulars of which, both, with the shyness natural to youth, had been silent; and finally, set forth in strong terms, the concern evinced by Everell while Esther's recovery was doubtful.

"Notwithstanding," the letter proceeded to say, "these circumstances are so favourable to my wishes, I have some apprehensions; and therefore, brother, I bespeak your immediate interposition in behalf of the future spiritual prosperity of this youth. He hath been assiduously courted by Miss Leslie's paternal connexions, and I have reason to believe, they have solicited him to marry her, and bring her to England. But without such solicitation the marriage is a probable one. Miss Leslie is reported here, to be wanting in grace, a want that I fear would not impoverish her in young Fletcher's estimation; and to be a maiden of rare comeliness, a thing precious in the eyes of youth—too apt to set a high price on that which is but dust and ashes. The young lady is of great estate too; but that I think will not weigh with the young man, for I discern a lofty spirit in him, that would spurn the yoke of mammon. Nor do I think, with some of our brethren, that 'gold and grace did never yet agree.' Yet there are some, who would make this alliance a ground of further scandal against our brother Fletcher. It is whispered that his worldly affairs are not so prosperous as we could wish. Mark me, brother—my confidence in him is unmoved, and I think, and am sure, that he would not permit his son to espouse this maiden, with the dowry of a queen, if thereby he endangered his spiritual welfare. But, brother, you in the new world, are as a city set on a hill. Many lie in wait for your halting, and all appearance of evil should be avoided. On this account and many others, brother Fletcher and all of us should duly prize that medium and safe condition for which Agur[7] prayed.

"One more reason I would suggest, and then commend the business to thy guidance, who art justly termed by friend and foe—the Moses of God's people in the wilderness.

"It seemeth to me, the motive of Miss Leslie's mother, in going with her offspring to the colony, should be duly weighed and respected. Could her purpose, in any other way, be so certainly accomplished, as by uniting her daughter speedily with a godly and approved member of the congregation?"

Every sentence of this letter stung Mr. Fletcher. He repeatedly threw it down, rose from his seat, and after taking two or three turns across the study, screwed his courage to the sticking point, and returned to it again. Governor Winthrop's attention appeared to be rivetted to a paper he was perusing, till he could no longer, from motives of delicacy to his friend, affect to abstract his attention from him. Mr. Fletcher finished the letter, and leaning over the table, covered his face with his hands. His emotion could not be hidden. The veins in his temples and forehead swelled almost to bursting, and his tears fell like rain-drops on the table. Governor Winthrop laid his hand on his friend's arm, and by a gentle pressure, expressed a sympathy that it would have been difficult to embody in words.

After a few moments' struggle with his feelings, Mr. Fletcher subdued his emotion, and turning to Governor Winthrop, he said, with dignity—"I have betrayed before you a weakness that I have never expressed, but in that gracious presence, where weakness is not degradation. Thus has it ever pleased Him, who knows the infirmity of my heart, to try me. From my youth, my path hath been hedged up with earthly affections. Is it that I have myself forged the fetters that bind me to the earth? Is it that I have given to the creature what I owed to the Creator, that one after another of my earthly delights is taken from me? that I am thus stripped bare? Oh! it has been the thought that came unbidden to my nightly meditations, and my daily reveries, that I might live to see these children of two saints in heaven united. This sweet child is the image of her blessed mother. She was her precious legacy to me, and she hath been such a spirit of love and contentment in my lone dwelling, that she hath inwrought herself with every fibre of my heart."

"This was natural," said Governor Winthrop.

"Ay, my friend—and was it not inevitable? I did think," he continued, after a momentary pause, "that in their childhood, their affections, as if instinct with their parents' feelings, mingled in natural union; if their hearts retain this bent, I think it were not right to put a force upon them."

"Certainly not," replied his friend; "but the affections of youth are flexible, and may be turned from their natural bent by a skilful hand. It is our known duty to direct them heavenward. In taking care for the spiritual growth of our young people, who are soon to stand in their father's places, we do, as we are bound, most assuredly build up the interests of our Zion. I should ill deserve the honourable name my brethren have given me, if I were not zealous over our youth. In fearing any opposition from the parties in question, I think, my worthy brother, you disquiet yourself in vain. It appeareth from Downing's letter, that there have been tender passages between your son and his daughter Esther; and even if Hope Leslie hath fed her fancies with thoughts of Everell, yet I think she would be forward to advance her friend's happiness, for, notwithstanding she doth so differ from her in her gay carriage, their hearts appear to be knit together."

"You do my beloved child but justice; what is difficult duty to others, hath ever seemed impulse in her; and I have sometimes thought that the covenant of works was to her a hindrance to the covenant of grace; and that, perhaps, she would hate sin more for its unlawfulness, if she did not hate it so much for its ugliness."

Governor Winthrop thought his friend went a little too far in magnifying the virtue of his favourite. "Pardon," he said, "the wounds inflicted by a friend—they are faithful. I have thought the child rests too much on *performances;* and you must allow, brother, that she hath not, I speak it tenderly, that passiveness, that, next to godliness, is a woman's best virtue."

"I should scarcely account," replied Mr. Fletcher, "a property of soulless matter, a virtue." This was spoken in a tone of impatience that indicated truly that the speaker, like an over fond parent, could better endure any reproach cast on himself, than the slightest imputation on his favourite. Governor Winthrop was not a man to shrink from inflicting what he deemed a salutary pain, because his patient recoiled from his touch, he therefore proceeded in his admonition.

"Partiality is dangerous, as we see in the notable history of David and Absalom,[8] and elsewhere; and perhaps it was your too great indulgence that emboldened the child to the daring deed of violating the law, by the secret release of the condemned."

"That violation rests on suspicion, not proof," said Mr. Fletcher, hastily.

"And why," replied Governor Winthrop, smiling, "is it permitted to rest on suspicion? from respect to our much suffering brother Fletcher, and consideration of the youth of the offender, we have winked at the offence. But we will pass that—I would be the last to lift the veil that hath fallen over it; I only alluded to it, to enforce the necessity of a stricter watch over this lawless girl. Would it not be wise and prudent to take my brother's counsel, and consign her to some one who should add to affection, the modest authority of a husband?"

Governor Winthrop paused for a reply, but receiving none, he proceeded—"One of our most promising youth hath this day discoursed to me of Hope Leslie, and expressed a matrimonial intent towards her."

"And who is this?" demanded Mr. Fletcher.

"William Hubbard[9]—the youth who hath come with so much credit from our prophets' school at Cambridge. He is a discreet young man, steeped in learning, and of approved orthodoxy."

"These be cardinal points with us," replied Mr. Fletcher, calmly, "but they are not like to commend him to a maiden of Hope Leslie's temper. She inclineth not to bookish men, and is apt to vent her childish gaiety upon the ungainly ways of scholars."

Thus our heroine, by her peculiar taste, lost at least the golden opportunity of illustrating herself by a union with the future historian of New-England.

After a little consideration, the governor resumed the conversation. "It is difficult," he said, "to suit a maiden who hath more whim, than reason—what think you of Sir Philip Gardiner?"

"Sir Philip Gardiner! a new-comer of to-day! and old enough to be the father of Hope Leslie!"

"The fitter guide for her youth. Besides, brother, you magnify his age—he is still on the best side of forty. He is a man of good family, who, after having fought on the side where his birth naturally cast him, hath been plucked, as a brand from the burning, by the preaching and exhortation of the godly Mr. Wilkins; and feeling, as he declares, a pious horror at the thought of imbruing his hands any further in blood, he hath come to cast his lot among us, instead of joining our friends in England."

"Hath he credentials to verify all these particulars?"

Governor Winthrop coloured, slightly, at an interrogatory that implied a deficiency of wariness on his part, and replied, "that he thought the gentleman scarcely needed other than he carried in his language and deportment, but that he had come furnished with a letter of introduction, satisfactory in all points."

"From whom?" inquired Mr. Fletcher.

"From one Jeremy Austin—who expresseth himself as, and Sir Philip says is, a warm friend to us."

"Is he known to you?"

"No—but I think I have heard him mentioned as a wellwiller to our colony."

This was not perfectly satisfactory to Mr. Fletcher, but he forbore to press the point further, and turned his attack to that part of the suggestion that appeared most vulnerable. "Methinks," he said, "you are over-hasty in proposing to match Hope Leslie with this stranger."

"Nay, I meant not a formal proposition. I noted that Sir Philip was struck with Hope's outward graces. He is an uncommon personable man, and hath that bearing that finds favour in maidens' eyes, and the thought came to me, that he may have been sent here, in good time, to relieve all our perplexities; and to confess the truth, brother, if I may use the sporting language of our youth, I am impatient to put jesses on this wild bird of yours, while she is on our perch. But to be serious, and surely the subject doth enforce us to it, I am satisfied that you will not oppose any means that may offer to secure the lambs of our flock in the true fold."

"I shall oppose nothing that will promote the spiritual prosperity of those dear to me as my own soul. I have no reason to doubt my son's filial obedience; he hath never been wanting, and though both he and I have fallen under censure, I see not that I erred in sending him from me, since I but complied with the last request of his sainted mother, and that compliance deprived me of the only child left of my little flock. I speak not vauntingly; but let not those who have remained in Egypt, condemn him who has drank of the bitterest waters of the wilderness." Mr. Fletcher, finding himself again yielding to irrepressible emotions, rose and hastily left his more equal-tempered and less interested friend.

Thus did these good men, not content with their magnanimous conflict with necessary evils, involve themselves in superfluous trials. Whatever gratified the natural desires of the heart was questionable, and almost every thing that was difficult and painful, assumed the form of duty. As if the benevolent Father of all had stretched over our heads a canopy of clouds, instead of the bright firmament, and its glorious host, and ever-changing beauty; and had spread under our feet a wilderness of bitter herbs, instead of every tree and plant yielding its good fruit. ——But we would fix our eyes on the bright halo that encircled the pilgrims' head; and not mark the dust that sometimes sullied his garments.

CHAPTER XII

"Then crush, even in their hour of birth
The infant buds of love,
And tread his glowing fire to earth,
Ere 'tis dark in clouds above."

HALLECK[1]

The observance of the Sabbath began with the puritans, as it still does with a great portion of their descendants, on Saturday night. At the going down of the sun on Saturday, all temporal affairs were suspended; and so zealously did our fathers maintain the letter, as well as the spirit of the law, that, according to a vulgar tradition in Connecticut, no beer was brewed in the latter part of the week, lest it should presume to *work* on Sunday.

It must be confessed that the tendency of the age is to laxity; and so rapidly is the wholesome strictness of primitive times abating, that, should some antiquary, fifty years hence, in exploring his garret rubbish, chance to cast his eye on our humble pages, he may be surprised to learn, that even now the Sabbath is observed, in the interior of New-England, with an almost judaical severity.

On Saturday afternoon an uncommon bustle is apparent. The great class of procrastinators are hurrying to and fro to complete the lagging business of the week. The good mothers, like Burns' matron, are plying their needles, making "auld claes look amaist as weel's the new;"[2] while the domestics, or help,[3] (we prefer the national descriptive term) are wielding with might and main, their brooms, and *mops,* to make all *tidy* for the Sabbath.

As the day declines, the hum of labour dies away, and after the sun is set, perfect stillness reigns in every well-ordered household, and not a foot-fall is heard in the village street. It cannot be denied, that even the most spiritual, missing the excitement of their ordinary occupations, anticipate their usual bed-time. The obvious inference from this fact, is skilfully avoided by certain ingenious reasoners, who allege that the constitution was originally so organised, as to require an extra quantity of sleep on every seventh night. We recommend it to the curious, to inquire, how this peculiarity was adjusted, when the first day of the week was changed from Saturday to Sunday.

The Sabbath morning is as peaceful as the first hallowed day. Not a human sound is heard without the dwellings, and but for the lowing of the herds, the crowing of the cocks, and the gossipping of the birds, animal life would seem to be extinct, till, at the bidding of the church-going bell, the old and young issue from their habitations, and with solemn demeanor, bend their measured steps to the *meeting-house.* The family of the minister—the squire—the doctor—the merchants—the modest gentry of the village, and the mechanic and labourer, all arranged in their best, all meeting on even ground, and all with that consciousness of independence and equality, which breaks down the pride of the rich, and rescues the poor from servility, envy, and discontent. If a morning salutation is reciprocated, it is in a suppressed voice; and if perchance, nature, in some reckless urchin, burst forth in laughter, "my dear, you forget it's Sunday!" is the ever ready reproof.

Though every face wears a solemn aspect, yet we once chanced to see even a deacon's muscles relaxed by the wit of a neighbour, and heard him allege in a half deprecating, half laughing voice, "the squire is so droll, that a body must laugh, though it be Sabbath-day."

The farmer's ample waggon, and the little one-horse vehicle, bring in all who reside at an inconvenient walking distance,— that is to say, in our riding community, half a mile from the church. It is a pleasing sight to those who love to note the happy peculiarities of their own land, to see the farmer's daughters blooming, intelligent, and well-bred, pouring out of these homely coaches, with their nice white gowns, prunel shoes, leghorn hats, fans, and parasols, and the spruce young men with their plaited ruffles, blue coats, and yellow buttons. The whole community meet as one religious family, to offer their devotions at the common altar. If there is an outlaw from the society—a luckless wight, whose vagrant taste has never been subdued, he may be seen stealing along the margin of some little brook, far away from the condemning observation, and troublesome admonitions of his fellows.

Towards the close of the day, or, (to borrow a phrase descriptive of his feelings who first used it) 'when the sabbath begins to *abate*,' the children cluster about the windows. Their eyes wander from their catechisms to the western sky, and though it seems to them as if the sun would never disappear, his broad disk does slowly sink behind the mountain; and while his last ray still lingers on the eastern summits, merry voices break forth, and the ground resounds with bounding footsteps. The village-belle arrays herself for her twilight walk; the boys gather on 'the green;' the lads and girls throng to the 'singing-school;' while some coy maiden lingers at home, awaiting her expected suitor —and all enter upon the pleasures of the evening with as keen a relish as if the day had been a preparatory penance.

After having favoured our readers with this long skipping-place, we resume the thread of our narrative. We have passed over eight days, which glided away without supplying any events to the historian of our heroine's life; though even then the thread was spinning that was to form the woof of her destiny.

Intent on verifying the prediction she had made to Esther, that Everell would soon declare himself her lover, she promoted the intercourse of the parties in every way she could, without making her motive apparent. While she treated Everell with frank sisterly affection, and was always easy and animated in his society, which she enjoyed above all other pleasures, she sedulously sought to bring Esther's moral and mental graces forth to the light. In their occasional walks, she took good care that Everell should be the companion of her friend, while she permitted Sir Philip Gardiner to attend her. He was a man of the world, au fait in all the arts of society, and though he sometimes offended her by the excess of his flattering gallantries, yet he often deeply interested her with his lively descriptions of countries and manners unknown to her.

It was just at twilight, on Saturday evening, when the elder Mr. Fletcher coming into Madam Winthrop's parlour, found his son sitting there alone, and interrupted a very delightful meditation on the eloquence of Hope Leslie, who had just been with him, descanting on the virtues of her friend Esther. The charms of the fair speaker had, we believe, a far larger share of his thoughts, than the subject of her harangue.

"We have a lecture extraordinary to-night," said Mr. Fletcher; "our rulers some time since, issued an order limiting our regular religious meetings to one, during the week. Shall you go, my son?"

"Sir—go to the lecture?" replied Everell, as if just waking from a dream, and then added, for then he caught a glimpse of Hope through the door, with her hat and mantle. "Oh, yes—certainly sir, I shall go to the lecture."

He snatched his hat, and would have joined Miss Leslie; but she saw his intention, and turning to him, as she passed the threshold of the door, she said, "You need not go with me, Everell; I have to call for aunt Grafton, at Mrs. Cotton's."

"May not I call with you?"

"No; I had rather you would not," she said decidedly, and hurried away without any explanation of her preference.

"What can have disturbed Hope?" asked Mr. Fletcher, for both he and his son had observed that her cheek was flushed, and her eye tearful.

"I cannot imagine," replied Everell; "she left me not half an hour since, all smiles and gaiety."

"It is but the April-temper of youth," said the father. "Hope is of a feeling make: she often reminds me of the Delta lands, where the fruits spring forth before the waters have retired. Smiles are playing on her lips before the tear is dry on her cheek.

But this sensitiveness should be checked; the dear child's feelings have too long been indulged."

"And as long as they are all innocent, Sir, why should they not be indulged?"

"Because, my son, she must be hardened for the cross-accidents and unkind events, or, rather I should say, the whole-some chastisements of life. She cannot—we can none of us —expect indulgence from the events of life." Mr. Fletcher paused for a moment, looked around, then shut the door, and returned to his son. "Everell," he said, "you have ever been dutiful to me."

"And ever shall be, my dear father," replied Everell with frank confidence, little thinking how soon the virtue might become difficult.

"Trust not, my son, to thine own strength; it may soon be put to a test that will make thee feel it to be but weakness. Everell, thou seest that Hope loves thee even as she loved thee in thy childhood. Let her affection remain of this temper, I charge thee, as thou respectest thy father's, and thine own honour. And, Everell, it were well if you fixed your eye on"——

"Stop, sir!—stop, I beseech you, and tell me—not because I have any thoughts—any intentions, I mean—any formed purpose, I would say—but tell me, I entreat you, why this prohibition?"

Everell spoke with such earnestness and ingenuousness, that his father could not refuse to answer him: but his reasons seemed even to himself to lose half their force as they emerged from their shroud of mystery. He acknowledged, in the first place, what his most cherished wishes had been, in relation to Hope, and Everell. He then communicated the intimations that had been thrown out, that his views for his son were mercenary.

Everell laughed at the idea. "No one," he said, "can so well afford such an imputation as you, sir, whose whole life has been a practical refutation of it: and for my own part, I am satisfied with the consciousness that I would not marry any woman with a fortune, whom I would not marry if the case were reversed, or even if we were both pennyless."

"I believe this is not an empty boast, my son; but we have

set ourselves up for a mark to the world, and, as brother Winthrop has said, and repeated to me, we cannot be too solicitous to avoid all appearance of evil. There are covetous souls, who, on the slightest ground, would suspect us of pursuing our own worldly by-ends."

"And so, sir, to win the approbation, or rather the good word of these covetous souls, we are to degrade ourselves to their level, and act as if we were capable of their mean passions."

"Everell! my son, you speak presumptuously; we are capable of all evil;—but we will waive that question at present. Our individual wishes must be surrendered to the public good. We who have undertaken this great work in the wilderness, must not live to ourselves. We have laid the foundation of an edifice, and our children must be so coupled together, as to secure its progress and stability when the present builders are laid low."

"And so, my dear father, a precious gem is to be mortared in like a common brick, wherever may best suit the purposes and views of the builders. You are displeased, Sir. Perhaps I spoke somewhat hastily. But, once for all, I entreat you not to dispose of us as if we were mere machines: we owe you our love and reverence."

"And obedience, Everell."

"Yes, sir, as far as it can be manifested by not doing what you command us not to do."

"Have I then strained parental authority so far, that you think it necessary thus to qualify your duty?"

"No, indeed, my dear father; and it is because your authority has ever been too gentle to be felt, that I wince at the galling of a new yoke. You will admit that my submission has not been less perfect, for being voluntary. Trust me, then, for the future; and I promise"——

Everell was perhaps saved from rashly committing himself, by the entrance of Madam Winthrop, who inquired if the gentlemen were ready to attend her to the lecture.

"Come, Mr. Everell," she said, "here is Esther to show you the way, than whom there can be no safer guide."

Miss Downing stood beside her aunt, but she shrunk back at Everell's approach, hurt at what seemed to her a solicitation for

his attention. He perceived her instinctive movement, but without appearing to notice it, he offered his arm to Madam Winthrop, saying, "As there is no skill in guiding one quite willing
to be led, I will not impose the trouble on Miss Downing, if
you will allow me the honour of attending you."

Madam Winthrop submitted with the best grace to this cross
purpose. The elder Fletcher offered his arm to Miss Downing,
and endeavoured to draw her into conversation; but she was
timid, downcast, and reserved; and mentally comparing her with
Hope Leslie, he felt how improbable it was that Everell would
ever prefer her. The old, even when grave and rigid, are said to
affect the young and gay; on the same principle, perhaps, that a
dim eye delights in bright colours.

"Is that Gorton's[4] company?" asked Everell, pointing towards several prisoners, who, in the custody of a file of soldiers,
appeared to be going towards the sanctuary.

"Yes," replied Madam Winthrop; "the governor and our ruling elders have determined, that as they are to be tried next week,
they shall have the benefit of all our public teaching in the mean
time."

"I should fear they would deem this punishment before trial,"
said Everell.

"They did reluct mightily at first; but on being promised that
if they had occasion to speak, after sermon, they should be permitted, provided they only spoke the words of sobriety and
truth, they consented to come forth."

This Gorton, whom Hubbard calls 'a prodigious minter of
exorbitant novelties,'[5] had been brought, with his adherents,
from Rhode-Island, by force of arms, to be tried for certain civil
and ecclesiastical offences, for which, according to the most
learned antiquary of our new world, (Mr. Savage,)[6] they were
not amenable to the magistracy of Massachusetts.

The prisoners were ushered into the church, and placed before
the ruling elders. The governor then entered, unattended by his
halberd-bearers,—(a ceremony dispensed with, except on
Sunday)—and, followed by his family, he walked slowly to his
pew, where Miss Leslie was already seated between Mrs. Grafton, and Sir Philip Gardiner. She rose, and contrived to exchange

her location for one next Miss Downing. "Look, Esther," she said in a whisper to her friend, "at that lad who stands in the corner of the gallery, just beside the lamp."

"I see him; but what of him?"

"Why, just observe how he gazes at me: his eye is like a burning-glass—it really scorches me. I wish the service were over. Do you think it will be long?"

"It may be long, but I trust not tedious," replied Esther, with a gravity which was the harshest rebuke she could ever command.

"Oh, it will be both!" said Hope, in a despairing tone; "for there is Mr. Wheeler in the pulpit, and he always talks of eternity till he forgets time."

"My dear Hope!" said Esther, in a voice of mingled surprise and reproof.

The service presently began, and Hope endeavoured dutifully to assume a decorous demeanour, and join Esther in singing the psalm; but her mind was soon abstracted, and her voice died away.

The preacher had not proceeded far in his discourse, before all her patience was exhausted. Even those who are the most strenuous advocates for the passive duties of the sanctuary, might have bestowed their pity on our heroine, who had really serious cause for her feverish impatience; obliged to sit, while a young man, accounted a 'universal scholar,' seemed determined, like many unfledged preachers, to tell all he knew in that one discourse, which was then called a prophesying—an extempore effusion. He was bent, not only on making 'root and branch work' of poor Gorton's heresies, but on eradicating every tare from the spiritual field. To Hope, he appeared to maintain one even pace straight forward, like the mortal in the fairy tale, sentenced to an eternal walk over a boundless plain.

"Do, Esther, look at the candles," she whispered; "don't you think it must be nine o'clock?"

"Oh hush!—no, not yet eight."

Hope sighed audibly, and once more resumed a listening attitude. All human labours have their end, and therefore had the preacher's. But, alas for our heroine! when he had finished, Gorton, whose face for the last hour had expressed that he felt much like a criminal condemned to be scourged before he is hung— Gorton rose, and, smarting under a sense of wrongs, he repeated all the points of the discourse, and made points where there were none; refuted and attacked, and proved (to his own satisfaction), 'that all ordinances, ministers, sacraments, &c. were but men's inventions—silver shrines of Diana.'

While this self-styled 'professor of mysteries' spoke, Hope was so much interested in his genuine enthusiasm and mysticism, (for he was the Swedenborg[7] of his day,) that she forgot her own secret subject of anxiety: but when he had finished, and half a dozen of the ruling elders rose at the same moment to prove the weapons of orthodoxy upon the arch heretic, she whispered to Esther, "I can never bear this;—I must make an apology to Madam Winthrop, and go home."

"Stay," said Esther; "do you not see Mr. Cotton is getting up?"

Mr. Cotton, the regular pastor, rose to remind his brethren of the decree, "that private members should be very sparing in their questions and observations after public sermons;" and to say, that he should postpone any farther discussion of the precious points before them, as it was near nine o'clock—after which it was not suitable for any christian family to be unnecessarily abroad.

Hope now, and many others instinctively rose, in anticipation of the dismissing benediction; but Mr. Cotton waved his hand for them to sit down, till he could communicate to the congregation the decision to which the ruling elders and himself had come, on the subject of the last Sabbath sermon. 'He would not repeat what he had before said upon that lust of costly apparel, which was fast gaining ground, and had already, as was well known, crept into godly families. He was pleased that there were among them gracious women, ready to turn at a rebuke, as was manifested in many veils being left at home, that were floating over the congregation like so many butterflies' wings in the morning. Economy, he justly observed, was, as well as simplicity, a christian grace; and therefore the rulers had determined, that those persons who had run into the excess of immoderate veils and sleeves, embroidered caps, and gold and silver lace, should be permitted to wear them out, but new ones should be forfeited.'

This sumptuary regulation announced, the meeting was dismissed.

Madam Winthrop whispered to Everell that she was going, with his father, to look in upon a sick neighbour, and would thank him to see her niece home. Everell stole a glance at Hope, and dutifully offered his arm to Miss Downing.

Hope, intent only on one object, was hurrying out of the pew, intending, in the jostling of the crowd, to escape alone; but she was arrested by Madam Winthrop's saying, "Miss Leslie, Sir Philip offers you his arm;" and at the same moment her aunt stooped forward, to beg her to wait a moment till she could send a message to Deacon Knowles' wife, that she might wear her new gown with the Turkish sleeves the next day.

"Oh martyrdom!" thought Hope, with indeed little of the spirit of a martyr. She dared not speak aloud, but she continued to whisper to Mrs. Grafton—"For pity's sake, do leave Mrs. Knowles to take care of herself; I am tired to death with staying here."

"No wonder," replied her aunt, in the same low tone, "it is enough to tire Job himself;—but just have a minute's patience, dearie; it is but doing as a body would be done by, to let Mistress Knowles know she may come out in her new gown to-morrow."

"Well, just as you please, ma'am; but I will go along with Sir Philip, and you can follow with Mr. Cradock. Mr. Cradock, you will wait for Mrs. Grafton?"

"Surely, surely," said the good man eagerly; "there is nothing you could ask me, Miss Hope, as you well know—be it ever so disagreeable—that I would not do."

"Thank you for nothing, Mr. Cradock," said the testy dame, with a toss of her head; "you are over civil, I think, to-night. It is very well, Miss Hope, it is very well;—you may go;—you know Cradock at best is purblind at night;—but it is very well; —you can go—I can get home alone. It is very peculiar of you, Mr. Cradock."

Poor Cradock saw he had offended, but how, he knew not;

and he looked imploringly to Hope to extricate him; but she was too anxious about her own affairs, to lend her usual benevolent care to his embarrassment.

"My dear aunt," said she, "I will not go without you, if you prefer to go with me; only do let us go."

Mrs. Grafton now acquiesced, for in her flurry she had lost sight of the messenger whom she intended to entrust with the important errand. Sir Philip arranged her hood and cloak, with a grace that she afterwards said "was so like her dear deceased," and in a few moments, the party was in the street, and really moving homeward.

Mrs. Grafton prided herself on a slow, measured step, which she fancied was the true gait of dignity. Hope, on the contrary, always moved, as the spirit moved her; and now she felt an ir- resistible impulse to hurry forward.

"My dear," said her aunt, "how can you fly so? I am sure, if they in England were to see you walk, they would think you had been brought up here to chase the deer in the woods."

Hope dared not confess her anxiety to get forward, and she could no longer check it.

"It is very undignified, and very unladylike, and very unbe- coming, Hope; and I must say, it is untoward and unfroward of you, to hurry me along so. Don't you think it is very peculiar of Hope, Sir Philip?"

The knight suspected that Miss Leslie's haste was merely im- patience of his society; and he could scarcely curb his chagrin, while he said, that "the young lady undoubtedly moved with uncommon celerity;—indeed he had before suspected she had invisible wings."

"Thank you for your hint, Sir Philip," exclaimed Hope. "It is a night," she continued, looking up at the bright moon, "to make one long to soar—so I will just spread my wings, and leave you to crawl on the earth." She withdrew her arm from Sir Philip's, and tripping on before them, she soon turned a corner, and was out of sight.

We must leave the knight, biting his lips with vexation, and feeling much like a merchant obliged to pay a heavy duty on a lost article. However, to do him justice, he did not make an

entire loss of it, but so adroitly improved the opportunity to win
the aunt's favour, that she afterwards said to Hope, that if she
must see her wedded to a puritan, she trusted it would be Sir
Philip, for he had nothing of the puritan but the outside.

Hope had not proceeded far, when she heard a quick step
behind her, and looking back, she saw the young man whose
gaze had disturbed her at the lecture. She had an indefinite womanly feeling of fear; but a second thought told her she had best
conceal it, and she slackened her pace. Her pursuer approached
till he was parallel to her, and slackened his also. He looked at
her without speaking; and as Hope glanced her eye at him, she
was struck with an expression of wretchedness and passion that
seemed unnatural, on a countenance so young and beautiful.
"Any thing is better than this strange silence," thought Hope;
so she stopped, looked the stranger full in the face, and said
inquiringly, "You have perhaps lost your way?"

"Lost my way?" replied the youth, in a half articulate voice:
"Yes, lady—I have lost my way."

The melancholy tone and mysterious look of the stranger, led
Hope to suspect that he meant to convey more than the natural
import of his words; but without seeming to understand more,
she said, "I perceive, by your foreign accent, that you are a
stranger here. If you will tell me where you wish to go, I will
direct you."

"And who will guide *you*, lady?" responded the stranger, in
a thrilling tone. "The lost may warn, but cannot guide."

"I need no guidance," said Hope hastily, still persisting in
understanding him literally: "I am familiar with the way; and if
I cannot be of service to you, must bid you good night."

"Stop one moment!" exclaimed the stranger, laying his hand
on Hope's arm, with an imploring look: "You look so good—
so kind—you may be of service to me;" and then bursting into
a passionate flood of tears, he added—"Oh, mon Dieu!——No,
no—there is no help for me!"

Hope now lost all thought for herself, in concern for the unhappy being before her. "Who—or what are you?" she asked.

"I!—what am I?" he replied in a bitter tone: "Sir Philip Gardiner's slave—or servant—or page—or—whatever he is pleased

to call me. Nay, lady, look not so piteously on me!—I love my master——at least, I did love him;—but I think innocence is the breath of love!—Heaven's mercy, lady! you will make me weep again, if you look at me thus."

"Nay, do not weep; but tell me," said Hope, "what I can do for you: I cannot remain here longer."

"Oh! you can do nothing for me—no one can do any thing for me. But, lady—take care for thyself."

"What do you mean?" demanded Hope, in a tone of mingled alarm and impatience: "do you mean any thing?"

The boy looked apprehensively about him, and approaching his lips close to Hope's ear, he said in a whisper—"Promise me you will not love my master. Do not believe him, though he pledge the word of a true knight always to love you;—though he swear it on the holy crucifix, do not believe it!"

Hope now began to think that the youth's senses were impaired; and, more impatient than ever to escape from him, she said—"Oh, I can promise all that, and as much more in the same way, as you will ask of me. But leave me now, and come to me again, when you want a much more difficult service."

"I never shall want any thing else, lady," he replied, shaking his head sorrowfully: "I want nothing else, but that you would pity me! You may, for angels pity; and I am sure you look like one. Pity me!—never speak of me, and forget me." He dropped on his knee—pressed her hand to his lips—rose to his feet, and left her so hastily, that she was scarcely conscious of his departure till he was beyond her sight.

Whatever matter for future reflection this interview might have afforded her, Hope had now no time to dwell on it; and she hastened forward, and surmounting a fence at the southeastern extremity of the burial ground, she entered the enclosure, now the church-yard of the stone chapel.[8] The moon was high in the heavens; masses of black clouds were driven by a spring gale over her bright disk, producing startling changes, from light to darkness, and from darkness to that gleamy, indefinite, illusive brightness, which gives to moonlight its dominion over the imagination.

At another time, Hope Leslie would have shrunk from going

alone, so late at night, to this region of silence and sad thoughts; and her fancy might have embodied the shadows that flitted over the little mounds of earth, but she was now so engrossed by one absorbing, anxious expectation, that she scarcely thought of the place where it was to be attained—and she pressed on, as if she was passing over common clods. Once, indeed, she paused, as the moon shot forth a bright ray—stooped down before a little hillock—pressed her brow to the green turf, and then raising her eyes to heaven, and clasping her hands, she exclaimed, "Oh, my mother! if ever thy presence is permitted to me, be with me now!"—After this solemn adjuration, she again rose to her feet, and looked anxiously around her for some expected object. "But I cannot know," she said, "till I have passed the thicket of evergreens;—that was the appointed spot."

She passed the thicket—and at that moment the intensity of her feelings spread a mist before her eyes. She faltered, and leaned on one of the grave-stones for support;—and there we must leave her for the present, to the secresy she sought.

END OF VOLUME FIRST.

VOLUME II

CHAPTER I

"There's nothing I have done yet o' my conscience,
Deserves a corner: would all other women
Could speak this with as free a soul as I do."

HENRY VIII[1]

While Hope Leslie was deeply engaged in the object of her secret expedition, Governor Winthrop's household was thrown into alarm at her absence.

Jennet was the only member of the family who did not admit that there was real cause of uneasiness. "Miss Hope," she said, "was always like a crazed body of moonlight nights; there was never any keeping her within the four walls of a house."

But a moonlight night it soon ceased to be. The clouds that had been scudding over the heavens, gathered in dark and terrific masses. A spring storm ensued; a storm to which winter and summer contribute all their elemental power—rain, lightning, wind, and hail.

Governor Winthrop naturally concluded, (for all persons not deeply interested are apt to be rational,) that Miss Leslie had taken refuge under some safe covert, and he summoned his family to their evening devotions. Both the Fletchers excused themselves, and braved the storm in quest of their lost treasure; and even old Cradock, in spite of Mrs. Grafton's repeated suggestions that he was a very useless person for such an enterprise, sallied forth; but all returned in the space of an hour to bring their various reports of fruitless inquiry and search. Everell remained but long enough to learn that there were no tidings of Hope, and was again rushing out of the house, when he met the object of his apprehensions at the hall door. "Thank heaven!" he exclaimed, on seeing her, "you are safe. Where have you been?—we were all in the most distressful alarm about you."

Hope had, by this time, advanced far enough into the entry for Everell to perceive, by the light of the lantern, that she was muffled in Sir Philip Gardiner's cloak. His face had kindled with joy at her appearance; all light now vanished from it, and he stood eyeing Hope with glances that spoke, though his lips refused again to move; while she, without observing or suspecting his emotion, did not reply to him, and was only intent on disengaging herself from the cloak. "Do help me, Everell," she said, impatiently; and he endeavoured to untie the string that fastened it, but in his agitation, instead of untying, he doubled the knot.

"Oh, worse and worse!" she exclaimed, and, without any farther ceremony, she broke the string and running back to the door, gave the cloak to Sir Philip, who stood awaiting it, till then unperceived by Everell, in the shadows of the portico.

Everell again looked at Miss Leslie in the natural expectation of some explanation, but she appeared only concerned to escape to her own apartment without any inquiries from the family. Her face was extremely pale; and her voice, still affected by recent agitation, trembled as she said to Everell, "be kind enough to tell your father, and all of them, that I have come in drenched with the rain, and have gone to my own room—that I am wearied, and shall throw off my wet garments, and get to bed as soon as possible;" and then adding, a "good night, Everell;" and without awaiting any answer, she was springing up the stairs when the parlour-door was thrown open, and half-a-dozen voices exclaimed, in the same breath, "oh, Hope!"—"Hope Leslie!"—"Miss Hope Leslie! is it you?"

"Come back, my child, and tell me where you have been," said Mr. Fletcher.

"Yes, Miss Leslie," said Governor Winthrop, but in a tone of kindness rather than authority, "render an account of thyself to thy rulers."

"Yes, come along Hope," said Mrs. Grafton, "and make due apologies to Madam Winthrop. A pretty hubbub you have put her house in, to be sure—though, I make no doubt, you can show good reason for it, and also for leaving Sir Philip and me in that rantipole way, which I must say was peculiar."

"For heaven's sake," said Hope to Esther, who had just joined her, "do go in and make an apology for me. Say I am wet and tired—say any thing you please, I care not what—will you?—that's a dear good girl."

"No, Hope—come in yourself—aunt Winthrop looked a little displeased—you had best come—I know she will expect it."

Thus beset, Hope dared not any longer hesitate, and with that feeling, half resolution and half impatience to have a disagreeable thing over which often impelled her, she descended the stairs as hastily as she had ascended them, and was in the parlour, confronting all the inquirers, before she had devised any mode of relieving herself from the disagreeable predicament of not being able to satisfy their curiosity.

"Verily, verily," exclaimed Cradock, who was the only one of the groupe, not even excepting Everell, whose sympathy mastered his curiosity—"verily, the maiden hath been in peril; she is as white as a snow-wreath, and as wet as a drowned kitten."

"Yes, Master Cradock, quite as wet," replied Hope, rallying her spirits, "and with almost as little discretion left, or I should not have entered the parlour in this dripping condition. Madam Winthrop, I beg you will have the goodness to pardon me for the trouble I have occasioned."

"Certainly, my dear, as I doubt not you will make it plain to us that you had sufficient reason for what appears so extraordinary, as a young woman wandering off by herself after nine o'clock on Saturday night."

Our heroine had never had the slightest experience in the nice art of diplomacy—that art that contrives to give such a convenient indistinctness to the boundary line between truth and falsehood. After a moment's reflection, her course seemed plain to her. To divulge the real motive of her untimely walk, was impossible—to invent a false excuse, to her, equally impossible. She turned to Governor Winthrop and said, with a smile, that

Everell, at least, thought might have softened the elder Brutus
—"I surrender myself to the laws of the land, having no hope,
but from the mercy of our magistrates. I have offended, I know;
but I should commit a worse offence—an offence against my
own conscience and heart—if I explained the cause of my absence."

Governor Winthrop was not accustomed to have his inquisitorial rights resisted by those of his own household, and he was
certainly more struck than pleased by Hope's moral courage.

Mrs. Grafton half muttered, half spoke, what she meant to be
an apology for her favourite. "It was not every body," she said,
"that thought as the Governor did about Saturday night."

"True, true," said Cradock, eagerly, "it is a doubtful point
with divines and gifted men."

"Master Cradock," said the Governor, "thou art too apt to
measure thy orthodoxy by thy charity. Saturday night is allowed
to be, and manifestly is, holy time; and therefore to be applied,
exclusively, to acts of mercy and devotion." Then turning to the
impatient culprit, he added, "I am bound to say to thee, Hope
Leslie, that thou dost take liberties unsuitable to thy youth, and
in violation of that deference due to the rule and observances of
my household, and discreditable to him who hath been entrusted
with thy nurture and admonition."

Hope received the first part of this reproof with her eyes
rivetted to the floor, and with a passiveness that had the sem-
blance of penitence; but at the implied reproach of her guardian,
for whom she had an affection that had the purity of filial and
the enthusiasm of voluntary love, she raised her eyes—their mild
lustre, for an instant, gave place to the passage of a flash of indignation direct from her heart. Her glance met Everell's—he
stood in a recess of the window, leaning his head against the
casement, looking intently on her. 'He too suspects me of evil,'
she thought, and she could scarcely command her voice to say,
as she turned and put her hand in the elder Fletcher's, "I have
done nothing to dishonour you. You believe me—do you not?"

"Yes, yes, my dear child; I must believe you, for you never
deceived me—but be not so impatient of reproof."

"I am not impatient for myself," she said; "I care not how

sternly—how harshly I am judged; but I see not why my fault, even if I had committed one, should cast a shadow upon you."

Madam Winthrop now interposed her good offices to calm the troubled waters. "There is no shadow any where, Miss Leslie, if there is sunshine in the conscience; and I can answer for the Governor, that he will overlook the disturbance of this evening, provided you are discreet in future. But we are wrong to keep you so long in your wet garments. Robin," she said, turning to a servant, "light a little fire in the young ladies' room, and tell Jennet to warm Miss Leslie's bed—let her strew a little sugar in the pan—an excellent thing, Mrs. Grafton, to take soreness out of the bones."

Madam Winthrop was solicitous to remove the impression from her guests that Miss Leslie was treated with undue strictness. Hope thanked her for her kindness; and protesting that she had no need of fire, or warming-pan, she hastily bade goodnight, and retired to her own apartment.

Miss Downing lingered a moment after her, and ventured to say, in a low timid tone, "that she trusted her uncle Winthrop would harbour no displeasure against her friend—she was sure that she had been on some errand of kindness; for, though she might sometimes indulge in a blameable freedom of speech, she had ever observed her to be strict in all duties and offices of mercy."

"You are right—right—marvellously right, Miss Downing," cried Cradock, exultingly rubbing his hands—and then added, in a lower tone, "a discerning young woman, Miss Esther."

"Humph!" said Mrs. Grafton, "I don't see any thing so *marvellously* right in what Miss Esther says—it's what every body knows, who knows Hope, that she never did a wrong thing."

Governor Winthrop suppressed a smile, and said to the good lady, "we should take heed, my worthy friend, not to lay too much stress on doing or not doing—not to rest unduly on duties and performances, for they be unsound ground."

Mrs. Grafton might have thought if she had enough such ground to stand on, it were terra firma to her; but, for once, she had the discretion of silence.

Neither Everell nor his father spoke, probably because they

felt more than all the rest; and Madam Winthrop, feeling the awkwardness of the scene, mentioned the hour, and proposed a general dispersion.

Everell followed Miss Downing to the staircase. "One word, Miss Downing," he said—Esther turned her face towards him, her pale face, for that instant illuminated—"did you," he asked, "in your apology for your friend, speak from knowledge or from generous faith?"

"From faith," she replied, "but not generous faith, for it was founded on experience."

Everell turned, disappointed, away. 'Faith,' he thought, 'there might be without sight—but faith against sight, never.' "Trifles light as air" are proverbially momentous matters to lovers. Everell had too noble a mind to indulge in that fretful jealousy which is far more the result of egregious self-love than love of another. But he had cherished for Hope a consecrating sentiment—he had invested her with a sacredness which the most refined, the purest, and most elevated love throws around the object of its devotion.

> "On magic ground that castle stoode,
> And fenc'd with many a spelle."

Were these "spelles" to be dissolved by the light of truth? 'Why should one,' thought Everell, 'who seemed so pure that she might dwell in light—so artless, confiding, and fearless—why should she permit herself to be obscured by mystery? If her meeting with Sir Philip Gardiner was accidental, why not say so?———But what right have I to scan her conduct?——What right to expect an explanation?——It is evident she feels nothing more for me than the familiar affection of her childhood. How she talked to me this evening of Esther Downing!—'if she had a brother, she would select her friend from all the world for his wife'—'Esther was not precise, she was only discreet'—'she was not formal, but timid.' Perhaps she sees I love her, and thus delicately tries to give a different bent to my affections; but that is impossible—every hope—every purpose has been concentrated in her. My affections may be blighted, but they cannot be transferred——Perhaps it is true, as some satirists say, that a woman's heart is wayward, fantastic, and capricious. This vagrant knight has scarcely turned his eyes from Hope since he first saw her, and I know he has addressed the most presumptuous flattery to her. Perhaps she favours his pretensions. I shrink even from his gazing on her, as if there were something sullying in the glance of his eye; and yet she violates the customs of the country—she braves severe displeasure—to walk alone with him—with him she is insensible to a gathering storm. He is incapable of loving her—he is intoxicated with her beauty—he seeks her fortune——Her fortune! I had forgotten that my father made that a bar between us. Fortune!—I never thought of any thing so mean as wealth in connexion with her. I would as soon barter my soul, as seek any woman for fortune—and Hope Leslie!—oh, I should as soon think of the dowry of a celestial spirit, as of your being enriched by the trappings of fortune."

These disjointed thoughts, and many others that would naturally spring up in the mind of a young lover, indicated the ardor, the enthusiasm, the disinterestedness of Everell's passion, and the restless and fearful state into which he had been plunged by the events of the evening.

While he was pursuing this train of fancies, in which some sweetness mingled with the bitter, Esther had followed Hope to her apartment, and having shut the door, turned on her friend a look of speaking inquiry and expectation, to which Hope did not respond, but continued in a hurried manner to disrobe herself, throwing her drenched shawl on one side, and her wet dress on the other.

Esther took a silver whistle from the toilet, and was opening the door to summon Jennet with its shrill call, when Hope, observing her intention, cried out, "If you love me, Esther, don't call Jennet to-night; I wish at least to be spared her croaking."

"As you please," replied Esther, quietly reclosing the door; "I thought Jennet had best come, and take care of your apparel, as, if your mind was not otherwise occupied, you would not choose to leave it in such disorder." While Esther spoke, she stood by the toilet, smoothing her kerchief, and restoring it to the laundress' folds.

"Yes," said Hope, "I prefer any disorder to the din of Jennet's tongue. I cannot, Esther—*I* cannot always be precise."

"Precision, I know, is not interesting," said Esther, with a slight tremulousness of voice; "but if you had a little more of it, Hope, it would save yourself, and your friends a vast deal of trouble."

"Now, do not you reproach me, Esther!—that is the drop too much!" said Hope, turning her face to the pillow, to hide the tears that gushed from her eyes: "I know I am vexed and cross—but I did not mean that you was too precise;—I do not know what I meant. I feel oppressed and wearied—and I want sympathy, and not reproof."

"Unburthen your heart then, to me," said Esther, kneeling by the bed-side, and throwing her arm over Hope: "most gladly would I pay back the debt of sympathy I owe you."

"And never, dear Esther, did a poor creditor receive a debt more joyfully than I should this. But others are concerned in my secret; a sacred promise requires me to preserve it inviolate. The Governor, and your aunt, and all of them might have known—and, most of all, Everell"—she continued, raising herself on her elbow—"they might have known, that I should not have been roaming about such a pitiless night as this, without good reason;—and Everell, I am sure, knows that I despise the silliness of making a secret out of nothing. I don't care so much for the rest; but it was very, very unkind of Everell!—I am sure my heart has been always open as the day to him."

Perhaps Miss Downing was not quite pleased with Hope's discriminating between the censure of Everell, and the rest of the family; for she said, with more even than her ordinary gravity—"There is but one thing, Hope, that ought to make you independent of the opinion of any of your friends."

"And what is that?"

"The acquittal of your conscience."

"My conscience!—Oh, my dear Esther, no mother Lois, nor grandmother Eunice, ever had a more quiet conscience than I have at this moment;—and I really wish that my tutors, governors—good friends all—would not think it necessary to keep quite so strict a guard over me."

"Hope Leslie," said Esther, "you do allow yourself too much liberty of thought and word: you certainly know that we owe implicit deference to our elders and superiors;—we ought to be guided by their advice, and governed by their authority."

"Esther, you are a born preacher," exclaimed Hope, with a sort of half sigh, half groan of impatience. "Nay, my dear friend, don't look so horridly solemn: I am sure, if I have wounded your feelings, I deserve to be preached to all the rest of my life. But really I do not entirely agree with you about advice and authority. As to advice, it needs to be very carefully administered, to do any good, else it's like an injudicious patch, which, you know, only makes the rent worse;—and as to authority, I would not be a machine, to be moved at the pleasure of anybody that happened to be a little older than myself. I am perfectly willing to submit to Mr. Fletcher, for he never"—and she smiled at her own sophistry—"he never requires submission. Now, Esther, don't look at me so, as if I was little better than one of the wicked. Come, kiss me good night; and when you say your prayers, Esther, remember me, for I need them more than you think."

This last request was made in a plaintive tone, and with unaffected seriousness, and Esther turned away to perform the duty, with a deep feeling of its necessity; for Hope, conscious of her integrity, had perhaps been too impatient of rebuke; and if to a less strict judge than Esther, she seems to have betrayed a little of the spoiled child, to her she appeared to be very far from that gracious state, wherein every word is weighed before it is uttered, and every action measured before it is performed.

CHAPTER II

"Those well seene natives in grave Nature's nests,
All close designs conceal in their deep brests."
                                        MORRELL[1]

It would be highly improper any longer to keep our readers in ignorance of the cause of our heroine's apparent aberration from the line of strict propriety. After her conversation with Everell, in which we must infer, from its effect on his mind, that she manifested less art than zeal in her friend's cause, she was retiring to her own apartment, when on passing through the hall, she saw an Indian woman standing there, requesting the servant who had admitted her, "to ask the young ladies of the house if they would look at some rare moccasins."

Miss Leslie was arrested by the uncommon sweetness of the stranger's voice; and fixing her eye on her, she was struck with the singular dignity and grace of her demeanor, a certain air indicating an "inborn royalty of soul," that even the ugly envelope of a blanket did not conceal.

The stranger seemed equally interested in Miss Leslie's appearance, and fixing her eye intently on her—"Pray try my moccasins, lady," she said earnestly.

"Oh, certainly, I should of all things like to buy a pair of you," said Hope, and advancing, she was taking them from her shoulder, over which they were slung, when she, ascertaining by a quick glance that the servant had disappeared, gently repressed Miss Leslie's hand, saying at the same time, "Tell me thy name, lady."

"My name!—Hope Leslie. But who art thou?" Hope asked in return, in a voice rendered almost inarticulate by the thought that flashed into her mind.

The stranger cast down her eyes, and for an half instant hesitated, then looking apprehensively around, she said, in low distinct accents, "Hope Leslie—I am Magawisca."

"Magawisca!" echoed Hope. "Oh, Everell!" and she sprang towards the parlour door to summon Everell.

"Silence—stay," cried Magawisca, with a vehement gesture, and at the same time turning to escape should Hope prosecute her intention.

Hope perceived this, and again approached her. "It cannot then be Magawisca," she said, and she trembled as she spoke, with doubts, hopes, and fears.

Magawisca might have at once identified herself, by opening her blanket, and disclosing her person; but that she did not, no one will wonder who knows that a savage feels more even than ordinary sensibility at personal deformity. She took from her bosom a necklace of hair and gold entwined together. "Dost thou know this?" she asked. "Is it not like that thou wearest?"

Hope grasped it, pressed it to her lips, and answered by exclaiming passionately—"My sister! my sister!"

"Yes—it is a token from thy sister. Listen to me, Hope Leslie—my time is brief—I may not stay here another moment; but come to me this evening at nine o'clock at the burial place, a little beyond the clump of pines, and I will give thee tidings of thy sister; keep what I say in thine own bosom; tell no one thou hast seen me; come *alone*, and fear not."

"Oh, I have no fear," exclaimed Hope, vehemently, "but tell me—tell me."

Magawisca put her finger on her lips in token of silence, for at this instant the door was again opened; not by the servant who had before appeared, but by Jennet. Magawisca instantly recognised her, and turned as if in the act of departing.

Time had indeed wrought little change on Jennet, save imparting a shriller squeak to her doleful voice, and a keener edge to her sharp features. "Madam Winthrop," she said, "is engaged now, but says you may call some other time with your moccasins; and I would advise you to let it be any other than the fag end of a Saturday; a wrong season for temporalities."

While Jennet was uttering this superfluous counsel, Hope sprang off the steps after Magawisca, anxious for some farther light on her dawning expectations. "Stay, oh stay," she said, "one moment, and let me try your moccasins."

At the same instant Mrs. Grafton appeared from the back parlour, evidently in a great flurry. "Here, you Indian woman," she screamed, "let me see your moccasins."

Thus beset, Magawisca was constrained to retrace her steps, and confront the danger of discovery. She drew her blanket closer over her head and face, and re-ascending the steps, threw her moccasins on the floor, and cautiously averted her face from the light. It was too evident to her, that Jennet had some glimmering recollections; for while she affected to busy herself with the moccasins, she turned her inquisitorial gray eye towards her, with a look of sharp scrutiny. Once Magawisca with a movement of involuntary disdain returned her glance. Jennet dropped the moccasins as suddenly as if she had received a blow, hemmed as if she were choking, and put her hand on the nob of the parlour door.

"Oh," thought Magawisca, "I am lost!" but Jennet, confused by her misty recollections, relinquished her purpose, whatever it was, and returned to the examination of the moccasins. In the meanwhile Hope stood behind her aunt and Jennet; her hands clasped, and her beautiful eyes bent on Magawisca with a supplicating inquiry.

Mrs. Grafton, as usual, was intent on her traffic. "It was odd enough of Madam Winthrop," she said, "not to let me know these moccasins were here; she knew I wanted them; at least she must know I might want them; and if I don't want them, that's nothing to the purpose. I like to look at every thing that's going. It is a diversion to the mind. A neat article," she continued, "I should like you to have a pair, Hope. Sir Philip said yesterday, they gave a trig look to a pretty foot and ankle. How much does she ask for them?"

"I do not know," replied Hope.

"Do not know! that's peculiar of you, Hope Leslie; you never inquire the price of any thing. I dare say, Tawney expects enough for them to buy all the glass beads in Boston. Ha, Tawney?"

Mrs. Grafton now, for the first time, turned from the articles to their possessor: she was struck with an air of graceful haughtiness in her demeanor, strongly contrasting with the submiss, dejected deportment of the natives whom she was in the habit of seeing, and dropping the moccasins and turning to Hope, she whispered—"Best buy a pair, dearie—by all means buy a pair —pay her any thing she asks—best keep peace with them, 'never affront dogs, nor Indians.' "

Hope wanted no urging, but anxious to get rid of the witnesses that embarrassed her, and quick of invention, she directed Jennet to go for her purse, "which she would find in a certain basket, or drawer, or some where else;" and reminded her aunt that she had promised to call in at Mrs. Cotton's, on her way to lecture, to look at her hyacinths, and that she had no time to lose.

Jennet obeyed, and Mrs. Grafton said, "that's true, and it's thoughtful of you to think of it, Hope; but," she added, lowering her voice, "I would not like to leave you alone, so I'll just open the parlour door."

Before Hope could intercept her, she set the door ajar, and through the aperture Magawisca had a perfect view of Everell, who was sitting musing in the window seat. An involuntary exclamation burst from her lips; and then shuddering at this exposure of her feelings, she hastily gathered together the moccasins that were strewn over the floor, dropped a pair at Hope's feet, and darted away.

Hope had heard the exclamation and understood it. Mrs. Grafton heard it without understanding it, and followed Magawisca to the door, calling after her—"Do stay and take a little something; Madam Winthrop has always a bone to give away.

Ah! you might as well call after the wind; she has already turned the corner. Heaven send she may not bear malice against us! What do you think, Hope?" Mrs. Grafton turned to appeal to her niece, but she, foreseeing endless interrogatories, had made good her retreat, and escaped to her own apartment.

Jennet, however, came to the good lady's relief; listened to all her conjectures and apprehensions, and reciprocated her own.

Jennet could not say what it was in the woman, but she had the strangest feeling all the time she was there; a mysterious beating of her heart that she could not account for; as to her disappearing so suddenly, that she did not think much of; the foresters were always impatient to get to their haunts; they were like the "wild ass," that the scripture saith, "scorneth the multitude of a city."[2]

But we leave Mrs. Grafton and Jennet to their unedifying conference, to follow our heroine to the privacy of her own apartment. There, in the first rush of her newly awakened feelings, till then repressed, she wept like a child, and repeated again and again, "Oh, my sister! my sister!" Her mind was in a tumult; she knew not what to believe—what to expect—what to hope.

But accustomed to diffuse over every anticipation the sunny hue of her own happy temperament, she flattered herself that she should even that night meet her sister—that she would be for ever restored to her—that the chord, severed by the cruel disaster at Bethel, would be refolded about their hearts. She had but a brief space to compose herself, and that was passed in fervent supplications for the blessing of God upon her hopes. She must go to the lecture, and after that trust to her ingenuity to escape to the rendezvous. The thought of danger or exposure never entered her mind, for she was not addicted to fear; and as she reflected on the voice and deportment of the stranger, she was convinced she could be none other than Magawisca; the heroine of Everell's imagination, whom he had taught her to believe, was one of those, who,

> "Without arte's bright lampe, by nature's eye,
> Keep just promise, and love equitie."[3]

Almost as impatient to go to the lecture, as she was afterwards to escape from it, (we trust our readers have absolved her for her apparent indecorum in the sanctuary,) she had tied and untied her hat twenty times before she heard the ringing of the bell for the assembling of the congregation. She refused, as has been seen, the escort of Everell, for she dared not expose to him, emotions which she could not explain.

After the various detentions, which have been already detailed, she arrived at the appointed rendezvous, and there saw Magawisca, and Magawisca alone, kneeling before an upright stake, planted at one end of a grave. She appeared occupied in delineating a figure on the stake, with a small implement she held in her hand, which she dipped in a shell placed on the ground beside her.

Hope paused with a mingled feeling of disappointment and awe; disappointment that her sister was not there—and awe inspired by the solemnity of the scene before her—the spirit-stirring figure of Magawisca—the duty she was performing —the flickering light—the monumental stones—and the dark shadows that swept over them, as the breeze bowed the tall pines. She drew her mantle, that fluttered in the breeze, close around her, and almost suppressed her breath, that she might not disturb, what she believed to be an act of filial devotion.

Magawisca was not unconscious of Miss Leslie's approach; but she deemed the office in which she was engaged, too sacred to be interrupted. She accompanied the movement of her hand with a low chant in her native tongue; and so sweet and varied were the tones of her voice, that it seemed to Hope they might have been breathed by an invisible spirit.

When she had finished her work, she leaned her head for a moment against the stake, and then rose and turned to Miss Leslie; a moonbeam shot across her face; it was wet with tears, but she spoke in a tranquil voice. "You have come—and alone?" she said, casting a searching glance around her.

"I promised to come alone," replied Hope.

"Yes—and I trusted you; and I will trust you further, for the good deed you did Nelema."

"Nelema then lived to reach you?"

"She did—wasted, faint, and dying, she crawled into my father's wigwam. She had but scant time, and short breath; with that she cursed your race, and she blessed you, Hope Leslie; her day was ended—the hand of death pressed her throat, and even then she made me swear to perform her promise to you."

"And you will, Magawisca," cried Hope impetuously; "you will give me back my sister."

"Nay, that she never promised—that I cannot do. I cannot send back the bird that has mated to its parent nest; the stream that has mingled with other waters to its fountain."

"Oh, do not speak to me in these dark sayings," replied Hope; her smooth brow contracting with impatience and apprehension, and her hurried manner and convulsed countenance contrasting strongly with the calmness of Magawisca; "what is it you mean?—where is my sister?"

"She is safe—she is near to you—and you shall see her, Hope Leslie."

"But when?—and where, Magawisca? Oh, if I could once clasp her in my arms, she never should leave me—she never should be torn from me again."

"Those arms," said Magawisca, with a faint smile, "could no more retain thy sister, than a spider's web. The lily of the Maqua's[4] valley, will never again make the English garden sweet."

"Speak plainer to me," cried Hope, in a voice of entreaty that could not be resisted. "Is my sister?"——she paused, for her quivering lips could not pronounce the words that rose to them.

Magawisca understood her, and replied. "Yes, Hope Leslie, thy sister is married to Oneco."

"God forbid!" exclaimed Hope, shuddering as if a knife had been plunged in her bosom. "My sister married to an Indian!"

"An Indian!" exclaimed Magawisca, recoiling with a look of proud contempt, that showed she reciprocated with full measure, the scorn expressed for her race. "Yes—an Indian, in whose veins runs the blood of the strongest, the fleetest of the children of the forest, who never turned their backs on friends or enemies, and whose souls have returned to the Great Spirit, stainless as they came from him. Think ye that your blood will be corrupted by mingling with this stream?

Long before Magawisca ceased to pour out her indignation, Hope's first emotion had given place to a burst of tears; she wept aloud, and her broken utterance of, "Oh, my sister! my sister! —My dear mother!" emitted but imperfect glimpses of the ruined hopes, the bitter feelings that oppressed her.

There was a chord in Magawisca's heart, that needed but the touch of tenderness to respond in harmony; her pride vanished, and her indignation gave place to sympathy. She said in a low soothing voice—"Now do not weep thus; your sister is well with us. She is cherished as the bird cherishes her young. The cold winds may not blow on her, nor the fierce sun scorch her; nor a harsh sound ever be spoken to her; she is dear to Mononotto as if his own blood ran in her veins; and Oneco—Oneco worships and serves her as if all good spirits dwelt in her. Oh, she is indeed well with us."

"There lies my mother," cried Hope, without seeming to have heard Magawisca's consolations, "she lost her life in bringing her children to this wild world, to secure them in the fold of Christ. Oh God! restore my sister to the christian family."

"And here," said Magawisca, in a voice of deep pathos, "here is my mother's grave; think ye not that the Great Spirit looks down on these sacred spots, where the good and the peaceful rest, with an equal eye; think ye not their children are His children, whether they are gathered in yonder temple where your people worship, or bow to Him beneath the green boughs of the forest?"

There was certainly something thrilling in Magawisca's faith, and she now succeeded in riveting Hope's attention. "Listen to me," she said; "your sister is of what you call the christian family. I believe ye have many names in that family. She hath been signed with the cross by a holy father from France; she bows to the crucifix."

"Thank God!" exclaimed Hope fervently, for she thought that any christian faith was better than none.

"Perhaps ye are right," said Magawisca, as if she read Hope's heart; "there may be those that need other lights; but to me, the Great Spirit is visible in the life-creating sun. I perceive Him in the gentle light of the moon that steals in through the forest boughs. I feel Him here," she continued, pressing her hand on her breast, while her face glowed with the enthusiasm of devotion. "I feel Him in these ever-living, ever-wakeful thoughts— but we waste time. You must see your sister."

"When, and where?" again demanded Hope.

"Before I answer you, you must promise me by this sign, and she pointed to the emblem of her tribe, an eagle, which she had rudely delineated on the post, that served as a head-stone to her mother's grave; "you must promise me by the bright host of Heaven, that the door of your lips shall be fast; that none shall know that you have seen me, or are to see me again."

"I promise," said Hope, with her characteristic precipitancy.

"Then, when five suns have risen and set, I will return with your sister. But hush," she said, suddenly stopping, and turning a suspicious eye towards the thicket of evergreens.

"It was but the wind," said Hope, rightly interpreting Magawisca's quick glance, and the slight inclination of her head.

"You would not betray me?" said Magawisca, in a voice of mingled assurance and inquiry. "Oh, more than ever entered into thy young thoughts, hangs upon my safety."

"But why any fear for your safety? why not come openly among us? I will get the word of our good Governor, that you shall come and go in peace. No one ever feared to trust his word."

"You know not what you ask."

"Indeed I do—but you, Magawisca, know not what you refuse—and why refuse? are you afraid of being treated like a recovered prisoner? Oh no! every one will delight to honour you, for your very name is dear to all Mr. Fletcher's friends— most dear to Everell."

"Dear to Everell Fletcher! Does he remember me? Is there a place in his heart for an Indian?" she demanded, with a blended expression of pride and melancholy.

"Yes—yes, Magawisca—indeed is there," replied Hope, for now she thought she had touched the right key. "It was but this morning, that he said he had a mind to take an Indian guide, and seek you out among the Maquas." Magawisca hid her face in the folds of her mantle, and Hope proceeded with increasing earnestness. "There is nothing in the wide world, there is nothing that Everell thinks so good, and so noble as you. Oh, if you could but have seen his joy, when after your parting on that horrid rock, he first heard you was living. He has described you so often and so truly, that the moment I saw you, and heard your voice, I said to myself, 'this is surely Everell's Magawisca.' "

"Say no more, Hope Leslie—say no more," exclaimed Magawisca, throwing back the envelope from her face, as if she were ashamed to shelter emotions she ought not to indulge. "I have promised my father—I have repeated the vow here on my mother's grave, and if I were to go back from it, those bright witnesses," she pointed to the heavens, "would break their silence. Do not speak to me again of Everell Fletcher."

"Oh, yes—once again, Magawisca; if you will not listen to me, if you will but give me this brief, mysterious meeting with my poor sister, at least let Everell be with me; for his sake—for my sake—for your own sake, do not refuse me."

Magawisca looked on Hope's glowing face for a moment, and then shook her head with a melancholy smile. "They tell me," she said, "that no one can look on you and deny you aught; that you can make old men's hearts soft, and mould them at your will; but I have learned to deny even the cravings of my own heart; to pursue my purpose like the bird that keeps her wing stretched to the toilsome flight, though the sweetest note of her mate recalls her to the nest. "But ah! I do but boast," she continued, casting her eyes to the ground. "I may not trust myself; that was a childish scream, that escaped me when I saw Everell; had my father heard it, his cheek would have been pale with shame. No, Hope Leslie, I may not listen to thee. You must come alone to the meeting, or never meet your sister—will you come?"

Hope saw in the determined manner of Magawisca, that there was no alternative but to accept the boon on her own terms, and she no longer withheld her compliance. The basis of their treaty being settled, the next point to be arranged, was the place of meeting. Magawisca had no objections to venture again within the town; but then it would be necessary to completely disguise Faith Leslie; and she hinted that she understood enough of Hope's English feelings, to know that she would wish to see her sister with the pure tint of her natural complexion.

Hope had too much delicacy, and too much feeling, even inadvertently to appear to lay much stress on this point; but the experience of the evening made her feel the difficulty of arranging a meeting, surrounded as she was by vigilant friends, and within the sphere of their observation. Suddenly it occurred to her, that Digby, her fast friend, and on more than one occasion her trusty ally, had the superintendence of the Governor's garden, on an island in the harbor, and within three miles of the town. The Governor's family were in the habit of resorting thither frequently. Digby had a small habitation there, of which he and his family were the only tenants, and indeed were the only persons who dwelt on the island. Hope was certain of permission to pass a night there, where she might indulge in an interview with her sister of any length, without hazard of interruption; and having explained her plan to Magawisca, it received her ready and full acquiescence.

Before they separated, Hope said, "you will allow me, Magawisca, to persuade my sister, if I can, to remain with me."

"Oh yes—if you can—but do not hope to persuade her. She and my brother are as if one life-chord bound them together; and besides, your sister cannot speak to you and understand you as I do. She was very young when she was taken where she has only heard the Indian tongue; some, you know, are like water, that retains no mark; and others, like the flinty rock, that never loses a mark." Magawisca observed Hope's look of disappointment; and in a voice of pity, she added, "your sister hath a face that speaketh plainly, what the tongue should never speak, her own goodness."

When these two romantic females had concerted every measure they deemed essential to the certainty and privacy of their meeting, Magawisca bowed her head, and kissed the border of Hope's shawl, with the reverent delicacy of an oriental salutation; she then took from beneath her mantle some fragrant herbs, and strewed them over her mother's grave, then prostrated herself in deep and silent devotion, feeling (as others have felt on earth thus consecrated) as if the clods she pressed were instinct with life. When this last act of filial love was done, she rose, muffled herself closely in her dark mantle, and departed.

Hope lingered for a moment. "Mysteriously," she said, as her eye followed the noble figure of Magawisca, till it was lost in the surrounding darkness, "mysteriously have our destinies been interwoven. Our mothers brought from a far distance to rest together here—their children connected in indissoluble bonds!"

But Hope was soon aware that this was no time for solitary meditation. In the interest of her interview with Magawisca, she had been heedless of the gathering storm. The clouds rolled over the moon suddenly, like the unfurling of a banner, and the rain poured down in torrents. Hope had no light to guide her, but occasional flashes of lightning, and the candle, whose little beam proceeding from Mr. Cotton's study window, pierced the dense sheet of rain.

Hope hurried her steps homewards, and as she passed the knot of evergreens, she fancied she heard a rattling of the boughs, as if there were some struggling within, and a suppressed voice saying, "hist—whish." She paused, and with a resolute step, turned towards the thicket; "we have been overheard," she thought, "this generous creature shall not be betrayed." At this instant a thunder-bolt burst over her head, and the whole earth seemed kindled with one bright illumination. She was terrified, and, perhaps, as much convinced by her fears, as her reason, that it was both imprudent, and useless, to make any further investigation, she again bent her quick steps towards home. She had scarcely surmounted the fence, which she passed more like a winged spirit, than a fine lady, when Sir Philip Gardiner joined her.

"Miss Leslie!" he exclaimed, as a flash of lightning revealed her person. "Now, thanks to my good stars, that I am so fortunate as to meet you; suffer me to wrap my cloak about you; you will be drenched with this pitiless rain."

"Oh no, no," she said, "the cloak will but encumber me. I

am already drenched, and I shall be at home directly," and she would have left him, but he caught her arm, and gently detained her, while he enveloped her in his cloak.

"It should not be a trifle, Miss Leslie, that has kept you out, regardless of this gathering storm," Sir Philip said inquiringly. Miss Leslie made no reply, and he proceeded. "You may have forgotten it is Saturday night—or, perhaps, you have a dispensation."

"Neither," replied Hope.

"Neither! then I am sure you are abroad in some godly cause, for you need to be one of the righteous, who, we are told, are as bold as a lion, to confront the Governor's family after trespassing on holy time."

"I have no fears," said Hope.

"No fears! that is a rare exemption, for a young lady; but I would that you possessed one still more rare; she who is incapable of fear, should never be exposed to danger; and if I had a charmed shield, I would devote my life to sheltering you from all harm—may not—may not love be such an one?"

"It's useless talking, Sir Philip," replied Hope; if that could be deemed a reply, which seemed to have rather an indirect relation to the previous address. "It is useless talking in this rattling storm, your words drop to the ground with the hail-stones."

"And every word you utter," said the knight, biting his lips with vexation, "not only penetrates my ear, but sinks into my heart; therefore, I pray you to be merciful, and do not make my heart heavy."

"The hail-stones melt as they touch the ground, and my words pass away as soon, I fancy," said Hope, with the most provoking nonchalance.

Sir Philip had no time to reply; they were just turning into the court in front of Governor Winthrop's house, when a flash of lightning, so vivid that its glare almost blinded them, disclosed the figure of the mysterious page leaning against the gate-post, his head inclined forward as if in the act of listening, his cap in his hand, his dark curls in wild disorder over his face and neck, and he apparently unconscious of the storm. They both recoiled—Hope uttered an exclamation of pity. "Ha, Roslin!" burst in a tone of severe reproach from Sir Philip; but instantly changing it for one of kindness, he added, "you should not have waited for me, boy, in such a storm."

"I cared not for the storm—I did not feel it," replied the lad, in a penetrating voice, which recalled to Miss Leslie all he had said to her, and induced her to check her first impulse to bid him in; she therefore passed him without any further notice, ascended the steps, and as has been related in the preceding chapter, met Everell in the hall.

It is necessary to state briefly to our readers, some particulars in relation to the re-appearance of Magawisca, which events have not as yet explained.

Her father, from the hour of his expulsion from his own dominion, had constantly meditated revenge. His appetite was not sated at Bethel—that massacre seemed to him but a retaliation for his private wrongs. The catastrophe on the sacrifice-rock disordered his reason for a time; and the Indians, who perceived something extraordinary in the energy of his unwavering and undivided purpose, never believed it to be perfectly restored. But this, so far from impairing their confidence, converted it to implicit deference, for they, in common with certain oriental nations, believe that an insane person is inspired; that the Divinity takes possession of the temple which the spirit of the man has abandoned. Whatever Mononotto predicted, was believed— whatever he ordered, was done.

He felt that Oneco's volatile unimpressive character was unfit for his purpose, and he permitted him to pursue without intermission, his own pleasure—to hunt and fish for his 'white bird,' as he called the little Leslie. But Magawisca was the constant companion of her father; susceptible and contemplative, she soon imbibed his melancholy, and became as obedient to the impulse of his spirit, as the most faithful are to the fancied intimations of the Divinity. She was the priestess of the oracle. Her tenderness for Everell, and her grateful recollections of his lovely mother, she determined to sacrifice on the altar of national duty.

In the years 1642 and 1643 there was a general movement

among the Indians. Terrible massacres were perpetrated in the English settlements in Virginia; the Dutch establishments in New-York were invaded, and rumours of secret and brooding hostility kept the colonies of New-England in a state of perpetual alarm. Mononotto determined to avail himself of this crisis, that appeared so favourable to his design, of uniting all the tribes of New-England in one powerful combination. He first applied to Miantunnomoh, hoping by his personal influence to persuade that powerful and crafty chief to sacrifice to the general good, his private feud with Uncas, the chief of the Mohegans.

Mononotto eloquently pressed those arguments, which, as is allowed by the historian of the Indian wars, "seemed to right reason, not only pregnant to the purpose, but also most cogent and invincible,"[5] and for a time, they prevailed over the mind of Miantunnomoh.

Vague rumours of conspiracy reached Boston; and the Governor summoned Miantunnomoh to appear before his court, and abide an examination there. The chief accordingly, (as has been seen) came to Boston; but so artfully did he manage his cause, as to screen from the English every just ground of offence. Their suspicions, however, were not removed; for Hubbard says, "though his words were smoother than oil, yet many conceived in his heart were drawn swords."[6]

It may appear strange, that while prosecuting so hazardous and delicate an enterprise, Mononotto should have encumbered himself with his family. Magawisca was necessary to him; and he submitted to be accompanied by Oneco and his bride, from respect to the dying declaration of Nelema, that his plans could never be accomplished till her promise to Hope Leslie had been redeemed—till, as she had sworn to her preserver, the sisters had met.

Had the Indians been capable of a firm combination, the purpose of Mononotto might have been achieved, and the English have been then driven from the American soil. But the natives were thinly scattered over an immense tract of country—the different tribes divided by petty rivalships, and impassable gulfs of long transmitted hatred. They were brave and strong, but it was brute force without art or arms: they had ingenuity to form, and they did form, artful conspiracies, but their best concerted plans were betrayed by the timid, or the treacherous.

But to return to our individual concerns. Mononotto trusted to his daughter the arrangement of the meeting of the sisters, which from his having a superstitious notion that it was in some way to influence his political purposes, he was anxious to promote. Magawisca left her companions at an Indian station on the Neponset river, and proceeded herself to Boston, to seek a private interview with Hope Leslie. The appearance of an Indian woman in Boston excited no observation, the natives being in the habit of resorting there daily with game, fish, and their rude manufactures. Aware of the necessity of disguising every peculiarity, she unbound her hair from the braids in which it was usually confined, and combed it thick over her forehead, after the fashion of the aborigines in the vicinity of Boston, whom Eliot describes as wearing this 'maiden veil.' She enveloped herself in a blanket that concealed the rich dress which it was her father's pride, (and perhaps her pleasure) that she should wear. Thus disguised, and favoured by the kind shadows of twilight, she presented herself at Governor Winthrop's, and was, as has already appeared, successful in her mission.

CHAPTER III

"I could find in my heart to disgrace my man's apparel, and to cry
like a woman."

As you like it[1]

Sir Philip Gardiner, by the kind offices of Governor Winthrop,
had obtained lodgings at one Daniel Maud's, the 'first recorded
schoolmaster' in Boston. Thither he went, followed by his
moody page, after receiving his cloak from our thankless
heroine.

Not one word passed between him and his attendant; and
after they reached their apartment, the boy, instead of performing the customary servile duties of his station, threw himself on
a cushion, and covering his face with his hands, he seemed lost
in his own sorrowful meditations.

There had been a little fire kindled on the hearth, on account
of the inclemency of the night. Sir Philip laid the fallen brands
together, lighted the candles, arranged his writing materials on
the table, and without permitting himself to be interrupted, or
in the least affected by the sobs that, at intervals, proceeded from
his companion, he indited the following epistle.

"To my good and trusty Wilton,
" 'In the name of Heaven, what sends you to New-England?'
were your last words to me. I had not time to answer your

question then, and perhaps, when I have finished, you will say I have not ability now; but who can explain the motives of his conduct? Who can always say, after an action is done, that he had sufficient motive? Not one of us, Wilton, sons of whim and folly that we are! But my motives, such as they were, are at your service—so here you have them.

"I was tired of playing a losing game; even rats, you know, have an instinct by which they flee a falling house. I had some compunctious visitings at leaving my king when he hath such cruel need of loyal servants—jeer not, Wilton,—I had my scruples. It was a saying of Father Baretti, that when Lucifer fell, conscience, that once guided, remained to torment him. My assertion thus modestly illustrated, have I not a right to say, I had scruples? I was wearied with a series of ill-luck, and as other men are as good to fill a ditch, I have retired till dame fortune shall see fit to give her wheel a turn in my royal master's favour. But why come hither?—to submit to 'King Winthrop and all his inventions—his Amsterdam fantastical ordinances—his preachings, marryings, and other abusive ceremonies?'² —Patience, my good gossip, and I will tell thee.

"You have heard of my old friend and patron, Thomas Morton³ of Furnival's Inn; and you know he was once master of a fine domain here, at Mount Wollaston, for which his revels obtained the name of the 'Merry Mount.' The ruling saintships of this "New-English Canaan" were so scandalized, because forsooth, he avowed and followed the free tastes of a gentleman, that they ejected him from his own territory.

"He once well-nigh obtained redress from the king, and a decree in his favour passed the privy-seal, but the influence of his enemies finally prevailed. He has had the consolation of sundry retaliations on his opponents; now, as he said, 'uncasing Medusa's head, and raising the old ghost of Sir F. George's patent,'⁴ and then thrusting home the keen point of his satiric verse. However, though this was a bitter draught to his adversaries, it was but lean satisfaction to him; and having become old, and poor, and lost his spirit, he came hither once more, last winter, in the hope of obtaining an act of oblivion of all past grievances, and a restitution of his rights.

"Immediately after his arrival, he wrote to me that *'Joshua* had promised to restore to him, and to his tribe, their lot in the inheritance of the faithful—that he was again to be king of the revels on the 'merry mount,' where he invited me to live with him, his prime minister, and heir apparent.' The letter came to hand at a moment when I was wearied with a bootless service, and willing to grasp any novelty; and accordingly I closed with the offer, but lo! on my arrival, I found that Morton, instead of being reinstated at Mount Wollaston, is in jail, and in honest opinion, is reputed crazy—as, doubtless, he is! Laugh at me, Wilton, even as the foul fiends laugh when their master is entangled in his own meshes—I defy your laugh; for though a dupe, I am not a victim; and Cæsar and his fortunes shall yet survive the storm.

"I have done with Morton; no one here knows or suspects our former alliance. My name is not like to reach his ear, and if it should, who would take the word of a ruined man, against an approved candidate for membership with the congregation, for such even, am I—a 'brother,' in this community of saints.

"Luckily, Morton, with that cunning incident to madness, cautioned me against appearing in this camp without the uniform of the church-militant, alleging, that we must play the part of pilgrims, till we were quite independent of the favour of the saints. Accordingly, I assumed the puritan habit, bearing, and language that so much amused you at our last meeting. But why, you will ask, prolong this dull masquerade? For an object, my good Wilton, that would make you or me, saint or devil, or any thing else whereby we might secure it—the most provoking, bewitching, and soul-moving creature that ever appeared in the form of woman, is my tempter. She is the daughter and sole heir of Sir Walter Leslie, who you may remember was noted for his gallantry in that mad expedition of Buckingham to the Isle of Rhée.[5]

"Is it not a shame that youth and beauty should be thrown away upon these drivelling, canting, preaching, praying, liberty-loving, lecture-going, *pilgrims!* Would it not be a worthy act to tear this scion of a loyal stock from these crabs of the wilderness, and set her in our garden of England? And would it not be a knightly feat to win the prize against a young gallant, a pink of courtesy, while the unfledged boy is dreaming of love's elysium?

"Marvel as you please, Wilton, goodly prospects are dawning on me—fortune smiles, as if inclined to pay the good turn she has so long owed me. I am in prime credit with guardians and governors—the beau-ideal of duenna-aunts and serving maids. Time and chance favour me—but—but there is always some devilish cross upon my line of luck.

"Rosa came with me to this barbarous land—a fit Houri,[6] you will say, for a Mahometan saint, but an odd appendage to a canting roundhead—even so she is, but what was to be done! She had no shelter but my protection. I had still some lingering of love for her, and pity (don't scoff!); and besides, Morton's representations had led me to believe that she would not be an inconvenient member of the household at Merry Mount, so I permitted her to disguise herself, and come over the rough seas with me. She is a fantastical wayward child, and a true woman withal. She loves me to distraction, and would sacrifice any to me but the ruling passion of her sex, her vanity; but in spite of my entreaties and commands, she persists in wearing a velvet Spanish hat, with a buckle and feathers, most audaciously cocked on one side; and indeed her whole apparel would better suit a Queen's page, than the humble serving-boy of a self-denying puritan.

"Luckily she is sad and dumpish, and does not incline to go abroad, but whenever she does appear I perceive, she is eyed with curiosity and suspicion; and suspicion once thoroughly awakened, discovery is inevitable, for you know her face gives the lie to her doublet and hose.

> Diana's lip is not more smooth and rubious,
> Her small pipe is as the maiden's organ, sound and shrill;
> And all is semblative a woman's part.[7]

"If we should be detected, I know not what punishment may be inflicted by the Draco-laws of these saints—a public whipping of poor Rosa—cropping of my ears—imprisonment—perhaps death, if peradventure some authority therefor should be found in the statutes of the land—that is to say, in the old Jewish records.

"But why expose myself to such peril? Ah! Wilton, you would not ask why if you could see my enchantress—but without seeing her, no man knows better than you, that

> "*Love is a sweet intice,*
> *'Gainst whom the wisest wits as yet*
> *Have never found devise.*"

"If I could but persuade Rosa to be prudent till we may both cast off these odious disguises; but she disdains all caution, and fears nothing but being supplanted in my favour.

"She is still in the fever of love—all eye and ear—irritable, jealous, watchful, and suspicious. One moment passionate, and the next dissolved in tears. So intense a flame must purify or consume the sentiment her beauty inspired—it cannot be purified and—the alternative—it is consumed.

"I cannot rid myself of her—I cannot control her, and in this jeopardy I stand; but I abandon all to my destiny. Even Jupiter, you know, was ruled by fate. It is folly to attempt to shape the events of life; as easily might we direct the course of the stars— those very stars, perhaps, govern the accidents of our being. The stars—destiny—Providence, what are they all but various terms for the same invisible, irresistible agency! But Heaven forbid I should lose myself in the bewildering mazes of these high speculations! It is a enough for me that I am a knight of the holy sepulchre, that I wear my crucifix, pray to all the saints and eat no flesh on Fridays. By the way, on the very first day of my arrival here, I came nigh to winning the crown of martyrdom by my saintly obedience to the canons of holy church. The Leslie, in simplicity or mischief, remarked on my confining myself to fish on Friday—rebel conscience, in spite of me tinged my cheeks, but thanks to my garb of hypocrisy, panoply of steel never did better service,—the light thrust glanced off and left me unharmed.

"You and I, Wilton, are too old to make, like dreaming boys, an Eldorado of our future, and you will ask me what are my rational chances of success in my present enterprise. I will not remind you of success on former similar occasions, for my vanity has been abated of its presumption this very evening by the indifference, real or affected, of this little sprite.

"Ladies must have lovers—idols must have worshippers, or they are no longer idols. I have but one rival here, and he, I think, is appointed by his wise guardians to another destiny; and being a right dutiful youth, he, no doubt, with management, and good fortune on my part, may be made to surrender his preference, (which by the way is quite obvious) and pass under the yoke of authority. Besides, the helpmate selected by these Judges in Israel, for the good youth might be, if she were a little less saint and more woman, a queen of love and beauty. But she is not to my taste. I covet not smiles cold as a sun-beam on arctic snows. Nothing in life is duller than mathematical virtue—nothing more paralyzing to the imagination than unaffected prudery. I detest a woman like a walled city, that can never be approached without your being reminded that it is inaccessible—a woman whose measured premeditated words sound always like the sentinel-cry, 'all is well!'

"Now the Leslie has a generous rashness, a thoughtless impetuosity, a fearlessness of the sanctimonious dictators that surround her, and a noble contempt of danger that stimulates me at least, to love and enterprise.

"My hope is bold, Wilton—my ambition is to win her heart—my *determination* to possess her hand; by fair means, if I can, but if fortune is adverse, if, as I sometimes fear, when I shrink from the falcon glance of her bright eye, as if the spear of Ithuriel[8] touched me, if she has already penetrated my disguise, and persists in disregarding my suit, why then, Necessity! parent of all witty inventions, come thou to my aid.

"Our old acquaintance Chaddock is riding in the harbour here, owner and commander of a good pinnace. I have heard him spoken of in the godly companies I frequent, as a 'notorious contemner of ordinances,' from which I infer he is the same bold desperado we knew him. My word for it, it does not require more courage to march up to the cannon's mouth, than to claim the independence of a gentleman in this pharasaic land. Now I think if I should have occasion to smuggle any precious freight, and convey it over the deep waters, convenient opportunity and fit agents will not be wanting. Time will ripen or blast my budding hopes; if ripen, why then I will cast my slough here, and present my beautiful bride to my royal master, or if, perchance, royalty should be in eclipse in England, there are, thank heaven, other asylums for beauty and fortune.

"Farewell, Wilton, yours in good faith,

"Gardiner."

As Sir Philip signed his name to this epistle, he felt Rosa's head drop upon his shoulder, an action that indicated, too truly, that she had been looking over the last paragraphs, at least, of his letter.

Fury flashed from his eyes, and he raised his hand to strike her, but before he had executed the unmanly act, she burst into a wild hysteric laugh, that changed his resentment to fear. "Rosa—Rosa," he said, in a soothing tone, "for Heaven's sake be quiet—you will be overheard—you will betray all."

She seemed not to hear him, but wringing her hands, she repeated again and again, "I wish I were dead! I wish I were dead!"

"Hush! foolish, mad child, or you will be discovered, and may indeed bring death upon yourself."

"Death! I care not; death would be heaven's mercy to what I suffer; what is death to shame!—to guilt! to the bitterness of disappointment!—to the rage of jealousy!—why should not I die!" she continued, overpowering Sir Philip's vain attempts to calm her; "why should not I die?—there is nobody to care for me if I live—and there is nobody to weep for me if I die."

"Patience—patience, Rosa."

"Patience! my patience is worn out; I am tired of this dreary world. Oh, that Lady Lunford had left me in my convent—I should have been happy there. She did not love me. Nobody has loved me since I left the good nuns—nobody but my poor little Canary bird, Mignonne; and she always loved me, and would always sing to me, and sing sweetest when my lady was cruellest. Cruel as my lady was, her cruelty was kindness to thine, Sir Philip. Oh, that you had left me with her!"

"You came to me with your own good-will, Rosa."

"Ay, Sir Philip—and will not the innocent babe stretch its arms to the assassin if he does but smile on it? You told me you loved me, and I believed you. You promised always to love me, and I believed that too; and there was nobody else that loved me, but Mignonne; and now I am all alone in the wide world, I do wish I were dead." She sunk down at Sir Philip's feet, laid her head on his knee, and sobbed as if her heart were breaking. "Oh, what shall I do," she said, "where shall I go! if I go to the good, they will frown on me, and despise me; and I cannot go to the wicked,—they have no pity."

Sir Philip's heart, depraved as it was, felt some motions of compassion as he looked on this young and beautiful creature, bowed to the earth with remediless anguish; some touches of remorse and pity, such as Milton's fallen angel felt, when he contemplated those "millions of spirits, for his fault amerc'd of Heav'n." "Poor child!" he said, laying his hand on her smooth brow, "would to God you had never left your convent!"

Rosa felt the blistering tears that flowed from the relicts of his better nature, drop on her cheek. She raised her heavy lids, and a ray of pleasure shot from her kindling eye. "Then you do love me," she said, "you would not weep only for pity—you do love me still?"

Sir Philip perceived the eagerness with which she caught at the first glimmering of returning tenderness, and well knew how to draw his advantage from it. He soothed her with caresses and professions, and when he had restored her to composure, he endeavoured to impress her with the necessity, for both their sakes, of more prudent conduct. He convinced her that their happiness, their safety, and perhaps their lives, depended on their escaping detection; and after explaining the defeat of his hopes in relation to Morton, he averred that the part of his letter relating to Miss Leslie, was mere badinage, written for his friend's amusement; and he concluded with reiterated promises, that he would return with her in the first ship bound to England.

Rosa was credulous—at least, she wished to believe—she was grateful for restored tenderness; and without daring to confess how nearly she had already betrayed him to Miss Leslie, she promised all the circumspection that Sir Philip required.

CHAPTER IV

"I should have been more strange I must confess,
But that thou overheard'st me, ere I was 'ware
My love's true passion: therefore, pardon me,
And not impute this yielding to light love."
ROMEO AND JULIET[1]

The week that succeeded Hope Leslie's interview with Maga-wisca, was one of anxiety to most of the members of Governor Winthrop's family.

The habitual self-possession of the Governor himself seemed somewhat disturbed; he was abstracted and thoughtful; frequently held secret conferences with Sir Philip Gardiner in his study; and in relation to this stranger, he appeared to have departed from his usual diplomatic caution, and to have admitted him to the most confidential intimacy. There were frequent private meetings of the magistrates; and it was quite evident from the external motions of these guardians of the colony, that some state secret was heaving in their bosoms.

The Governor was in the habit of participating with his wife his most secret state-affairs; moved to this confidence, no doubt, by his strict views of her rights as his help-mate; for it cannot be supposed, even for a moment, that one of the superior sex should find pleasure in telling a secret.

But in this instance, he communicated nothing to his trust-worthy partner, excepting some obscure intimations, that might be gathered from the significant utterance of such general truths as, "that it was impossible for human foresight to foresee every thing; that those who stood at the helm of state could not be too vigilant; that ends were often brought about by unexpected means;" and similar truisms, which, enunciated by grave and dignified lips, are invested with importance from the source whence they proceed.

Madam Winthrop was happily too much absorbed with the feminine employment of watching the developement of her niece's affairs, to have much curiosity in relation to cabinet secrets. She naturally concluded that some dangerous adherent of that arch-heretic Gorton, had been discovered; or, perhaps, some new mode of faith had demanded magisterial interference; whatever her mental conclusions were, it is certain her thoughts all ran in another channel. In all ages of the world, in every condition, and at every period of life, a woman's interest in the progress of a love affair, masters every other feeling.

Esther Downing was a favourite of her aunt; and as it had been urged by Mr. Downing, as an objection to his removal to New-England, that his daughters would have small chance of being eligibly married there, it became a point of honour with Madam Winthrop, after he had been persuaded to overlook this objection, to prove to him that it was unfounded.

Madam Winthrop was too upright, intentionally to do a wrong to any one; but, without being herself conscious of it, she was continually setting off the lights of her niece's character, by what she deemed the shades of Hope Leslie's. Our heroine's independent temper, and careless gaiety of heart, had more than once offended against the strict notions of Madam Winthrop, who was of the opinion, that the deferential manners of youth, which were the fashion of the age, had their foundation in immutable principles.

Nothing was farther from Miss Leslie's intention, than any disrespect to a woman whom she had been taught to venerate; but unfortunately, she would sometimes receive what Madam Winthrop meant for affability, as if it were simply the kindness of an equal; she had been seen to gape in the midst of the good lady's most edifying remarks; and once she ran away to gaze on a brilliant sunset, at the moment Madam Winthrop was condescendingly relating some very important particulars of her early life. This was certainly indecorous; but her offences were trifling, and were probably forgotten by Madam Winthrop herself, long before their effects were effaced from her mind.

Esther was always respectful, always patient; always governed by the slightest intimation of her aunt's wishes; and it must be confessed, that even to those who were less partial and prejudiced than Madame Winthrop, Miss Downing appeared far more lovely than our heroine during the week, when she was suffering the extremes of anxiety and apprehension. No one, who did not know that there was a secret and sufficient cause for her restlessness, her seeming indifference to her friends, and to every thing about her, could have escaped the conclusion, that forced itself on Everell's mind; that fortune, and beauty, and indulgence, had had their usual and fatal effect on Hope Leslie. In the bitterness of his disappointment, he wished he had never returned to have the vision of her ideal perfection expelled from his imagination by the light of truth.

With the irritable feeling of a lover, he watched the devoted attentions of Sir Philip Gardiner to Hope, which she, almost unconscious of them, received passively, but as Everell thought, favourably. Utterly engrossed in one object, she never reflected that there had been any thing in her conduct to excite Everell's distrust; and feeling more than ever, the want of that sympathy and undisguised affection which she had always received from him, she was hurt at his altered conduct; and her manner insensibly conforming to the coldness and constraint of his, he naturally concluded that she designed to repel him, and he would turn from her, to repose in the calm and twilight quiet that was shed about the gentle Esther, whom he knew to be pure, disinterested, humble, and devoted.

Poor Hope, the subject of his unjust condemnation, was agitated, not only by impatience for the promised meeting with her unfortunate sister, but by fear that some unforeseen circumstance might prevent it. She was also harassed with a sense of conflicting duties. She sometimes thought that the duty of restoring her sister to the condition in which she was born, was paramount to the obligation of her promise to Magawisca. She would waver and resolve to disclose her secret appointment; but the form of Magawisca would rise to her recollection with its expression of truth and sweetness and confidence, as if to check her treacherous purpose.

A thousand times she condemned herself for the rashness of her promise to Magawisca, by which she had reduced herself, surrounded as she was by wise and efficient friends, to act without their counsel and aid. Had Everell treated her with his accustomed kindness, the habitual confidence of their intercourse might have led her to break through the restriction of her promise, but she dared not deliberately violate her word so solemnly pledged. Oppressed with these anxieties, the hours rolled heavily on; and when Friday, the appointed day arrived, it seemed to Hope that an age had intervened since her interview with Magawisca.

She had taken care previously to propose an excursion on Friday to the Governor's garden; and contrary to usual experience, when a long projected pleasure is to be realized, every circumstance was propitious. The day was propitious, one of nature's holidays—the governor too was propitious, and even promoted the party with unprecedented zeal.

After various delays, which, however trifling, had increased Hope's nervous impatience, they were on the point of setting forth, when Madam Winthrop, who was not one of the party, came into the parlour, and said, after a slight hesitation, "I am loath, my young friends, to interfere with what you seem to have set your hearts on—but really,"—she paused.

"Really what, Ma'am?" asked Hope impatiently.

Madam Winthrop was not inclined to be spurred by Miss Leslie, and she answered very deliberately, "I have a feeling as if something were to happen to-day. I am a coward on the water, at all times, more than becomes one who fully realizes that the same Providence that watches over us on the land, follows us on the great deep."

"But your fears, Madam," said Sir Philip, "did not prevent your crossing the stormy Atlantic."

"Nay, Sir Philip, and I know not what metal that woman is made of, that would not go hand in hand with her husband in so glorious a cause as ours."

"Are we not all ready?" asked Hope, anxious to escape before Madam Winthrop proposed, as she apprehended she was about to do, a postponement of the party.

"Yes, all ready, I believe, Miss Leslie, but not *all* too impatient to await a remark I was about to make, namely, Sir Philip, that a party of pleasure is very different from a voyage of duty."

"Certainly, madam," replied Sir Philip, who trusted that assent would end the conversation, "widely different."

"It is not necessary for me," resumed Madam Winthrop, "to state all the points of difference."

"Oh! not in the least, Ma'am," exclaimed Hope.

"Miss Leslie!" said Madam Winthrop, in a tone of surprise, and then turning her eye to Everell, who was standing next Esther, she said, resuming her measured tone, "my responsibility is so great to my brother Downing—I had an uncommon dream about you, Esther, last night—and if any thing should happen to you—"

"If it is me, you are concerned about, aunt," said Esther, untying her bonnet, "I will remain at home,—do not let me detain you," she added, turning to Hope, "another moment."

Nothing seemed to Hope of any importance, in comparison with the prosecution of her plans, and nodding a pleased assent to Esther, she took her aunt's arm in readiness to depart.

"How changed," thought Everell, as his eye glanced towards her, "thus selfishly and impatiently to pursue her own pleasure without the slightest notice of her friend's disappointment." His good feelings were interested to compensate for the indifference of Hope. "If," he said to Madam Winthrop, "you will commit Miss Downing to my care, I will promise she shall encounter no danger that my caution may avoid, or my skill overcome."

Madam Winthrop's apprehensions vanished. "If she is in your particular charge, Mr. Everell," she said, "I shall be greatly relieved. I know, I am of too anxious a make. Go, my dear Esther, Mr. Everell will be constantly near you; under Providence, your safe-guard. I believe it is not right to be too much influenced by dreams. See that she keeps her shawl round her, Mr. Everell, while on the water. I feel quite easy in confiding her to your care."

Everell bowed, and expressed his gratitude for Madam Winthrop's confidence, and Esther turned on him a look of that meek and pleased dependence, which it is natural for woman to feel, and which men like to inspire, because—perhaps—it seems to them an instinctive tribute to their natural superiority.

"Miss Leslie has become so sedate of late," continued Madam Winthrop, with a very significant smile, "that I scarcely need request that no unwonted sounds of revelry and mirth may proceed from any member of the governor's family, which ever has been, as it should be, a pattern of gospel sobriety to the colony."

Mrs. Grafton dropped a bracelet she was clasping on her niece's arm, but Madam Winthrop's remark—half reproof, and half admonition, excited no emotion in Hope, whose heart was throbbing with her own secret anxieties, and who was now in some measure relieved, by Sir Philip making a motion for their departure, by adroitly availing himself of this first available pause, and offering her his arm.

As soon as they were fairly out of the house, "revelry and mirth," exclaimed Mrs. Grafton, as if the words blistered her tongue, "revelry and mirth indeed! I think poor Hope will forget how to laugh, if she stays here much longer. I wonder, Sir Philip, if it is such a mighty offence to use one's laughing faculties, what they were given for?"

"I believe, madam," replied the knight, with well sustained gravity, "that ingenious theologians impute this convulsion of the muscles to some disorganization occasioned by Adam's transgression, and in support of their hypothesis, they maintain that there is no allusion to laughter in scripture. Madam Winthrop, I fancy, intends that her house shall be a little heaven on earth."

Honest Cradock, who had taken his favourite station at Miss Leslie's side, replied, without in the least suspecting the knight's irony. "Now, Sir Philip, I marvel whence you draw that opinion. I have studied all masters in theology, from the oldest down to the youngest, and, greatest of all, Master Calvin, with whose precious sentences I 'sweeten my mouth always before going to bed,' yet did I never see that strange doctrine concerning laughter. To me it appears—the Lord preserve me from advancing novelties—but to me it appears, that there is no human sound so pleasant and so musical as the laugh of a little child—and of such are the kingdom of heaven. I have heard the walls at Bethel ring with bursts of laughter from Miss Hope, and the thought came to me, (the Lord forgive me, if I erred therein,) that it was the natural voice of innocence, and therefore, pleasing to him that made her."

Hope was touched with the pure sentiment of her good tutor, and she involuntarily slipped her arm into his. Sir Philip was also touched, and for once, speaking without forethought, he said, "I would give a kingdom for one of the laughs of my boyhood."

"I dare say, Sir Philip," said Cradock, "for truly there is no heart-work in the transgressor's laugh."

"Sir!" exclaimed Sir Philip angrily.

The simple man started as if he had received a blow, and Hope said, "you did not mean to call Sir Philip a transgressor."

"Oh, certainly not, in particular, certainly not; Sir Philip's professions are great, and I doubt not, practice correspondent; but all of us add daily transgression to transgression, which, I doubt not, Sir Philip will allow."

"Yes," said Hope archly, "it is far easier, as is said in one of your good books, Master Cradock, 'to subscribe to a sentence of universal condemnation, than to confess individual sins.'"

"What blessed times we have fallen on," retorted Sir Philip, "when youthful beauties, instead of listening to the idle songs of troubadours, or the fantastic flatteries of vagrant knights, or announcing with their ruby lips the rewards of chivalry, are exploring the mines of divinity with learned theologians like Master Cradock, and bringing forth such diamond sentences, as the pithy saying Miss Leslie has quoted."

"Heaven preserve us! Sir Philip," exclaimed Mrs. Grafton, "Hope Leslie study theology! you are as mad as a March hare —all her theology she has learned out of the Bible and common prayer-book, which should always go together, in spite of what the Governor says. It is peculiar that a man of his commodity of sense, should bamboozle himself with that story he told at breakfast. Oh, you was not there, Sir Philip—well, he says, that in his son's library, there are a thousand books, and among them, a Bible and prayerbook bound together—one jewel in the dunghill—but that is not what he says—it seems this unlucky prayerbook is gnawed to mince-meat by the mice, and not another book in the library touched.[2] I longed to commend the instinct of the little beasts, that knew what good food was; but every body listened with such a solemn air, and even you, Hope Leslie, who are never afraid to smile, even you, did not move your lips."

"I did not hear it," said Hope.

"Did not hear it! that is peculiar—why it was just when Robin was coming in with the rolls—just as I had taken my second cup—just as Everell gave Esther Downing that bunch of rosebuds; did you take notice of that?"

"Yes," replied Hope, and a deep blush suffused her cheek. She had noticed the offering with pain, not because her friend was preferred, but because it led her mind back to the time when she was the object of all Everell's little favors, and impressed her with a sense of his altered conduct.

The tell-tale blush did not escape the watchful eye of Sir Philip, and determined to ascertain if the "bolt of Cupid," had fallen on this "little western flower," he said, "I perceive Miss Leslie is aware that rose-buds, in the vocabulary of lovers, are made to signify a declaration of the tender passion."

Secret springs of the heart are sometimes suddenly touched, and feelings disclosed, that have been hidden even from our own self-observation. Hope had been moved by Miss Downing's story, and taking a generous interest in her happiness, she had, with that ardent feeling with which she pursued every object that interested her, resolved to promote it in the only mode by which it could be attained. But now, at the first intimation that her romantic wishes were to be fulfilled, strange to tell, and still stranger to her to feel, there was a sudden rising in her heart of disappointment—a sense of loss, and, we shrink from recording it, but the truth must be told, tears, honest tears, gushed from her eyes. Oh, pardon her, all ye youthful devotees to secret self-immolation!—all ye youthful Minervas, who hide with an impenetrable shield of wisdom and dignity, the natural workings of your hearts! Make all due allowance for a heroine of the seventeenth century, who had the misfortune to live before there was a system of education extant, who had not learned, like some young ladies of our enlightened days, to prattle of metaphysics —to quote Reid, and Stewart, and Brown,[3] and to know (full as well as they perhaps) the springs of human action—the mysteries of mind—still profound mysteries to the unlearned.

Hope Leslie was shocked, not that she had betrayed her feelings to her companions, but at her own discovery of their existence—not that they had appeared, but that they were. The change had been so gradual, from her childish fondness for Everell, to a more mature sentiment, as to be imperceptible even to herself. She made no essay to explain her emotion. Mrs. Grafton, though not remarkably sagacious, was aware of its obvious interpretation, and of the pressing necessity of offering some ingenious reading. "What a miserable nervous way you have fallen into, Hope," she said, "since you was caught out in that storm; she must have taken an inward cold, Sir Philip."

"The symptoms," replied the knight significantly, "would rather, I should think, indicate an internal heat."

"Heat or cold, Hope," continued Mrs. Grafton, "I am determined you shall go through a regular course of medicine; valerian tea in the morning, and lenitive drops at night. You have not eaten enough for the last week to keep a humming-bird alive. Hope has no kind of faith in medicine, Sir Philip, but I can tell her it is absolutely necessary, in the spring of the year, to sweeten the blood."

Sir Philip looked at Hope's glowing face, and said, "he thought such blood as mantled in Miss Leslie's cheek, needed no medical art to sweeten it."

Hope, alike insensible to the good natured efforts of her aunt, and the flatteries of Sir Philip, was mentally resolving to act most heroically; to expel every selfish feeling from her heart, and to live for the happiness of others.

The experienced smile sorrowfully at the generous impulses, and fearless resolves of the young, who know not how costly is the sacrifice of self-indulgence—how difficult the ascent to the heights of disinterestedness; but, let not the youthful aspirant be discouraged; the wing is strengthened by use, and the bird that drops in its first flutterings about the parent nest, may yet soar to the sky.

Our heroine had rallied her spirits, by the time she joined her companions in the boat that was awaiting them at the wharf; and in the effort to veil her feelings, she appeared to Everell extravagantly gay; and he, being unusually pensive, and seeing no cause for her apparent excitement, attributed it to Sir Philip's devotion—a cause that certainly had no tendency to render the effect agreeable to him.

When they disembarked, they proceeded immediately to the single habitation on the island—Digby's neat residence. The faithful fellow welcomed Everell with transports of joy. He had a thousand questions to ask, and recollections to recall; and while Everell lingered to listen, and Hope and Esther, from a very natural sympathy, to witness the overflowings of the good fellow's affectionate heart, their companions left them to stroll about the island.

As soon as his audience was thus reduced "it seems but a day," he said, "since you, Mr. Everell, and Miss Leslie, were but children."

"And happy children, Digby, were we not?" said Everell with a suppressed sigh, and venturing a side glance at Hope; but her face was averted, and he could not see whether Digby had awakened any recollections in her bosom responding to his own.

"Happy! that were you," replied Digby, "and the lovingest," he continued, little thinking that every word he uttered was as a talisman to his auditors; "the lovingest that ever I saw. Young folks for the most part, are like an April day, clouds and sunshine: there are my young ones, though they look so happy, now they have your English presents, Mr. Everell, yet they must now and then fall to their little battles; show out the natural man, as the ministers say; but with you and Miss Hope, it was always sunshine: it was not strange either, seeing you were all in all to one another, after that terrible sweep off at Bethel. It is odd what vagaries come and go in a body's mind; time was, when I viewed you as good as mated with Magawisca; forgive me for speaking so, Mr. Everell, seeing she was but a tawny Indian after all."

"Forgive you, Digby! you do me honour, by implying that I rightly estimated that noble creature; and before she had done the heroic deed, to which I owe my life—Yes, Digby, I might have loved her—might have forgotten that nature had put barriers between us."

"I don't know but you might, Mr. Everell, but I don't believe you would; things would naturally have taken another course after Miss Hope came among us; and many a time, I thought it was well it was as it was, for I believe it would have broken Magawisca's heart, to have been put in that kind of eclipse by Miss Leslie's coming between you and her. Now all is as it should be; as your mother—blessed be her memory—would have wished, and your father, and all the world."

Digby seemed to have arranged every thing in his own mind, according to what he deemed natural and proper; and too self-complacent at the moment, to receive any check to his garrulity, from the silence of his guests, he proceeded. "The tree follows the bent of the twig; what think you, Miss Esther, is not there a wedding a brewing?" Miss Downing was silent—Digby looked round and saw confusion in every face, and feeling that he had ventured on forbidden ground, he tried to stammer out an apology. "I declare now," he said, "it's odd—it's a sign I grow old; but I quite entirely forgot how queer young people feel about such things. I should not have blundered on so, but my wife put it into my head; she is equal to Nebuchadnezar for dreaming dreams; and three times last night she waked me to tell me about her dreaming of a funeral, and that, she said, was a sure forerunner of a wedding, and it was natural I should go on thinking whose wedding was coming—was not it, Miss Esther?"

Everell turned away to caress a chubby boy. Miss Downing fidgetted with her bonnet strings, threw back her shawl, and disclosed the memorable knot of rose-buds. If they had a meaning, they seemed also to have a voice, and they roused Hope Leslie's resolution. Some pride might have aided her, but it was maidenly pride, and her feelings were as near to pure generosity as our infirm nature can approach.

"Digby," she said, "it was quite natural for you both to think and speak of Mr. Everell's wedding; we are to have it, and that right soon, I hope; you have only mistaken the bride; and as neither of the parties will speak to set you right," and she glanced her eyes from Esther to Everell, "why, I must."

Esther became as pale as marble. Hope flew to her side, took her hand, placed it in Everell's, threw her arm around Esther, kissed her cheek, and darted out of the house. Digby half articulated an expression of disappointment and surprise, and impelled by an instinct that told him this was not a scene for witnesses, he too disappeared.

Never were two young people left in a more perplexing predicament. To Everell, it was a moment of indescribable confusion and embarrassment. To Esther, of overwhelming recollections, of apprehension, and hope, and above all, shame.

She would gladly have buried herself in the depths of the earth. Everell understood her feelings. There was no time for deliberation—and with emotions that would have made self-immolation at the moment easy, and impelled, as it seemed to him, by an irresistible destiny, he said something about the happiness of retaining the hand he held.

Miss Downing confused by her own feelings, misinterpreted his. She was, at the moment, incapable of estimating the disparity between his few, broken, disjointed, half-uttered words, and the natural, free, full expressions of an ardent and happy lover. She only spoke a few words, to refer him to her aunt Winthrop; but her hand, passive in his, her burning cheeks, and throbbing heart, told him what no third person could tell, and what her tongue could not utter.

Thus had Hope Leslie, by rashly following her first generous impulses, by giving to "an unproportioned thought its act," effected that, which the avowed tenderness of Miss Downing, the united instances of Mr. Fletcher and Governor Winthrop, and the whole colony and world beside, could never have achieved. Unconscious of the mistake by which she had put the happiness of all parties concerned in jeopardy, she was exulting in her victory over herself, and endeavouring to regain in solitude the tranquillity which she was surprised to find had utterly forsaken her; and to convince herself that the disorder of her spirits, which in spite of all her efforts, filled her eyes with tears, was owing to the agitating expectation of seing her long-lost sister.

The eastern extremity of the island being sheltered by the high ground on the west, was most favourable for horticultural experiments, and had, therefore been planted with fruit trees and grape vines; here Hope had retired, and was flattering herself she was secure from interruption and observation, when she was startled by a footstep, and perceived Sir Philip Gardiner approaching. "I am fortunate at last," he said. "I have just been vainly seeking you, where I most unluckily broke in upon the lovers, at a moment of supreme happiness, if I may judge from the faces of both parties; but what are you doing with that vine, Miss Leslie?" he continued, for Hope had stooped over a grape vine, which she seemed anxiously arranging.

"I am merely looking at it," she said; "it seems drooping."

"Yes—and droop and die it must. I am amazed that the wise people of your colony should hope to rear the vine in this cold and sterile land; a fit climate it is not for any delicate plant."

The knight's emphasis and look gave a particular significance to his words; but Miss Leslie, determined to take them only in their literal sense, coldly replied, "that it was not the part of wisdom to relinquish the attempt to cultivate so valuable a production, till a fair experiment had been made."

"Very true, Miss Leslie. The Governor himself could not have spoken it more sagely. Pardon me for smiling—I was thinking what an admirable illustration of your remark, your friend, Miss Downing, afforded you. Who would have hoped to rear such a hot-bed plant as love, amidst her frosts and ice? Nay, look not so reproachfully. I admit there are analogies in nature—in my rambles in the Alpine country, I have seen herbage and flowers fringing the very borders of perpetual snows."

"Your analogy does not suit the case, Sir Philip," replied Miss Leslie coldly, "but I marvel not at your ignorance of my friend; the waters gushed from the rock only at the prophet's touch"

—Hope hesitated; she felt that her rejoinder was too personal, and she added, in a tone of calmer defence, "surely she who has shown herself capable of the fervour of devotion, and the tenderness of friendship, may be susceptible of an inferior passion."

"Most certainly; and your philosophy, fair reasoner, agrees with experience and poetry. An old French lay well sets forth the harmony between the passions; thus it runs, I think"—and he trilled the following stanzas.

> *"Et pour verité vous record*
> *Dieu et amour sont d'un accord,*
> *Dieu aime sens et honorance,*
> *Amour ne l'a pas en viltance;*
> *Dieu hait orgueil et fausseté,*
> *Et Amour aime loyauté*
> *Dieu aime honneur et courtoisie*
> *Et bonne Amour ne hait-il mie;*
> *Dieu écoute belle prière*
> *Amour ne la met pas arrière."*

Sir Philip dropped on his knee, and, seizing Hope's hand, repeated,

> *"Dieu écoute belle prière*
> *Amour ne la met pas en arrière."*[4]

At this moment, when Hope stood stock still from surprise, confusion, and displeasure, Everell crossed the walk. The colour mounted to his cheeks and temples, he quickened his footsteps, and almost instantly disappeared. This apparition, instead of augmenting Miss Leslie's embarrassment, restored all her powers. "Reserve your gallantries, Sir Philip," she said, quietly withdrawing her hand, "and your profane verses for some subject to whom they are better suited; if you have aught of the spirit of a gentleman in you, you must feel that I have neither invited the one, nor provoked the other."

Sir Philip rose mortified and disconcerted, and suffered Miss Leslie to walk slowly away from him without uttering a word to urge or defend his suit. He would have been better pleased if he had excited more emotion of any sort; he thought he had never seen her, on any occasion, so calm and indifferent. He was piqued, as a man of gallantry, to be thus contemptuously repelled; and he was vexed with himself that by a false step, he had retarded, perhaps endangered, the final success of his projects. He had been too suddenly elated by the removal of his rival; he deemed his path quite clear; and with due allowance for natural presumption and self-love, it was not perhaps strange that an accomplished man of the world should, in Sir Philip's circumstances, have counted sanguinely on success.

He remained pulling a rose to pieces, as a sort of accompaniment to his vexed thoughts, when Mrs. Grafton made an untimely appearance before him. "Ah ha!" she said, picking up a bracelet Hope had unconsciously dropped, "I see who has been here—I thought so—but, Sir Philip, you look downcast." Sir Philip, accustomed as he was to masquerade, had not been able to veil his feelings even from the good dame, whose perceptions were neither quick nor keen; but what was defective in them, she made up in abundant good nature. "Now, Sir Philip," she said, "there is nothing but the wind so changeful as a woman's mind; that's what every body says, and there is both good and bad in it: for if the wind is dead ahead, we may look for it to turn."

Sir Philip bowed his assent to the truism, and secretly prayed that the good lady might be just in her application of it. Mrs. Grafton continued, "Now, what have you been doing with that rose, Sir Philip? one would think it had done you an ill turn, by your picking it to pieces; I hope you did not follow Everell's fashion; such a way of expressing one's ideas should be left to boys." Sir Philip most heartily wished that he had left his sentiments to be conveyed by so prudent and delicate an interpreter; but, determined to give no aid to Mrs. Grafton's conjectures, he threw away the rose-stem, and plucking another, presented it to her, saying, that 'he hoped she would not extend her proscription of the language of flowers so far as to prevent their expressing his regard for her.'

The good lady curtsied, and said, 'how much Sir Philip's ways did remind her of her dear deceased husband.'

The knight constrained himself to say, 'that he was highly flattered by being thus honourably associated in her thoughts.'

"And you may well be, Sir Philip," she replied, in the honesty of her heart, "for my poor dear Mr. Grafton was called the most elegant man of his time; and the best of husbands he proved: for, as Shakespeare says, he never let the winds of heaven visit me."⁵ She paused to wipe away a genuine tear, and then continued, "it was not for such a man to be disheartened because a woman seemed a little offish at first. Nil desperandum⁶ was his motto; and he, poor dear man, had so many rivals! Here, you know, the case is quite different. If any body were to fall in love with any body—I am only making a supposition, Sir Philip— there is nobody here but these stiff-starched puritans—a thousand pardons, Sir Philip—I forgot you was one of them. Indeed, you seem so little like them, that I am always forgetting it."

Sir Philip dared not trust Mrs. Grafton's discretion so far as to cast off his disguises before her, but he ventured to say that 'some of his brethren were over zealous.'

"Ay, ay, quite too zealous, aren't they? a kind of mint, anise, and cummin Christians."

Sir Philip smiled—'he hoped not to err in that particular; he must confess a leaning of the heart towards his old habits and feelings.'

"Quite natural; and I trust you will finally lean so far as to fall into them again—all in good time—but as I was saying— skittishness isn't a bad sign in a young woman. It was a long, long time before I gave poor dear Mr. Grafton the first token of favour; and what do you surmise that was, Sir Philip? Now just guess—it was a trick of fancy, really worth knowing."

Sir Philip was wearied beyond measure with the old lady's garrulity, but he said, with all the complaisance he could assume, 'that he could not guess—the ingenuity of a lady's favour baffled conjecture.'

"I thought you would not guess; well, I'll tell you. There's a little history to it, but, luckily, we've plenty of time on hand. Well, to begin at the beginning, you must know I had a fan—a French fan, I think it was—there were two cupids painted on it; and exactly in the middle, between them, a figure of hope—I don't mean Hope Leslie," she continued, for she saw the knight's eye suddenly glancing towards the head of the walk, past which Miss Leslie was just walking, in earnest conversation with Everell Fletcher.

Sir Philip felt the urgent necessity, at this juncture of affairs, of preventing, if possible, a confidential communication between Miss Leslie and Fletcher; and his face expressed unequivocally that he was no longer listening to Mrs. Grafton.

"Do you hear, Sir Philip," she continued, "I don't mean Hope Leslie."

"So I understand, Madam," replied the knight, keeping his face towards her, but receding rapidly in the direction Miss Leslie had passed, till almost beyond the sound of her voice, he laid his hand on his heart, bowed, and disappeared.

"Well, that is peculiar of Sir Philip," muttered the good lady; then suddenly turning to Cradock, who appeared, making his way through some snarled bushes—"What is the matter now, master Cradock?" she asked. Cradock replied by informing her that the tide served for their return to town, and that the Governor had made it his particular request that there might be no delay.

Mrs. Grafton's spirit was always refractory to orders from head-quarters; but she was too discreet or too timid for any overt act of disobedience, and she gave her arm to Cradock, and hastened to the appointed rendezvous.

When Sir Philip had emerged from the walk, he perceived the parties he pursued at no great distance from him, and was observed by Hope, who immediately, and manifestly to avoid him, motioned to Everell to take a path which diverged from that which led to the boat, to which they were now all summoned by a loud call from the boatmen.

We must leave the knight to digest his vexation, and follow our heroine, whose face could now claim nothing of the apathy that had mortified Sir Philip.

"You are then fixed in your determination to remain on the island to-night?" demanded Fletcher.

"Unalterably."

"And is Digby also to have the honour of Sir Philip's company?"

"Everell!" exclaimed Hope, in a tone that indicated surprise and wounded feeling.

"Pardon me, Miss Leslie."

"Miss Leslie again! Everell, you are unkind; you but this moment promised you would speak to me as you were wont to do."

"I would, Hope: my heart has but one language for you, but I dare not trust my lips. I may—I *must* now speak to you as a brother; and before we part, let me address a caution to you, which that sacred, and, thank God, permitted love, dictates. My own destiny is fixed—fixed by your act, Hope; heaven forgive me for saying so. It is done. For myself, I can endure any thing, but I could not live to see you the prey of a hollow-hearted adventurer." The truth flashed on Hope; she was beloved—she loved again—and she had rashly dashed away the happiness within her grasp. Her head became dizzy; she stopped, and gathering her veil over her face, she leaned against a tree for support. Everell grievously misunderstood her agitation.

"Hope," he said, with a faltering voice, "I have been slow to believe that you could thus throw away your heart. I tried to shut my eyes against that strange Saturday night's walk—that mysterious, unexplained assignation with a stranger—knowing, as I did, that his addresses had received the Governor's full approbation—my father's, my poor father's reluctant assent; I still trusted that your pure heart would have revolted from his flatteries. I believe he is a heartless hypocrite. I would have told you so, but I was too proud to have my warning attributed, even for a moment, to the meanness of a jealous rival. I have been accused of seeking you from"—interested motives, he would have added; but it seemed as if the words blistered his tongue, and he concluded, "it matters not now; now I may speak freely, without distrusting myself, or being distrusted by others. Hope, you have cast away my earthly happiness, trifle not with your own."

Hope perceived that events, conspiring with her own

thoughtless conduct, had rivetted Everell's mistake—but it was now irremediable. There was no middle path between a passive submission to her fate, and a full, and now useless explanation. She was aware that plighted friendship and troth were staked on the resolution of the moment; and when Everell added, "Oh, I have been convinced against my will—against my hopes —what visions of possible felicity have you dispersed—what dreams!"——

"Dreams—dreams all," she exclaimed, interrupting him, and throwing back her veil, she discovered her face drenched with tears. "Hark—they call you; let the past be forgotten; and for the future—the future, Everell—all possible felicity does await you, if you are true to yourself; true to—" her voice faltered, but she articulated, "Esther," and turning away, she escaped from his sight, as she would have rushed from the brink of a precipice.

"Oh!" thought Everell, as his eye and heart followed her, with the fervid feeling of love, "Oh, that one, who seems all angel, should have so much of woman's weakness!" while he lingered for a moment to subdue his emotion, and obtain a decent composure to fit him to appear before Esther, and less interested observers, Sir Philip joined him, apparently returning from the boat. "Your friends stay for you, sir," he said, and passed on.

"Then he does remain with her," concluded Everell; and the conviction was forced more strongly than ever on his mind, that Hope had lent a favourable ear to Sir Philip's suit. "The illusion must be transient," he thought; "vanity cannot have a lasting triumph over the noble sentiments of her pure heart." This was the language of his affection; but we must confess, that the ardor of his confidence was abated by Miss Leslie's apparently wide departure from delicate reserve, in permitting (as he believed she had) her professed admirer to remain on the island with her.

He now hastened to the boat, in the hope that he should hear some explanation of this extraordinary arrangement; but no such consolation awaited him. On the contrary, he found it the subject of speculation to the whole party. Faithful Cradock expressed simple amazement. Mrs. Grafton was divided between her pleasure in the probable success of her secret wishes, and her consciousness of the obvious impropriety of her niece's conduct, and her flurried and half articulated efforts at explanation, only served, like a feeble light, to make the darkness visible; and Esther's downcast and tearful eye intimated her concern and mortification for her friend.

CHAPTER V

"The sisters' vows, the hours that we have spent,
When we have chid the hasty-footed time
For parting us—Oh, and is all forgot?"
                    MIDSUMMER NIGHT'S DREAM[1]

On quitting Everell, our heroine, quite unconscious that she was
the subject of painful suspicion or affectionate anxiety, sought a
sequestered spot, where she might indulge and tranquilize her
feelings.

It has been said that the love of a brother and sister is the
only platonic affection. This truth, (if it be a truth) is the conviction of an experience far beyond our heroine's. She had seen
in Esther the pangs of repressed and unrequited love, and mistaking them for the characteristic emotions of that sentiment, it
was no wonder that she perceived no affinity to it, in the joyous
affection that had animated her own soul. "After a little while,"
she said, "I shall feel as I did when we lived together in Bethel;
if all that I love are happy, I must be happy too." If the cold
and selfish laugh to scorn what they think the reasoning of ignorance and inexperience, it is because they have never felt, that
to meditate the happiness of others, is to enter upon the ministry, and the joy of celestial spirits. Not one envious or repining
thought intruded into the heaven of Hope Leslie's mind. Not
one malignant spirit passed the bounds of that paradise, that was

filled with pure and tender affections, with projects of goodness, and all their cheerful train.

Hope was longer absorbed in her reverie than perhaps was quite consistent with her philosophy; and when she was roused from it by Digby's voice, she blushed from the consciousness that her thoughts had been too long withdrawn from the purpose of her visit to the island. Digby came to say that his wife's supper-table was awaiting Miss Leslie. Hope embraced the opportunity, as they walked together towards his dwelling, to make her arrangements for the evening. "Digby," she said, "I have something to confide to you, but you must ask me no questions."

"That's crossing human nature," replied the good fellow; "but I think I can swim against the current for you, Miss Hope."

"Thank you, Digby. Then, in the first place, you must know, I expect some friends to meet me here this evening; all that I ask of you is, to permit me to remain out unmolested as long as I may choose. You may tell your wife that I like to stroll in the garden by moonlight—or to sit and listen to the waves breaking on the shore—as you know I do, Digby."

"Yes, Miss Hope, I know your heart always linked into such things; but it will be heathen Greek to my wife—so you must make out a better reason for her."

"Then tell her, that I like to have my own way."

"Ah, that will I," replied Digby chuckling, "that is what every woman can understand. I always said, Miss Hope, it was a pure mercy you chose the right way, for you always had yours."

"Perhaps you think, Digby, I have been too headstrong in my own way."

"Oh, no! my sweet mistress—no—why this having our own way, is what every body likes; it's the privilege we came to this wilderness world for; and though the gentles up in town there, with the Governor at their head, hold a pretty tight rein, yet I can tell them, that there are many who think what blunt Master Blackstone said, 'that he came not away from the Lords-bishops, to put himself under the Lord's-brethren.' No, no, Miss Hope, I watch the motions of the straws—I know which way the wind blows. Thought and will are set free. It was but the other day, so to speak, in the days of good queen Bess, as they called her, when, if her majesty did but raise her hand, the parliament folks were all down on their knees to her; and now, thank God, the poorest and the lowest of us only kneel to Him who made us. Times are changed—there is a new spirit in the world—chains are broken—fetters are knocked off—and the liberty set forth in the blessed word, is now felt to be every man's birth-right. But shame on my prating tongue, that wags so fast when I might hear your nightingale voice."

Hope's mind was pre-occupied, and she found it difficult to listen to Digby's speculations with interest, or to respond with animation; but she was too benignant to lose herself in sullen abstraction, and when they arrived at the cottage, she roused her faculties to amuse the children, and to listen to the mother's stories of their ominous smartness. She commended the good wife's milk and cakes, and sat for an half hour after the table was removed, talking of the past, and brightening the future prospects of her good friends, with predictions of their children's prosperity and respectability—predictions, which, Digby afterwards said, the sweet young lady's bounty brought to pass.

Suddenly she sprang from her chair—"Digby," she exclaimed, "I think the east is lighting up with the rising moon—is it not?"

"If it is not, it soon will," replied Digby, understanding and favouring her purpose.

"Then," said Hope, "I will take a walk round the island, and do not you, Betsy, sit up for me." Betsy, of course, remonstrated. The night air was unwholesome; and though the sky overhead was clear, yet she had heard distant thunder; the beach birds had been in flocks on shore all the day; and the breakers on the east side of the island made a boding sound. These, and other signs, were urged as arguments against the unseasonable walk. Of course they were unheeded by our heroine, who, declaring that with shelter so near she was in no danger, muffled herself in her cloak, and sallied forth. She bent her steps around the cliff which rises at the western extremity of the island, leaving at its base a few yards of flat rocky shore, around which the

waters of the bay sweep, deeply indenting it, and forming a natural cove or harbour for small boats. As Hope passed around a
ledge of rocks, she fancied she saw a shadow cast by a figure
that seemed flying before her. "They are here already," she
thought, and hastened forward, expecting to catch a glimpse of
them as soon as she should turn the angle of the rock—but no
figure appeared; and though Hope imagined she heard stones
rattling, as if displaced by hurried steps, she was soon convinced
the sound was accidental. Alive only to one expectation, she
seated herself, without any apprehension, to await in this solitude the coming of her sister.

The moon rose unclouded, and sent her broad stream of light
across the beautiful bay, kindling in her beams the islands that
gemmed it, and disclosing, with a dim indefinite light, the distant
town rising over this fair domain of sea and land—hills, heights,
jutting points, and islands, then unknown to fame, but now consecrated in domestic annals, and illustrious in the patriot's story.

Whatever charms the scene might have presented to our heroine's eye at another moment, she was now only conscious of
one emotion of feverish impatience. She gazed and listened till
her senses ached; and at last, when anticipation had nearly
yielded to despair, her ear caught the dash of oars; and at the
next moment, a canoe glanced around the headland into the cove;
she darted to the brink of the water—she gazed intently on the
little bark—her whole soul was in that look. Her sister was
there. At this first assurance, that she really beheld this loved,
lost sister, Hope uttered a scream of joy; but when, at a second
glance, she saw her in her savage attire, fondly leaning on Oneco's shoulder, her heart died within her; a sickening feeling came
over her, an unthought of revolting of nature; and instead of
obeying the first impulse, and springing forward to clasp her in
her arms, she retreated to the cliff, leaned her head against it,
averted her eyes, and pressed her hands on her heart, as if she
would have bound down her rebel feelings.

Magawisca's voice aroused her. "Hope Leslie," she said, "take
thy sister's hand."

Hope stretched out her hand, without lifting her eyes; but
when she felt her sister's touch, the energies of nature awoke,

she threw her arms around her, folded her to her bosom, laid her cheek on hers, and wept as if her heart would burst in every sob.

Mary (we use the appellative by which Hope had known her sister,) remained passive in her arms. Her eye was moistened, but she seemed rather abashed and confounded, than excited; and when Hope released her, she turned towards Oneco with a look of simple wonder. Hope again threw her arm around her sister, and intently explored her face for some trace of those infantine features that were impressed on her memory. "It is— it is my sister!" she exclaimed, and kissed her cheek again and again. "Oh! Mary, do you not remember when we sat together on mother's knee? Do you not remember, when with her own burning hand, the very day she died, she put those chains on our necks? Do you not remember when they held us up to kiss her cold lips?" Mary looked towards Magawisca for an explanation of her sister's words. "Look at *me*, Mary—speak to *me*," continued Hope.

"No speak Yengees," replied Mary, exhausting in this brief sentence, all the English she could command.

Hope, in the impetuosity of her feelings, had forgotten that Magawisca had forewarned her not to indulge the expectation that her sister could speak to her; and the melancholy truth, announced by her own lips, seemed to Hope to open a new and impassable gulf between them. She wrung her hands; "Oh what shall I do! what shall I say?" she exclaimed.

Magawisca now advanced to her, and said in a compassionate tone, "Let me be thy interpreter, Hope Leslie; and be thou more calm. Dost thou not see thy sister is to thee as the feather borne on the torrent?"

"I will be more calm, Magawisca; but promise me you will interpret truly for me."

A blush of offended pride overspread Magawisca's cheek. "We hold truth to be the health of the soul," she said: "thou mayest speak, maiden, without fear that I will abate one of thy words."

"Oh, I fear nothing wrong from you, Magawisca—forgive me—forgive me—I know not what I say or do." She drew her sister to a rock, and they sat down together. Hope knew not how to address one so near to her by nature, so far removed by habit and education. She thought that if Mary's dress, which was singularly and gaudily decorated, had a less savage aspect, she might look more natural to her; and she signed to her to remove the mantle she wore, made of birds' feathers, woven together with threads of the wild nettle. Mary threw it aside, and disclosed her person, light and agile as a fawn's, clothed with skins, neatly fitted to her waist and arms, and ambitiously embellished with bead work. The removal of the mantle, instead of the effect designed, only served to make more striking the aboriginal peculiarities; and Hope, shuddering and heart-sick, made one more effort to disguise them by taking off her silk cloak and wrapping it close around her sister. Mary seemed instantly to comprehend the language of the action, she shook her head, gently disengaged herself from the cloak, and resumed her mantle. An involuntary exclamation of triumph burst from Oneco's lips. "Oh tell her," said Hope to Magawisca, "that I want once more to see her in the dress of her own people—of her own family—from whose arms she was torn to be dragged into captivity."

A faint smile curled Magawisca's lip, but she interpreted faithfully Hope's communication, and Mary's reply, " 'she does not like the English dress,' she says."

"Ask her," said Hope, "if she remembers the day when the wild Indians sprung upon the family at Bethel, like wolves upon a fold of lambs?—If she remembers when Mrs. Fletcher and her innocent little ones were murdered, and she stolen away?"

"She says, 'she remembers it well, for then it was Oneco saved her life.' "

Hope groaned aloud. "Ask her," she continued with unabated eagerness, "if she remembers when we played together, and read together, and knelt together at our mother's feet; when she told us of the God that made us, and the Saviour that redeemed us?"

"She remembers something of all this, but she says, 'it is faint and distant, like the vanishing vapour on the far-off mountain.' "

"Oh, tell her, Magawisca, if she will come home and live with me, I will devote my life to her. I will watch over her in sickness and health. I will be mother; sister, friend to her—tell her, that our mother, now a saint in heaven, stoops from her happy place to entreat her to return to our God, and our father's God."

Mary shook her head in a manner indicative of a more determined feeling than she had before manifested, and took from her bosom a crucifix, which she fervently pressed to her lips.

Every motive Hope offered was powerless, every mode of entreaty useless, and she leaned her head despondently on Mary's shoulder. The contrast between the two faces thus brought together, was most striking. Hope's hat had slipped back, and her rich brown tresses fell about her neck and face; her full eye was intently fixed on Mary, and her cheek glowing with impassioned feeling. She looked like an angel touched with some mortal misery; while Mary's face, pale and spiritless, was only redeemed from absolute vacancy by an expression of gentleness and modesty. Hope's hand was lying on her sister's lap, and a brilliant diamond ring caught Mary's attention. Hope perceived this, and instantly drew it from her own finger and placed it on Mary's; "and here is another—and another—and another," she cried, making the same transfer of all her rings. "Tell her, Magawisca, if she will come home with me, she shall be decked with jewels from head to foot, she shall have feathers from the most beautiful birds that wing the air, and flowers that never fade—tell her that all I possess shall be hers."

"Shall I tell her so?" asked Magawisca, with a mingled expression of contempt and concern, as if she herself despised the lure, but feared that Mary might be caught by it, for the pleased girl was holding her hand before her, turning it, and gazing with child-like delight on the gems, as they caught and reflected the moon-beams. "Shall I ask your sister to barter truth and love, the jewels of the soul, that grow brighter and brighter in the land of spirits, for these poor perishing trifles?—Oh, Hope Leslie, I had better thoughts of thee."

"I cannot help it, Magawisca; I am driven to try every way to win back my sister—tell her, I entreat you, tell her what I have said."

Magawisca faithfully repeated all the motives Hope had urged, while Hope herself clasped her sister's hand, and looked in her face with a mute supplication, more earnest than words could express. Mary hesitated, and her eye turned quickly to Oneco, to Magawisca, and then again rested on her sister. Hope felt her hand tremble in hers. Mary, for the first time, bent towards her, and laid her cheek to Hope's. Hope uttered a scream of delight, "Oh, she does not refuse, she will stay with me," she exclaimed. Mary understood the exclamation, and suddenly recoiled, and hastily drew the rings from her fingers. "Keep them—keep them," said Hope, bursting into tears, if "we must be cruelly parted again, they will sometimes speak to you of me."

At this moment, a bright light as of burning flax, flamed up from the cliff above them, threw a momentary flash over the water, and then disappeared. Oneco rose, "I like not this light," he said, "we must begone, we have redeemed our promise," and he took Hope's cloak from the ground, and gave it to her as a signal that the moment of separation had arrived.

"Oh, stay one moment longer," cried Hope. Oneco pointed to the heavens, over which black and threatening clouds were rapidly gathering, and Magawisca said, "do not ask us to delay, my father has waited long enough." Hope now for the first time observed there was an Indian in the canoe, wrapped in skins, and listlessly waiting in a recumbent position the termination of the scene. "Is that Mononotto?" said she, shuddering at the thought of the bloody scenes with which he was associated in her mind; but before her inquiry was answered, the subject of it sprang to his feet, and uttering an exclamation of surprise, stretched his hand towards the town. All at once perceived the object towards which he pointed. A bright strong light streamed upward from the highest point of land, and sent a ruddy glow over the bay. Every eye turned inquiringly to Hope. "It is nothing," she said to Magawisca, "but the light that is often kindled on Beacon-Hill to guide the ships into the harbour. The night is becoming dark, and some vessel is expected in—that is all, believe me."

Whatever trust her visitors might have reposed in Hope's good faith, they were evidently alarmed by an appearance which they did not think sufficiently accounted for; and Oneco hearing, or imagining he heard, approaching oars, said in his own language to Magawisca, "we have no time to lose—I will not permit my white bird to remain any longer within reach of the net."

Magawisca assented: "We must go," she said; "we must not longer hazard our father's life." Oneco sprang into the canoe, and called to Mary to follow him.

"Oh, spare her one single moment!" said Hope, imploringly to Magawisca, and she drew her a few paces from the shore, and knelt down with her, and in a half articulate prayer, expressed the tenderness and sorrow of her soul, and committed her sister to God. Mary understood her action, and feeling that their separation was for ever, nature for a moment asserted her rights; she returned Hope's embrace, and wept on her bosom.

While the sisters were thus folded in one another's arms, a loud yell burst from the savages; Magawisca caught Mary by the arms, and Hope turning, perceived that a boat filled with armed men, had passed the projecting point of land, and borne in by the tide, it instantly touched the beach, and in another instant Magawisca and Mary were prisoners. Hope saw the men were in the uniform of the Governor's guard. One moment before she would have given worlds to have had her sister in her power; but now, the first impulse of her generous spirit, was an abhorrence of her seeming treachery to her friends. "Oh, Oneco," she cried, springing towards the canoe, "I did not—indeed I did not know of it." She had scarcely uttered the words, which fell from her neither understood nor heeded, when Oneco caught her in his arms, and shouting to Magawisca to tell the English, that as they dealt by Mary, so would he deal by her sister; he gave the canoe the first impulse, and it shot out like an arrow, distancing and defying pursuit.

Oneco's coup-de-main seemed to petrify all present. They were roused by Sir Philip Gardiner, who, coming round the base of the cliff, appeared among them; and learning the cause of their amazement, he ordered them, with a burst of passionate exclamation, instantly to man the boat, and proceed with him in pursuit. This, one and all refused. "Daylight, and calm water," they said, "would be necessary to give any hope to such a pursuit, and the storm was now gathering so fast, as to render it dangerous to venture out at all."

Sir Philip endeavoured to alarm them with threats of the Governor's displeasure, and to persuade them with offers of high reward; but they understood too well the danger and hopelessness of the attempt to risk it, and they remained inexorable. Sir Philip then went in quest of Digby, and at the distance of a few paces met him. Alarmed by the rapid approach of the storm, he was seeking Miss Leslie; when he learned her fate from Sir Philip's hurried communication, he uttered a cry of despair. "Oh! I would go after her," he said, "if I had but a cockle shell; but it seems as if the foul fiends were at work: my boat was this morning sent to town to be repaired. And yet what could we do?" He added, shuddering, "the wind is rising to that degree, that I think no boat could live in the bay; and it is getting as dark as Egypt—Oh, God save my precious young lady!—God have mercy on her!" he continued. A sudden burst of thunder heightened his alarm—"man can do nothing for her. Why in the name of heaven," he added, with a natural desire to appropriate the blame of misfortune, "why must they be for ever meddling; why not let the sisters meet and part in peace?"

'Oh! why not?' thought Sir Philip, who would have given his right hand to have retraced the steps that had led to this most unlooked for and unhappy issue of the affair. They were now joined by the guard with their prisoners. Digby was requested to lead them instantly to a shelter. He did so; and, agitated as he was with fear and despair for Miss Leslie, he did not fail to greet Magawisca, as one to whom all honour was due. She heeded him not—she seemed scarcely conscious of the cries of Faith Leslie, who was weeping like a child, and clinging to her. The treachery that had betrayed her wrapt her soul in indignation, and nothing roused her but the blasts of wind and flashes of lightning, that seemed to her the death-knell of her father.

The storm continued for the space of an hour, and then died away as suddenly as it had gathered. In another hour, the guard had safely landed at the wharf, and were conveying their prisoners to the Governor. He, and his confidential counsellors, who had been awaiting at his house, the return of their emissaries, solaced themselves with the belief that all parties were safely sheltered on the island; and probably would remain there during the night. While they were whispering this conclusion to one another, at one extremity of the parlour, Everell sat beside Miss Downing, in the recess of a window, that overlooked the garden. The huge projecting chimney formed a convenient screen for the lovers. The evening was warm—the window-sash thrown up. The moon had come forth, and shed a mild lustre through the dewy atmosphere; the very light that the young and senti-mental—and above all, young and sentimental lovers, most delight in. But in vain did Everell look abroad for inspiration; in vain did he turn his eyes to Esther's face, now more beautiful than ever, flushed as it was with the first dawn of happiness; in vain did he try to recall his truant thoughts, to answer words to her timid but bright glances; he would not—he could not say what he did not feel; and the few sentences he uttered fell on his own ear like the cold abstractions of philosophy. While he was in this durance his father was listening—if a man stretched on a rack can be said to listen—to Madam Winthrop's whispered and reiterated assurances of her entire approbation of her niece's choice.

This was the position of all parties, when a bustle was heard in the court, and the guard entered. The foremost advanced to the Governor and communicated a few sentences in a low tone. The Governor manifested unusual emotion, turned round sud-denly, and exclaimed, "here, Mr. Fletcher—Everell;" and then motioning to them to keep their places, he said in an under voice to those near to him, "we must first dispose of our prisoner—come forward, Magawisca."

"Magawisca!" echoed Everell, springing at one bound into the hall. But Magawisca shrunk back, and averted her face. "Now God be praised!" he exclaimed, as he caught the first glance of a form never to be forgotten—"it is—it is Magawisca!" She did not speak, but drew away, and leaned her head against the wall. "What means this?" he said, now for the first time espying Faith Leslie, and then looking round on the guard, "what means it, sir?" he demanded, turning somewhat imperiously to the Gov-ernor.

"It means, sir," replied the Governor coldly, "that this Indian woman is the prisoner of the Commonwealth."

"It means that I am a prisoner, lured to the net, and betrayed."

"You a prisoner—here, Magawisca!" Everell exclaimed—"impossible; justice, gratitude, humanity, forbid it. My father—Governor Winthrop, you will not surely suffer this outrage."

The elder Fletcher had advanced, and scarcely less perplexed and agitated than his son, was endeavouring to draw forth Faith Leslie, who had shrunk behind Magawisca. Governor Winthrop seemed not at all pleased with Everell's interference. "You will do well, young Mr. Fletcher, to bridle your zeal; private feelings must yield to the public good; this young woman is suspected of being an active agent in brewing the conspiracy forming against us among the Indian tribes; and it is somewhat bold in you to oppose the course of justice—to intermeddle with the public welfare—to lift your feeble judgment against the wisdom of Providence, which has led by peculiar means, to the apprehension of the enemy. Conduct your prisoner to the jail," he added, turning to the guard; "and bid Barnaby have her in close and safe keeping, till further orders."

"For the love of God, sir," cried Everell, "do not this injustice. At least suffer her to remain in your own house, on her promise—more secure than the walls of a prison." Governor Winthrop only replied by signing to the guards to proceed to their duty.

"Stay one moment," exclaimed Everell; "permit her, I beseech you, to remain here; place her in any one of your apartments, and I will remain before it, a faithful warder, night and day. But do not—do not, I beseech you, sully our honour by committing this noble creature to your jail."

"Listen to my son, I entreat you," said the elder Fletcher, unable any longer to restrain his own feelings—"certainly we owe much to this woman."

"You owe much, undoubtedly," replied the Governor, "but it yet remains to be proved, my friend, that your son's redeemed life is to be put in the balance against the public weal."

Esther, who had observed the scene with an intense interest, now overcame her timidity so far, as to penetrate the circle that surrounded the Governor, and to attempt to enforce Everell's prayer. "May not Magawisca," she said, "share our apartment, Hope's and mine; she will then, in safe custody await your further pleasure."

"Thanks, Esther—thanks," cried Everell, with an animation that would have rewarded a far more difficult effort; but all efforts were unavailing; but not useless, for Magawisca said to Everell, "you have sent light into my darkened soul—you have truth, and gratitude, and for the rest, they are but what I deemed them. Send me," she continued, proudly turning to the Governor, "to your dungeon—all places are alike to me, while I am your prisoner; but for the sake of Everell Fletcher, let me tell you, that she, who is dearer to him than his own soul, if indeed she has lived out the perils of this night, must answer for my safe keeping."

"Hope Leslie!" exclaimed Everell; "what has happened—what do you mean, Magawisca?"

"She was the decoy bird," replied Magawisca calmly; "and she too is caught in the net."

"Explain, I beseech you!" The Governor answered Everell's appeal by a brief explanation. A bustle ensued—every other feeling was now lost in concern for Hope Leslie; and Magawisca was separated from her weeping and frightened companion, and conducted away without further opposition; while the two Fletchers, as if life and death hung on every instant, were calling on the Governor to aid them in the way and means of pursuit. But as we hope our readers sympathise in their apprehensions, we must leave them to return to our heroine.

CHAPTER VI

"But, oh, that hapless virgin, our lost sister,
Where may she wander now, whither betake her?"
                                                    COMUS[1]

Hope Leslie, on being forced into the canoe, sunk down, over-powered with terror and despair. She was roused from this state by Oneco's loud and vehement appeals to his father, who only replied by a low inarticulate murmur, which seemed rather an involuntary emission of his own feelings, than a response to Oneco. She understood nothing but the name of Magawisca, which he often repeated, and always with a burst of vindictive feeling, as if every other emotion were lost in wrath at the treachery that had wrested her from him. As the apparent contriver, and active agent in this plot, Hope felt that she must be the object of detestation, and the victim of vengeance; and all that she had heard or imagined of Indian cruelties, was present to her imagination; and every savage passion seemed to her to be embodied in the figure of the old chief, when she saw his convulsed frame and features, illuminated by the fearful lightning that flashed athwart him. "It is possible," she thought, "that Oneco may understand me;" and to him she protested her innocence, and vehemently besought his compassion. Oneco was not of a cruel nature, nor was he disposed to inflict unnecessary suffering on the sister of his wife; but he was determined to retain so valuable a hostage, and his heart was steeled against her, by his conviction that she had been a party to the wrong done him; he, therefore, turned a deaf ear to her entreaties, which her supplicating voice and gestures rendered intelligible, though he had nearly forgotten her language. He made no reply by word or sign, but continued to urge on his little bark with all his might, redoubling his vigorous strokes as the fury of the storm increased.

Hope cast a despairing eye on her receding home, which she could still mark through the mirky atmosphere, by the lurid flame that blazed on Beacon-hill. Friends were on every side of her, and yet no human help could reach her. She saw the faint light that gleamed from Digby's cottage-window, and on the other hand, the dim ray that, struggling through the misty atmosphere, proceeded from the watch-tower on Castle-Island. Between these lights from opposite islands, she was passing down the channel, and she inferred that Oneco's design was to escape out of the harbour. But heaven seemed determined to frustrate his purpose, and to show her how idle were all human hopes and fears, how vain "to cast the fashion of uncertain evils."

The wind rose, and the darkness deepened at every moment; the occasional flashes of lightning only serving to make it more intense. Oneco tasked his skill to the utmost to guide the canoe; he strained every nerve, till exhausted by useless efforts, he dropped his oars, and awaited his resistless fate. The sublime powers of nature had no terrors for Mononotto. There was something awe-striking in the fixed, unyielding attitude of the old man, who sat as if he were carved in stone, whilst the blasts swept by him, and the lightnings played over him. There are few who have not at some period of their lives, lost their consciousness of individuality—their sense of this shrinking, tremulous, sensitive being, in the dread magnificence—the "holy mystery" of nature.

Hope, even in her present extremity, forgot her fear and danger in the sublimity of the storm. When the wild flashes wrapped the bay in light, and revealed to sight the little bark leaping over the "yesty waves," the stern figure of the old man, the graceful

form of Oneco, and Hope Leslie, her eye upraised, with an instinctive exaltation of feeling, she might have been taken for
some bright vision from another sphere, sent to conduct her dark
companions through the last tempestuous passage of life. But the
triumphs of her spirit were transient; mortal danger pressed on
life. A thunderbolt burst over their heads. Hope was, for a moment, stunned. The next flash showed the old man struck down
senseless. Oneco shrieked—raised the lifeless body in his arms,
laid his ear to the still bosom, and chafed the breast and limbs.
While he was thus striving to bring back life, the storm abated
—the moon-beams struggled through the parting clouds, and the
canoe, driven at the mercy of the wind and tide, neared a little
island, and drifted on to the beach. Oneco leaped out, dragged
his father's lifeless body to the turf, and renewed and redoubled
his efforts to restore him; and Hope, moved by an involuntary
sympathy with the distress of his child, stooped down and
chafed the old man's palms. Either from despair, or an impulse
of awakened hope, Oneco suddenly uttered an exclamation,
stretched himself on the body, and locked his arms around it.
Hope rose to her feet, and seeing Mononotto unconscious, and
Oneco entirely absorbed in his own painful anxieties and efforts,
the thought occurred to her, that she might escape from her
captors.

    She looked at the little bark: her strength, small as it was,
might avail to launch it again; and she might trust the same Providence that had just delivered her from peril, to guide her in
safety over the still turbulent waters. But a danger just escaped,
is more fearful than one untried; and she shrunk from adven-
turing alone on the powerful element. The island might be inhabited. If she could gain a few moments before she was missed
by Oneco, it was possible she might find protection and safety.
She did not stop to deliberate; but casting one glance at the
brightening heavens, and ejaculating a prayer for aid, and ascertaining by one look at Oneco that he did not observe her, she
bounded away. She fancied she heard steps pursuing her; but
she pressed on without once looking back, or faltering, till she
reached a slight elevation, whence she perceived, at no great distance from her, a light placed on the ground; and on approaching

a little nearer, she saw a man lying beside it; and at a few paces from him several others stretched on the grass, and, as she thought, sleeping. She now advanced cautiously and timidly, till she was near enough to conclude that they were a company of sailors, who had been indulging in a lawless revel. Such, in truth, they were; the crew belonging to the vessel of the notorious Chaddock.[2] The disorders of both master, and men, had given such offence to the sober citizens of Boston, that they had been prohibited from entering the town; and the men having been on this occasion allowed by their captain to indulge in a revel on land, they had betaken themselves to an uninhabited island, where they might give the reins to their excesses, without dread of restraint or penalty. As they now appeared to the eye of our heroine, they formed a group from which a painter might have sketched the triumphs of Bacchus.

Fragments of a coarse feast were strewn about them, and the ground was covered with wrecks of jugs, bottles, and mugs. Some of them had thrown off their coats and neck-cloths in the heat of the day, and had lain with their throats and bosoms bared to the storm, of which they had been unconscious. Others, probably less inebriated, had been disturbed by the vivid flashes of lightning, and had turned their faces to the earth. While Hope shuddered at the sight of these brutalized wretches, and thought any fate would be better than

> "To meet the rudeness and swilled insolence
> Of such late wassailers."

One of them awoke, and looked up at her. He had but imperfectly recovered his senses, and he perceived her but faintly and indistinctly, as one sees an object through mist. Hope stood near him, but she stood perfectly still; for she knew from his imbecile smile, and half articulated words, that she had nothing to fear. He laid his hand on the border of her cloak, and muttered, "St. George's colours—Dutch flag—no, d—n me, Hanse, I say—St. George's—St. George's—nail them to the mast head—I say, Hanse, St. George's—St. George's"—and then his words died

away on his tongue, and he laughed in his throat, as one laughs
in sleep.

While Hope hesitated for an instant, whether again to expose
herself to the thraldom from which she had with such joy escaped, one of the other men, either aroused by his comrade's
voice, or having outslept the fumes of the liquor, started up, and,
on perceiving her, rubbed his eyes, and stared as if he doubted
whether she were a vision of his sleep or a reality. Hope's first
impulse was to fly; but, though confused and alarmed, she was
aware that escape would be impossible if he chose to pursue, and
that her only alternative was to solicit his compassion.

"Friend," she said, in a fearful, tremulous voice, "I come to
beg your aid."

"By the lord Harry, she speaks," exclaimed the fellow, interrupting her—"she is a woman—wake boys—wake!"

The men were now roused from their slumbers: some rose to
their feet, and all stared stupidly, not one, save him first awakened, having the perfect command of his senses. "If ye have the
soul of a man," said Hope imploringly, "protect me—convey
me to Boston. Any reward that you will ask or take shall be
given to you."

"There's no reward could pay for you, honey," replied the
fellow, advancing towards her.

"In the name of God, hear me!" she cried: but the man continued to approach with a horrid leer on his face. "Then save
me, heaven!" she screamed, and rushed towards the water. The
wretch was daunted; he paused but for an instant, then calling
on his comrades to join him, they all, hooting and shouting,
pursued her.

Hope now felt that death was her only deliverance; if she
could but reach the waves that she saw heaving and breaking on
the shore—if she could but bury herself beneath them. But
though she flew as if she were borne on the wings of the wind,
her pursuers gained on her. The foremost was so near, that she
expected at every breath his hand would grasp her, when his
foot stumbled, and he fell headlong, and as he fell, he snatched
her cloak. By a desperate effort she extricated herself from his
hold, and again darted forward. She heard him vociferate curses,

and understood he was unable to rise. She cast one fearful glance behind her—she had gained on the horrid crew. 'Oh! I may escape them,' she thought; and she pressed on with as much eagerness to cast away life, as ever was felt to save it. As she drew near the water's edge, she perceived a boat attached to an upright post that had been driven into the earth at the extremity of a narrow stone pier. A thought like inspiration flashed into her mind: she ran to the end of the pier, leaped into the boat, uncoiled the rope that attached it to the post, and seizing an oar, pushed it off. There was a strong tide; and the boat, as if instinct with life, and obedient to her necessities, floated rapidly from the shore. Her pursuers had now reached the water's edge, and finding themselves foiled, some vented their spite in jeers and hoarse laughs, and others in loud and bitter curses. Hope felt that heaven had interposed for her, and sinking on her knees, she clasped her hands, and breathed forth her soul in fervent thanksgivings. Whilst she was thus absorbed, a man, who had been lying in the bottom of the boat, unobserved by her, and covered by various outer garments, which he had so disposed as to shelter himself from the storm, lifted up his head, and looked at her with mute amazement. He was an Italian, and belonged to the same ship's company with the revellers on the shore; but not inclining to their excesses, and thinking, on the approach of the storm, that some judgment was about to overtake them, he had returned to the boat, and sheltered himself there as well as he was able. When the tempest abated, he had fallen asleep, his imagination probably in an excited state; and on awaking, and seeing Hope in an attitude of devotion, he very naturally mistook her for a celestial visitant. In truth, she scarcely looked like a being of this earth: her hat and gloves were gone; her hair fell in graceful disorder about her neck and shoulders, and her white dress and blue silk mantle had a saint-like simplicity. The agitating chances of the evening had scarcely left the hue of life on her cheek; and her deep sense of the presence and favour of heaven heightened her natural beauty with a touch of religious inspiration.

"Hail, blessed virgin Mary!" cried the catholic Italian, bending low before her, and crossing himself: "Queen of heaven!—

Gate of paradise!—and Lady of the world!—O most clement!
—most pious! and most sweet virgin Mary! bless thy sinful servant." He spoke in his native tongue, of which Hope fortunately
knew enough to comprehend him, and to frame a phrase in return. The earnestness of his countenance was a sure pledge of
his sincerity; and Hope was half inclined to turn his superstition
to her own advantage; but his devotion approached so near to
worship, that she dared not; and she said, with the intention of
dissipating his illusion, "I am not, my friend, what you imagine
me to be."

"Thou art not, thou art not, holy queen of virgins, and of all
heavenly citizens—then most gracious lady, which of all the
martyrs and saints of our holy church art thou? Santa Catharina
of Siena, the blessed bride of a holy marriage?" Hope shook her
head. "Santa Helena then, in whose church I was first signed
with holy water? nay, thou art not?—then art thou, Santa Bi-
biani? or Santa Rosa? thy beauteous hair is like that sacred lock
over the altar of Santa Croce."

"I am not any of these," said Hope with a smile, which the
catholic's pious zeal extorted from her.

"Thou smilest!" he cried exultingly; "thou art then my own
peculiar saint—the blessed lady Petronilla. Oh, holy martyr!
spotless mirror of purity!" and he again knelt at her feet and
crossed himself. "My life! my sweetness! and my hope! to thee
do I cry, a poor banished son of Eve—what wouldst thou have
thy dedicated servant, Antonio Batista, to do, that thou hast, oh,
glorious lady! followed him from our own sweet Italy to this
land of heathen savages and heretic English?"

This invocation was long enough to allow our heroine time
to make up her mind as to the course she should pursue with
her votary. She had recoiled from the impiety of appropriating
his address to the holy mother, but protestant as she was, we
hope she may be pardoned for thinking that she might without
presumption, identify herself with a catholic saint. "Good Antonio," she said, "I am well pleased to find thee faithful, as thou
hast proved thyself, by withdrawing from thy vile comrades. To
take part in their excesses would but endanger thine eternal
welfare—bear this in mind. Now, honest Antonio, I will put

honour on thee; thou shalt do me good service. Take those oars and ply them well till we reach yon town, where I have an errand that must be done."

"Oh, most blessed lady! sacred martyr, and sister of mercy! who, entering into the heavenly palace, didst fill the holy angels with joy, and men with hope, I obey thee," he said, and then taking from his bosom a small ivory box, in which, on opening it, there appeared to be a shred of linen cloth, he added, "but first, most gracious lady, vouchsafe to bless this holy relic, taken from the linen in which thy body was enfolded, when, after it had lain a thousand years in the grave, it was raised therefrom fresh and beautiful, as it now appeareth to me."

Our saint could not forbear a smile at this startling fact in her history, but she prudently took the box, and unclasping a bracelet from her arm, which was fastened by a small diamond cross, she added it to the relic, whose value though less obvious, could not be exceeded in Antonio's estimation. "I give thee, this," she said, "Antonio, for thy spiritual and temporal necessities, and shouldst thou ever be in extreme need, I permit thee to give it into the hand of some cunning artificer, who will extract the diamonds for thee, without marring that form which thou rightly regardest as blessed." Antonio received the box as if it contained the freedom of Paradise, and replacing it in his bosom, he crossed himself again and again, repeating his invocations till his saint, apprehensive that in his ecstasy he would lose all remembrance of the high office for which she had selected him, gently reminded him that it was the duty of the faithful to pass promptly from devotion to obedience; on this hint he rose, took up the oars, and exercised his strength and skill with such exemplary fidelity, that in less than two hours, his boat touched the pier which Hope designated as the point where she would disembark.

Before she parted from her votary, she said, "I give thee my blessings and my thanks, Antonio, and I enjoin thee, to say nought to thy wicked comrades, of my visitation to thee; they would but jeer thee and wound thy spirit by making thy lady their profane jest. Reserve the tale, Antonio, for the ears of the faithful who marvel not at miracles."

Antonio bowed in token of obedience, and as long as Hope saw him, he remained in an attitude of profound homage.

Our heroine's elastic spirit, ever ready to rise when pressure was removed, had enabled her to sustain her extempore character with some animation, but as soon as she had parted from Antonio, and was no longer stimulated to exertion by the fear that his illusion might be prematurely dissipated, she felt that her strength had been overtaxed by the strange accidents and various perils of the evening. Her garments were wet and heavy, and at every step, she feared another would be impossible. Her head became giddy, and faintness and weariness, to her, new and strange sensations, seemed to drag her to the earth. She looked and listened in vain for some human being to call to her assistance: the streets were empty and silent; and unable to proceed, she sunk down on the steps of a warehouse, shut her eyes, and laid down her head to still its throbbings.

She had not remained thus many minutes, when she was started by a voice saying, "Ha! lady, dost *thou* too wander alone?—is *thy* cheek pale—*thy* head sick—*thy* heart fluttering?—yet thou art not guilty nor forsaken!"

Hope looked up, and perceived she was addressed by Sir Philip Gardiner's page. She had repeatedly seen him since their first meeting, but occupied as she had been with objects of intense interest to her, she thought not of their first singular interview, excepting when it was recalled by the supposed boy's keen, and as she fancied, angry glances. They seemed involuntary, for when his eye met hers, he withdrew it, and his cheek was dyed with blushes. There was now a thrilling melancholy in his tone; his eye was dim and sunken; and his apparel, usually elaborate, and somewhat fantastical, had a neglected air. His vest was open; his lace ruff, which was ordinarily arranged with a care that betrayed his consciousness how much it graced his fair delicate throat, had now been forgotten, and the feathers of his little Spanish hat dangled over his face. Hope Leslie was in no condition to note these particulars; but she was struck with his haggard and wretched appearance, and was alarmed when she saw him lay his hand on the hilt of a dagger that gleamed from beneath the folds of his vest.

"Do not shrink, lady," he said, "the pure should not fear death, and I am sure the guilty need not dread it—there is nothing worse for them than they may feel walking on the fair earth with the lights of heaven shining on them. I had this dagger of my master, and I think," he added with a convulsive sob, "he would not be sorry, if I used it to rid him of his troublesome page."

"Why do you not leave your master, if he is of this fiendish disposition towards you?" asked Hope, "leave him and return to your friends."

"Friends!—friends!" he exclaimed; "the rich—the good—the happy—those born in honour, have friends. I have not a friend in the wide world."

"Poor soul!" said Hope, losing every other thought in compassion for the unhappy boy; and some notion of his real character and relation to Sir Philip darting into her mind, "then leave this wretched man, and trust thyself to heaven."

"I am forsaken of heaven, lady."

"That cannot be. God never forsakes his creatures: the miserable, the guilty, from whom every human face is turned away, may still go to him, and find forgiveness and peace. His compassions never fail."

"Yes—but the guilty must forsake their sinful thoughts, and I cannot. My heart is steeped in this guilty love. If my master but looks kindly on me, or speaks one gentle word to me, I again cling to my chains and fetters."

"Oh, this is indeed foolish and sinful; how can you love him, whom you confess to be so unworthy?"

"We must love something," replied the boy in a faint voice, his head sinking on his bosom. "My master did love me, and nobody else ever loved me. I never knew a mother's smile, lady, nor felt her tears. I never heard a father's voice; and do you think it so very strange that I should cling to him who was the first, the only one that ever loved me?" He paused for a moment, and looked eagerly on Hope, as if for some word of encouragement; but she made no reply, and he burst into a passionate flood of tears, and wrung his hands, saying, "Oh, yes, it is—I know it is foolish and sinful, and I try to be penitent. I say my paternosters," he added, taking a rosary from his bosom, "and my ave-maries, but I get no heart's ease; and betimes my head is wild, and I have horrid thoughts. I have hated you, lady; you who look so like an angel of pity on me; and this very day, when I saw Sir Philip hand you into that boat, and saw you sail away with him over the bright water so gay and laughing, I could have plunged this dagger into your bosom; and I made a solemn vow that you should not live to take the place of honour beside my master, while I was cast away a worthless thing."

"These are indeed useless vows, and idle thoughts," said Hope. "I cannot longer listen to you now, for I am very sick and weary; but do not grieve thus,—come to me to-morrow, and tell me all your sorrows, and be guided by me."

"Oh, not to-morrow!" exclaimed the boy, grasping her gown as she rose to depart; "not to-morrow—I hate the light of day —I cannot go to that great house—I have no longer courage to meet the looks of the happy, and answer their idle questions; stay now, lady, for the love of heaven! my story is short."

Hope had no longer the power of deliberation, she did not even hear the last entreaty. At the first movement she made, the sensation of giddiness returned, every object seemed to swim before her, and she sunk, fainting, into Roslin's arms. The page had now an opportunity to gratify his vindictive passions if he had any; but his mad jealousy was a transient excitement of feelings in a disordered, almost a distracted state, and soon gave way to the spontaneous emotions of a gentle and tender nature. He carefully sustained his burden, and while he pressed his lips to Hope's cold brow, with an undefinable sensation of joy that he might thus approach angelic purity, he listened eagerly to the sound of footsteps, and as they came nearer, he recognised the two Fletchers, with a company of gentlemen, guards, and sailors, whom, with the Governor's assistance, they had hastily collected to go in pursuit of our heroine.

Everell was the first to perceive her. He sprang towards her, and when he saw her colourless face, and lifeless body, he uttered an exclamation of horror. All now gathered about her, listening eagerly to Roslin's assurance that she had just fainted, complaining of sickness and extreme weariness. He, as our readers well know, could give no further explanation of the state in which Miss Leslie was found; indeed, her friends scarcely waited for any. Everell wrapped her in his cloak, and assisted by his father, carried her in his arms to the nearest habitation, whence she was conveyed, as soon as a carriage could be obtained, to Governor Winthrop's.

CHAPTER VII

"He that questions whether God made the world, the Indian will teach him. I must acknowledge I have received in my converse with them, many confirmations of those two great points; first, that 'God is;' second, 'that he is a rewarder of all them that diligently seek him.'"

ROGER WILLIAMS[1]

Our readers' sagacity has probably enabled them to penetrate the slight mystery, in which the circumstances that led to the apprehension of Magawisca have been shrouded. Sir Philip Gardiner, after attending Mrs. Grafton home on the Saturday night, memorable in the history of our heroine, saw her enter the burial-place. Partly moved by his desire to ascertain whether there was any cause for her running away from him that might soothe his vanity, and partly, no doubt, by an irresistible attraction towards her; he followed at a prudent distance, till he saw her meeting with Magawisca; he then secreted himself in the thicket of evergreens, where he was near enough to hear and observe all that passed; and where, as may be remembered, he narrowly escaped being exposed by his dog.

Sir Philip had heard the rumour of a conspiracy among the natives; and when he saw Magawisca's extreme anxiety to secure a clandestine interview with Miss Leslie, the probable reason for her secresy at once occurred to him. If he conjectured rightly, he was in possession of a secret that might be of value to the state, and of course, be made the means of advancing him in the favour of the Governor. But might he not risk incurring Miss

Leslie's displeasure by this interposition in her affairs, and thus forfeit the object of all his present thoughts and actions? He believed not. He saw that she yielded reluctantly, and because she had no alternative, to Magawisca's imposition of secrecy. With her romantic notions, it was most probable that she would hold her promise inviolate; but would she not be bound in everlasting gratitude to him, who by an ingenious manœuvre should, without in the least involving her honour, secure the recovery of her sister? Thus he flattered himself he should, in any event, obtain some advantage. To Miss Leslie he would appear solely actuated by zeal for her happiness; to the Governor, by devotion to the safety and welfare of the commonwealth.

Accordingly, on the following Monday morning, he solicited a private interview with the magistrates, and deposed before them, "that on returning to his lodgings on Saturday night, he had seen Miss Leslie enter the burying-ground alone; that believing she had gone to visit some spot consecrated by the interment of a friend, and knowing the ardent temper of the young lady, he feared she might forget, in the indulgence of her feelings, the lateness of the hour. He had, therefore, with the intention of guarding her from all harm, without intruding on her meditations, (which though manifestly unseasonable, might, he thought, tend to edifying by withdrawing her thoughts from worldly objects,) followed her, and secluded himself in the copse of evergreens, where, to his astonishment, he had witnessed her interview with the Indian woman." The particulars of their conversation he gave at length.

Unfortunately for Magawisca, Sir Philip's testimony coincided with the story of a renegado Indian, formerly one of the counsellors and favourites of Miantunnomoh. This savage, stung by some real or fancied wrongs, deserted his tribe, and vowing revenge, he repaired to Boston, and divulged to the Governor the secret hostility of his chief towards the English; which, he said, had been stimulated to activity by the old Pequod chief, and the renowned maiden Magawisca.

He stated also, that the chiefs of the different tribes, moved by the eloquence and arguments of Mononotto, were forming a powerful combination. Thus far the treacherous savage told the truth; but he proceeded to state plots and underplots, and art-fully to exaggerate the number and power of the tribes. The magistrates lent a believing ear to the whole story. They were aware that the Narragansetts, ever since they had witnessed the defeat and extinction of their ancient enemies the Pequods, had felt a secret dread and jealousy of the power and encroachments of the English, and that they only waited for an opportunity to manifest their hostility. Letters had been recently received from the magistrates of Connecticut, expressing their belief that a gen-eral rising of the Indians was meditated. All these circumstances combined to give importance to Sir Philip's and the Indian's communications. But the Governor felt the necessity of pro-ceeding warily.

Miantunnomoh had been the faithful friend and ally of the English. He is described by Winthrop, as a "sagacious and subtle man, who showed good understanding in the principles of jus-tice and equity, and ingenuity withal."[2] Such a man it was ob-viously the policy of the English not unnecessarily to provoke; and the Governor hoped, by getting possession of the Pequod family, to obtain the key to Miantunnomoh's real designs, and to crush the conspiracy before it was matured.

We have been compelled to this digression, in order to explain the harsh reception and treatment of Magawisca; to account for the zeal with which the Governor promoted the party to the garden; and for the signal which guided the boat directly to the Pequod family, and which Sir Philip remained on the island to give. The knight had now gotten very deep into the councils and favour of the magistrates, who saw in him the selected medium of a special kindness of Providence to them. He took good care,

> "That all his circling wiles should end
> In feigned religion, smooth hypocrisy;"[3]

and by addressing his arts to the predominant tastes and prin-ciples of the honest men whom he deluded, he well sustained his accidental advantage.

It would be vain to attempt to describe the various emotions of Governor Winthrop's family at the return of Hope Leslie. Madam Winthrop, over excited by the previous events of the evening, had fortunately escaped any further agitation by retiring to bed, after composing her nerves with a draught of valerian tea. Mrs. Grafton, who had been transported with joy at the unlooked for recovery of Faith Leslie, was carried to the extreme of despair, when she saw the lifeless body of her beloved niece borne to her apartment. Poor old Cradock went like the bird of poetic fame, "up stairs and down stairs," wringing his hands, and sobbing like a whipt boy. The elder Fletcher stood bending in mute agony over the child of his affections, whom he loved with even more than the tenderness of a parent. His tears, like those of old and true Menenius, seemed "salter than a younger man's, and venemous to his eyes;"[4] and his good friend Governor Winthrop, when he saw his distress, secretly repented that he had acquiesced in a procedure that had brought such misery upon this much enduring man. Jennet bustled about, appearing to do every thing, and doing nothing; and hoping 'to goodness' sake, the young lady would come to herself, long enough, at least, to tell what had befallen her'—'she always thought, she did, what her harem-scarem ways would bring her to at last.' Miss Downing, without regarding, or even hearing, these and many other similar mutterings, proceeded with admirable presence of mind to direct and administer all the remedies that were at hand; while Everell, almost distracted, went in quest of medical aid.

A delirious fever succeeded to unconsciousness; and for three days Hope Leslie's friends hung over her in the fear that every hour would be her last. For three days and nights, Esther Downing never quitted her bedside, except to go to the door of the apartment to answer Everell's inquiries. Her sweet feminine qualities were now called into action: she watched and prayed over her friend; and, though her cheek was pale, and her eye dim, she had never appeared half so lovely to Everell, as when in her simple linen dressing gown, she for an instant left the invalid to announce some favourable symptom. On the fourth morning, Hope's fever abated; her incoherent ravings ceased, and . she sunk, for the first time, into a tranquil sleep. Esther sat perfectly still by her bedside, fearing to move, lest the slightest noise should disturb her—she heard Everell walking in the entry, as he had done incessantly, and stopping, at every turn, to listen at the door. Till now, all her faculties had been in requisition—her mind and body devoted to her friend—she had not thought of herself; and if sometimes the thought of Everell intruded, she blushed at what she deemed the unsubdued selfishness of her heart. "Alas!" she said, "I am far from that temper which leads us to 'weep with those that weep,' if I suffer thoughts of my own happy destiny to steal in when my friend is in this extremity." But these were but transient emotions: her devotion to Hope was too sincere and unremitting to afford occasion of reproach even to her watchful and accusing conscience. But now, as she listened to Everell's perturbed footsteps, a new train of thoughts passed through her mind. "Everell has scarcely quitted that station. With what eagerness he has hung on my words when I spoke of Hope! What a mortal paleness has overspread his face at every new alarm! It would not, perhaps, have been right—but, methinks, it would have been natural—that he should have expressed some concern for me—I cannot remember that he has. How often has he said to me, 'dear Esther, you will not leave her?' and, 'for the love of heaven, trust her not a moment to the discretion of her aunt'—'do not confide in Jennet'—'Madam Winthrop has too many cares for so delicate a charge—all depends on you, dear Esther.' Yes—he said *dear* Esther; but how many times he has repeated it, as if his life were suspended by the same thread as hers. If I were in Hope's condition, would he feel thus? I could suffer death itself for such proofs of tenderness. Sinful worm that I am, thus to doat on any creature." The serenity of her mind was disturbed—she rose involuntarily—as she rose, her gown caught in her chair, and overthrew it. The chair fell against a little stand by the bedside, covered with phials, cups, and spoons, and all were overthrown, with one of those horrible clatters, that are as startling in a sickroom as the explosion of a magazine at midnight.

Everell, alarmed by the unwonted noise, instinctively opened the door—Hope awoke from her profound sleep, and drew aside the curtain—she looked bewildered; but it was no longer the wildness of fever: thronging and indistinct recollections oppressed her; but after an instant, a perfect consciousness of the past and the present returned; she covered her eyes, and sunk back on the pillow, murmuring, "thank God!" and tears of gratitude and joy stole over her cheeks.

Esther lost every other emotion in unmixed joy. She went to the door to Everell, who was still standing there, as if he were transfixed. "It is as you see," she said, "the danger is past—she has slept sweetly for three hours, and was now only disturbed by my carelessness; go to your father with the good news; your face will tell it even if your lips refuse, as they do now, to move."

They did now move, and the joy of his heart broke forth in the exclamation, "You are an angel, Esther! my father owes to you the preservation of his dearest treasure; and I—I—my life, Esther, shall prove to you my sense of what I owe you."

There was an enthusiasm in his manner, that for the first time satisfied Esther's feelings; but her religious sentiments habitually predominating over every other, "I have been a poor but honoured instrument," she said; "let us all carry our thanksgivings to that altar where they are due." Then, after allowing Everell to press her hand to his lips, she closed the door, and returned to Hope's bedside. Hope again put aside the bed-curtain—"Is not my sister here?" she asked; "she must be here, and yet I can scarcely separate my dreams from the strange accidents of that night."

"She is here, safe and well, my dear Hope; but for the present, you must be content not to see her; you have been very ill, and need perfect rest."

"I feel that I need it, Esther, but I must first know how it has fared with Magawisca; she came on my solemn promise—I trust she has been justly dealt by—she has been received as she deserved, Esther?"

Esther hesitated—but seeing Hope's lip quivering with apprehension, and fearing the effects, in her weak state, of any new agitation, she, for the first time in her life, condescended to an equivocation, solacing herself with thinking that she ought to believe that perfectly right which her uncle Winthrop appointed: she said, "Magawisca has had a merited reception—now ask no more questions, Hope, but compose yourself again to sleep." If Hope had had the will, she had not the power to disobey, for nature will not be rifled of her dues. But we must leave her to the restoring influence of the kindest of all nature's provisions, to visit one from whom care and sorrow banished sleep.

At an advanced hour of the following evening, Sir Philip Gardiner repaired to the town jail, and was admitted by its keeper, Barnaby Tuttle. The knight produced a passport to the cell of Thomas Morton, and pointing to the Governor's signature and seal, "you know that, friend," he said.

"As well as my own face; but I am loath to lead a gentleman of your bearing to such an unsavory place."

"Scruple not, honest master Tuttle, duty takes no note of time and place."

"You shall be served, sir; and with the better will, since you seem to be, as it were, of a God-serving turn,—but walk in, your worship, and sit down in my bit of a place; which, though a homely one, and within the four walls of a jail, is, I thank the Lord, like that into which Paul and Silas were thrust, a place where prayers and praises are often heard."

Barnaby now lighted a candle, and while Sir Philip was awaiting his dilatory preparations, he could not but wonder that a man of his appearance should have been selected for an office that is usually supposed to require a muscular frame, strong nerves, and a hardy spirit. Barnaby Tuttle had none of these; but, on the contrary, was a man of small stature, meagre person, and a pale and meek countenance, that bespoke the disposition that lets "I dare not, wait upon I would."

"Have you been long in this service of jailer?" asked Sir Philip.

"Six years, an please your worship, come the 10th day of next October, at 8 o'clock of the morning. I had been long a servant in the Governor's own household; and he gave me the office, as he was pleased to say, because he knew me trust worthy, and a merciful man."

"But mercy, master Barnaby, is not held to be a special qualification for those of your calling."

"It is not sir? Well, I can tell your honour, there's no place it's more wanted; and here, in our new English colony, we have come, as it were, under a new dispensation. Our prisoners are seldom put in for those crimes that fill the jails in Old England. Since I have been keeper—six years next October, as I told you it is—I have had but few in for stealing, and one for murder; and that was a disputed case, there being no clear testimony; but as he was proved to have lived an atheist life, he was condemned to die, and at the last confessed many sore offences, which, as Mr. Cotton observed in his sermon, preached the next Lord's day, were each and all held worthy of death by the laws of Moses. No sir, our prisoners are chiefly those who are led astray of the devil into divers errors of opinions, or those who commit such sins as are named at length in the Levitical law."

"Ah," said Sir Philip, with a well pitched groan, "the depravity of man will find a channel: stop it at one place and it will out at another.[5] But come, friend Barnaby—time is going on—I'll follow you." The jailer now led the way through a long narrow passage, with doors on each side, which opened into small apartments. "Hark!" said Barnaby, laying his hand on Sir Philip's arm—"hear you that? It's Gorton praying; he and his company are all along in these wards; and betimes I hear them calling on the Lord, like Daniel in the lion's den, for hours together. I hope it's not a sin to feel for such woful heretics, for I have dropped salt tears for them. Does not your honour think our magistrates may have some way opened up for their pardon?"

"I see not how they can, master Barnaby, unless these sore revilers should renounce their heresies, or—" he added, with an involuntary sneer, fortunately for him, unobserved by his simple companion, "or, their title to the Indian lands."

They had now arrived at one extremity of the passage, and Barnaby selected a key from his bunch; but before putting it in the lock, he said, "Morton is in a little room within the Indian woman's, taken the other day."[6]

"So I understand; and by your leave, master Tuttle, I would address a private admonition to this Indian woman, who, as report saith, is an obstinate heathen."

"I suppose she is, your honour; they that should know, say

so. But she hath truly a discreet and quiet way with her, that I would was more common among Christian women. But as you say you wish to speak in private, I must beg your honour's pardon for turning my bolt on you. I will give you the light, and the key to the inner room; and when you desire my attendance, you have but to pull a cord that hangs by the frame of the door inside, and rings a bell in the passage—one word more, your honour—be on your guard when you go into Morton's cell. He raves, betimes, as if all the fiends possessed him; and then again, he sings and dances, as if he were at his revels on the merry mount; and betimes he cries—the poor old man—like a baby, for the twenty-four hours round; so that I cannot but think a place in the London hospital would be fitter for him than this."

"Your feelings seem not to suit with the humour of your profession, Master Tuttle."

"May be not, sir; but there is a pleasure in a pitiful feeling, let your outward work be ever so hard, as, doubtless, your worship well knows."

Sir Philip felt that conscience sent a burning blush to his hardened cheek; and he said, with an impatient tone, "I have my instructions—let me pass in, master Tuttle." Barnaby unlocked the door, gave him the candle, and then turned the bolt upon him.

Magawisca was slowly pacing the room, to and fro; she stopped, and uttered a faint exclamation at the sight of her visitor, then turned away, as if disappointed, and resumed her melancholy step. Sir Philip held up his candle to survey the apartment. It was a room of ordinary size, with one small grated window; and containing a flock-bed, and a three-legged stool, on which stood a plate of untasted provisions.

"Truly," said he, advancing into the room, "generous entertainment this, for a hapless maiden." Magawisca made no reply, and gave no heed to him, and he proceeded, "a godly and gallant youth, that Everell Fletcher, to suffer one who risked her life, and cast away a precious limb for him, to lie forgotten here. Methinks if he had a spark of thy noble nature, maiden, he would burn the town, or batter down this prison wall, for you." An irrepressible groan escaped from Magawisca, but she spoke not.

"He leaves you here alone and helpless to await death," continued the knight; thus venting his malignity against Everell, though he saw that every word was a torturing knife to the innocent maiden. "Death, the only boon you can expect from these most christian magistrates, while he, with a light heart and smirking face, is dancing attendance on his lady love."——

"On whom?" interrupted Magawisca, in a tone of fearful impatience.

"On her who played so faithfully the part of decoy-pigeon to thee."

"Hope Leslie!—my father then is taken," she screamed.

"Nay, nay, not so; thy father and brother, both, by some wondrous chance escaped."

"Dost thou speak truth?" demanded Magawisca in a thrilling voice, and looking in Sir Philip's face as if she would penetrate his soul—"I doubt thee."

The knight opportunely bethought himself of having heard Magawisca during her interview with Hope Leslie, allude to the Romish religion; he took a crucifix from his bosom and pressed it to his lips. "Then by this holy sign," he said, "of which if you know aught, you know that to use it falsely would bring death to my soul, I swear I speak truly."

Magawisca again turned away, and drawing her mantle, which, in her emotion, had fallen back, close over her shoulders, she continued to pace the apartment, without bestowing even a look on Sir Philip, who felt himself in an awkward predicament, and found it difficult to rally his spirits to prosecute the object of his visit. But habitually confident, and like all bad men, distrusting the existence of incorruptible virtue, he soon shook off his embarrassment, and said, "I doubt, maiden, you would breathe more freely in the wild wood than in this stifling prison; and sleep more quietly on the piled leaves of your forests, than on that bed that christian love has spread for you." Magawisca neither manifested by word or sign that she heard him, and he proceeded more explicitly,—"Do you sigh for the freedom of nature?—would you be restored to it?"

"Would I! would the imprisoned bird return to its nestlings?" she now stopped, and looked with eager inquiry on Sir Philip.

"Then listen to me, and you shall learn by what means, and on what terms you may escape from this prison, and beyond the reach of your enemies. Here," he continued, producing from beneath his cloak, a rope-ladder, and a file and wrench, "here are instruments by which you can remove those bars, and by which you may safely descend to the ground."

"Tell me," cried Magawisca, a ray of joy lighting her eyes, "tell me how I shall use them."

Sir Philip explained the mode, enjoined great caution, and then proceeded to say,—"By tomorrow night at twelve you can remove the bars; the town will then be still; proceed directly to the point where you last landed, and a boat shall there be in readiness, well manned, to convey you beyond danger."

"Well—well," she replied, with breathless eagerness, "now tell me what I am to do; what a poor Indian prisoner can do to requite such a favour as this?"

Sir Philip began a reply—stammered, and paused. He seemed to turn and turn his purpose, and endeavoured to shelter it in some drapery that should hide its ugliness; but this was beyond his art, and summoning impudence to his aid, he said, "I have a young damsel with me, who for silly love followed me out of England. Now you foresters, maiden, who live according to the honesty of nature, you could not understand me, if I were to tell you of the cruel laws of the world, which oblige this poor girl to disguise herself in man's apparel, and counterfeit the duties of a page, that she may conceal her love. She hath become somewhat troublesome to me: all that I ask as the price of your liberty is, that she may be the companion of your flight."

"Doth she go willingly?"

"Nay, not willingly; but she is young, and like a tender twig, you can bend her at will; all I ask is, your promise that she return not."

"But if she resist?"

"Act your pleasure with her; yet I would not that she were harmed. You may give her to your brother in the place of this fair-haired damsel they have stolen from him; or," he added, for he saw that Magawisca's brow contracted, "or, if that suits not you, nor him, you may take her to your western forests, and give her to a Romish priest, who will guide her to the Hotel Dieu, which our good lady of Bouillon has established in Canada." Magawisca dropped at his feet the instruments which she had grasped with such delight. "Nay, nay, bethink you, maiden, it is a small boon to return for liberty and life; for, trust me, if you remain here, they will not spare your life."

"And dost thou think," she replied, "that I would make my heart as black as thine, to save my life?—life! Dost thou not know, that life can only be abated by those evil deeds forbidden by the Great Master of life?—The writing of the Great Spirit has surely vanished from thy degraded soul, or thou wouldst know, that man cannot touch life! Life is nought but the image of the Great Spirit—and he hath most of it, who sends it back most true and unbroken, like the perfect image of the clear heavens, in the still lake."

Sir Philip's eye fell, and his heart quailed before the lofty glance, and unsullied spirit of the Indian maiden. Once he looked askance at her, but it was with such a look as Satan eyed the sun in his "high meridian tower." With a feeling of almost insupportable meanness he collected, and again concealed beneath his cloak the ladder and other instruments, which he had been at no small pains to procure, and was turning to summon Barnaby by ringing the bell, when he suddenly recollected, that Thomas Morton had been the ostensible motive of his visit, and that it was but a prudent precaution to look in upon him for an instant; and feeling too, perhaps, a slight curiosity to see the companion of his former excesses, he changed his purpose, turned to Morton's door, unlocked and opened it.

The old man seemed to have shrunk away as if frightened, and was gathered up almost into a ball in one corner of his miserable little squalid den. A few remnants of his garments hung like shreds about him. Every particle of his hair had dropped out; his grisly beard was matted together; his eyes gleamed like sparks of fire in utter darkness. Sir Philip was transfixed. 'Is this,' he thought, 'Morton! the gentleman—the gallant cavalier—the man of pleasure—Good God! the girl hath truly spoken of life!' While he stood thus, the old man sprang on him like a cat, pulled him within the door, and then, with the action of madness, swift as thought, he seized the key, locked the door on the inside, and threw the key through the bars of the window without the prison. The candle had fallen and was extinguished, and Sir Philip found himself immured with his scarcely human companion in total darkness, without any means of rescue, excepting through Magawisca. His first impulse was to entreat her to ring the bell, but he delayed for a moment, lest he should heighten the old man's paroxysm of madness.

In this interval of silence, Magawisca fancied she heard a sound against her window, and on going to it, perceived, though the night was extremely dark, a ladder resting against the bars; she listened and heard a footstep ascending; then there was a wrestling in Morton's room; and screams—"He'll kill me—ring the bell." Again all was still, and she heard from the ground below, "Come down, Mr. Everell, for the love of heaven come down." The words were uttered in a tone hardly above a whisper.

"Hush, Digby, I will not come down."

"Then you are lost; those cries will certainly alarm the guard."

"Hush! the cries have ceased." Everell mounted quite to the window, quick as if he had risen on wings.

'He is true!' thought Magawisca, and it seemed to her that her heart would burst with joy, but she could not speak. He applied an instrument to one of the iron bars, and wrenched it off. Repeated and louder cries of "murder!—help—ring the bell!" now proceeded from Gardiner, and the old maniac seemed determined to outroar him. Again the noise ceased, and again Digby spoke in a more agitated voice than before. "Oh, they are stirring in the yard—come away, Mr. Everell."

"I will not—I had rather die—stand fast, Digby—one bar more, and she is free;" and again he applied the instrument.

"Are you mad?" exclaimed Digby, in a more raised and eager voice; "I tell you the lights are coming; if you do not escape now, nothing can ever be done for her."

This last argument had the intended effect: Everell felt that all hope of extricating Magawisca depended on his now eluding discovery; and with an exclamation of bitter disappointment, he relinquished the enterprise for the present, and, descending a few rounds of the ladder, leaped to the ground, and, with Digby, disappeared before the guard reached the spot of operations. Magawisca saw two of the men go off in pursuit, while the other remained picking up the implements that Everell had dropped, and muttering something of old Barnaby sleeping as if he slept his last sleep.

Relieved from the sad conviction of Everell's desertion and ingratitude, Magawisca seemed for a moment to float on happiness, and in her exultation to forget the rocks and quicksands that encompassed her. Another outcry from Sir Philip recalled her thoughts, and obeying the first impulse of humanity, she rang the bell violently. Barnaby soon appeared with a lamp and keys, and learning the durance of Sir Philip, he hastened to his relief. A key was found to unlock the door, and on opening it, the knight's terror and distress were fully explained. Morton had thrown him on his back, and pinned him to the floor, by planting his knee on Sir Philip's breast, and had interrupted his cries, and almost suffocated him, by stuffing his cloak into his mouth. At the sight of his keeper, the maniac sprang off, and with a sort of inarticulate chattering and laughing, resumed his old station in the corner, apparently quite unconscious that he had moved from it.

Sir Philip darted out and shut the door, as if he were closing a tiger's cage; and then, in wrath that overswelled all limits, he turned upon poor Barnaby, and, shaking him till his old bones seemed to rattle in their thin casement, he poured out on him curses deep and loud, for leading him into that 'devil's den.' Magawisca interposed, but instead of calming his wrath, she only drew it on herself. He swore 'he would be revenged on her, d—d Indian that she was, to stand by and not lift her hand, when she knew he was dying by torture.' Magawisca did not vouchsafe any other reply to this attack, than a look of calm disdain; and Barnaby, now recovering from the fright and amazement into which Sir Philip's violence had thrown him, held up his lamp, and reconnoitring the knight's face and person,

"It is the same," he said, resolving his honest doubts, "the same I let in—circumstances alter cases—and men too, I think; why, I took him for as godly a seeming man as ever I laid my eyes on; a yea and nay pilgrim; but such profane swearing exceedeth Chaddock's men, or Chaddock either, or the master they serve."

"Prate not, you canting villain; why did not you come when you heard my cries? or where was you that you heard them not?"

"Just taking a little nap in my rocking chair; and I said to myself, as I set myself down, 'now Barnaby, if you should happen to fall out of your meditation into sleep, remember to wake at the ringing of the bell;' and, accordingly, at the very first touch of it I was on my feet, and coming hitherward."

Sir Philip's panic and wrath had now so far subsided, that he perceived there was an alarming discordance between his extempore conduct, and his elaborate pretensions; and re-assuming his mask, with an awkward suddenness, he said, "Well, well, friend Barnaby, we will both forgive and forget. I will say nothing of your sleeping soundly at your post, when you have such dangerous prisoners in ward, that the Governor has thought it necessary to give you a guard; and you, good Barnaby, you will say nothing of my having for a moment lost the command of my reason; though being so sorely bestead, and having but a poor human nature, I think I should not be hardly judged by merciful men."

"As to forgiving and forgetting, your worship," replied the good-natured fellow, "that I can do as easily as another man, but not from any dread of your tale-bearing; for I think the Governor hath sent the guard here partly in consideration of my age and feebleness; and I fear not undue blame. Therefore, not for my own by-ends will I keep close, but that I hold it not neighbourly to speak to another's hurt; and I well know it is but the topmost saints that are always in the exercise of grace. But I marvel, your worship, that ye spoke those evil words so glibly: it seemed like one casting away stilts, and going on his own natural feet again."

"All the fault of an ungodly youth, worthy master Tuttle," replied Sir Philip, rolling up his eyes sanctimoniously, "and he who ensnared my soul, thy miserable prisoner there, is now reaping the Lord's judgments therefor."

"I think it is not profitable," said the simple man, as he led the way out of the prison, "to cast up judgments at any one; we are all—as your worship has just suddenly and wofully experienced—we are all liable to falls in this slippery world; and I have always thought it a more prudent and Christian part, to lend a helping hand to a fallen brother, than to stand by, and laugh at him, or flout him."

Sir Philip hurried away; every virtuous sentiment fell on his ear like a rebuke. Even in an involuntary comparison of himself with the simple jailer, he felt that genuine goodness, dimmed and sullied though it may be by ignorance and fanaticism, like a good dull guinea, rings true at every trial; while hypocrisy, though it show a face fair and bright, yet, like a new false coin, betrays at every scratch the base metal.

Perhaps no culprit ever turned his back on a jail with a more thorough conviction that he deserved there to be incarcerated, than did Sir Philip. Detection in guilt is said marvellously to enlighten men's consciences: there may be a kindred virtue in disappointment in guilty projects. The knight had become impatient of his tedious masquerade. He was at first diverted with a new, and, as it seemed to him, a fantastical state of society; and amused at the success with which he played his assumed character. He soon became passionately enamoured of Hope Leslie, and pursued her with a determined, unwavering resolution, that, vacillating as he had always been, astonished himself. In the eagerness of the chase, he underrated the obstacles that opposed him, and above all, the insuperable obstacle, the manifest indifference of the young lady; which his vanity (must we add, his experience) led him to believe was affectation, whim, or accident—any or all of these might be successfully opposed and overcome. He had tried to probe her feelings in relation to Everell, and though he was puzzled by the result, and knew not what it meant, he trusted it did not mean love. But if it did, what girl of Hope Leslie's spirit, he asked himself, would remain attached to a drivelling fellow, who, from complaisance to the wishes of prosing old men, had preferred to her such a statue of formality and puritanism as Esther Downing? and Everell removed, Sir Philip feared no other competitor; for he counted for nothing those gentlemen who might aspire to Miss Leslie's hand, but whose strict obedience to the canons of puritanism left them, as he thought, few of the qualities that were likely to interest a romantic imagination. For himself, determined not to jeopard his success by wearing his sanctimonious mask to Hope, he played the magician with two faces, and to her he was the gay and gallant chevalier; his formality, his preciseness, and every badge and insignia of the puritan school, were dropped, and he talked of love and poetry like any carpet knight of those days, or drawing-room lover of our own. But this was a dangerous game to play, and must not be protracted. Some untoward accident might awaken the guardians of the colony from their credulous confidence; and to this danger his wayward page continually exposed him.

As our readers are already acquainted with the real character of this unhappy victim of Sir Philip's profligacy, it only remains to give the few untold circumstances of her brief history. She was the natural child of an English nobleman. Her mother was a distinguished French actress, who, dying soon after her birth, committed the child to some charitable sisters of the order of St. Joseph. Her father on his death bed, seized with pangs of remorse, exacted a promise from his sister, the Lady Lunford, that she would receive the orphan under her protection. The lady performed the promise à la lettre, and no more. She withdrew the unfortunate Rosa from her safe asylum, but she kept from her, and from all the world, the secret of their relationship, and made the dependence and desolateness of the poor orphan, a broad foundation for her own tyranny. Lady Lunford was a woman of the world—a waning; Rosa, a ripening beauty. Her house was the resort of men of fashion. Sir Philip paid his devotions there ostensibly to the noble mistress, but really to the young creature, whose melting eyes, naiveté, and strong and irrepressible feelings, enchanted him. Probably Lady Lunford found the presence of the young beauty inconvenient. She certainly never threw any obstacle in Sir Philip's way; indeed, he afterwards cruelly boasted to Rosa, that her patroness had persuaded him to receive her; but this was long after; for many months he treated her with the fondest devotion; and she, poor credulous child, was first awakened from dreams of love and happiness by pangs of jealousy.

From her own confessions, Sir Philip learned how far she had divulged her sorrows to Hope Leslie; and from that moment, he meditated some mode of secretly and suddenly ridding himself of her; and finally, determined on the project which, as we have seen, was wofully defeated; and he was compelled to retreat from Magawisca's prison, with the tormenting apprehension that he might himself fall into the pit he had digged.

Let those who have yet to learn in what happiness consists, and its actual independence of external circumstances, turn from the gifted and accomplished man of the world, to the Indian prisoner; from the baffled tempter, to the victorious tempted. Magawisca could scarcely have been made happier if Everell had achieved her freedom, than she was by the certain knowledge of his interposition for her. The sting of his supposed ingratitude had been her sharpest sorrow. Her affection for Everell Fletcher had the tenderness, the confidence, the sensitiveness of woman's love; but it had nothing of the selfishness, the expectation, or the earthliness of that passion. She had done and suffered much for him, and she felt that his worth must be the sole requital for her sufferings. She felt too, that she had received much from him. He had opened the book of knowledge to her—had given subjects to her contemplative mind, beyond the mere perceptions of her senses; had in some measure dissipated the clouds of ignorance that hung over the forest-child, and given her glimpses of the past and the distant; but above all, he had gratified her strong national pride, by admitting the natural equality of all the children of the Great Spirit; and by allowing that it was the knowledge of the Englishman—an accidental superiority that forced from the uninstructed Indian the exclamation, "Manittoo!—Manittoo!"—he is a God."[7]

CHAPTER VIII

—————"My heart is wondrous light,
Since this same wayward girl is so reclaimed."
ROMEO AND JULIET[1]

The next morning opened on Boston with that boon to all small societies, a new topic of interest and conversation. The attempt on the prison the preceding night, was in every one's mouth; and as the community had been much agitated concerning the heresies and trial of Gorton and his company, they did not hesitate to attribute the criminal outrage to some of his secret adherents, who, as the sentence that had passed on the unfortunate men, was the next day to take effect, had made this desperate effort to rescue them. It was not even surmised by the popular voice, that the bold attempt had been made on account of the Indian woman. The magistrates had very discreetly refrained from disclosing her connection with state affairs, as every alarm about the rising of the Indians, threw the colony, especially the women and children, into a state of the greatest agitation. The imprisonment of Magawisca was, therefore, looked upon as a transient and prudential and domiciliary arrangement, to prevent the possibility of any concert between her and the recovered captive, Faith Leslie, who was known to be pining for her Indian friends.

That the Governor's secret conclusions were very different

from those of the people, was indicated by a private order, which
he sent to Barnaby Tuttle, to remove the Indian maiden from
the upper apartment, to the dungeon beneath the prison; but by
no means to inflict any other severity on her, or to stint her of
any kindness consistent with her safe keeping. Gorton's company were, on the same day, removed from the prison; and, as
is well known to the readers of the chronicles of the times, dis-
tributed separately to the towns surrounding Boston, where,
notwithstanding they were jealously guarded and watched, they
proved dangerous leaven, and were soon afterwards transported
to England.[2]

Whatever secret suspicions the Governor entertained in relation to Everell Fletcher, his kind feelings, and the delicate relation in which he stood to that young man, as the son of his
dearest friend, and the betrothed husband of his niece, induced
him to keep them within his own bosom; without even intimat-
ing them to his partners in authority, who, he well knew, whatever infirmities they, frail men, might have of their own, were
seldom guilty of winking at those of others.

But to return to our heroine, whom we left convalescing; the
energies of a youthful and unimpaired constitution, and the un-
wearied care of her gentle nurse, restored her in the space of two
days, to such a degree of strength, that she was able to join the
family in the parlour at the evening meal, to which we cannot
give the convenient designation of "tea," as Asia had not yet
supplied us with this best of all her aromatic luxuries.

Hope entered the parlour leaning on Esther's arm. All rose
to welcome her, and to offer their congratulations, more or less
formal, on her preservation and recovery. Everell advanced with
the rest, and essayed to speak, but his voice failed him. Hope
with natural frankness gave him her hand, and all the blood in
her heart seemed to gush into her pale cheeks, but neither did
she speak. In the general movement their reciprocal emotion
passed unobserved, excepting by Esther; she noted it. After the
meal was finished, and the Governor had returned thanks, in
which he inserted a clause expressive of the general gratitude
"for the mercies that had been vouchsafed to the maiden near
and dear to many present, in that she had been led safely through

perils by water, by land, and by sickness," Madame Winthrop kindly insisted that Hope should occupy her easy-chair, but Hope declined the honour, and seating herself on the window-seat, motioned to her sister to come and sit by her. The poor girl obeyed, but without any apparent interest, and without even seeming conscious of the endearing tenderness with which Hope stroked back her hair, and kissed her cheek. "What shall we do with this poor home-sick child?" she asked, appealing to her guardian.

"In truth, I know not," he replied. "All day, and all night, they tell me, she goes from window to window, like an imprisoned bird fluttering against the bars of its cage; and so wistfully she looks abroad, as if her heart went forth with the glance of her eye."

"I have done my best," said Mrs. Grafton, now joining in the conversation, "to please her, but it's all working for nothing, and no thanks. In the first place, I gave her all her old playthings, that you saved so carefully, Hope, and shed so many tears over, and at first they did seem to pleasure her. She looked them over and over, and I could see by the changes of her countenance as she took up one and another, that some glimmerings of past times came over her; but as ill luck would have it, there was among the rest, in a little basket, a string of bird's eggs, which Oneco had given her at Bethel. I remembered it well, and so did she, for as soon as she saw it, she dropped every thing else, and burst into tears."

"Poor child!" said Mr. Fletcher, "these early affections are deeply rooted." Everell, who stood by his father, turned and walked to the other extremity of the apartment; and Hope involuntarily passed her hand hastily over her brow; as she did so, she looked up and saw Esther's eye fixed on her. Rallying her spirits, "I am weak yet, Esther," she said, "and this sudden change from our still room confuses me." Mrs. Grafton did not mark this little interlude, and replying to Mr. Fletcher's last observation, "Poor child! do you call her? I call it sheer foolishness. Her early affections indeed! you seem to forget she had other and earlier than for that Indian boy; but this seems to be the one weed that has choked all the rest. Hope, my dear, you have no idea what a non compos mentis she has got to be. I showed her all my ear-rings, and gave her her choice of all but the diamonds that are promised for your wedding gift, dearie, you know, and do you think, she scarcely looked at them? while she won't let me touch those horrid blue glass things she wears, that look so like the tawnies, it makes me all of a nerve to see them. And then just look for yourself, though I have dressed her up in that beautiful Lyon's silk of yours, with the Dresden tucker, she will—this warm weather too—keep on her Indian mantle in that blankety fashion."

"Well, my dear aunt, why not indulge her for the present? I suppose she has the feeling of the natives, who seem to have an almost superstitious attachment to that oriental costume."

"Oriental fiddlestick! you talk like a simpleton, Hope. I suppose you would let her wear that string of all coloured shells round her neck, would you not," she asked, drawing aside Faith's mantle, and showing the savage ornament, "instead of that beautiful rainbow necklace of mine, which I have offered to her in place of it?"

"If you ask me seriously, aunt, I certainly would, if she prefers it."

"Now that is peculiar of you, Hope. Why, Miss Esther Downing, mine is a string of stones that go by sevens—yellow, topaz—orange, onyx—red, ruby—and so on, and so on. Master Cradock wrote the definitions of them all out of a latin book for me once; and yet, though it is such a peculiar beauty, that silly child will not give up those horrid shells for it. Now," she continued, turning to Faith, and putting her hand on the necklace, "now that's a good girl, let me take it off."

Faith understood her action, though not her words, and she laid her own hand on the necklace, and looked as if obstinately determined it should not be removed.

Hope perceived there was something attached to the necklace, and on a closer inspection, which her position enabled her to make, she saw it was a crucifix; and dreading lest her sister should be exposed to a new source of persecution, she interposed: "Let her have her own way at present, I pray you, aunt: she may have some reason for preferring those shells that we do

not know; and if she has not, I see no great harm in her preferring bright shells to bright stones; at any rate, for the present we
had best leave her to herself, and say nothing at all to her about
her dress or ornaments."

"Well—very well, take your own way, Miss Hope Leslie."

Hope smiled—"Nay, aunt," she said, "I cannot be *Miss* Hope
Leslie till I get quite well again."

"Oh, dearie, I meant nothing, you know," said the good lady,
whose displeasure never held out against one of her niece's
smiles. "If Miss Esther Downing," she added, lowering her
voice, "had told me to say nothing of dress and ornaments, I
should not have been surprised; but it is an unheard of simple-
ness for you, Hope. Dress and ornaments! they are the most
likely things in the world to take the mind off from trouble. Till
I came to this New English colony, where every things seems,
as it were, topsy turvy, I never saw that woman whose mind
could not be diverted by dress and ornaments."

"You strangely dishonor your memory, mistress Grafton, or
Hope's noble mother," said the elder Fletcher; "methinks I have
heard you often say that Alice Fletcher had no taste for these
vanities."

"No, you never heard me say that, Mr. Fletcher. Vanities!—
no, never, the longest day I had to live; for I never called them
vanities—no—I did say Alice always went as plain as a pike
staff, after you left England; and a great pity it was, I always
thought; for when queen Henrietta came from France, we had
such a world of beautiful new fashions, it would have cured
Alice of moping if she would have given her mind to it. There
was my lady Penyvére, how different it was with her after her
losses: let's see, her husband, and her son Edward, heir to the
estate; and her daughter-in-law—that was not so much—but
we'll count her; and Ulrica, her own daughter—all died in one
week. And for an aggravation, her coachman, horses, coach and
all, went off London Bridge, and all were drowned—killed—
smashed to death; and yet, in less than a week, my lady gave
orders for every suit of mourning—and that is the great use
of wearing mourning, as she said: it takes the mind off from
trouble."

Hope felt, and her quick eye saw, that her aunt was running on sadly at her own expense; and to produce an effect similar to the painter, when, by his happy art, he shifts his lights, throwing defects into shadow, and bringing out beauties, she said, "You are very little like your friend, lady Penyvére, dear aunt, for I am certain, if, as you feared, I had lost my life the other day, all the mourning in the king's realm would not have turned your thoughts from trouble."

"No, that's true—that's true, dearie," replied the good lady, snuffling, and wiping away the tears that had gathered at the bare thought of the evil that had threatened her. "No, Hope, touch you, touch my life; but then," she added, lowering her voice for Hope's ear only, "I can't bear to have you give in to this outcry against dress; we have preaching and prophesying enough, the Lord knows, without your taking it up."

Lights were now ordered, and after the bustle, made by the ladies drawing around the table, and arranging their work, was over, Governor Winthrop said, "if your strength is equal to the task, Miss Leslie, we would gladly hear the particulars of your marvellous escape, of which Esther has been able to give us but a slight sketch; though enough to make us all admire at the wonderful Providence that brought you safely through."

The elder Fletcher, really apprehensive for Hope's health, and still more apprehensive that she might, in her fearless frankness, discredit herself with the Governor, by disclosing all the particulars of her late experience, which he had already heard from her lips, and permitted to pass uncensured, interposed, and hoped to avert the evil, by begging that the relation might be deferred. But Hope insisted that she felt perfectly well, and began by saying, 'she doubted not her kind friends had made every allowance for the trouble she had occasioned them. She was conscious that much evil had proceeded from the rash promise of secresy she had given.' She forbore to name Magawisca, on her sister's account, who was still sitting by her; the Governor, by a significant nod, expressed that he comprehended her; and she went on to say, 'that she trusted she had been forgiven for that, and for all the petulant and childish conduct of the week that followed it.' "I scarcely recollect any thing of those days, that then seemed to me interminable," she said, "but that I tried to mask my troubled spirit with a laughing face, and in spite of all my efforts I was rather cross than gay. I believe, Madam Winthrop, I called forth your censure, and I pray you to forgive me for not taking it patiently and thankfully, as I ought."

Madam Winthrop, all astonishment at Hope's exemplary humility and deference, graces she had not appeared to abound in, assured her with unassumed kindness, that she had her cordial forgiveness; though, indeed, she was pleased to say, 'Hope's explanation left her little to forgive.'

"And you, sir," said Hope, turning to the Governor, "you, I trust, will pardon me for selecting your garden for a secret rendezvous."

"Indeed, Hope Leslie, I could pardon a much heavier transgression in one so young as thee; and one who seems to have so hopeful a sense of error," replied the Governor, while the goodwill beaming in his benevolent face, shewed how much more accordant kindness was with his nature, than the austere reproof which he so often believed the letter of his duty required from him.

"Then you all—all forgive me; do you not?" Hope asked; and glancing her eye around the room, it involuntarily rested, for a moment, on Everell. All but Everell, who did not speak, were warm in their assurances that they had nothing to forgive; and the elder Fletcher tenderly pressed her hand, secretly rejoicing that her graceful humility enabled her to start with her story from vantage ground.

"I did not see you, I believe, Esther," continued Hope, "after we parted at Digby's cottage?"

"Speak a trifle louder, if you please, Miss Leslie," said the Governor. Hope was herself conscious that her voice had faltered, at the recollection of the definitive scene in Digby's cottage, and making a new effort, she said in a firmer and more cheerful tone, "you, Esther, were happily occupied. I was persecuted by Sir Philip Gardiner, whose ungentlemanly interference in my concerns, will, I trust, relieve me from his society in future."

"Pardon me, Miss Leslie," said the Governor, interrupting

Hope, "our friend, Sir Philip, hath deserved your thanks rather than your censure. There are, as you well know, duties paramount to the courtesies of a gentleman, which are, for the most part, but a vain show: mere dress and decoration;" and he vouchsafed a smile, as he quoted the words of Mrs. Grafton, "Sir Philip believed he was consulting your happiness, when he took measures to recover your sister, which your promise forbade your taking."

"Sir Philip strangely mistakes me," replied Hope, "if he thinks any thing could console me for apparently betraying one who trusted me, to sorrowful, fearful imprisonment."

There was a pause, during which Mrs. Winthrop whispered to Esther, "then she knows all about it?"

"Yes—she would not rest till she heard all."

Hope proceeded. "I believe I am not yet strong enough to speak on this point." She then went on to narrate circumstantially all that took place after she was parted from Magawisca, till she came to Antonio. Cradock, when she began, had laid aside a little Greek book, over which he was conning, and had at every new period of her relation given his chair a hitch towards her, till he sat directly before her, on the edge of his chair, his knees pressed close together, and his palms resting upright on them, his head stooped forward, so as to be at right angles with his body, and his parting lips creeping round to his ears, with an expression of complacent wonder. Thus he sat and looked, while Hope described her politic acquiescence in Antonio's error, and repeated her first reply to him in Italian. At this the old man threw his head back, and burst into a peal of laughter, that resembled the neighing of a horse more than any human sound; and as soon as he could recover his voice, "did not I teach her the tongues?" he asked, with a vehement gesture to the company—"did not I teach her the tongues?"

"Indeed you did, kind master Cradock," said Hope, laying her hand on his; "and many a weary hour it cost you."

"Never—never one—thou wert always a marvellous quick witted damsel." He then resumed his seat and his former attitude, and, closing his eyes, said in his usual low, deliberate tone, "I bless the Lord that the flower and beauty of my youth were spent in Padua: a poor blind worm that I am, I deemed it a loss, but it hath saved her most precious and sweet life." And here he burst into a paroxysm of tears and sobbing, almost as violent as his laughter had been: his organs seemed moved by springs which, if touched by an emotion, were quite beyond his control, and only ceased their operation when their mechanical force was exhausted.

Hope had little more to relate: she prudently suppressed the private concerns of Sir Philip's page, and attributed their accidental meeting to his having come abroad, as in truth he had, in quest of his master. When she had finished, the Governor said, "Thou hast indeed been brought through many dangers, Hope Leslie; delivered from the hand of thy strong enemy, and thy feet made like hinds' feet; and I joy to say, that thy experience of the Lord's mercies seemeth to have wrought a becoming sobriety in thee. I would fain pass over that last passage in thy evening's adventures without remark, but duty bids me say, thou didst err, lamentably, in permitting, for a moment, the idol worship of that darkened papistical youth."

"Worship, sir!" said Hope: "I did not esteem it worship; I thought it merely an affectionate address to one who—and I hope I erred not in that—might not have been a great deal better than myself."

"I think she erred not greatly," said Mr. Fletcher, who at this moment felt too tenderly for Hope, patiently to hear her rebuked; "the best catholic doctors put this interpretation on the invocations to saints."

"Granted," replied the Governor, "but did she right to deepen and strengthen the superstition of the Romish sailor?"

"It does not appear to me," said Mr. Fletcher, "that it was a seasonable moment for meddling with his superstitions. We do not read that Paul rebuked the Melitans, even when they said he was a god." This was but negative authority; but while the Governor hesitated how he should answer it, Mr. Fletcher turned to Esther: "Miss Downing," he said, "thou art the pattern maiden of the commonwealth,—in Hope's condition, wouldst thou have acted differently? out of thy mouth she shall be justified or condemned."

"Speak, dear Esther," said Hope; "why do you hesitate? If I were to choose an external conscience, you should be my rule; though I think the stern monitor could never be embodied in so gentle a form. Now tell us, Esther, what would you have done?"

"What I should have done, if left to my own strength, I know not," replied Esther, speaking reluctantly.

"Then, Esther, I will put the question in a form to spare your humility; I will not ask what you would have done, but what I ought to have done?"

Esther's strictness was a submission to duty; and it cost her an effort to say, "I would rather, Hope, thou hadst trusted thyself wholly to that Providence that had so wonderfully wrought for thee thus far."

"I believe you are quite right, Esther," said Hope, who was disposed to acquiesce in whatever her friend said, and glad to escape from any further discussion; and, moreover, anxious to avert Esther's observation from Everell, who, during the conversation, had been walking the room, his arms folded, to and fro, but had narrowly watched Esther during this appeal; and when she announced her opinion, had turned disappointed away.

Mrs. Grafton now arose with a trifling apparent vexation, and, taking Faith by the arm, she signified her intention to retire to her own apartment. While crossing the room she said, "It is not often I quote scripture, as you all know; because, as I have said before, I hold a text from scripture, or a sample of chintz, to be a deceptive kind of specimen; but I must say now, that I think the case of David, in eating the shew bread, instead of looking for manna, upholds Hope Leslie in using the means the Lord chose to place in her hands."

Having the last word is one of the tokens of victory, and the good lady, content with this, withdrew from the field of discussion. Governor Winthrop retired to his study. Hope followed him thither, and begged a few moments audience; which was, of course, readily granted. When the door was closed, and he had seated himself, and placed a large arm-chair for her, all the tranquillity which she had just before so well sustained, forsook her; she sunk, trembling, on her knees, and was compelled to rest her forehead on the Governor's knee: he laid his hand kindly on her head, "what does this mean?" he asked; "I like not, and it is not fitting, that any one should kneel in my house, but for a holy purpose,—rise, Hope Leslie, and explain yourself—rise, my child," he added in a softened tone, for his heart was touched with her distress; "tyrants are knelt to—and I trust I am none."

"No, indeed, you are not," she replied, rising and clasping her hands with earnest supplication; "and therefore, I hope—nay, I believe, you will grant my petition for our poor Indian friend."

"Well, be calm—what of her?"

"What of her! Is she not, the generous creature, at this moment in your condemned dungeon? is she not to be tried tomorrow—perhaps sentenced to death—and can I, the cause of bringing her into this trouble—can I look calmly on?"

"Well, what would you have, young lady?" asked the Governor, in a quiet manner, that damped our heroine's hopes, though it did not abate her ardour.

"I would have your warrant, sir," she replied boldly, "for her release; her free passage to her poor old father, if indeed he lives."

"You speak unadvisedly, Miss Leslie. I am no king; and I trust the Lord will never send one in wrath on his chosen people of the new world, as he did on those of old. No, in truth, I am no king. I have but one voice in the commonwealth, and I cannot grant pardons at pleasure; and besides, on what do you found your plea?"

"On what?" exclaimed Hope. "On her merits, and rights."

"Methinks, my young friend, you have lost right suddenly that humble tone, that but now in the parlour graced you so well. I trusted that your light afflictions, and short sickness, had tended to the edification of your spirit."

"I spoke then of myself, and humility became me; but surely you will permit me to speak courageously of the noble Magawisca."

"There is some touch of reason in thy speech, Hope Leslie," replied the Governor, his lips almost relaxing to a smile. "Sit down, child, and tell me of these merits and rights, for I would be possessed of every thing in favour of this unhappy maiden."

"I have not to tell you, sir," said Hope, struggling to speak in a dispassionate tone, "but only to *remind* you of what you were once the first to speak of—the many obligations of the English to the family of Mononotto—a debt, that has been but ill paid."

"That debt, I think, was cancelled by the dreadful massacre at Bethel."

"If it be so, there is another debt that never has been—that scarce can be cancelled."

"Yes, I know to what you allude: it was a noble action for a heathen savage; and I marvel not that my friend Fletcher should think it a title to our mercy; or, that young Mr. Everell, looking with a youthful eye on this business, should deem it a claim on our justice. They have both spoken much and often to me, and it were well, if Everell Fletcher were content to leave this matter with those who have the right to determine it." Hope perceived the Governor looked very significantly, and she apprehended that he might think her intercession was instigated by Everell.

"I have not seen Everell Fletcher," she said, "till this evening, since we parted at the garden; and you will do both him and me the justice to believe, I have not now spoken at his bidding."

"I did not think it. I know thou art ever somewhat forward to speak the dictates of thy heart," he continued with a smile; "but now let me caution you both, especially Everell, not to stir in this matter, any private interference will but prejudice the Pequod's cause. They have ever been a hateful race to the English. And as the old chief and his daughter are accused, and I fear justly, of kindling the enmity of the tribes against us, and attempting to stir up a war that would lay our villages in ruins, it will be difficult to make a private benefit outweigh such a public crime. At any rate, the prisoner must be tried for her life; afterwards, we may consider if it be possible, and suitable, to grant her a pardon." Hope rose to withdraw: the sanguine hopes that had sustained her were abated, her limbs trembled, and her lips quivered, as she turned to say "good-night." The Governor took her hand, and said compassionately,—"Be not thus disquieted, my child; cast thy care upon the Lord, He can bring light out of this darkness."

'And he alone,' she thought, as she slowly crept to her room. A favourite from her birth, Hope had been accustomed to the gratification of her wishes; innocent and moderate they had been; but uniform indulgence is not a favourable school, and our heroine had now to learn from that stern teacher experience, that events and circumstances cannot be moulded to individual wishes. She must sit down and passively await the fate of Magawisca. 'She had done all she could do, and without any effect—had she done all?' While she still meditated on this last clause of her thoughts, Esther entered the room. Absorbed in her own reverie, Hope did not, at first, particularly observe her friend, and when she did, she saw that she appeared much disturbed. Esther, after opening and shutting drawers and cupboards, and seeking by these little devices to conceal or subdue her agitation, found all unavailing, and throwing herself into a chair, she gave way to hysterical sobbings.

This in almost any young lady would have been a common expression of romantic distress; but in the disciplined, circumspect Esther, uncontrolled emotion was as alarming, to compare small things to great, as if an obedient planet were to start from its appointed orbit.

Hope hastened to her, and folding her arms around her tenderly, inquired what could thus distress her? Esther disengaged herself from her friend, and turned her face from her.

"I cannot bear this," said Hope, "I can bear any thing better than this: are you displeased with me, Esther?"

"Yes, I am displeased with you—with myself—with every body—I am miserable."

"What do you mean, Esther? I have done nothing to offend you; for pity's sake tell me what you mean? I have never had a feeling or thought that should offend you."

"You have most cruelly, fatally injured me, Hope Leslie."

"Here is some wretched mistake," cried Hope; "for heaven's sake explain, Esther: if I had injured you knowingly, I should be of all creatures most guilty; but I have not. If I have innocently injured you, speak, my dear friend, I beseech you," she added, again putting her arm around Esther; "have not you yourself, a thousand times, said there should be no disguises with friends; no untold suspicions; no unexplained mysteries."

Again Esther repressed Hope. "I have been unfairly dealt by," she said. "I have been treated as a child."

"How—when—where—by whom?" demanded Hope impetuously.

"Ask me no questions now, Hope. I will answer none. I will no longer be played upon."

"Oh, Esther, you are cruel," said Hope, bursting into tears. "You are the one friend that I have loved gratefully, devotedly, disinterestedly, and I cannot bear this."

There was a pause of half an hour, during which Esther sat with her face covered with her handkerchief, and sobbing violently, while Hope walked up and down the room; her tender heart penetrated to the very core with sorrow, and her mind perplexed with endless conjectures about the cause of her friend's emotions.

She sometimes approached near the truth, but that way she could not bear to look. At last Esther became quiet, and Hope ventured once more to approach her, and leaned over her without speaking. Esther rose from her chair, knelt down, and drew Hope down beside her, and in a low, but perfectly firm voice, supplicated for grace to resist engrossing passion, and selfish affections. She prayed they might both be assisted from above, so that their mutual forgiveness, and mutual love, might be perfected, and issue in a friendship which should be a foretaste of heaven. She then rose, and folded her arms around her friend, saying, "I have given way to my sinful nature; but I feel already an earnest of returning peace. Do not say any thing to me now, Hope—the future will explain all."

There was an authority in her manner, that Hope could not, and did not, wish to resist. "If you speak to me so, Esther," she said, "I would obey you, even though it were possible obedience should be more difficult. Now we will go to bed, and forget all this wearisome evening; but first kiss me, and tell me you love me as well as ever."

"I do," she replied; but her voice faltered; and governed by the strictest law of truth, she changed her form of expression— "I mean that I shall again love you as well—I trust better than ever—be content with this, for the present, Hope, and try me no further."

Once, while they were undressing, Esther said, but without any emotion in her voice,—her face was averted from Hope,— "Everell has been proposing to me to assist him in a clandestine attempt to get Magawisca out of prison."

"To get her out!" exclaimed Hope, with the greatest animation—"to-night?"

"To-night or to-morrow night."

"And is there any hope of effecting it?"

"I thought it not right for me to undertake it," Esther replied in the same tone, quite calm, but so deliberate, that Hope detected the effort with which she spoke, and dared not venture another question.

They both went to bed, but not to sleep; mutual and secret anxieties kept them for a long time restless, and a strange feeling of embarrassment, as distant as the width of their bed would allow; but, finally, Hope, as if she could no longer bear this estrangement, nestled close to Esther, folded her arms around her, and fell asleep on her bosom.

Madam Winthrop had very considerately, in the course of the evening, left Everell and her niece alone together; and he had availed himself of this first opportunity of private communication, to inform her, that after being frustrated in all his efforts for Magawisca's rescue, he had, at length, devised a plan which only wanted her co-operation to insure it success. Her agency would certainly, he believed, not be detected; and, at any rate, could not involve her in any disagreeable consequences.

'Any consequences to herself,' Esther said, 'she would not fear.' Everell assured her, that he was certain she would not; but he was anxious she should see he would not expose her to any even to attain an object for which he would risk or sacrifice his own life. He then went on eagerly to detail his plan of operations, till Esther summoned courage to interrupt him. Perhaps there is not on earth a more difficult duty, than for a woman to place herself in a disagreeable light before the man she truly loves. Esther's affections were deep, fixed, and unpretending, capable of any effort, or any sacrifice, that was not proscribed by religious loyalty; but no earthly consideration could have tempted her to waver from the strictest letter of her religious duty as that duty was interpreted by her conscience. It cost her severe struggles, but after several intimations, which Everell did not understand, she constrained herself to say, 'that she thought they had not scripture warrant for interfering between the prisoner and the magistrates.'

"Scripture warrant!" exclaimed Everell with surprise and vexation he could not conceal. "And are you to do no act of mercy, or compassion, or justice, for which you cannot quote a text from scripture?"

"Scripture hath abundant texts to authorise all mercy, compassion, and justice, but we are not always the allowed judges of their application; and in the case before us we have an express rule, to which, if we submit, we cannot err; for thou well knowest, Everell, we are commanded in the first of Peter, 2d chapter, to 'submit ourselves to every ordinance of man, for the Lord's sake: whether it be to the king, as supreme; or into governors, as unto them that are sent by him for the punishment of evil doers, and for the praise of them that do well.' "[3]

"But surely, Esther, there must be warrant, as you call it, for sometimes resisting legitimate authority, or all our friends in England would not be at open war with their king. With such a precedent, I should think the sternest conscience would permit you to obey the generous impulses of nature, rather than to render this slavish obedience to the letter of the law."

"Oh, Everell! do not seek to blind my judgment. Our friends at home are men who do all things in the fear of the Lord, and are, therefore, doubtless guided by the light of scripture, and the inward testimony. But they cannot be a rule for us, in any measure; and for me, Everell, it would be to sin presumptuously, to do aught, in any way, to countervail the authority of those chosen servants of the Lord, whose magistracy we are privileged to live under."

Everell tried all argument and persuasion to subdue her scruples, but in vain; she had some text, or some unquestioned rule of duty, to oppose to every reason and entreaty.

To an ardent young man, there is something unlovely, if not revolting, in the sterner virtues; and particularly when they oppose those objects which he may feel to be authorised by the most generous emotions of his heart. Everell did not mean to be unjust to Esther—his words were measured and loyal—but he felt a deep conviction that there was a painful discord between them; that there was, to use the modern German term, no elective affinity. In the course of their conversation, he said, "you would not, you could not, thus resist my wishes, if you knew Magawisca."

"Everell," she replied, "those who love you need not know this maiden, to feel that they would save her life at the expense of their own, if they might do it;" and then blushing at what she feared might seem an empty boast, she added, "but I do know Magawisca; I have visited her in her prison every day since she has been there."

"God bless you for that, Esther—but why did you not tell me?"

"Because my uncle only permitted me access to her, on condition that I kept it a secret from you."

"Methinks that prohibition was as useless as cruel."

"No, Everell; my uncle, doubtless, anticipated such applications as you have made to-night, and he was right to guard me from temptation."

'He might securely have trusted you to resist it,' thought Everell. But he tried to suppress the unkind feeling, and asked Esther 'if she had any motive in visiting Magawisca thus often, beyond the gratification of her compassionate disposition?'

"Yes," replied Esther, "I heard my uncle say, that if Magawisca could be induced to renounce her heathenish principles, and promise, instead of following her father to the forest, to remain here, and join the catechised Indians, he thought the magistrates might see it to be their duty to overlook her past misdemeanors, and grant her Christian privileges." Esther paused for a moment, but Everell made no comment, and she proceeded, in a tone of the deepest humility: "I knew I was a poor instrument, but I hoped a blessing on the prayer of faith, and the labour of love. I set before her, her temporal and her eternal interest—life, and death. I prayed with her—I exhorted her—but, oh! Everell, she is obdurate; she neither fears death, nor will believe that eternal misery awaits her after death!"

To Esther's astonishment, Everell, though he looked troubled, neither expressed surprise or disappointment at the result of her labours, but immediately set before her the obvious inference from it. "You see, yourself," he said, "by your own experience, there is but one way of aiding Magawisca."

"It is unkind of you, Everell," she replied, with a trembling voice, "to press me further; that way, you know, my path is hedged up;" and without saying any thing more, she abruptly left the room; but she had scarcely passed the threshold of the door, when her gentle heart reproached her with harshness, and she turned to soften her final refusal. Everell did not hear her returning footsteps; he stood with his back to the door; and Esther heard him make this involuntary apostrophe. "Oh, Hope Leslie! how thy unfettered soul would have answered such an appeal! why has fate cruelly severed us?"

Esther escaped hastily, and without his observation; and the scene already described, in the apartment of the young ladies, ensued.

Everell Fletcher must not be reproached with being a disloyal knight. The artifices of Sir Philip Gardiner, the false light in which our heroine had been placed by her embarrassments with Magawisca—the innocent manœuvrings of Madam Winthrop, and finally, the generous rashness of Hope Leslie, had led him step by step, to involve himself in an engagement with Miss Downing; that engagement had just been made known to her protectors, and ratified by them, when the denouement of the mysterious rendezvous at the garden, explained his fatal mistake. When he recurred to all that had passed since his first meeting with Hope Leslie, and particularly to their last interview at the garden, when he had imputed her uncontrollable emotion to her sensibility in relation to Sir Philip, he had reason to believe, he was beloved by the only being he had ever loved. But in what cruel circumstance did this discovery find him! His troth plighted to one whose pure and tender heart he had long possessed. There was but one honourable course for him to pursue, and on that he firmly resolved; to avoid the presence of Hope Leslie—to break the chain of affection wrought in youth, and rivetted in manhood, and whose links seemed to him, to encompass and sustain his very life; in fine, to forget the past—but alas! who can convert to Lethe the sweetest draughts of memory?

Hope's dangerous illness had suspended all his purposes; he could not disguise his interest—and indeed, its manifestation excited neither surprise nor remark, for it seemed sufficiently accounted for by their long and intimate association. While Hope's life was in peril, even Magawisca was forgotten; but the moment Hope's convalescence restored the use of his faculties, they were all devoted to obtaining Magawisca's release, and he had left no means untried, either of open intercession, or clandestine effort; but all as yet was without effect.

CHAPTER IX

"What trick, what device, what starting hole canst thou now find out, to hide thee from this open and apparent shame?"

HENRY IV[1]

The day appointed for Magawisca's trial, arose on Boston one of the brightest and most beautiful of summer. There are moments of deep dejection and gloom in every one's experience, when the eye closes against the beauty of light, when the silence of all those great powers that surround us, presses on the soul like the indifference of a friend, and when their evolving glories overpower the wearied spirit, as the splendours of the sun offend the sick eye. In this diseased state of mind, Everell wandered about Boston, till the ringing of the bell, the appointed signal, gave notice that the court was about to open for the trial of the Indian prisoner. He then turned his footsteps towards the house where the sittings of the magistrates were held; and on reaching it, he found a crowd had already assembled in the room assigned for the trial.

At one extremity of the apartment was a platform of two or three feet elevation, on which sat the deputies and magistrates, who constituted the court; and those elders who had, as was customary on similar occasions, been invited to be present as advisory counsel. The New-England people have always evinced a fondness for asking advice, which may, perhaps, be explained

by the freedom with which it is rejected. A few seats were provided for those who might have claims to be selected from the
ordinary spectators; two of these were occupied by the elder
Fletcher, and Sir Philip Gardiner. Everell remained amidst the
multitude unnoticed and unnoticing; his eye roving about in that
vague and inexpressive manner that indicates the mind holds no
communion with external objects, till he was roused by a buz
of "there she comes!" and a call of "make room for the prisoner." A lane was opened, and Magawisca appeared, preceded
and followed by a constable. A man of middle age walked beside
her, whose deep set and thoughtful eye, pale brow, ascetic complexion, and spare person, indicated a life of self-denial, and of
physical and mental labour; while an expression of love, compassion, and benevolence, seemed like the seal of his Creator
affixed to declare him a minister of mercy to His creatures. Everell was struck with the aspect and position of the stranger, and
inquired of the person standing next to him, "who he was?"

The man turned on him a look of astonishment which expressed, "who are you that ask so strange a question?" and
replied,—"That gentleman, sir, is the 'apostle of New-England,'²
though it much offendeth his modesty to be so called."

'God be praised!' thought Everell. 'Eliot, (for he was familiar
with the title, though not with the person of that excellent man)
my father's friend! this augurs well for Magawisca.'

"I marvel," continued his informant, "that Mr. Eliot should,
in a manner, lend his countenance to this Jezabel. See, with what
an air she comes among her betters, as if she were queen of
us all."

There was certainly nothing of the culprit, or suitor in the
aspect of Magawisca: neither guilt, nor fearfulness, nor submission. Her eyes were downcast, but with the modesty of her
sex—her erect attitude, her free and lofty tread, and the perfect
composure of her countenance, all expressed the courage and
dignity of her soul. Her national pride was manifest in the care
with which, after rejecting with disdain the Governor's offer of
an English dress, she had attired herself in the peculiar costume
of her people. Her collar—bracelet—girdle—embroidered moccasins, and purple mantle with its rich border of bead-work, had

been laid aside in prison, but were now all resumed and displayed with a feeling resembling Nelson's,[3] when he emblazoned himself with stars and orders to appear before his enemies, on the fatal day of his last battle.

The constable led her to the prisoner's bar. There was a slight convulsion of her face perceptible as she entered it, and when her attendant signed to her to seat herself, she shook her head and remained standing. Everell moved by an irresistible impulse, forced his way through the crowd, and placed himself beside her. Neither spoke—but the sudden flush of a sun-beam on the October leaf is not more bright nor beautiful than the colour that overspread Magawisca's olive cheek. This speaking suffusion and the tear that trembled on her eye-lids, but no other sign, expressed her consciousness of his presence. The Magistrates looked at Everell, and whispered together, but they appeared to come to the conclusion that this expression of his feeling was natural and harmless, and it was suffered to pass unreproved.

The Governor, as chief Magistrate, now rose and requested Mr. Eliot to supplicate divine assistance in the matter they were about to enter on. The good man accordingly performed the duty with earnestness and particularity. He first set forth the wonder-working providence of God in making their enemies to be at peace with them. He recounted in the narrative style, then much used in public devotions, the various occasions on which they had found their fears of the savages groundless, and their alarms unfounded. He touched on divers instances of 'kindness and neighbourlike conduct that had been shown them by the poor heathen people, who having no law, were a law unto themselves.' He intimated that the Lord's chosen people had not now, as of old, been selected to exterminate the heathen, but to enlarge the bounds of God's heritage, and to convert these strangers and aliens, to servants and children of the most High! He alluded to the well known and signal mercies received from the mother of the prisoner, and to that valiant act of the prisoner herself, whereby she did redeem from death, and captivity worse than death, the child—the only child, of a sorely bereaved man. He hinted at the authorities for the merciful requital of these deeds in the promises of the spies of Joshua to the heathen woman of

Jericho, that when the Lord had given them the land, they would deal truly with her, and show kindness to her, and to her father's house; and in the case of David's generosity to Mephibosheth, the son of Jonathan, the son of Saul, wherein he passed by the evil that Saul had done him, and only remembered the favours of Jonathan. He alluded to the ruined chief, the old father, on whom 'the executed wrath of God had fallen so heavily, that, as divers testified, the light of reason was quite put out, and he was left to wander up and down among the tribes, counselling revenges to which none listened.' And finally, he dwelt on 'the gospel spirit of forgiveness as eminently becoming those who, being set on a hill in the wilderness, were to show their light to the surrounding nations," and concluded with the prayer that on this occasion, justice and mercy might be made publicly to kiss each other.

When he had done, all eyes turned again on Magawisca, and many who had regarded her with scorn, or at best, idle curiosity, now looked at her with softened hearts, and moistened eyes. Not so Sir Philip, who had his own reasons for being apprehensive of any advance Magawisca might make in the favour of her Judges. He whispered to a Magistrate near whom he sat, "is it not a singular procedure thus to convert a prayer into an ex parte statement of the case?"

"Very singular," replied the good man, with an ominous shake of the head, "but brother Eliot hath an overweening kindness towards the barbarians. We shall set all right," he added with one of those sagacious nods, so expressive of soi-disant infallibility. The Governor now proceeded to give an outline of the charges against Magawisca, and the testimony that would be adduced to support them. He suppressed nothing, but gave a colour to the whole, which plainly indicated his own favourable dispositions, and Everell felt lightened of half his fears. Sir Philip was then requested to relate the circumstances that had, through his instrumentality, led to the taking of the prisoner, and so much of the conversation he had heard between her and Miss Leslie, as might serve to elucidate the testimony of the Indian, who had pretended, by his information, to reveal a direful conspiracy. Sir Philip rose, and Magawisca, for the first time, raised her eyes, and fixed them on him; his met hers, and he quailed before her glance. As if to test the power of conscience still further, at this critical moment, his unhappy page, poor Rosa, pressed through the crowd, and giving Sir Philip a packet of letters just arrived from England, she seated herself on the steps of the platform, near where the knight stood.

Sir Philip threw the packet on the table before the Governor, and stood for a few moments silent, with his eyes downcast, in profound meditation. The trial was assuming an unexpected and startling aspect. Sir Philip now feared he had counted too far on the popular prejudices, which he knew were arrayed against Magawisca, as one of the diabolical race of the Pequods. He perceived that all the weight of Eliot's influence would be thrown into the prisoner's scale, and that the Governor was disposed, not only to an impartial, but to a merciful investigation of her case.

Reposing confidently on the extraordinary favour that had been manifested towards him by the magistrates, he had felt certain of being able to prevent Magawisca's disclosure of their interview in the prison, or to avert any evil consequence to himself, by giving it the air of a malignant contrivance, to be expected from a vengeful savage, against one who had been the providential instrument of her detection. But he now felt that this might be a difficult task.

He had at first, as has been seen, enlisted against Magawisca, not from any malignant feeling towards her, but merely to advance his own private interests. In the progress of the affair, his fate had, by his own act, become singularly involved with hers. Should she be acquitted, he might be impeached; perhaps exposed and condemned by her testimony. Alliances like his with Rosa, were by the laws of the colony, punished by severe penalties. These would be aggravated by the discovery of his imposture. At once perceiving all his danger, he mentally cursed the fool-hardiness with which he had rushed, unnecessarily and unwittingly, to the brink of a precipice.

He had observed Magawisca's scrutinizing eye turn quickly from him to Rosa, and he was sure from her intelligent glances, that she had at once come to the conclusion, that this seeming page was the subject of their prison interview. Rosa herself appeared to his alarmed imagination, to be sent by heaven as a witness against him. How was he to escape the dangers that encompassed him? He had no time to deliberate on the most prudent course to be pursued. The most obvious was to inflame the prejudices of Magawisca's judges, and by anticipation to discredit her testimony; and quick of invention, and unembarrassed by the instincts of humanity, he proceeded, after faithfully relating the conversation in the churchyard, between the prisoner and Miss Leslie, to detail the following gratuitous particulars.

He said, 'that after conducting Miss Leslie to the Governor's door, he had immediately returned to his own lodgings, and that induced by the still raging storm to make his walk as short as possible, he took a cross-cut through the burial ground; that on coming near the upper extremity of the enclosure, he fancied he heard a human voice mingling with the din of the storm; that he paused, and directly a flash of lightning discovered Magawisca kneeling on the bare wet earth, making those monstrous and violent contortions, which all who heard him, well knew characterized the devil-worship of the powwows; he would not—he ought not repeat to christian ears, her invocations to the Evil-one to aid her in the execution of her revenge on the English; nor would he, more particularly describe her diabolical writhings and beatings of her person. His brethren might easily imagine his emotions at witnessing them by the sulphureous gleams of lightning, on which, doubtless, her prayers were sped.'

Sir Philip had gained confidence as he proceeded in his testimony, for he perceived by the fearful and angry glances that were cast on the prisoner, that his tale was credited by many of his audience, and he hoped by all.

The notion that the Indians were the children of the devil, was not confined to the vulgar; and the belief in a familiar intercourse with evil spirits, now rejected by all but the most ignorant and credulous, was then universally received.

All had, therefore, listened in respectful silence to Sir Philip's extraordinary testimony, and it was too evident that it had the effect, to set the current of feeling and opinion against the prisoner. Her few friends looked despondent; but for herself, true

to the spirit of her race, she manifested no surprise, nor emotion
of any kind.

The audience listened eagerly to the magistrate, who read
from his note-book, the particulars which had been received
from the Indian informer, and which served to corroborate and
illustrate Sir Philip's testimony. All the evidence being now before the court, the Governor asked Magawisca, "if she had aught
to allege in her own defence."

"Speak humbly maiden," whispered Mr. Eliot, "it will grace
thy cause with thy judges."

"Say," said Everell, "that you are a stranger to our laws and
usages, and demand some one to speak for you."

Magawisca bowed her head to both advisers, in token of acknowledgment of their interest, and then raising her eyes to her
judges, she said,—"I am your prisoner, and ye may slay me, but
I deny your right to judge me. My people have never passed
under your yoke—not one of my race has ever acknowledged
your authority."

"This excuse will not suffice thee," answered one of her
judges: "thy pride is like the image of Nebuchadnezar's dream
—it standeth on feet of clay—thy race have been swift witnesses
to that sure word of prophecy. 'Fear thou not, O Jacob, my
servant, for I am with thee, and I will make a full end of the
people whither I have driven thee'⁴—thy people truly—where
are they?"

"My people! where are they?" she replied, raising her eyes to
heaven, and speaking in a voice that sounded like deep-toned
music, after the harsh tones addressed to her,—"my people are
gone to the isles of the sweet south-west; to those shores that
the bark of an enemy can never touch: think ye I fear to follow
them?"

There was a momentary silence throughout the assembly; all
seemed, for an instant, to feel that no human power could touch
the spirit of the captive. Sir Philip whispered to the magistrate
who last spoke,—"Is it not awful presumption for this woman
thus publicly to glory in her heathen notions?"

The knight's prompting had the intended effect. "Has this
Pequod woman," demanded the magistrate, "never been in-

structed in the principles of truth, that she dares thus to hold
forth her heathenisms before us? Dost thou not know, woman,"
he continued, holding up a Bible, "that this book contains the
only revelation of a future world—the only rule for the present
life?"

"I know," she replied, "that it contains thy rule,[5] and it may
be needful for thy mixed race; but the Great Spirit hath written
his laws on the hearts of his original children, and we need
it not."

"She is of Satan's heritage, and our enemy—a proved conspirator against the peace of God's people, and I see not why
she should not be cut off," said the same gentleman, addressing
his brethren in office.

"The testimony," said another of the magistrates, in a low
voice, in which reason and mildness mingled, and truly indicated
the disposition of the speaker; "the testimony appeareth to me
insufficient to give peace to our consciences in bringing her to
extremity. She seems, after her own manner, to be guided by the
truth. Let the Governor put it to her, whether she will confess
the charges laid against her."

The Governor accordingly appealed to the prisoner: "I neither confess nor deny aught," she said, "I stand here like a deer
caught in a thicket, awaiting the arrow of the hunter."

Sir Philip again whispered to his next neighbour, who, unconsciously obeying the knight's crafty suggestions, seemed to
have become the conductor of the prosecution. "She hath the
dogged obstinacy of all the Pequod race," said he, "and it hath
long been my opinion, that we should never have peace in the
land till their last root was torn from the soil."

"You may be right, brother," replied the Governor, "but it
becometh us, as Christian men, to walk circumspectly in this
matter:" then opening a note-book, elevating his voice, and turning to the knight, he added, "I observe that your present
testimony, Sir Philip, hath not kept equal pace with that taken
down from your lips on a former occasion. I have looked over
these memoranda with a careful eye, and I do not perceive even
an intimation of your having seen the prisoner after parting with
Hope Leslie."

The knight had anticipated this scrutiny, and was prepared to answer it: "I was not upon oath then," he replied, "and, of course, was not required to disclose the whole truth; and, besides, it was then, as your excellency may remember, doubtful whether the prisoner would be taken, and I was reluctant to magnify, unnecessarily, the apprehensions of the paternal guardians of the people."

Though this insinuated compliment was enforced by a deferential bow to the Governor, he passed it over, and replied to the first clause of Sir Philip's rejoinder: "You allege, Sir Philip Gardiner, that you were not then on oath—neither have you been now; we do not require a member of the congregation to take the oath, unless charged by the party against whom he testifies. What sayest thou, maiden, shall I administer the oath to him?"

"Certainly—require the oath of him," whispered Everell to Magawisca.

Magawisca bowed her assent to the Governor.

Sir Philip would not probably have been so prompt in his false testimony, if he had anticipated being put on his oath; for he was far enough from having one of those religious consciences that regard truth as so sacred that no ceremonies can add to its authority. But now, his word being questioned, it became necessary for him to recede from it, or to maintain it in the usual legal form; and, without hesitating, he advanced to the table, raised his hand, and went through the customary form of the oath. The collectedness and perfect equanimity of Magawisca, to this moment, had seemed to approach to indifference to her fate; but the persevering falsehood of Sir Philip, and the implicit faith in which it was apparently received, now roused her spirit, and stimulated that principle of retaliation, deeply planted in the nature of every human being, and rendered a virtue by savage education. She took a crucifix from her bosom—Everell whispered, "I pray thee hide that, Magawisca, it will ruin thy cause." Magawisca shook her head, and held up the crucifix.

"Put down that idolatrous sign," said the Governor.

"She hath, doubtless, fallen under popish enchantments,"

whispered one of the deputies; "the French priests have spread their nets throughout the western forests."

Magawisca, without heeding the Governor's command, or observing the stares of astonishment that her seeming hardihood drew upon her, addressed herself to Sir Philip: "This crucifix," she said, "thou didst drop in my prison. If, as thou saidst, it is a charmed figure, that hath power to keep thee in the straight path of truth, then press it to thy lips now, as thou didst then, and take back the false words thou hast spoken against me."

"What doth she mean?" asked the Governor, turning to Sir Philip.

"I know not," replied the knight, his reddening face and embarrassed utterance indicating he knew that which he dared not confess—"I know not; but I should marvel if this heathen savage were permitted, with impunity, to insult me in your open court. I call upon the honourable magistrates and deputies," he continued, with a more assured air, "to impose silence on this woman, lest her uttered malignities should, in the minds of the good people here assembled, bring scandal upon one whose humble claims to fellowship with you, you have yourselves sanctioned."

The court were for a moment silent: every eye was turned towards Magawisca, in the hope that she would be suffered to make an explanation; and the motions of curiosity coinciding with the dictates of justice, in the bosoms of the sage judges themselves, were very like to counteract the favour any of them might have felt for Sir Philip. Everell rose to appeal to the court to permit Magawisca to invalidate, as far as she was able, the testimony against her, but Mr. Eliot laid his hand on his arm, and withheld him. "Stay, my young friend," he whispered, "I may speak more acceptably." Then, addressing the court, he 'prayed the prisoner might be allowed liberty to speak freely, alleging that it was for the wisdom of her judges to determine what weight was to be attached to her testimony;' and glancing his eye at Sir Philip, he added, "the upright need not fear the light of truth."

Sir Philip again remonstrated; he asked 'why the prisoner should be permitted further to offend the consciences of the godly? Surely,' he said, 'none of her judges would enforce her demand; surely, having just sworn before them in the prescribed form, they would not require him to repeat his oath on that symbol of popish faith, that had been just styled an idolatrous sign.'

"This, I think, brother Eliot, is not what thou wouldst ask?" said Governor Winthrop.

"Nay, God forbid that I should bring such scandal upon our land. It is true, I have known many misguided sons of the Romish church who would swear freely on the holy word, what they dared not verify on the crucifix; which abundantly showeth that superstition is with such, stronger than faith. But we, I think, have no warrant for using such a test—neither do we need it. The prisoner hath asserted that this symbol belongeth to Sir Philip Gardiner, and that he did use it to fortify his word; if so, the credit of his present testimony would be mainly altered; and it seemeth to me but just, that the prisoner should not only be allowed, but required, to state in full that to which she hath but alluded."

A whispered consultation of the magistrates followed this proposition, during which Sir Philip seemed virtually to have changed places with the prisoner, and appeared as agitated as if he were on the verge of condemnation: his brow was knit, his lips compressed, and his eye, whose movement seemed beyond his control, flashed from the bench of magistrates to Magawisca, and then fixed on Rosa, as if he would fain have put annihilation in its glance. This unhappy girl still sat where she had first seated herself; she had taken off her hat, laid it on her lap, and rested her face upon it.

There was a vehement remonstrance, from some of the members of the court, against permitting the prisoner to criminate one who had shown himself well and zealously affected towards them. And it was urged, with some plausibility, that the hints she had received of the advantage to be gained by disqualifying Sir Philip, would tempt her to contrive some crafty tale that might do him a wrong, which they could not repair. The Governor answered this argument by suggesting that they, being forewarned, were forearmed, and might certainly rely on their own sagacity to detect any imposture. Of course, no individual was forward to deny, for himself, such an allegation, and the Governor proceeded to request Magawisca to state the circumstances to which she alluded as having transpired in the prison. Magawisca now, for the first time, appeared to hesitate, to deliberate, and to feel embarrassed.

"Why dost thou falter, woman?" demanded one of her judges; "no time shall be allowed now to contrive a false testimony—proceed—speak quickly."

"Fear not to speak, Magawisca," whispered Everell.

"I do fear to speak," she replied aloud; "but it is such fear as he hath, who, seeing the prey in the eagle's talons, is loath to hurl his arrow, lest, perchance, it should wound the innocent victim."

"Speak not in parables, Magawisca," said Governor Winthrop, "but let us have thy meaning plainly."

"Then," replied Magawisca, "let me first crave of thy mercy, that that poor youth, (pointing to Rosa,) withdraw from this presence."

All eyes were now directed to Rosa, who, herself, conscious that she had become the object of attention, raised her head, threw back the rich feminine curls that drooped over her face, and looked wildly around her. On every side her eye encountered glances of curiosity and suspicion; her colour deepened, her lips quivered and, like a bewildered, terrified child, that instinctively flies to its mother's side, she sprang up the steps, grasped Sir Philip's cloak, as if she would have hidden herself in its folds, and sunk down at his feet. Sir Philip's passions had risen to an uncontrollable pitch: "Off boy," he cried, spurning her with his foot. A murmur of "shame! cruelty!" ran through the house. The unhappy girl rose to her feet, pressed both her hands on her forehead, stared vacantly about, as if her reason were annihilated, then darting forward, she penetrated through the crowd, and disappeared.

There were few persons present so dull as not to have solved Magawisca's *parable,* at the instant the clue was given by Rosa's involuntary movements. Still, all they had discovered was, that the page was a disguised girl; and a hope darted on Sir Philip, in the midst of his overwhelming confusion, that if he could gain time, he might escape the dangers that menaced him. He rose, and, with an effrontery that, with some, passed for the innocence he would fain have counterfeited, said, 'that circumstances had just transpired in that honourable presence, which, no doubt, seemed mysterious; that he could not then explain them without uselessly exposing the unhappy; for the same reason, namely, to avoid unnecessary suffering, he begged that no interrogatories might, at the present time, be put to the prisoner, in relation to the hints she had thrown out; that if the Governor would vouchsafe him a private interview, he would, on the sure word of a Christian man, clear up whatever suspicions had been excited by the dark intimations of the prisoner, and the very singular conduct of his page.'

The Governor replied, with a severe gravity, ominous to the knight, 'that the circumstances he had alluded to certainly required explanation; if that should not prove satisfactory, they would demand a public investigation. In the mean time, he should suspend the trial of the prisoner, who, though the decision of her case might not wholly depend on the establishment of Sir Philip's testimony, was yet, at present, materially affected by it.'

'He expressed a deep regret at the interruption that had occurred, as it must lead,' he said, 'to the suspension of the justice to be manifested either in the acquittal or condemnation of the prisoner. Some of the magistrates being called away from town on the next morning, he found himself compelled to adjourn the sitting of the court till one month from the present date.'

"Then," said Magawisca, for the first time speaking, with a tone of impatience, "then, I pray you, send me to death now. Any thing is better than wearing through another moon in my prison-house, thinking," she added, and cast down her eye-lids, heavy with tears, "thinking of that old man—my father. I pray thee," she continued, bending low her head, "I pray thee now to set my spirit free. Wait not for his testimony"—she pointed to Sir Philip—"as well may ye expect the green herb to spring up in your trodden streets, as the breath of truth to come from his false lips. Do you wait for him to prove that I am your enemy? Take my own word, I am your enemy; the sun-beam and the shadow cannot mingle. The white man cometh—the Indian vanisheth. Can we grasp in friendship the hand raised to strike us? Nay—and it matters not whether we fall by the tempest that lays the forest low, or are cut down alone, by the stroke of the axe. I would have thanked you for life and liberty; for Mononotto's sake I would have thanked you; but if ye send me back to that dungeon—the grave of the living, feeling, thinking soul, where the sun never shineth, where the stars never rise nor set, where the free breath of heaven never enters, where all is darkness without and within"—she pressed her hand on her breast—"ye will even now condemn me to death, but death more slow and terrible than your most suffering captive ever endured from Indian fires and knives." She paused—passed unresisted without the little railing that encompassed her, mounted the steps of the platform, and advancing to the feet of the Governor, threw back her mantle, and knelt before him. Her mutilated person, unveiled by this action, appealed to the senses of the spectators. Everell involuntarily closed his eyes, and uttered a cry of agony, lost indeed in the murmurs of the crowd. She spoke, and all again were as hushed as death. "Thou didst promise," she said, addressing herself to Governor Winthrop, "to my dying mother, thou didst promise, kindness to her children. In her name, I demand of thee death or liberty."

Everell sprang forward, and clasping his hands exclaimed, "In the name of God, liberty!"

The feeling was contagious, and every voice, save her judges, shouted "liberty!—liberty! grant the prisoner liberty!"

The Governor rose, waved his hand to command silence, and would have spoken, but his voice failed him; his heart was touched with the general emotion, and he was fain to turn away to hide tears more becoming to the man, than the magistrate.

The same gentleman who, throughout the trial, had been most forward to speak, now rose; a man of metal to resist any fire. "Are ye all fools, and mad!" he cried; "ye that are gathered here together, that like the men of old, ye shout 'great is Diana of the Ephesians!'⁶ For whom would you stop the course of justice? for one who is charged before you, with having visited every tribe on the shores and in the forests, to quicken the savages to diabolical revenge!—for one who flouts the faith once delivered to the saints, to your very faces!—for one who hath entered into an open league and confederacy with Satan against you!—for one who, as ye have testimony within yourselves, in that her looks and words do so prevail over your judgments, is presently aided and abetted by the arch enemy of mankind!—I call upon you, my brethren," he added, turning to his associates, "and most especially on you, Governor Winthrop, to put a sudden end to this confusion by the formal adjournment of our court."

The Governor bowed his assent. "Rise, Magawisca," he said, in a voice of gentle authority, "I may not grant thy prayer; but what I can do in remembrance of my solemn promise to thy dying mother, without leaving undone higher duty, I will do."

"And what mortal can do, I will do," said Everell, whispering the words into Magawisca's ear as she rose. The cloud of despondency that had settled over her fine face, for an instant vanished, and she said aloud,—"Everell Fletcher, my dungeon will not be, as I said, quite dark, for thither I bear the memory of thy kindness."

Some of the magistrates seemed to regard this slight interchange of expressions between the prisoner and her champion as indecorous: the constables were ordered immediately to perform their duty, by re-conducting their prisoner to jail; and Magawisca was led out, leaving in the breasts of a great majority of the audience, a strange contrariety of opinion and feelings. Their reason, guided by the best lights they possessed, deciding against her—the voice of nature crying out for her.

Before the parties separated, the Governor arranged a private interview with Sir Philip Gardiner, to take place at his own house immediate-after dinner.

CHAPTER X

"Ye're like to the timmer o' yon rotten wood,
Ye're like to the bark o' yon rotten tree,
Ye'll slip frae me like a knotless thread,
And ye'll crack your credit wi' mae nor me."
BURNS[1]

At the period of our history, twelve o'clock was the hour appointed for dinner: we believe in the mother country—certainly in the colony then, as now, every where in the interior of our states, this natural division of time was maintained. Our magistrates did not then claim any exemption from the strict rules of simplicity and frugality that were imposed on the humble citizens, and Governor Winthrop's meridian meal, though it might have been somewhat superior in other luxuries, had no more of the luxury of time bestowed on it, than that of the honest artisans and tradesmen about him.

In order to explain what follows, it is necessary to state to our readers, that adjoining the parlour of Governor Winthrop's mansion, was that sine qua non of all thrifty housekeepers, an ample pantry. In the door of this pantry, was a glazed panel, over the parlour side of which, hung a green curtain. The glass, as glasses will, had been broken, and not yet repaired; and let housewives take the admonition if they like, on this slight accident depended life and death.

The pantry beside the door already described, had another which communicated with the kitchen; through this, Jennet, (who in housewife skill resembled the "neat-handed Phillis" of poetic fame, though, in other respects, prosaic enough) had entered to perform within the sanctum certain confidential services for Madam Winthrop.

It now drew near the hour of two, the time appointed for the interview of the Governor with Sir Philip; the dinner was over, the table removed, and all orderly and quiet in the parlour, when Jennet, in her retreat, heard Miss Leslie and Mr. Everell Fletcher enter, and though the weather was warm, close the door after them. A slight hint is sufficient for the wary and wise, and Jennet, on hearing the door shut, forbore to make any noise, which should apprise the parties of her proximity.

The young people, as if fearful of being overheard without, withdrew to the furthest extremity from the entry door, and came into the corner adjoining the pantry. They spoke, though in low tones, yet in the most earnest and animated manner; and Jennet, tempted beyond what she was able to bear, drew nigh to the door with a cat's tread, and applied her ear to the aperture, where the sounds were only slightly obstructed by the silk curtain.

While speakers and listener stood in this interesting relation to each other, Sir Philip Gardiner was approaching the mansion, his bad mind filled with projects, hopes, and fears. He had, after much painful study, framed the following story, which he hoped to impose on the credulity of the Governor, and through him, of the public. His sole care was to avoid present investigation and detection; like all who navigate winding channels, he regarded only the difficulties directly before him.

He meant that, in the first place, by way of a coup de grace, the Governor should understand he had intentionally acquiesced in the discovery of Rosa's disguise. He would then, as honest Varney[2] did, confess there had been some love-passages between the girl and himself, in the days of his folly. He would state, that subsequent to his conversion, he had placed her in a godly school in England, and that to his utter confusion, he had discovered after he had sailed from London, that she had, in the disguise she still wore, secreted herself on board the ship. He had, perhaps, felt too much indulgence for the girl's youth, and unconquerable affection for him; but he should hope that was not an unpardonable sin. He had been restrained from divulging her real character on ship-board, from his reluctance to expose her youth to insult, or further temptation. On his arrival, he was conscious it was a manifest duty, to have delivered her over to the public authorities, but pity—pity still had ruled him. He scrupled—perhaps that was a temptation of the enemy who knew well to assail the weakest points; he scrupled to give over to public shame one, of whose transgressions he had been the cause. Besides, she had been bred in France a papist; and he had hoped—trusting, perhaps, too much in his own strength—that he might convert her from the error of her ways; snatch the brand from the burning; he had indeed felt a fatherly tenderness for her, and weakly indulging that sentiment, he had still, when he found her obstinately persisting in her errors, devised a plan to shelter her from public punishment; and in pursuance of it, he had taken advantage of the opportunity afforded him by his visit to Thomas Morton, to propose to Magawisca, that in case she should obtain her liberty from the clemency of her judges, she should undertake to convey Rosa to a convent in Montreal, of the order to which she had been in her childhood attached.

He meant to plead guilty, as he thought he could well afford to do, if he was exculpated on the other points, to all the sin of acquiescence in Rosa's devotion to an unholy and proscribed religion; and to the crucifix Magawisca had produced, and which he feared would prove a "confirmation strong," to any jealousies the Governor might still harbour against him, he meant to answer, that he had taken it from Rosa to explain to Magawisca that she was of the Romish religion.

With this plausible tale, not the best that could have been devised, perhaps, by one accustomed to all the sinuosities of the human mind and human affairs, but the best that Sir Philip could frame in his present perplexity, he bent his steps towards the Governor's, a little anticipating the appointed hour, in the hope of obtaining a glimpse of Miss Leslie, whom he had not seen since their last interview at the island; and who was still the bright cynosure by which, through all the dangers that beset him, he trusted to guide himself to a joyous destiny.

Never was he more unwelcome to her sight, than when he opened the parlour door, and interrupted the deeply interesting conversation in which we left her engaged. She coldly bowed without speaking, and left him, without making any apology, in the midst of his flattering compliments on the recovery of her health.

Sir Philip and Everell were much on the terms of two un-friendly dogs, who are, by some coercion, kept from doing bat-tle, but who never meet without low growls and sullen looks, that intimate their deadly enmity. Everell paced the room twice or thrice, then snatched up his hat, left the house, and sauntered up the street.

No sooner had he disappeared, than Jennet emerged from her seclusion, her hands uplifted, and her eyes upturned—"Oh, Sir Philip! Sir Philip!" she said, as soon as she could get her voice, a delay never long with Jennet—"truly is the heart deceitful— and the lips too. Oh! who would have thought it?—such a dar-ing, presumptuous, and secret sin, too! Where is the Governor? he must know it. But first, Sir Philip, I will tell you—that will do—as you and the Governor are one in counsel."

'Heaven grant we may be so,' thought Sir Philip, and he closed the door, and turned to Jennet, eager to hear her com-munication; for her earnestness, and still more the source whence the intelligence emanated, excited his curiosity.

Jennet drew very close to him, and communicated her secret in a whisper.

At first, the listener's face did not indicate any particular emo-tion, but merely that courteous attention that a sagacious man would naturally lend to intelligence which the relator deemed of vital importance. Suddenly a light seemed to flash across him; he started away from Jennet, stood still for a moment, with a look of intense thought, then turning to his informer, he said, "Mrs. Jennet, I think we had best, for to-day, confine within our own bosoms the knowledge of this secret. As you say, Mr. Ev-erell's is a presumptuous sin; but it will not be punished unless it proceeds to the overt act."

"Overt act! what kind of act is that?" inquired Jennet.

Sir Philip explained, and Jennet soon comprehended the difference, in its consequences to the offender, between a meditated, and an executed crime. Jennet hesitated for a few moments; she had a sort of attachment to the family she had long served, much like that of an old cat for its accustomed haunts, but towards Everell she had a feeling of unqualified hostility. From his boyhood, he had been rebellious against her petty domiciliary tyranny, and had never manifested the slightest deference for her canting pretensions. Still she was loath in any way to be accessory to an act that would involve the family, with which she was herself identified, in any disgrace or distress. Sir Philip divined the cause of her hesitation, and, impatient for her decision, he essayed to resolve her doubts: "Of course, Mrs. Jennet," he said, "you are aware that any penalty Mr. Everell Fletcher would incur, will not be of a nature to touch life or limb."

"Ay—that's what I wanted to know; and that being the case, it appears to me plain duty to let him bake as he has brewed. Faithful are the wounds of a friend, Sir Philip; and this may prove a timely rebuke to his youth, and to this quicksilver, fearnought, Hope Leslie. But you will take care to have your hand come in in time, for if there should be any miss in the matter, it would prove a heavy weight to our consciences."

"Oh certainly, certainly," said Sir Philip, with undisguised exultation, "I shall, you know, command the springs, and can touch them at pleasure. Now, Mrs. Jennet, will you favour me with pen and ink; and do me still another favour"—and he took a guinea from his purse—"expend this trifle in some book for your private edification; I hear much of a famous one just brought from England, entitled, 'Food for saints, and Fire for sinners.'"

"Many thanks, Sir Philip," replied Jennet, graciously accepting the gift; "such savory treatises are as much wanted among us just now, as rain upon the parched earth: it's but a sickly and a moral time with us. You put me in mind, Sir Philip," she continued, while she was collecting the writing materials, "you put me in mind of Mr. Everell's oversight; or, rather, I may say, of his making me a mark in that unhandsome way that I can never forget. When he came from England, there was not, save myself, one of the family—no, nor an old woman or child, in

Springfield but what he had some keepsake for; not that I care
for the value of the thing—as I told Digby, at his wedding, when
he saluted every woman in the room but me. But, then, one does
not like to be slighted."

Sir Philip, by this time, was fortunately bending over his paper, and Jennet did not perceive his smile at her jumble of selfish,
and feminine resentments; and observing that he had at once
become quite abstracted from her, she withdrew, half satisfied
herself that she had acted conscientiously in her conspiracy
against her young master, and quite sure that she should appear
a pattern of wisdom and duty.

Sir Philip, mentally thanking heaven that he had not yet encountered Governor Winthrop, addressed a hasty note to him,
saying that he had come to his house, true to his appointment,
and impatient for the explanation, which, he might say without
presumption, he was sure would remove the displeasure under
which he (Sir Philip) was at this moment suffering; but that, in
consequence of a sudden and severe indisposition, the effect of
the distressful agitation of his feelings, he found himself obliged
to return to his lodgings, and defer their interview till the next
day; till then, he humbly hoped the Governor would suspend
his judgment. He then directed the note, and left it on the table,
and passed the threshold of the Winthrop mansion, as he believed, and hoped, for the last time.

CHAPTER XI

"This murderous shaft that's shot,
 Hath not yet lighted; and our safest way
Is to avoid the aim. Therefore to horse,
And let us not be dainty of leave-taking."
                                    MACBETH[1]

The Greeks and Romans had their lucky and unlucky days; and whatever name we give to the alternations of life, we believe that the experience of every family, and individual, will attest the clustering of joys or woes at marked periods. The day of Magawisca's trial was eventful, and long remembered in the annals of the Fletcher family. Indeed, every one in any way associated with them, seems to have participated in the influences of their ruling star. Each member of Governor Winthrop's household appeared to be moving in a world of his own, and to be utterly absorbed in his own projects and hopes.

Miss Downing was for a long time closeted with her uncle and aunt; then a great bustle ensued, and emissaries went to and fro, from Madam Winthrop's apartment; Madam Winthrop herself forgot her usual stateliness and dignified composure, and hurried from one apartment to another with quick footsteps and a disturbed countenance. The Governor was heard pacing up and down his study, in earnest conversation with the elder Fletcher. Everell had gone out, leaving directions with a servant to say to his father, or any one who should inquire for him, that he should not return till the next day. Hope Leslie resisted all her aunt's efforts to interest her in a string of pearls, which she intended for a wedding gift for Esther; "but," Mrs. Grafton said, wreathing them into Hope's hair, "her heart misgave her, they looked so much prettier peeping out from among Hope's wavy locks, than they would on Esther's sleek hair." The agitation of Hope's spirits was manifest, but (we grieve to unveil her infirmities) that, in her, excited no more attention than a change of weather in an April day. She read one moment—worked the next—and the next, was devoting herself with earnest affection to the amusement of her pining sister; then she would suddenly break off from her, and take a few turns in the garden: in short, confusion had suddenly intruded within the dominion of order, and usurped the government of all his subjects.

In the evening the surface of affairs, at least, bore a more tranquil aspect. The family all assembled in the parlour as usual, excepting Miss Leslie and Cradock, who had retired to the study, to look over a translation from the Italian, which Hope just recollected her tutor had never revised.

Faith Leslie sat on a cushion beside the door, in a state of vacancy and listlessness, into which she seemed to have hopelessly sunk, after the first violent emotions that succeeded her return. The ladies were plying their needles at the table: Miss Downing, pale as a statue, moved her hand mechanically, and Mrs. Grafton had just remarked, that she had seen her put her needle twelve times in the same place, when fortunately for her, any further notice of her abstraction was averted by a rap at the outer door, and a servant admitted a stranger who, without heeding a request that he would remain in the portico till the Governor should be summoned, advanced to the parlour door. He sent a keen scrutinizing glance around the room, and on every individual in it, and then fixing his eye on the Governor, he bent his head low, with an expression of deferential supplication.

His appearance was that of extreme wretchedness, and, as all who saw him thought, indicated a shipwrecked sailor. His face and figure were youthful, and his eye bright, but his skin was of a sickly ashen hue. He had on his head a sailor's woollen cap, drawn down to his eyes in part, as it seemed, to defend a wound he had received on his temple, and about which, and to the rim of his cap that covered it, there adhered clotted blood. His dress was an over-coat of coarse frieze cloth, much torn and weather beaten, and strapped around his waist with a leathern girdle; his throat was covered with a cotton handkerchief, knotted in sailor-fashion, and his legs and feet were bare.

To the Governor's inquiry of "who are you, friend?" and "what do you want?" he replied, in an unknown language, and with a low rapid enunciation. At the first sound of his voice, Faith Leslie sprang to her feet, but instantly sunk back again on the cushion, and apparently returned to her former abstraction.

Governor Winthrop eyed the stranger narrowly. "I think, brother Fletcher," he said, "this man has the Italian lineaments; perhaps, Master Cradock may understand his language, as he is well versed in all the dialects of the kingdoms of Italy. Robin," he added, "bid Master Cradock come hither."

"Master Cradock has gone out, sir, an please you, some minutes since, with Miss Leslie."

"Gone out—with Miss Leslie—whither?"

"I do not know, sir. The young lady bid me say she had gone to a friend's, and should not return till late. She begged Mrs. Jennet might be in waiting for her."

"This is somewhat unseasonable," said the Governor, looking at his watch; "it is now almost nine; but I believe," he added, in kind consideration of Mr. Fletcher's feelings, "we may trust your wild-wood bird; her flights are somewhat devious, but her instincts are safer than I once thought them."

"Trust her—yes, indeed," exclaimed Mrs. Grafton, catching the word that implied distrust. "But I wonder," she added, going to the window, and looking anxiously abroad, "that she should venture out this dark night, with nobody but that blind beetle of a Cradock to attend her; however, I suppose she is safe, if she but keep on the main land, as I think you say the wolves come no more over the neck."

"They certainly will not come any where within the bounds that our lamb is likely to stray," said Mr. Fletcher.

The Governor's care again recurred to the mendicant stranger, who now signified, by intelligible gestures, that he both wanted food and sleep. Every apartment in the Governor's house was occupied; but it was a rule with him, that admitted of no exception, that his shelter should never be denied to the wanderer, nor his charities to the poor; and, accordingly, after some consultation with the executive department of his domestic government, a flock-bed was ordered to be spread on the kitchen floor, and a meal provided, on which, we observe en passant, the stranger did extraordinary execution.

When the result of these charitable deliberations was signified to him, he expressed his gratitude by the most animated gestures, and, seeming involuntarily to recur to the natural organ of communication, he uttered, in his low and rapid manner, several sentences, which appeared, from the direction of his eye, and his repeated bows, to be addressed to his benefactor.

"Enough, enough," said the Governor, interpreting his words by a wave of his hand, which signified to the mendicant that he was to follow Robin to the kitchen. There we must leave him to achieve, in due time, an object involving most momentous consequences, while we follow on the trail of our heroine, whose excursive habits have so often compelled us to deviate from the straight line of narration.

Hope had retired to the study with Master Cradock, where she delighted her tutor with her seemingly profound attention to his criticisms on her Italian author. "You see, Miss Hope Leslie," he said, intent on illustrating a difficult passage, "the point here lies in this, that Orlando hesitates whether to go to the rescue of Beatrice."

"Ah, stop there, Master Cradock, you speak an admonition to me. You have yourself told me, the Romans believed that words spoken by those ignorant of their affairs, but applicable to them, were good or bad omens."

"True, true—you do honour your tutor beyond his deserts, in treasuring these little classical notices, that it hath been my rare privilege to plant in your mind. But how were my words an admonition to you, Miss Hope Leslie?"

"By reminding me of a duty to a friend who sadly needs my help—and thine too, my good tutor."

"My help!—your friend! It shall be as freely granted as Jonathan's was to David, or Orpheus' to Eurydice."[2]

"The task to be done," said Hope, while she could not forbear laughing at Cradock's comparing himself to the master of
music, "is not very unlike that of Orpheus. But we have no time
to lose—put on your cloak, Master Cradock, while I tell Robin
what to say if we are inquired for."

"My cloak! you forget we are in the summer solstice; and the
evening is somewhat over sultry, so that even now, with my
common habiliments, I am in a drip."

"So much the more need to guard against the evening air,"
said Hope, who had her own secret and urgent reasons for insisting on the cloak; "put on the cloak, Master Cradock, and
move quick, and softly, for I would pass out without notice from
the family."

A Moslem would as soon have thought of resisting fate, as
Cradock of opposing a wish of his young mistress, which only
involved his own comfort, so he cloaked himself, while Hope
flew to the kitchen, gave her orders, and threw on her hat and
shawl, which she had taken care to have at hand. They then
passed through the hall, and beyond the court, without attracting
observation.

Cradock was so absorbed in the extraordinary happiness of
being selected as the confidential aid and companion of his favourite, that he would have followed her to the world's end,
without question, if she had not herself turned the direction of
his thoughts.

"It is like yourself," she said, "my good tutor, to obey the
call of humanity, without inquiring in whose behalf it comes;
and I think you will not be the less prompt to follow the dictates
of your own heart, and my wishes, when I tell you that I am
leading you to poor Magawisca's prison."

"Ah! the Indian woman, concerning whom I have heard
much colloquy. I would, in truth, be fain to see her, and speak
to her such comfortable words and counsels, as may, with a
blessing, touch the heathen's heart. You have, doubtless, Miss
Hope, provided yourself with a passport from the Governor,"
he added, for almost the first time in his life looking at the business part of a transaction.

"Master Cradock, I did not esteem that essential."

"Oh! but it is; and if you will abide here one moment, I will hasten back and procure it," he said, in his simplicity never suspecting that Miss Leslie's omission was any thing other than an oversight.

"Nay, nay, Master Cradock," she replied, laying her hand on his arm, "it is too late now: my heart is set on this visit to the unhappy prisoner—and if you were to go back, Madam Winthrop, or my aunt, or somebody else, might deem the hour unseasonable. Leave it all to me—I will manage with Barnaby Tuttle; and when we return, be assured, I will take all the blame, if there is any, on myself."

"No, that you shall not—it shall fall on my grey head, where there should be wisdom, and not on your youth, which lacketh discretion"—'and lacketh nought else,' he murmured to himself; and, without any further hesitation, he acquiesced in proceeding onward.

They arrived, without hindrance, at the jail, and knocked a long time for admittance at that part of the tenement occupied by our friend Barnaby, without his appearing. Hope became impatient, and bidding Cradock follow her, she passed through the passage, and opened the door of Barnaby's apartment.

He was engaged in what he still called his 'family exercise;' though, by the death of his wife, and the marriage of his only child, he was the sole remnant of that corporation. On seeing our heroine, he gave her a familiar nod of recognition, and by an equally intelligible sign, he demonstrated his desire that she should seat herself, and join in his devotions, which he was just closing, by singing a psalm, versified by himself; for honest Barnaby, after his own humble fashion, was a disciple of the tuneful Nine. Hope assented, and, with the best grace she could command, accompanied him through twelve stanzas of long, and very irregular metre, which he obligingly, gave out, line by line. When this, on Hope's part, extempore worship was finished, "Welcome here, and many thanks, Miss Leslie," said Barnaby, "it's a good sign to find a prepared heart and ready voice. Service to you, Master Cradock, you are not gifted in psalmody, I see."

"Not in the outward manifestation, but the inward feeling is,

I trust, vouchsafed to me. My heart hath taken part in the fag
end of your feast."

"A pretty similitude truly, Master Cradock, and a token for
good is it when the appetite is always sharp set for such a feast.
But come, Miss Leslie," raking open the embers, "draw up your
chair, and warm your dear little feet. She looks pale yet after her
sickness, ha, Master Cradock? You should not have come forth
in the evening air—not but what I am right glad to see you—
the sight of you always brings to mind your kindness to the
dead and the living. You have not been here, I think, since the
night of Ruthy's wedding—that puts me in mind that I got a
letter from Ruthy to-day. I'll read it to you," he continued, taking off his spectacles, and giving them a preparatory wipe—
"Ruthy is quite handy with her pen—takes after the Tuttles in
that: you know, Miss Leslie, my great-grandfather wrote a
book."

"Yes," said Hope, interrupting him, and rising, "and I trust
his great-grandson will live to write another."

"Sit down, Miss Leslie—it may be—those of as humble a
degree as Barnaby Tuttle have written books; and writing runs
in families, like the king's evil"—and Barnaby laughed at his
own witty illustration—"but sit down, Miss Leslie, I must read
Ruthy's letter to you."

"Not now, good Barnaby; let me take it home with me; it is
getting late, and I have a favour to ask of you."

"A favour to ask of me!—ask any thing, my pretty mistress,
that's in the power of Barnaby Tuttle to grant. Ah! Mr. Cradock,
there's nobody knows what I owe her—what she did for my
wife when she laid on her death-bed, and all for nothing but our
thanks and prayers."

"Oh, you forget that your wife had once been a servant to
my dear mother."

"Yes, yes, but only in the common way, and there's few that
would have thought of it again. It's not my way to speak with
flattering lips, but truly, Miss Hope Leslie, you seem to be one
of those that does not to others that it may be done to you
again."

"Oh, my good friend Barnaby, you speak this praise in the wrong time, for I have even now come, as I told you, to beg a favour on the score of old friendship."

"It shall be done—it shall be done," said Barnaby, snapping his fingers, his most energetic gesture; "be it what it may, it shall be done."

"Oh, it is not so very much, but only, Barnaby, I wish it quickly done, that we may return. I want you to conduct Master Cradock and myself to your Indian prisoner, and leave us in her cell for a short time."

"Is that all! certainly—certainly," and anxious to make up for the smallness of the service by the avidity of his compliance, Barnaby prepared his lamp with unwonted activity. "Now we are ready," he said, "just show me your permit, and we'll go without delay."

Hope had flattered herself, that her old friend in his eagerness to serve her, would dispense with the ceremony of a passport from the Governor. Agitated by this new and alarming obstacle, she commanded her voice with difficulty to reply in her usual tone. "How could I think it necessary to bring a permit to you, who know me so well, Barnaby?"

"Not *necessary!* that was an odd thought for such an all-witted damsel as thou art, Miss Hope Leslie. Not *necessary,* indeed! why I could not let in the king if he were to come from his throne—the king truly, he is but as his subjects now; but if the first parliament man were to come here, I could not let him in without a permit from the Governor."

Hope walked up and down the room, biting her lips with vexation and disappointment. Every moment's delay hazarded the final success of her project. Poor Cradock now interposed with one of his awkward movements which, though made with the best will in the world, was sure to overturn the burden he essayed to bear. "Be comforted, Miss Hope Leslie," he said, "I am not so nimble as I was in years past, but it is scarce fifteen minutes walk to the Governor's, and I will hasten thither, and get the needful paper."

"Ay, ay, so do," said Barnaby, "that will set all right."

"No," cried Hope; "no, Master Cradock, you shall not go. If Barnaby cannot render me this little kindness, there is an end of it. I will give it up. I shall never ask another favour of you, Barnaby," and she sat down, anxious and disappointed, and burst into tears. Honest Barnaby could not stand this. To see one so much his superior—one who had been an angel of mercy to his habitation—one who had a right to command him in all permitted service, thrown into such deep distress by his refusal of a favour which, after all, there could be no harm in granting, he could not endure.

"Well, well," he said, after hesitating and jingling his keys for a moment, "dry up your tears, my young lady; a 'wayward child,' they say, 'will have its way;' and they say too, 'men's hearts melt in women's tears,' and I believe it; come, come along, you shall have your way."

Hope now passed to the extreme of joy and gratitude. "Bless you—bless you, Barnaby," she said, "I was sure you would not be cross to me."

"Lord help us, child, no, there's no denying you; but I do wish you was as thoughtful as Miss Esther Downing; she never came without a permit—a good thing is consideration—you have made me to do that which I trust not to do again—step aside from known duty—but we're erring creatures."

Hope had the grace to pause one instant, and to meditate a retreat before she had involved others in sinning against their consciences; but she had the end to be attained so much at heart, and the faults to be committed by her agents were of so light a dye, that the scale of her inclinations soon preponderated, and she proceeded. When they came to the door of the dungeon,— "Hark to her," said Barnaby; "is not that a voice for psalmody?" Magawisca was singing in her own language, in the most thrilling and plaintive tones. Hope thought there could not be darkness or imprisonment to such a spirit. "It is in truth, Barnaby," she replied, "a voice fit to sing the praises of God." Barnaby now turned the bolts and opened the door, and as the feeble ray of his lamp fell athwart the dungeon's gloom, Hope perceived Magawisca sitting on her flock bed, with a blanket wrapped around her. On hearing their voices she had ceased her singing, but she gave no other sign of her consciousness of the presence of her visitors.

Miss Leslie took the lamp from Barnaby. "How much time will you allow us?" she asked.

"Ten minutes."

"Ten minutes! oh, more than that I pray you, good Barnaby."

"Not one second more," replied Barnaby, resolute not to concede another inch of ground. "There may be question of this matter—you must consider, my dear young lady."

"I will—always in future, I will, Barnaby; now you may leave me."

"Yes, yes, I understand," said Barnaby, giving a knowing nod. "You mind the scripture rule about the right and the left hand —some creature comfort to be given to the prisoner. I marvel that ye bring Master Cradock with you, but in truth, he hath no more eye nor ear than the wall."

"Marvel not at any thing, Barnaby, but leave me, and let my ten minutes be as long as the last ten minutes before dinner."

Hope, quick as she was in invention and action, felt that she had a very brief space to effect her purposed arrangements, and while she hesitated as to the best mode of beginning, Cradock, who nothing doubted he had been brought hither as a ghostly teacher, asked whether "he should commence with prayer or exhortation?"

"Neither—neither, Master Cradock—do just as I bid you; you will not hesitate to help a fellow creature out of deep, un-merited distress?" this was uttered in a tone of half inquiry and half-assertion, that enforced by Hope's earnest imploring man-ner, quickened Cradock's slow apprehension. She perceived the light was dawning on his mind, and she turned from him to Magawisca: "Magawisca," she said, stooping over her, "rouse yourself—trust me—I have come to release you." She made no reply, nor movement: "Oh! there is not a moment to lose. Ma-gawisca, listen to me—speak to me."

"Thou didst once deceive and betray me, Hope Leslie," she replied, without raising her head.

Hope concisely explained the secret machinations of Sir

Philip, by which she had been made the unconscious and innocent instrument of betraying her. "Then, Hope Leslie," she exclaimed, rising from her abject seat, and throwing off her blanket, "thy soul is unstained, and Everell Fletcher's truth will not be linked to falsehood."

Hope would have explained that her destiny and Everell's were not to be interwoven, but she had neither time nor heart for it. "You are too generous, Magawisca," she said, in a tremulous tone, "to think of any one but yourself, now—we have not a breath to lose—take this ribbon," and she untied her sash; "bind your hair tight with it, so that you can draw Master Cradock's wig over your head—you must exchange dresses with him."

"Nay, Hope Leslie, I cannot leave another in my net."

"You must not hesitate, Magawisca—you will be freed—he runs no risk, will suffer no harm—Everell awaits you—speed, I pray you." She turned to Cradock, "now, my good tutor," she said, in her most persuasive tones, "lend me your aid, quickly—Magawisca must have the loan of your wig, hat, boots, and cloak, and you must sit down there on her bed, and let me wrap you in her blanket."

Cradock retreated to the wall, planted himself against it, shut his eyes, and covered his ears with his hands, that temptation might, at every entrance, be quite shut out. "Oh! I scruple, I scruple," he articulated in a voice of the deepest distress.

"Scruple not, dear Master Cradock," replied Hope, pulling down one of his hands, and holding it between both hers, "no harm can, no harm shall befall you."

"Think not, sweet Miss Hope, it's for the perishing body I am thoughtful; for thy sake I would bare my neck to the slayer; to thy least wish I would give the remnant of my days; but I scruple if it be lawful for a Christian man to lend this aid to an idolater."

"Oh! is that all? we have no time to answer such scruples now, but to-morrow, master Cradock, I will show you that you greatly err;" and as she said this, she proceeded, without any further ceremony, to divest the old man of his wig, which she very carefully adjusted on Magawisca's head. Both parties were

passive in her hands, Magawisca not seeming to relish much better than Cradock, the false character she was assuming. Such was
Cradock's habitual deference to his young mistress, that it was
morally impossible for him to make any physical resistance to
her movements: but neither his conscience, nor his apprehensions for her, would permit him to be silent when he felt a conviction that she was doing, and he was suffering, an act that was
a plain transgression of a holy law.

"Stay thy hand," he said, in a beseeching voice, "and let not
thy feet move so swiftly to destruction."

"Just raise your foot, while I draw off this boot, Master
Cradock."

He mechanically obeyed, but at the same time continued his
admonition: "Was not Jehoshaphat reproved of Micaiah the
prophet, for going down to the help of Ahab?"[3]

"Now the other foot, Master Cradock—there, that will do.
Draw them on, Magawisca, right over your moccasins—quick,
I beseech you."

"Was not the good king Josiah reproved in the matter of
Pharaoh-nechoh?"

"Oh, Magawisca! how shall I ever make your slender
shoulders and straight back look any thing like Master Cradock's broad, round shoulders? One glance of Barnaby's dim
old eyes will detect you. Ah! this will do—I will bind the pillow
on with the sheet." While she was uttering the device, she accomplished it. She then threw Magawisca's mantle over her expanded shoulders, and Cradock's cloak over all; and, finally, the
wig was surmounted by the old man's steeple-crowned hat.
"Now," she said, almost screaming with joy at the transformation so suddenly effected, "now, Magawisca, all depends on
yourself: if you will but contrive to screen your face, and shuffle
a little in your gait, all will go well."

The hope of liberty—of deliverance from her galling
imprisonment—of escape beyond the power and dominion of
her enemies, had now taken full possession of Magawisca; and
the thought that she should owe her release to Everell and to
Hope, who in her imagination was identified with him, filled her
with emotions of joy, resembling those a saint may feel, when

she sees in vision the ministering angels sent to set her free from her earthly prison: "I will do all thou shalt command me, Hope Leslie; thou art indeed a spirit of light, and love, and beauty."

"True, true, true," cried Cradock, losing, in the instincts of his affection, the opposition he had so valorously maintained, and his feelings flowing back into their accustomed channel, "Thou woman in man's attire, it is given to thee to utter truth, even as of old, lying oracles were wont to speak words of prophecy."

Hope had not, as may be imagined, stood still to listen to this long sentence, uttered in her tutor's deliberate, entrecoupé manner, but in the meanwhile she had, with an almost supernatural celerity of movement, arranged every thing to present the same aspect as when Barnaby first opened the door of the dungeon. She drew Cradock to the bed, seated him there, and wrapped the blanket about him as it had enveloped Magawisca. "Oh! I hear Barnaby," she exclaimed; "dear Master Cradock, sit a little straighter—there—that will do—turn a little more side ways, you will not look so broad—there—that's better."

"Miss Hope Leslie, ye have perverted the simple-minded."

"Say not another word, Master Cradock; pray do not breathe so like a trumpet; ah, I see it is my fault." She readjusted the blanket, which she had drawn so close over the unresisting creature's face as almost to suffocate him. "Now, Magawisca, sit down on this stool—your back to the door, close to Master Cradock, as if you were talking with him." All was now arranged to her mind, and she spent the remaining half instant in whispering consolations to Cradock: "Do not let your heart fail you, my good kind tutor—in one hour you shall be relieved." Cradock would have again explained that he was regardless of any personal risk, but she interrupted him: "Nay, you need not speak; I know that is not your present care, but do not be troubled; we are commanded to do good to all—the rain falleth on the just and the unjust—and if we are to help our enemy's ox out of the pit, much more our enemy. This best of all thy kind services shall be requited. I will be a child to thy old age—hush—there's Barnaby."

She moved a few steps from the parties, and when the jailer

opened the door, she appeared to be awaiting him: "Just in season, good Master Tuttle; my tutor has nothing more to say, and I am as impatient to go, as you are to have me gone."

"It is only for your own sake that I am impatient, Miss Hope; let us make all haste out." He took up the lamp which he had left in the cell, trimmed it, and raised the wick, that it might better serve to guide them through the dark passage.

Hope was alarmed by the sudden increase of light—"lend me the lamp, Barnaby," she said, "to look for my glove—where can I have dropped it? It must be somewhere about here. I shall find it in a minute, Master Cradock, you had best go on while I am looking."

Magawisca obeyed the hint, while Hope in her pretended search, so skilfully managed the light, that not a ray of it touched Magawisca's face. She had passed Barnaby—Hope thought the worst danger escaped. "Ah, here it is," she said, and by way of precaution, she added, in the most careless tone she could assume, "I will carry the lamp for you, Barnaby."

"No, no, thank you, Miss Leslie, I always like to carry the light myself; and besides, I must take a good look at you both before I lock the door. It is a rule I always observe in such cases, lest I should be left to 'brood the eggs the fox has sucked.' It is a prudent rule I assure you, always to be sure you take out the same you let in. Here, Master Cradock, turn round, if you please, to the light, just for form's sake."

Magawisca had advanced several steps into the passage, and Hope's first impulse was to scream to her to run, but a second, and happier thought prevailed, and taking her shawl, which was hanging negligently over her arm, she contrived in throwing it over her head, to sweep it across Barnaby's lamp, in such a way as to extinguish the light beyond the possibility of recovery, as Barnaby proved, by vainly trying to blow it again into a flame.

"Do not put yourself to any further trouble about it, Barnaby, it was all my fault; but it matters not, you know the way—just give me your arm, and Master Cradock can take hold of my shawl, and we shall grope through this passage without any difficulty."

Barnaby arranged himself as she suggested, and then hoping

her sudden action had broken the chain of his thoughts, and determined he should not have time to resume it, she said,— "When you write to Ruth, Barnaby, be sure you commend me kindly to her; and tell her, that I have done the baby linen I promised her, and that I hope little Barnaby will prove as good a man as his grandfather."

"Oh, thank ye, Miss Hope, I trust, by the blessing of the Lord, much better; but they do say," added the old man, with a natural ancestral complacency, "they do say he favours me; he's got the true Tuttle chin, the little dog!"

"You cannot tell yet whether he is gifted in psalmody, Barnaby?"

"La, Miss Hope, you must mean to joke. Why little Barnaby is not five weeks old till next Wednesday morning, half past three o'clock. But I'm as sure he will take to psalmody as if I knew; there never was a Tuttle that did not."

Our heroine thus happily succeeded in beguiling the way to the top of the staircase, where a passage diverged to the outer door, and there with many thanks, and assurances of future gratitude, she bade Barnaby good night; and anticipating any observation he might make of Cradock's silence, she said, "my tutor seems to have fallen into one of his reveries; but never mind, another time he will remember to greet and thank you."

Barnaby was turning away from the door, when he recollected that the sudden extinction of the candle had prevented his intended professional inspection. "Miss Hope Leslie," he cried, "be so good as to stay one moment, while I get a light; the night is so murky that I cannot see, even here, the lineaments of Master Cradock's complexion."

"Pshaw, Barnaby, for mercy's sake do not detain us now for such an idle ceremony; you see the *lineaments* of that form, I think; we must have been witches indeed, to have transformed Magawisca's slender person into that enormous bulk; but one sense is as good as another—speak, Master Cradock," she added, relying on Magawisca's discretion. "Oh, he is in one of his silent fits, and a stroke of lightning would scarcely bring a sound from him, so good night, Barnaby," she concluded, gently putting him back and shutting the door.

'It is marvellous,' thought Barnaby, as he reluctantly acquiesced in relinquishing the letter of his duty, 'how this young creature spins me round, at her will, like a top. I think she keeps the key to all hearts.'

With this natural reflection he retired to rest, without taking the trouble to return to the dungeon, which he would have done, if he had really felt one apprehension of the fraud that had been there perpetrated.

At the instant the prison door was closed, Magawisca divested herself of her hideous disguise, and proceeded on with Hope, to the place where Everell was awaiting them, with the necessary means to transport her beyond the danger of pursuit. But while our heroine is hastening onward, with a bounding step and exulting heart, we must acquaint our readers with the cruel conspiracy that was maturing against her.

CHAPTER XII

"Sisters! weave the web of death:
Sisters! cease; the work is done."
THE FATAL SISTERS[1]

The conversation overheard by the faithless Jennet, and communicated with all its particulars to Sir Philip Gardiner, was, as must have been already conjectured by our readers, the contrivance for Magawisca's liberation. It appeared by her statement, that Hope and Magawisca unattended, would, at a late hour of the evening, pass through an uninhabited and unfrequented part of the town near the water-side, and that Everell, with assistants, would be in waiting for them at a certain landing-place. Before they reached there, Sir Philip knew there were many points where they might be intercepted, without the possibility of Everell's coming to their rescue.

Sir Philip was entangled in the meshes of his own weaving; extrication was possible—nay, he believed probable; but there was a fearful chance against him. He had now to baffle well-founded suspicions—to disprove facts—to double his guard over his assumed and tiresome character—and after all, human art could not secure him from accidents, which would bring in their train immediate disgrace and defeat. His passion for Miss Leslie had been stimulated by the obstacles which opposed it. His hopes were certainly abated by her indifference; but self-love, and its minister vanity, are inexhaustible in their resources; and Sir Philip trusted for better success in future to his own powers, and to feminine weakness; for he, like other profligates, believed that there was no woman, however pure and lofty her seeming, but she was commanded

> "By such poor passion as the maid that milks,
> And does the meanest chares;"[2]

yet this process of winning the prize was slow, and the result, alas! uncertain.

Jennet's information suggested a master-stroke by which he could at once achieve his object; a single coup de main by which he could carry the citadel he had so long and painfully besieged. If an evil spirit had been abroad on a corrupting mission, he could not have selected a subject more eager to grasp temptation than Sir Philip; nor a fitter agent than Jennet, nor have contrived a more infernal plot against an "innocent and aidless lady," than that which we must now disclose.

Chaddock (whose crew had occasioned such danger and alarm to Miss Leslie) was still riding in the bay with his vessel. Sir Philip had formerly some acquaintance with this man. He knew him to be a desperate fellow—that he had once been in confederacy with the bucaniers of Tortuga[3]—the self-styled "brothers of the coast," and he believed that he might be persuaded to enter upon any new and lawless enterprise.

Accordingly, from Governor Winthrop's he repaired to Chaddock's vessel, and presented such motives to him, and offered such rewards, as induced the wretch to enter heartily into his designs. Fortunately for their purposes, the vessel was ready for sea, and they decided to commence their voyage that very night. All Miss Leslie's paternal connexions were on the royal side—her fortune was still in their hands, and subject to their control. "If the lady's reluctance to accept his hand was not subdued before the end of the voyage," (a chance scarcely worth consideration) Sir Philip said, "she must then submit to stern necessity, which even a woman's will could not oppose." After their arrival in England, he meant to abandon himself to the disposal of fortune; but he promised Chaddock, that he, with certain other cavaliers, whom he asserted had already meditated such an enterprise, would, with the remnant of their fortunes, embark with him, and enrol themselves among the adventurers of Tortuga.

It may be remembered by our readers, that early in our history, some glimmerings of a plot of this nature appear, from a letter of Sir Philip's, even then to have dawned on his mind; but other purposes had intervened and put it off till now, when it was ripened by sudden and fit opportunity.

The detail of operations being all settled by these worthy confederates, Sir Philip, at nightfall, went once more to the town, secretly withdrew his baggage from his lodgings, and bidding Rosa, who, in sorrow and despair, mechanically obeyed, to follow, he returned to the vessel, humming, as he took his last look at the scene where he had played so unworthy a part,

> *"Kind Boston, adieu! part we must, though 'tis pity,*
> *But I'm made for mankind—all the world is my city."*

Sir Philip, in his arrangements with Chaddock, excused himself from being one of the party who were to effect the abduction of Miss Leslie. Perhaps the external habits of a gentleman, and it may be, some little remnant of human kindness, (for we would not believe that man can become quite a fiend,) rendered him reluctant to take a personal part in the cruel outrage he had planned and prepared. Chaddock himself commanded the enterprise, and was to be accompanied by four of the most daring of his crew.

The night was moonless, and not quite clear. "It is becoming dark, extremely dark, Captain," Sir Philip said, in giving his last instructions, "but it is impossible you should make a mistake. Miss Leslie's companion, as I told you, may be disguised—she may wear a man's or woman's apparel, but you have an infallible guide in her height: she is at least a half head taller than Miss Leslie. It may be well, when you get to the wharf, to divide your party, agreeing on the signal of a whistle. But I rely on your skill and discretion."

"You may rely on it," replied the hardy desperado. "He who has boarded Spanish Galleons, stormed castles, pillaged cities, violated churches, and broken open monasteries, may be entrusted with the capture of a single defenceless girl."

Sir Philip recoiled from trusting his prey in the clutches of this tiger; but there was no alternative. "Have a care, Chaddock," he said, "that she is treated with all due and possible gentleness."

"Ay, ay, Sir Philip—kill, but not wound"—a smile of derision accompanied his words.

"You have pledged me the honour of a gentleman," said Sir Philip, in an alarmed tone.

"Ay—the only bond of free souls. Remember, Sir Philip," he added, for he perceived the suspicion the knight would fain have hidden in his inmost soul, "remember our motto, 'Trusted, we are true—suspected, we betray.' I have pledged my honour, better than parchment and seal——if you confide in it."

"Oh, I do—entirely—implicitly—I have not the shadow of a doubt, my dear fellow."

Chaddock turned away, laughing contemptuously at the ineffectual hypocrisy of Sir Philip, and ordered his men, who were to be left in charge of the vessel, to have every thing in readiness to sail at the moment of his return. "And whither bound, Captain?" demanded one of his sailors.

"To hell," was his ominous reply. This answer, seemingly accidental, was long remembered and repeated, as a proof that the unhappy wretch was constrained, thus involuntarily, to pronounce his approaching doom.

Once more, before he left the vessel, Sir Philip addressed him: "Be in no haste to return," he said; "the lady was not to leave Governor Winthrop's before half-past eight—she may meet with unforeseen detentions—you will reach the dock a few minutes before nine. Take your stations as I have directed, and fortune cannot thwart us, if you are patient—wait till ten—eleven—twelve, or one, if need be. Again, I entreat there may be no unnecessary haste; I shall have no apprehensions—I repose on your fidelity."

"D—n him," muttered Chaddock, as he turned away, "he reposes on my fidelity!—while he has my vessel in pledge."

Sir Philip remained standing by the side of the vessel, listening to the quick strokes of the oars, till the sounds died away in the distance, then he spoke aloud and exultingly, "shine out my good star, and guide this prize to me."

"Oh! rather," exclaimed Rosa, who stood unobserved beside him, "rather, merciful heaven, let thy lightnings blast her, or thy waves swallow her. Oh, God!" she continued, sinking on her knees, and clasping her hands, "shield the innocent—save her from the hand of the destroyer."

Sir Philip recoiled, it seemed to him there was something prophetic in the piercing tones of the unhappy girl, and, for a moment, he felt as if her prayer must penetrate to heaven, but soon collecting courage, "hush that mockery, Rosa," he said, "your words are scorpions to me."

Rosa remained for a few moments on her knees, but without again giving voice to her feelings, then rising, and sobbing as she spoke, "I thought," she said, "no prayer of mine would ever go upward again. I have tried to pray, and the words fell back like stones upon my heart; but now I pray for the innocent, and they part from me winged for heaven." She folded her arms, looked upwards, and continued to speak as if it were the involuntary utterance of her thoughts: "How wildly the stars shoot their beams through the parting clouds! I have sometimes thought that good spirits come down on those bright rays to do their messages of love. They may even now be on their way to guard a pure and helpless sister—God speed them!"

Sir Philip's superstitious fears were awakened: "What do you mean, Rosa?" he exclaimed; "what, are you talking of stars! I see nothing but this cursed hazy atmosphere, that hangs like a pall over the water. Stars indeed! are you mad, Rosa?"

Rosa replied, with a touching simplicity, as if the inquiry were made in good faith, "Yes—betimes I think I am mad. Thoughts rush so fast, so wildly through my poor head—and then, again, all is vacancy. Yes," she continued, as if meditating her case, "I think my brain is touched; but this—this, Sir Philip, is not madness. Do you not know that all the good have their ministering spirits? Why, I remember reading in the 'Legends of the Saints,' which our good Abbess gave me, of a chain, invisible to mortal senses, that encompassed all the faithful, from the bright spirits that wait around the throne of heaven, to the lowliest that walk upon the earth. It is of such exquisite temper that nought but sin can harm it; but if that but touch it, it falls apart like rust-eaten metal."

"Away with these fantastic legends, inventions of hypocritical priests and tiresome old women. You must curb these foolish vagaries of your imagination, Rosa. I have present and urgent work for you; do but this good service for me, and I will love you again, and make you as happy as you were in your brightest days."

"You make me *happy*, Sir Philip! Alas! alas! there is no happiness without innocence; if that be once lost, like the guilty Egyptian's pearl, you told me of, melted in the bowl of pleasure, happiness cannot be restored."

"As you please, girl—if you will not be happy, you may play the penitent Magdalen the rest of your life. You shall select your own convent, and tell your beads, and say your prayers, and be as demure and solemn as any seeming saint of them all. I will give you a penance to begin with,—nay, I am serious—hear me. In spite of your prayers, and visions, and silly fancies, Miss Leslie must soon be here; the snare is too well prepared to be escaped. After this one violence, to which she and cruel fate have driven me, I will be a true knight, as humble and worshipful as any hero of chivalry."

"But she does not now love you, and do you not fear she will hate you for this outrage?"

"Ay, but there is a potent alchymy at work for us in the hearts of you women, that turns hate to love. You shall yet hear her say, like the lady of Sir Gawaine, 'Oh! how it is befallen me, that now I love him whom I before most hated of all men living.'⁴ But you must aid me, Rosa—this proud queen must have her maid of honour."

"And I must be the poor slave to do her bidding!" said Rosa, impatiently, interrupting him, and all other feelings giving way to the rising of womanly pride.

"Nay, not so, Rosa," replied Sir Philip; and added, in a voice which he hoped might soothe her petulance, "render to her all maidenly service; for a little while do the tasks of the bond-woman, and you shall yet have her wages—nay, start not—you remember the good Patriarch's affections manifestly leaned to the side of Hagar."[5]

"Yes, yes—and I remember too what her fate was—the fate of all who follow in her footsteps—to be cast out to wander forth in a desert, where there is not one sign of God's bounty left to them."—She burst into tears, and added, "I would give my poor life, and a thousand more, if I had them, to save Hope Leslie, but I will never do her menial service."

Sir Philip continued to offer arguments and entreaties, but nothing that he said had the least effect on Rosa; he could not extort a promise from her, nor perceive the slightest indication of conformity to his wishes. But trusting that when the time came she would of necessity submit to his authority, he relinquished his solicitations, and quitting her side, he paced the deck with hurried impatient footsteps.

There is no solitude to the good or bad. Nature has her ministers that correspond with the world within the breast of man. The words, "my kingdom is within you," are worth all the metaphysical discoveries ever made by unassisted human wisdom. If all is right in that "kingdom," beautiful forms and harmonious voices surround us, discoursing music; but if the mind is filled with guilty passions—recollections of sin—and purposes of evil, the ministering angels of nature are converted into demons, whose "monstrous rout are heard to howl like stable wolves." Man cannot live in tranquil disobedience to the law of virtue, inscribed on his soul by the finger of God. "Our torments" cannot "become our elements." To Sir Philip's disordered imagination the heavy mist seemed like an infolding shroud—there was a voice of sullen menace in the dashing of the waves against the vessel—the hooting of the night-bird was ominous—and Rosa's low sobs, and the horrid oaths of the misruled crew, rung in his ears like evil prophecies.

Time wore away heavily enough till ten, the earliest moment he had calculated on the return of the boat, but after that it appeared to stand stock-still. He ordered the signal lights attached to the mast to be doubled—he strained his eyes in the vain attempt to descry an approaching object, and then cursed the fog that hemmed in his sight. Suddenly a fresh breeze came off the shore, the fog dispersed, and he could discern the few lights that still glimmered from the habitations of the town, but no boat was seen or heard. "What folly," he repeated to himself a hundred times, "to be thus impatient; they certainly have not failed in their object, or relinquished it, for in that case they would have been here—it is scarcely time to expect them yet;" but, as every one must have experienced, when awaiting with intense anxiety an expected event, the suggestions of reason could not calm the perturbations of impatience. For another hour he continued to stride the deck, approaching the light at every turn to look at his watch. The sailors now began to fret at the delay. "Every thing was ready," they said, "good luck had sent them a fair breeze, and the tide had just turned in their favor." And in Sir Philip's favour too, it appeared, for at this moment the longed-for boat was both heard and seen rapidly nearing the vessel. He gazed towards it, as if it contained for him a sentence of life or death—and life it was, for he soon perceived a female form wrapped in Chaddock's watch-cloak.

The boat came to the side of the vessel.—"Has the scoundrel dared to put his arm around Hope Leslie?" thought the knight, as he saw the captain's arm encircling the unfortunate girl; but a second reflection told him that this, which seemed even to him profanity, was but a necessary precaution! "He dared not trust her—she would have leaped into the waves rather than have come to me—ungracious girl!"

"What hath kept you?" called out one of the sailors.

"The devil and Antonio," replied the captain. "We left him with the boat, and while we were grappling the prize he ran away. I had to be chains and fetters to the prisoner—we had not hands to man our oars, so we waited for the fellow, but he came not, and has, doubtless, ere this, given the alarm. Weigh your anchor and spread your sails, boys—starting with this wind and tide we'll give them a devil of a chace, and bootless at last."

While this was saying, the unhappy victim was lifted up the side of the vessel, and received in Sir Philip's arms. She threw back the hood that had been drawn over her head, and attempted to speak, but was prevented by her shawl, which the ruffians had bound over her face to prevent the emission of any sound. Sir Philip was shocked at the violence and indignity she had suffered. "Did I not order you, Chaddock," he said, "to treat the lady with all possible respect?"

"D—n your orders," replied the captain, "was I to let her scream like forty sea-mews, and raise the town upon us."

"A thousand—thousand pardons!" whispered Sir Philip, in a low imploring voice, and then aloud to Chaddock, "but after you left the town, captain, you surely should have paid more respect to my earnest and repeated injunctions."

"D—n your injunctions. John Chaddock is yet master of his vessel and boat too. I tell you when the fishing-smacks hailed us, that even with that close-reefed sail, she made a noise like a creaking mast in a gale."

"Oh forgive—forgive," whispered Sir Philip, "this horrible —necessary outrage. Lean on me, I will conduct you away from these wretches—a room is prepared for you—Rosa shall attend you—you are queen here—you command us all. Forgive— forgive—and fear nothing. I will not remove your skreen till you are beyond the lawless gaze of these fellows—here, Roslin!" he called, for he still kept up the farce of Rosa's disguise in the presence of the ship's company, "here, Roslin!—take the lamp, and follow me."

Rosa obeyed, her bosom heaving with struggling emotions, and her hand trembling so that she could scarcely hold the lamp. "Bear the light up, and more steadily, Roslin. Nay, my beloved—adored mistress, do not falter; hasten forward—in one minute more we shall be below, in your own domain, where you may admit or exclude me at pleasure. Do not struggle thus—you have driven me to this violence—you must forgive the madness you have caused. I am your slave for life."

They had just passed down the steps that served as a companion way, when Sir Philip observed on his right hand, an uncovered barrel of gunpowder. It had been left in this exposed situation by a careless fellow, entrusted with the preparation of the fire arms for the expedition to the town. "Have a care," cried Sir Philip to Rosa, who was just coming down the stairs; "stay where you are—do not approach that gunpowder with the light." He heard a footstep above. "Here, friend," he called, "lend us a hand; come down and cover this powder. We cannot discretely move an inch." The footsteps ceased, but there was no reply to the call. "I cannot leave Miss Leslie," continued Sir Philip, "she leans on me as if she were fainting. Set down your lamp, Rosa, and come yourself, and cover the barrel."

Rosa did not set down the lamp, but moved forward one or two steps with it in her hand, and then paused. She seemed revolving some dreadful purpose in her mind. Her eyes glanced wildly from Sir Philip to his helpless victim—then she groaned aloud, and pressed her hand upon her head as if it were bursting.

Sir Philip did not observe her—he was intent upon his companion. "She is certainly fainting," he said, "it is the close air and this cursed shawl." He attempted to remove it, but the knot by which it was tied baffled his skill, and he again shouted to Rosa, "Why do you not obey me? Miss Leslie is suffocating—set down the lamp, I say, and call assistance. Damnation!" he screamed, "what means the girl?" as Rosa made one desperate leap forward, and shrieking, "it cannot be worse for any of us!" threw the lamp into the barrel.

The explosion was instantaneous—the hapless, pitiable girl—her guilty destroyer—his victim—the crew—the vessel, rent to fragments, were hurled into the air, and soon engulfed in the waves.[6]

CHAPTER XIII

"And how soon to the bower she loved, they say,
Returned the maid that was borne away
From Maquon, the fond and the brave."

BRYANT[1]

After Miss Leslie's escape from Oneco on the island, he remained for some time unconscious of her departure, and entirely absorbed in his efforts to quicken the energy of reviving life in his father; and when he discovered that his prisoner had left him, he still deemed her as certainly within his power on the sea-girt island, as if she had been enclosed by the walls of a prison. He felt that his father's life depended on his obtaining an asylum as soon as possible, and he determined to abandon his plan of going to Narragansett, and instead, to cross the bay to Moscutusett,[2] the residence of the son and successor of Chicatabot, an avowed ally of the English, but really, in common with most of the powerful chiefs, their secret enemy.

If, availing himself of the sheltering twilight of the morning, he could convey his father safely to the wigwam of his friend, Oneco believed he might securely remain there for the present. In the mean time, he should himself be at liberty to contrive and attempt the recovery of his wife. The instrumentality of Hope Leslie might be important to effect this object, and she also might remain in safe custody with the Indian chief.

Thus having digested his plans, before the morning dawned, and by the sufficient light of the moon, he went in quest of his

343

prisoner, but was destined, as our readers know, to be disappointed.

He encountered Chaddock's crew, much in the situation in which they were first discovered by Miss Leslie, for after having been baffled in their pursuit of her, they returned and recomposed themselves to await the light of day, when they might give a signal to some boat to take them off the island.

Oneco apprehending that in the prosecution of his search over the island, he might meet with some straggler from this gang, very prudently disguised himself in certain of the cast-off garments belonging to the men, which would enable him to escape, at least, immediate detection. This disguise, though useless then, proved afterwards of important service to him.

Compelled by the approach of day to abandon his search, he returned to his canoe, placed his father in it, and rowed him to Sachem's-head, where he was kindly received and cherished, though with the utmost secresy, for the Indians had long ere this been taught, by painful experience, to guard against the most dispiriting of all dangers—a danger to which the weak, in the neighbourhood of a powerful and comparatively rich foe, are always exposed—the treachery of their own people.

The chief of Moscutusett obtained, from day to day, intelligence of whatever transpired in Boston; and in this way Monocutto was apprised of the imprisonment and probable fate of Magawisca. This was the last drop in his cup of bitterness; worse, far worse, than to have borne on his body the severest tortures ever devised by human cruelty. Magawisca had obtained an ascendency over her father's mind by her extraordinary gifts and superior knowledge. He loved her as his child—he venerated her as an inspired being. He might have endured to have had her cut off by the chances of war, but to have her arraigned before the tribunal of his enemies, as amenable to their laws—to have her die by the hands of the executioner, as one of their own felon subjects, pierced his national pride as well as his affection, and he resigned himself to overwhelming grief. Oneco sorrowed for himself, and he sorrowed for the old man's tears, but he felt nothing very deeply but the loss of his "white bird."

All his ingenuity was employed to devise the means of her

escape. After having painted his face, hands, and legs, so as ef-
fectually to conceal his tawny hue, he appeared a foreign sailor,
in Madam Winthrop's parlour. All succeeded better than his
most sanguine expectations. He contrived to give every necessary hint to Faith Leslie; and so happily veiled his language by
his indistinct and rapid utterance, that Governor Winthrop, familiar as he was with the sound of the Indian dialects, did not
suspect him. The family retired immediately after their evening
devotions: he laid himself down on the bed that had been hospitably spread for him, and soon feigned himself asleep. He
watched the servants make their last preparations for bed—the
lights were extinguished, and the fire raked up, though enough
still glimmered through the ashes, to afford him a competent
light when he should need it. The menials withdrew—their footsteps had hardly ceased to vibrate on his ear, when his wife,
impatient of any further delay, stole from her aunt's side, threw
on her dress, and with the light bounding tread of a fawn, passed
down the stairs, through the hall, and into the kitchen. Oneco
started up, and in a transport of joy would have locked her in
his arms, when Jennet—Jennet, our evil genius, appeared. She,
like some other disagreeable people, seemed to be gifted with
ubiquity, and always to be present where happiness was to be
interrupted, or mischief to be done.

She stood for an instant, her hands uplifted in silent amazement, hesitating whether to alarm the family with her outcries,
or more quietly to give them notice of the character of their
guest. Oneco put a sudden end to her deliberations. He first
darted to the door and closed it; then drew a knife from his
bosom, and pointing it at Jennet's heart, he told her in very bad
English, but plainly interpreted by his action, that if she moved
or uttered a sound, his knife should taste her life-blood.

Jennet saw determination in his aspect, and she stood as still
as if she were paralyzed or transfixed, while Oneco proceeded
to tell her, that to make all sure, she should go with him to his
canoe. He bade her calm her fears, for then he would release her,
provided that in the mean time, she made no effort, by voice or
movement, to release herself.

There was no alternative, but she did beg to be allowed to go to her room to get her bonnet and shawl. Oneco smiled deridingly at the weak artifice by which she hoped to elude him; but deigning no other reply to it; he caught a shawl which hung over a chair, threw it over her, and without any further delay, compelled her to follow him.

Oneco took care to avoid the danger, slight though it was, of encountering any passengers, by directing his way through an unfrequented part of the town. Impatience to be beyond the bounds of danger, and the joy of escape and reunion, seemed to lend wings to Jennet's companions, while she followed breathless and panting, enraged at her compelled attendance, and almost bursting with spite, to which she could not give its natural vent by its customary outlet the tongue, the safety-valve of many a vexed spirit.

They had arrived very near to the cove where Oneco had moored his canoe. He good naturedly pointed towards it, and told Jennet that there she should be released. But the hope of release by a mode much more satisfactory to her feelings, inasmuch as it would involve her companions in danger, had dawned on Jennet. She had just perceived some men, (how many she could not tell, for the night was then dark) who were, unobserved by Oneco, stealing towards them. She withdrew a few inches, as far as she dared from his side, lest he should execute sudden vengeance with the weapon which he still held in his hand. Her conjectures were now converted to certainty, and she already mentally exulted in the retaliation she should inflict on her companions, but alas!—

> *"Esser vicino al lido*
> *Molti fra naufragar;"*[3]

or, to express the same truth by our vernacular adage,—"There's many a slip between the cup and the lip." The men did approach, even to her side, and without listening to her protestations of who she was, and who her companions were—without even hearing them, they seized on her, and suffering the other parties to escape without any annoyance, they bound her shawl over her head and face, and as our readers have already anticipated, conveyed her to that awful destiny, which she had herself indirectly prepared.

It may excite some surprise that Chaddock, forewarned as he had been, that the lady whom he was to intercept would have no male attendant, should not have hesitated when he saw Oneco. But that may be explained by Oneco wearing the dress of the ship's crew, and the natural conclusion on Chaddock's part, that Antonio, whom he had left in the boat, had come on shore, and probably just joined these females. Chaddock's only care was, to select the shortest of the two women, and obscure as the night was, their relative height was apparent.

CHAPTER XIV

"Basta cosi t'intendo
Già ti spiegasti à pieno;
E mi diresti meno
Se mi dicessi più."
                    METASTASIO[1]

We trust we have not exhausted the patience of our readers, and that they will vouchsafe to go forth with us once more, on the eventful evening on which we have fallen, to watch the safe conduct of the released prisoner.

The fugitives had not proceeded many yards from the jail, when Everell joined them. This was the first occasion on which Magawisca and Everell had had an opportunity freely to interchange their feelings. Everell's tongue faltered when he would have expressed what he had felt for her: his manly, generous nature, disdained vulgar professions, and he feared that his ineffectual efforts in her behalf had left him without any other testimony of the constancy of his friendship, and the warmth of his gratitude.

Magawisca comprehended his feelings, and anticipated their expression. She related the scene with Sir Philip, in the prison; and dwelt long on her knowledge of the attempt Everell then made to rescue her. "That bad man," she said, "made me, for the first time, lament for my lost limb. He darkened the clouds that were gathering over my soul; and, for a little while, Everell,

I did deem thee like most of thy race, on whom kindness falls like drops of rain on the lake, dimpling its surface for a moment, but leaving no mark there—but when I found thou wert true," she continued in a swelling, exulting voice—"when I heard thee in my prison, and saw thee on my trial, I again rejoiced that I had sacrificed my precious limb for thee; that I had worn away the days and nights in the solitudes of the forest musing on the memory of thee, and counting the moons till the Great Spirit shall bid us to those regions where there will be no more gulfs between us, and I may hail thee as my brother."

"And why not now, Magawisca, regard me as your brother? True, neither time nor distance can sever the bonds by which our souls are united, but why not enjoy this friendship while youth, and as long as life lasts? Nay, hear me, Magawisca—the present difference of the English with the Indians, is but a vapour that has, even now, nearly passed away. Go, for a short time, where you may be concealed from those who are not yet prepared to do you justice, and then—I will answer for it—every heart and every voice will unite to recall you; you shall be welcomed with the honour due to you from all, and always cherished with the devotion due from us."

"Oh! do not hesitate, Magawisca," cried Hope, who had, till now, been only a listener to the conversation in which she took a deep interest. "Promise us that you will return and dwell with us—as you would say, Magawisca, we will walk in the same path, the same joys shall shine on us, and, if need be that sorrows come over us, why, we will all sit under their shadow together."

"It cannot be—it cannot be," replied Magawisca, the persuasions of those she loved, not, for a moment, overcoming her deep invincible sense of the wrongs her injured race had sustained. "My people have been spoiled—we cannot take as a gift that which is our own—the law of vengeance is written on our hearts—you say you have a written rule of forgiveness—it may be better—if ye would be guided by it—it is not for us—the Indian and the white man can no more mingle, and become one, than day and night."

Everell and Hope would have interrupted her with further entreaties and arguments: "Touch no more on that," she said, "we must part—and for ever." Her voice faltered for the first time, and, turning from her own fate to what appeared to her the bright destiny of her companions, "my spirit will joy in the thought," she said, "that you are dwelling in love and happiness together. Nelema told me your souls were mated—she said your affections mingled like streams from the same fountain. Oh! may the chains by which He, who sent you from the spirit land, bound you together, grow brighter and stronger till you return thither again."

She paused—neither of her companions spoke—neither could speak—and, naturally, misinterpreting their silence, "have I passed your bound of modesty," she said, "in speaking to the maiden as if she were a wife?"

"Oh, no, Magawisca," said Everell, feeling a strange and undefinable pleasure in an illusion, which, though he could not for an instant participate, he would not for the world have dissipated—"oh, no, do not check one expression, one word, they are your last to us." 'And may not the last words of a friend, be, like the sayings of a death-bed, prophetic?' he would have added, but his lips refused to utter what he felt was the treachery of his heart.

To Hope it seemed that too much had already been spoken. She could be prudent when any thing but her own safety depended on her discretion. Before Magawisca could reply to Everell, she gave a turn to the conversation: "Ere we part, Magawisca," she said, "cannot you give me some charm, by which I may win my sister's affections? she is wasting away with grief and pining."

"Ask your own heart, Hope Leslie, if any charm could win your affections from Everell Fletcher?"

She paused for a reply. The gulf from which Hope had retreated, seemed to be widening before her, but, summoning all her courage, she answered with a tolerably firm voice, "yes—yes, Magawisca, if virtue, if duty to others required it, I trust in heaven I could command and direct my affections."

We hope Everell may be forgiven, for the joy that gushed through his heart when Hope expressed a confidence in her own strength, which at least implied a consciousness that she needed it. Nature will rejoice in reciprocated love, under whatever adversities it comes.

Magawisca replied to Hope's apparent meaning: "Both virtue and duty," she said, "bind your sister to Oneco. She hath been married according to our simple modes, and persuaded by a Romish father, as she came from Christian blood, to observe the rites of their law. When she flies from you, as she will, mourn not over her, Hope Leslie—the wild flower would perish in your gardens—the forest is like a native home to her—and she will sing as gaily again as the bird that hath found its mate."

They now approached the place where Digby, with a trusty friend, was awaiting them. A light canoe had been provided, and Digby had his instructions from Everell to convey Magawisca to any place she might herself select. The good fellow had entered into the confederacy with hearty good will, giving, as a reason for his obedience to the impulse of his heart, 'that the poor Indian girl could not commit sins enough against the English to weigh down her good deed to Mr. Everell.'

Everell now inquired of Magawisca whither he should direct the boat: "To Moscutusett," she said; "I shall there get tidings, at least, of my father."

"And must we now part, Magawisca? must we live without you?"

"Oh! no, no" cried Hope, joining her entreaties, "your noble mind must not be wasted in those hideous solitudes."

"Solitudes!" echoed Magawisca, in a voice in which some pride mingled with her parting sadness. "Hope Leslie, there is no solitude in me; the Great Spirit, and his ministers, are every where present and visible to the eye of the soul that loves him; nature is but his interpreter; her forms are but bodies for his spirit. I hear him in the rushing winds—in the summer breeze —in the gushing fountains—in the softly running streams. I see him in the bursting life of spring—in the ripening maize—in the falling leaf. Those beautiful lights," and she pointed upward, "that shine alike on your stately domes and our forest homes, speak to me of his love to all,—think you I go to a solitude, Hope Leslie?"

"No, Magawisca; there is no solitude, nor privation, nor sorrow, to a soul that thus feels the presence of God," replied Hope. She paused—it was not a time for calm reflection or protracted solicitation; but the thought that a mind so disposed to religious impressions and affections, might enjoy the brighter light of Christian revelation—a revelation so much higher, nobler, and fuller, than that which proceeds from the voice of nature—made Hope feel a more intense desire than ever to retain Magawisca; but this was a motive Magawisca could not now appreciate, and she could not, therefore, urge: "I cannot ask you," she said, "I do not ask you, for your sake, but for ours, to return to us."

"Oh! yes, Magawisca," urged Everell, "come back to us and teach us to be happy, as you are, without human help or agency."

"Ah!" she replied, with a faint smile, "ye need not the lesson, ye will each be to the other a full stream of happiness. May it be fed from the fountain of love, and grow broader and deeper through all the passage of life."

The picture Magawisca presented, was, in the minds of the lovers, too painfully contrasted with the real state of their affairs. Both felt their emotions were beyond their control; both silently appealed to heaven to aid them in repressing feelings that might not be expressed.

Hope naturally sought relief in action: she took a morocco case from her pocket, and drew from it a rich gold chain, with a clasp containing hair, and set round with precious stones: "Magawisca," she said, with as much steadiness of voice as she could assume, "take this token with you, it will serve as a memorial of us both, for I have put in the clasp a lock of Everell's hair, taken from his head when he was a boy, at Bethel—it will remind you of your happiest days there."

Magawisca took the chain, and held it in her hand a moment,

as if deliberating. "This is beautiful," she said, "and would, when I am far away from thee, speak sweetly to me of thy kindness, Hope Leslie. But I would rather—if I could demean myself to be a beggar"—she hesitated, and then added, "I wrong thy generous nature in fearing thus to speak; I know thou wilt freely give me the image when thou hast the living form."

Before she had finished, Hope's quick apprehension had comprehended her meaning. Immediately after Everell's arrival in England, he had, at his father's desire, had a small miniature of himself painted, and sent to Hope. She attached it to a ribbon, and had always worn it. Soon after Everell's engagement to Miss Downing, she took it off to put it aside, but feeling, at the moment, that this action implied a consciousness of weakness, she, with a mixed feeling of pride, and reluctance to part with it, restored it to her bosom. While she was adjusting Magawisca's disguise in the prison, the miniature slid from beneath her dress, and she, at the time, observed that Magawisca's eye rested intently on it. She must not now hesitate—Everell must not see her reluctance, and yet, such are the strange contrarieties of human feeling, the severest pang she felt in parting with it, was the fear that Everell would think it was a willing gift. Hoping to shelter all her feelings in the haste of the action, she took the miniature from her own neck, and tied it around Magawisca's. "You have but reminded me of my duty," she said; "nay, keep them both, Magawisca, do not stint the little kindness I can show you."

Digby had at this moment come up to urge no more delay; and we leave to others to adjust the proportions of emotion that were indicated by Hope's faltering voice, and an irrepressible burst of tears, between her grief at parting, and other and secret feelings.

All stood as if they were rivetted to the ground, till Digby again spoke, and suggested the danger to which Magawisca was exposed by this delay. All felt the necessity of immediate separation, and all shrunk from it as from witnessing the last gasp of life. They moved to the water's edge, and, once more prompted by Digby, Everell and Hope, in broken voices, expressed their last wishes and prayers. Magawisca joined their hands, and bowing her head on them,—"The Great Spirit guide ye," she said, and then turning away, leaped into the boat, muffled her face in her mantle, and in a few brief moments disappeared for ever from their sight.

Everell and Hope remained immoveable, gazing on the little boat till it faded in the dim distance; for a few moments, every feeling for themselves was lost in the grief of parting for ever from the admirable being, who seemed to her enthusiastic young friends, one of the noblest of the works of God—a bright witness to the beauty, the independence, and the immortality of virtue. They breathed their silent prayers for her; and when their thoughts returned to themselves, though they gave them no expression, there was a consciousness of perfect unity of feeling, a joy in the sympathy that was consecrated by its object, and might be innocently indulged, that was a delicious spell to their troubled hearts.

Strong as the temptation was, they both felt the impropriety of lingering where they were, and they bent their slow, unwilling footsteps homeward. Not one word during the long protracted walk was spoken by either; but no language could have been so expressive of their mutual love and mutual resolution, as this silence. They both afterwards confessed, that though they had never felt so deeply as at that moment, the bitterness of their divided destiny, yet neither had they before known the worth of those principles of virtue, that can subdue the strongest passions to their obedience. An experience worth a tenfold suffering.

As they approached Governor Winthrop's, they observed that instead of the profound darkness and silence that usually reigned in that exemplary mansion at eleven o'clock, the house seemed to be in great bustle. The doors were open, and they heard loud voices, and lights were swiftly passing from room to room. Hope inferred, that notwithstanding her precautions, the apprehensions of the family had probably been excited in regard to her untimely absence, and she passed the little distance that remained with dutiful haste. Everell attended her to the gate of the court, and pressing her hand to his lips, with an emotion

HOPE LESLIE 355

that he felt he might indulge for the last time, he left her and went, according to a previous determination, to Barnaby Tuttle's, where, by a surrender of himself to the jailer's custody, he expected to relieve poor Cradock from his involuntary confinement.

CHAPTER XV

"Quelque rare que soit le véritable amour il l'est encore moins que la véritable amitié."

ROCHEFOUCAULD[1]

Hope Leslie met Mr. Fletcher at the threshold of the door. He was sallying forth with hasty steps and disordered looks. He started at the sight of her, and then clasping her in his arms, exclaimed, "My child! my child! my precious child!"

At the sound of his voice the whole family rushed from the parlour. "Praised be the Lord for thy deliverance, Hope Leslie," cried Governor Winthrop, clasping his hands with astonishment. Mrs. Grafton gave vent to her feelings in hysterical sobbings, and inarticulate murmurs of joy. Madam Winthrop said,—"I thought it was impossible—I told you the Lord would be better to you than your fears:" and Esther Downing embraced her friend with deep emotion, whispering as she did so, "the Lord is ever better to us than our fears, or our deservings."

It was obvious to our heroine, that all this excitement and overflowing of tenderness could not be occasioned merely by her unseasonable absence, and she begged to know what had caused so much alarm.

The Governor was beginning, in his official manner, a formal statement, when, as if the agitations of this eventful evening were never to end, the explosion of Chaddock's vessel broke in upon their returning tranquillity, and spread a panic through the town of Boston.

The occurrence of the accident, at this particular moment, was fortunate for Magawisca, as it prevented a premature discovery of her escape; a discovery by which the Governor would have felt himself obliged to take measures for her recapture, that might then have proved effectual. The explosion of course withdrew his attention from all other subjects, and both he and Mr. Fletcher went out to ascertain whence it had proceeded, and what ill consequences had ensued.

In the mean time, Hope learned the following particulars from the ladies. The family had retired to bed at the accustomed time, and about half an hour before her return, were alarmed by a violent knocking at the outer door. The servant first awakened let in a stranger, who demanded an immediate audience of the Governor, concerning matters of life and death. The stranger proved to be Antonio, and his communication, the conspiracy with which our readers are well acquainted, or rather, as much of it as had fallen within the knowledge of the subordinate agents. Antonio declared, that having within the harbour of Boston been favoured with an extraordinary visitation from his tutelar saint, who had vouchsafed to warn him against his sinful comrades, he had determined from the first, that he would, if possible, prevent the wicked designs of the conspirators; and for that purpose, had solicited to be among the number who were sent on shore, intending to give notice to the Governor, in time for him to counteract the wicked project: he averred that after quitting the boat, he had heard the screams of the unhappy girl, when she was seized by the sailors; he had been spurred to all possible haste, but unhappily, ignorant of the town, he had strayed out of his way in coming from the cove, and finally, had found it almost impossible to rouse any of the sleeping inhabitants to guide him to the Governor's.

Antonio knew the name of the author of this guilty project to be Sir Philip Gardiner, and its victim, Miss Leslie. These names were fearful hints to the Governor, and had prevented his listening with utter incredulity to the tale of the stranger. As the easiest means of obtaining its confirmation or refutation, a messenger was despatched to Sir Philip's lodgings, who almost instantly returned with the intelligence, that he, his page, and baggage, had clandestinely disappeared during the evening. This was a frightful coincidence; and while the Governor's orders that all the family should be called were executing, he made one further investigation.

He recollected the packet of letters which Rosa had given to her master during the trial. Sir Philip had laid them on the table, and forgetting them in the confusion that followed, the Governor had taken possession of them, intending to restore them at the first opportunity. He felt himself now, not only authorised to break the seals, but compelled to that discourtesy. The letters were from a confidential correspondent, and proved, beyond a doubt, that Sir Philip had formerly been the protegé, and ally of Thomas Morton, the old political enemy of the colony; that he was a Roman catholic; of course, that the Governor and his friends had been duped by his religious pretensions; and in short, that he was an utter profligate, who regarded neither the laws of God nor man.

And into the power of this wretch the friends of Miss Leslie were left, for a few agonizing moments, to believe she had fallen; and their joy at her appearance was, as may be believed, commensurate with their previous distress.

Some of the minor incidents of the evening now transpired. One of the servants reported that the young sailor had disappeared; and Mrs. Grafton suddenly recollected to have observed that Faith Leslie was not with her when she was awakened, a circumstance she had overlooked in her subsequent agitation. By a single clew an intricate maze may be threaded. Madam Winthrop now recalled Faith Leslie's emotion at the first sound of the sailor's voice, and the ladies soon arrived at the right conclusion, that he was in reality Oneco, and that they had effected their escape together. Jennet (if Jennet had survived to hear it, she never would have believed the tale,) the only actual sufferer, was the only one neither missed nor inquired for. Good Master Cradock was not forgotten; but his friends were satisfied with Miss Leslie's assurance that he was safe, and would, probably, not return before the morning.

The final departure of her sister cost Hope many regrets and tears. But an inevitable event, of such a nature, cannot seriously disturb the happiness of life. There had been nothing in the intercourse of the sisters to excite Hope's affections. Faith had been spiritless, woe-begone—a soulless body—and had repelled, with sullen indifference, all Hope's efforts to win her love. Indeed, she looked upon the attentions of her English friends but as a continuation of the unjust force by which they had severed her from all she held dear. Her marriage, solemnized as it had been by prescribed Christian rites, would probably have been considered by her guardian, and his friends, as invalidated by her extreme youth, and the circumstances which had led to the union. But Hope took a more youthful, romantic, and, perhaps, natural view of the affair; and the suggestions of Magawisca, combining with the dictates of her own heart, produced the conclusion that this was a case where 'God had joined together, and man might not put asunder.'

All proper (though it may be not very vigorous) measures were taken by Governor Winthrop, on the following day, to discover the retreat of the fugitives; but the secret was faithfully kept while necessary to their security.

The return of his children, and, above all, of Magawisca, seemed to work miracles on their old father: his health and strength were renewed, and, for a while, he forgot, in the powerful influence of her presence, his wrongs and sorrows. He would not hazard the safety of his protector, and that of his own family, by lingering a single day in the vicinity of his enemies.

Before the dawn of the next morning, this little remnant of the Pequod race, a name at which, but a few years before, all within the bounds of the New-England colonies—all, English and Indians, 'grew pale,' began their pilgrimage to the far western forests. That which remains untold of their story, is lost in the deep, voiceless obscurity of those unknown regions.

The terrors her friends had suffered, on account of our heroine, induced them to overlook every thing but the joy of her safety. She was permitted to retire with Esther to their own apartment, without any inquisition being made into the cause of her extraordinary absence. Even her friend, when they were alone together, made no allusion to it, and Hope rightly concluded that she was satisfied with her own conjectures as to its object.

Hope could scarcely refrain from indulging the natural frankness of her temper, by disclosing, unsolicited, the particulars of her successful enterprise; and she only checked the inclinations of her heart from the apprehension that Esther might deem it her duty to extend her knowledge to her uncle, and thus Magawisca might be again endangered. 'She certainly conjectures how it is,' thought Hope, making her own mental comments on Esther's forbearance; 'and yet she does not indicate the least displeasure at my having combined with Everell to render the delightful service that her severe conscience would not allow her to perform.' 'She never spoke to me with more tenderness—how could I ever suspect her of jealousy, or distrust?—she is incapable of either—she is angelic—far, far more deserving of Everell than I am.'

At this last thought, a half stifled, but audible, sigh escaped her, and reached her friend's ear. Their eyes met. A deep, scorching blush suffused Hope's cheeks, brow, and neck. Esther's face beamed with ineffable sweetness and serenity. She looked as a mortal can look only when the world and its temptations are trampled beneath the feet, and the eye is calmly, steadily, immovably fixed on heaven. She folded Hope in her arms, and pressed her fondly to her heart, but not a word, tear, or sigh escaped her. Her soul was composed to a profound stillness, incapable of being disturbed by her friend's tears and sobs, the involuntary expression of her agitated, confused, and irrepressible feelings.

Hope turned away from Esther, and crept into her bed; feeling, like a condemned culprit, self-condemned. It seemed to her that a charm had been wrought on her; a sudden illumination had flashed from her friend's face into the most secret recesses of her heart, and exposed—this was her most distressful apprehension—to Esther's eye, feelings whose existence, till thus revealed to another, (and the last person in the world to whom they should be revealed,) she had only, and reluctantly, acknowledged to herself.

Deeply mortified and humbled, she remained wakeful, weeping and lamenting this sudden exposure of emotions that she feared could never be explained or forgotten, long after her friend had encircled her in her arms, and fallen into a sweet and profound sleep.

We must leave the apartment of the generous and involuntary rivals, to repair to the parlour, where Governor Winthrop, after having ascertained that Chaddock's vessel had been blown up by the explosion, was listening to Barnaby Tuttle's relation of the transaction at the prison.

The simple jailer, on learning from Everell's confessions how he had been cajoled, declined increasing his responsibilities by making the exchange Everell proposed, but very readily acceded to his next proposition, namely, that he should be permitted to share the imprisonment of Cradock. On entering the dungeon, they found the good old man sleeping as soundly on Magawisca's pallet, as if he were in his own apartment; and Everell rejoicing that he had suffered so little, in the good cause to which it had been necessary to make him accessory, and exulting in the success of his enterprise, took possession of his dark and miserable cell, with feelings that he would not have bartered for those of a conqueror mounting his triumphal car.

Barnaby had a natural feeling of vexation at having been outwitted by Hope Leslie's stratagems; but it was a transient emotion, and not strong enough to check the habitual current of his gratitude and affection for her, nor did it at all enter into his relation of the facts to the Governor. On the contrary, his natural kind-heartedness rendered the statement favourable towards all parties.

He did not mention Magawisca's name without a parenthesis, containing some commendation of her deportment in the prison. He spoke of Hope Leslie, as the "thoughtless child," or, the "feeling young creature." Master Cradock was, "the poor witless old gentleman;" and "for Mr. Everell, it was not within the bounds of human nature, in his peculiar case, not to feel as he did; and as to himself, he was but an old dotard, ill fitted to keep bars and bolts, when a child—the Lord and the Governor forgive her!—could guide him with a wisp of straw."

Nothing was further from Barnaby Tuttle's thoughts, than any endeavour to blind or pervert a ruler's judgment; but the Governor found something infectious in his artless humanity. Besides, he had one good, sufficient, and state reason for extenuating the offence of the young conspirators, and of this he made a broad canopy to shelter his secret and kind dispositions towards them. A messenger had that day arrived, from the chief of the Narragansetts, with the information that a war had broken out between Miantunnomoh and Uncas, and an earnest solicitation that the English would not interfere with their domestic quarrels.[2]

To our ancestors, it appeared their melancholy policy to promote, rather than to allay these feuds among the tribes; and a war between these rival and powerful chieftains assured, while it lasted, the safety of the English settlements. It became, therefore, very important to avoid any act that might provoke the universal Indian sentiment against the English, and induce them to forego their civil quarrel, and combine against the common enemy. This would be the probable effect of the condemnation of the Pequod girl, whose cause had been espoused by several of the tribes: still, on a further investigation of her case, the laws might require her condemnation—and the puritans held firmly to the principle, that good must be done, though evil ensue.

Governor Winthrop perceived that Magawisca's escape relieved them from much and dangerous perplexity; and though Everell Fletcher's interposition had been unlawful and indecorous, yet, as Providence had made him the instrument of certain good, he thought his offence might be pardoned by his associates in authority.

He dismissed Barnaby, with an order to appear before him with his prisoners, at six o'clock the following morning. At that hour he assembled together such of the magistrates and deputies as were in Boston, deeming it, as he said, proper to give them the earliest notice of the various important circumstances that had occurred since the morning of the preceding day.

He opened the meeting with a communication of the important intelligence received from the Narragansett chief; intimated the politic uses to which the wisdom of his brethren might apply it; then, after some general observations on the imperfection of human wisdom, disclosed at full the iniquitous character and conduct of Sir Philip Gardiner; lamented in particular, that he had been grievously deceived by that crafty son of Belial—and then dwelt on the wonderful interposition of Providence in behalf of Hope Leslie, which clearly intimated, as he said, and all his auditors acknowledged, that the young maiden's life was precious in the sight of the Lord, and was preserved for some special purpose. He called their attention to the light thrown on the testimony of Sir Philip against the Indian prisoner by his real character—and last of all, he communicated the escape of Magawisca, and the means by which it had been accomplished, with this comment simply, that it had pleased the Lord to bring about great good to the land by the rash act of two young persons, who seemed to have been wrought upon by feelings natural to youth; and the foolishness of an old man, whose original modicum of sense was greatly diminished by age, and excess of useless learning; for, he said, Master Cradock not only wrote Greek and Latin, and talked Hebrew like the Rev. Mr. Cotton, but he was skilled in Arabic, and the modern tongues.

The Governor then proceeded to give many and plausible reasons, with the detail of which it is not necessary to weary the patience of our readers, why this case, in the absence of a precise law, should be put under the government of mercy. His associates lent a favourable ear to these suggestions. Most of them considered the offence very much alleviated by the youth of the two principal parties, and the strong motives that actuated them. Some of the magistrates were warm friends of the elder Fletcher, and all of them might have been quickened in their decision, by the approach of the breakfast hour; for as modern philosophy has discovered, the mind and sensibilities are much under the dominion of these periodical returns of the hours of refection.

The conclusion of the whole matter was, that Miss Leslie and Master Cradock should receive a private admonition from the Governor, and a free pardon; and that Mr. Everell Fletcher should be restored to liberty, on condition that, at the next sitting of the court, he appeared in the prisoner's bar, to receive a public censure, and be admonished as to his future carriage. To this sentence Everell submitted at the proper time, with due humility, and a very becoming, and, as said the elders, edifying modesty.

Throughout the whole affair, Governor Winthrop manifested those dispositions to clemency, which were so beautifully illustrated by one of the last circumstances of his life, when being, as is reported of him, upon his death-bed, Mr. Dudley pressed him to sign an order of banishment of an heterodox person, he refused, saying,—"*I have done too much of that work already.*"³

Everell and Master Cradock, who had awaited in an adjoining apartment the result of these deliberations, were now informed of the merciful decision of their judges, and summoned to take their places at the breakfast-table. While all this business was transpiring, Hope Leslie, wearied by the fatigues, agitations, and protracted vigil of the preceding night, was sleeping most profoundly. She awoke with a confused sense of her last anxious waking thoughts, and naturally turned to look for Esther, but Esther had already risen. This excited no surprise, for it must be confessed that our heroine was often anticipated in early-rising, as in other severe duties, by her friend. Admonished by a broad sun-beam that streamed aslant her apartment, that she had already trespassed on the family breakfast hour, she rose, and despatched her toilet duties. Her mind was still intent on Esther, and suddenly she missed some familiar objects: Esther's morocco dressing-case and Bible, that always laid at hand on the dressing-table. Hope was at that moment adjusting her hair; she dropped her comb—cast a hasty survey around the room. Esther's trunks, bandboxes, every article belonging to her had disappeared. "What could this mean?" Some solution of the mystery might have dawned from the recollections of the preceding night, but impatient for a full explanation, she seized her whistle, opened the door, and blew for Jennet, till its shrill notes had penetrated every recess of the house. But no Jennet appeared; and without waiting to adjust her hair, which she had left in what is called disorder, but according to the natural and beautiful order of nature, and with a flushed cheek and beating heart she hastily descended to the parlor, and dispensing with the customary morning salutations, eagerly demanded—"Where is Esther?"

The family were all assembled at the breakfast-table. Her sudden appearance produced an apparent sensation—every eye turned towards her. Mrs. Grafton would have impulsively answered her question, but she was prevented by an intimation from Madam Winthrop. Everell's eye, on seeing her, flashed a bright intelligent glance, but at her interrogatory it fell, and then turned on Madam Winthrop inquiringly, indicating that he now, for the first time, perceived that there was something extraordinary in the absence of her niece.

Hope still stood with the door half open, her emotions in no degree tranquillized by the reception of her inquiry.

Governor Winthrop turned to her with his usual ceremony. "Good morning, Miss Hope Leslie—be good enough to close the door—the wind is easterly this morning. You are somewhat tardy, but we know you have abundant reason; take your seat, my child—apologies are unnecessary."

Madam Winthrop beckoned to Hope to take a chair next her, and Hope moved to the table mechanically, feeling as if she had been paralyzed by some gorgon influence. Her question was not even adverted to—no allusion was made to Esther. Hope observed that Madam Winthrop's eyes were red with weeping, and she also observed that in offering the little civilities of the table, she addressed her in a voice of unusual kindness.

She dared not look again at Everell, whose unexpected release from confinement would, at any other time, have fully occupied her thoughts; and her perplexity was rather increased by seeing her guardian's eyes repeatedly fill with tears while they rested on her with even more than their usual fondness.

Impatient, and embarrassed as she was, it seemed to her the breakfast would never end; and she was in despair when her aunt asked for her third, and her fourth cup of chocolate, and when the dismissal of the table awaited old Cradock's discussion of a replenished plate of fish, from which he painfully and patiently abstracted the bones. But all finite operations have their period —the breakfast did end, the company rose, and all left the parlour, one after another, save the two Fletchers, Madam Winthrop, and our heroine.

Hope would have followed her aunt—any further delay

seemed insupportable, but Madam Winthrop took her hand, and detained her.—"Stay, my young friend," she said, "I have an important communication which could not be suitably made till this moment." She took a sealed letter from her pocket. "Nay, Hope Leslie, grow not so suddenly pale, no blame is attached to thee—nor to thee, Mr. Everell Fletcher, who art even more deeply concerned in this matter. Both the Governor and myself have duly weighed all the circumstances, and have most heartily approved of that which she hath done, who near and dear as she is to us in the flesh, is still nearer and dearer by those precious gifts and graces that do so far exalt her (I would offend none present,) above all other maidens. Truly, 'if many do virtuously,' Esther 'excelleth them all.' "

Hope was obliged to lean against the wall for support. The elder Fletcher looked earnestly at Madam Winthrop, as if he would have said—"for Heaven's sake do not protract this scene." Perhaps she understood his glance—perhaps she took counsel from her own womanly feelings.—"This letter, my young friends," she said, "is addressed to you both, and it was my niece's request that you should read it at the same time."

Madam Winthrop kindly withdrew. Everell broke the seal, and both he and Hope, complying faithfully with Miss Downing's injunction, read together, to the very last word, the letter that follows:

"To my dear and kind friends, Everell Fletcher and Hope Leslie. "When you read these lines, the only bar to your earthly happiness will be removed. With the advice and consent of my honoured uncle and aunt, I have taken passage in the "Lion," which, as you know, is on the eve of sailing for London. With God's blessing on my present purposes, I shall remain there, with my father, till he has closed his affairs in the old world, and then come hither again.

"Do not think, my dear friends, I am fleeing away, because, as matters stand between us, I cannot abide to stay here. For your sakes, for I would not give you needless pain, I go for a little while. For myself, I have contentment of mind. It hath pleased God to give me glimpses of christian happiness, the foundations of which are not laid on the earth, and therefore cannot be removed or jostled by any of the cross accidents of life.

"There have been some notable errors in the past. We have all erred, and I most of all. My error hath been exceeding humbling to the pride of woman; yours, Hope Leslie, was of the nature of your disposition—rash and generous; and you, Everell (I speak it not reproachfully, but as being truth-bound,) have not dealt with gospel sincerity. I appeal to thine own heart—would it not have been better, as well as kinder, to have said, 'Esther, I do not love thee,' than to have permitted me to follow my silly imaginings, and thereby have sacrificed my happiness for this world—and thine—and Hope Leslie's?—for I think, and am sure, you never did me the wrong to believe I would knowingly have taken thy hand without thy affections—all of them (at least such measure as may be given to an earthly friend,) being poor and weak enough to answer to the many calls of life.

"It is fitting, that, having been guided to a safe harbour by the good providence of God, we should look back—not reproachfully—God forbid—but with gratitude and humility, on the dark and crooked passages through which we have passed. Neither our virtue—I speak it humbly—nor our happiness, have been wrecked. Ye will in no wise wonder that I speak thus assuredly of your happiness, but, resting your eye on the past, you might justly deem that, for myself, I have fallen into the 'foolishness of boasting'⁴—not so. In another strength than mine own, I have overcome, and am of good cheer, and well assured that, as the world hath not given me my joy, the world cannot take it away.

"For the rest, I shall ever rejoice that my affections settled on one worthy of them—one for whom I shall hereafter feel a sister's love, and one who will not withhold a brother's kindness. And to thee, my loving—my own sweet and precious Hope Leslie—I resign him. And may He, who, by his signal providence, hath so wonderfully restored in you the sundered affections of your parents, knitting, even from your childish years, your hearts together in love—may He make you his own dear and faithful children in the Lord.

"Thus—hoping for your immediate union, and worldly well-
being—ever prays your true and devoted friend,
                                             "*Esther Downing.*"

Hope Leslie's tears fell, like rain drops, on her friend's letter;
and when she had finished it, she turned and clasped her arms
around her guardian's neck, and hid her face on his bosom. Feelings for which words are too poor an expression, kept all parties
for some time silent. To the elder Fletcher it was a moment of
happiness that requited years of suffering. He gave Hope's hand
to Everell: "Sainted mothers!" he said, raising his full eyes to
heaven, "look down on your children, and bless them!" And,
truly, celestial spirits might look with complacency, from their
bright spheres, on the pure and perfect love that united these
youthful beings.

Mr. Fletcher withdrew, and we, following his example, must
permit the curtain to fall on this scene, as we hold it a profane
intrusion for any ear to listen to the first confessions of reciprocated, happy love.

Events have already meted 'fit retribution' to most of the parties
who have figured in our long story. A few particulars remain.

There was one man of Chaddock's crew left alive to tell the
tale; the same whose footsteps, it may be recollected, Sir Philip
heard, and on whom he had vainly called for assistance. This
man was lingering to observe the principal actors in the tragedy,
when the explosion took place, and, with the rest, was blown
into the air; but he escaped with his life, gained the boat, and
came, the next day, safely to the shore, where he related all he
knew, to the great relief of the curiosity of the good people of
Boston.

Strict search was, by the Governor's order, made for the bodies of the unhappy wretches who had been so suddenly sent to
their doom.

Jennet's was one of the first found: the shawl that had been
bound over her head still remained, the knot which defied Sir
Philip's skill having also resisted the lashing of the waves. When
this screen was removed, and the body identified, the mystery

of her disappearance was at once explained. "Death wipes out all scores." And even Jennet, *dead*, was wrapped in the mantle of charity; but all who had known her living, mentally confessed that Death could not have been more lenient in selecting a substitute for the precious life he had menaced.

Poor Rosa's remains were not

> *"Left to float upon their wat'ry bier*
> *Unwept, and welter to the parching wind."*[5]

Her youth, her wrongs and sufferings, combined with the pleadings of Hope Leslie, obtained for her the rites of a separate and solemn burial. Tears, of humility and pity, were shed over her grave; a fit tribute, from virtuous and tender woman, to a fallen, unhappy sister.

All the bodies of the sufferers were finally recovered, except that of Sir Philip Gardiner; and the inference of our pious forefathers, that Satan had seized upon that as his lawful spoil, may not be deemed, by their skeptical descendants, very unnatural.

We leave it to that large, and most indulgent class of our readers, the misses in their teens, to adjust, according to their own fancy, the ceremonial of our heroine's wedding, which took place in due time, to the joy of her immediate friends, and the entire approbation of all the inhabitants of Boston, who, in those early times, manifested a friendly interest in individual concerns, which is said to characterise them to the present day.

The elder Fletcher remained with his children, and permitted himself to enjoy, to the full, the happiness which, it was plain, Providence had prepared for him. The close of his life was as the clear shining forth of the sun after a stormy and troubled day.

Dame Grafton evinced some mortification at the discovery of the fallibility of her judgment in relation to Sir Philip Gardiner; but she soon dubbed him Sir *Janus;* a name that implied he had two faces, and her sagacity was not at fault if she judged by the one presented to her. Her trifling vexation was soon forgotten in her participation in her niece's felicity, and in her busy preparations for the wedding; and after that event, she was made so happy by the dutiful care of Hope and Everell, that she ceased to regret Old England, till, falling into her dotage, her entreaties, combining with some other motives, induced them to visit their mother country, where the old lady died, and was buried in the tomb of the Leslies, the church burial service being performed by the bishop of London. Her unconsciousness of this poetic justice must be regretted by all who respect innocent prejudices.

We hope that class of our readers, above alluded to, will not be shocked at our heroine's installing Master Cradock as a life-member of her domestic establishment. We are sure their kind hearts would reconcile them to this measure if they could know with what fidelity, and sweetness, and joy to the good man, she performed the promise she gave in Magawisca's prison, "that she would be a child to his old age." If they are still discontented with the arrangement, let them perform an action of equal kindness, and they will learn from experience that our heroine had her reward.

Digby never ceased, after the event had verified them, to pride himself on his own presentiments, and his wife's dreams. A friendship between him, and Everell and Hope subsisted through their lives, and descended, a precious legacy, through many generations of their descendants, fortified by favours, and gratitude, and reciprocal affection. -

Barnaby Tuttle, and his timely compliance with her wishes, were not forgotten by our heroine. Persuaded by her advice, and enabled by an annual stipend from her to do so, he retired from his solitary post of jailer, and passed his old age comfortably with his daughter Ruth, versifying psalms, and playing with the little Tuttles.

After the passage of two or three years, Miss Downing returned to New-England, and renewed her intercourse with Everell and Hope, without any other emotions, on either side, than those which belong to warm and tender friendship. Her personal loveliness, Christian graces, and the high rank she held in the colony, rendered her an object of very general attraction.

Her hand was often and eagerly sought, but she appears never to have felt a second engrossing attachment. The current of her purposes and affections had set another way. She illustrated a truth, which, if more generally received by her sex, might save a vast deal of misery: that marriage is not *essential* to the contentment, the dignity, or the happiness of woman. Indeed, those who saw on how wide a sphere her kindness shone, how many were made better and happier by her disinterested devotion, might have rejoiced that she did not

"Give to a party what was meant for mankind."[6]

EXPLANATORY NOTES

Volume I

Preface

1. Sedgwick's Sir Philip Gardiner is named after two historical associates of Thomas Morton's—Sir Christopher Gardiner and Philip Ratcliff—but based on accounts of the former. According to William Bradford's *Of Plymouth Plantation,* Chap. 22, Sir Christopher Gardiner emigrated to Massachusetts "under pretence of forsaking the world and to live a private life in a godly course." While claiming interest in joining one of the local Puritan churches, he was in fact a Catholic, as revealed by "a little notebook that by accident had slipped out of his pocket." He brought with him "a comely young woman whom he called his cousin; but it was suspected she, after the Italian manner, was his concubine." Bradford paid some Indian allies to capture Gardiner. After being deported to England, Gardiner testified against the Plymouth and Massachusetts Bay colonists and sought—to have their charter revoked unsuccessfully—which Winthrop regarded as evidence that "the Lord hath care of His people here." His "cousin" remained in New England, where she married and settled in Maine. In *Three Episodes of Massachusetts History,* Chap. 15, Charles Francis Adams quotes sources accusing Gardiner of bigamy and identifying his "cousin" as a " 'known harlot,' Mary Grove by name." Sedgwick's chief "liberties" with the historical record consist in bringing both Gardiner and his mistress to a violent end.

2. Puritan accounts of the Pequot war present the English massacre of the Pequots at Mystic in 1637 as a retaliation for previous Pequot atrocities against the English. As Philip Gould has pointed out, by reversing this chronology, Sedgwick recasts the English as the initial aggressors and the Pe-

quots as engaging in a reprisal. Historians Francis Jennings and Neal Salisbury bear out Sedgwick's reinterpretation of the historical record. The spelling *Pequod* was prevalent until the twentieth century.

3. Indians were in fact enslaved by the Spaniards in the Southwest and, on a smaller scale, in many English colonies as well. In Chap. 2 of *Hope Leslie*, Sedgwick herself mentions that some Pequot captives were sold into slavery in the West Indies.

Chapter I

1. *Comus* (1637), a masque by John Milton (1608–74), takes place in a wilderness where Comus, son of the enchantress Circe and of the god of wine, Bacchus, tries to tempt a Lady with drink, riches, and other temporal pleasures. She resists, with the help of "a hidden strength," chastity. The lines Sedgwick quotes in her epigraph (589–92) articulate Milton's moral and apply in different ways to William Fletcher and his cousin Alice.

2. Quoted freely from Proverbs 26.17, attributed to the wise King Solomon.

3. Quoted freely from Habakkuk 2.2.

4. John Winthrop (1588–1649) founded the colony of Massachusetts Bay in 1630 and served as its governor for twelve years, playing a key role in shaping its policies toward religious dissenters and Indian nations. His journal, published in 1825–26 as *The History of New England from 1630 to 1649*, was one of Sedgwick's main sources.

5. The Congregationalist missionary John Eliot (1604–90), known as the "Apostle to the Indians," is hailed by most nineteenth-century writers for his efforts to convert the Indians (see Sedgwick's portrayal of him as the Indians' advocate in Vol. 2, Chap. 9 and in her accompanying note). He began his proselytizing in 1646 and formed his converts into separate towns of "Praying Indians." Historian Francis Jennings presents a less favorable assessment of Eliot.

6. The quotation is from William Bradford's *Of Plymouth Plantation*, Chap. 7.

Chapter II

1. Roger Williams (1603?–1683), who arrived in Massachusetts with Winthrop in 1630, founded the colony of Rhode Island after his banishment from Massachusetts Bay in 1636. Williams advocated religious toleration, separation of church and state, and respect for Indian rights. The epigraph (slightly reworded) comes from his *Key into the Language of America* (1643), Chap. 7, "Of their Persons and parts of body." A dictionary and phrase book, the *Key* was designed both to teach the Algonkian language and to describe native customs and beliefs. Williams was instrumental in persuading the Narragansetts of Rhode Island to ally themselves with the English against the Pequots, rather than with the Pequots against the English.

2. William Pynchon (c. 1590–1662) founded Springfield, Massachusetts in 1636. Samuel Chapin (c. 1598–1675) and Elizur Holioke or Holyoke (no dates available), held key offices in the town from the 1640s on.

3. In Genesis 12.1–2, 7–8, God commands Abram (later renamed Abraham): "Get thee out of thy country, and from thy kindred, and from thy father's house, unto a land that I will shew thee: And I will make of thee a great nation, and I will bless thee, and make thy name great." A native of Ur in Chaldea, Abraham went to Canaan, where God promised: "Unto thy seed will I give this land." Abraham pitched his tent at Bethel, the name Fletcher chooses for his own homestead.

4. Anne Hutchinson (1591–1643) held religious meetings in her home and attracted a large following among both men and women. The clergy regarded her as a threat because she maintained that the elect could communicate directly with God and did not need the mediation of ministers, some of whom she denounced as unregenerate. She was tried, condemned, and banished for heresy by the Massachusetts Gen-

eral Court in 1637, while the colony was mobilizing against the Pequots.

5. "We would take the liberty to refer those, who may think we have here violated probability, to Winthrop, who speaks of a Pequod maiden, who attended Miantunnomoh as interpreter, and 'spoke English perfectly' " (Sedgwick's note; see Winthrop's *History*, ed. Savage, 2:16).

6. Quoted freely from Ecclesiastes 3.13.

7. "For those who disbelieve the existence in savage life, of the virtues which we have ascribed to this Indian woman, we quote our authority—

"'Among the Pequot captives was the wife and children of Mononotto. She was particularly noticed by the English for her great modesty, humanity, and good sense. She made it as her only request, that she might not be injured, either as to her offspring or personal honour. As a requital for her kindness to the captivated maids, her life and the lives of her children were not only spared, but they were particularly recommended to the care of Governor Winthrop. He gave charge for their protection and kind treatment.'—*Trumbull's Hist. Connecticut.* See also, *Hubbard's Indian Wars*, p. 47" (Sedgwick's note).

Sedgwick's sources are Benjamin Trumbull's *A Complete History of Connecticut, Civil and Ecclesiastical* (1797); and William Hubbard's *A Narrative of the Indian Wars in New-England* (Brattleborough, Vt., 1814), originally titled *The Present State of New-England, Being a Narrative of the Troubles with the Indians in New-England* (1677). Neither source names Mononotto's wife and children or supplies any further details about them.

Trumbull alludes here to an earlier episode in English-Pequot hostilities when the Pequots retaliated against English attacks by raiding Wethersfield, Connecticut, in April 1637, killing nine colonists and capturing two women. He describes that episode as follows: "[T]hrough the humanity and mediation of Mononotto's squaw, [the two maids had] been spared from death, and kindly treated" (1:82). This episode is fictionalized in Harriet Vaughan Cheney's *A Peep at the Pilgrims in Sixteen Hundred Thirty-Six*, which names Mononotto's wife "Mioma."

8. Acts 10.35.

9. Winthrop's *History of New England* identifies Sassacus and Mononotto as the Pequots' "two chief sachems" (1:233). A later entry reports that "Mr. Ludlow, Mr. Pincheon, and about twelve more . . . brought with them a part of the skin and lock of hair of Sasacus and his brother, and five other Pequod sachems, who, being fled to the Mohawks for shelter, with their wampom, being to the value of five hundred pounds, were by them surprised and slain, with twenty of their best men. Mononottoh was also taken, but escaped wounded" (1:235).

10. Judges 1.5–7 tells of how the tribe of Judah defeated the Canaanites and hunted down their king, Adonibezek, cutting "off his thumbs and his great toes. And Adonibezek said, Threescore and ten kings, having their thumbs and their great toes cut off, gathered their meat under my table: as I have done, so God hath requited me." The Puritans commonly equated the Indians with the Canaanites and themselves with the Israelites. Hubbard cites this passage in his *Narrative* 43.

Chapter III

1. From *The Faerie Queene* (1596) III.4.27, by Edmund Spenser (1552–99). The sea nymph Cymoënt tries to save her son, Marinell, from his fated murder at the hands of "A virgin straunge" by warning him against entertaining the love of women, but Marinell proves unable to "avoyd his fate." The epigraph applies to Martha Fletcher as well.

2. Sedgwick quotes freely from *The Simple Cobler of Aggawam in America* (1647) by Nathaniel Ward (1578–1652). An influential preacher and lawyer, Ward adopted the persona of a homespun frontier shoemaker to satirize deviations from the true religion in England and to plead for a compromise between the King and Parliament in the hope of

averting the rupture that led to the execution of Charles I in 1649.

3. The doctrine of metempsychosis, or transmigration, attributed to the Greek philosopher Pythagoras, held that after death the soul passed into the body of another human being or animal.

4. John Cotton (1584–1652) was one of the most revered and influential ministers in Massachusetts. Anne Hutchinson claimed him as her mentor, though he ultimately repudiated her.

5. The apocryphal book of Judith tells of how this Jewish heroine cut off the head of the Babylonian general Holofernes after gaining access to his tent. The Old Testament book of Esther tells of how the Jewish queen of the Persian king, Ahasuerus, saved her people from massacre by his wicked prime minister, Haman, causing Haman to be hanged on the gallows he had intended for his Jewish enemy. In contrast, the Old Testament heroine Ruth is a Moabite; when her Jewish mother-in-law, Naomi, decides to return from Moab to Israel after both women are widowed, Ruth says: "whither thou goest, I will go; . . . thy people shall be my people, and thy God my God."

Chapter IV

1. John Robinson (c. 1576–1625) had served as pastor of William Bradford and his fellow "pilgrims" during their exile in Leyden, Holland. Sedgwick's epigraph is adapted from his letter of Dec. 19, 1623 to Bradford (*Of Plymouth Plantation* Appendix 5), protesting against Miles Standish's entrapment and murder of a group of Massachusett sachems. Robinson goes on to point out that "where blood is once begun to be shed, it is seldom staunched of a long time after" and that any violence the Indians may have committed was probably in response to "provocations and invitements by . . . heathenish Christians."

2. Sentinel.

3. Historian Francis Jennings argues rather that it was the En-

glish who were "cowardly" in deliberately choosing to "avoid attacking Pequot warriors" and to target instead an encampment of women and children. He contends that the "Narragansett allies had dissented sharply" from this strategy, hundreds of them withdrawing. "Not trusting the remainder to be sufficiently ruthless, Mason and Underhill surrounded Mystic with two concentric rings, relegating the remaining Indian allies to the outer one" (*Invasion* 220–23).

4. " 'But finding that the sachems whom they had spared, would give them no information, they beheaded them on their march at a place called Mekunkatuck, since Guilford.' —*Ibid.*" (Sedgwick's note, referring to Trumbull's *History of Connecticut* 1: 83.)

5. "The language of the Indians as reported by Heckewelder, verifies, so strongly, the sentiment in our text, and is so powerful an admonition to Christians, that we here quote it for those who may not have met with the interesting work of this excellent Moravian missionary.—' "And yet," say those injured people, "these white men would always be telling us of their great Book which God had given to them. They would persuade us that every man was good who believed in what the Book said, and every man was bad who did not believe in it. They told us a great many things, which they said were written in the good Book, and wanted us to believe it all. We would probably have done so, if we had seen them practise what they pretended to believe, and act according to the *good words* which they told us. But no! while they held their big Book in one hand, in the other they had murderous weapons, guns and swords wherewith to kill us poor Indians. Ah! and they did so too!" ' " (Sedgwick's note; she is quoting from Heckewelder's *Account of the History, Manners, and Customs of the Indian Nations* 188.)

6. Sedgwick is quoting from Bradford's *Of Plymouth Plantation*, Chap. 28.

7. Hubbard 46.

8. *Ibid.*

9. On the murders of the English traders John Stone, John Norton, and John Oldham, see Hubbard's *Narrative* (16–

21), Trumbull's *History of Connecticut* (1:60–62), and
Winthrop's *History* (1:122–23, 189–92). Although the Puri-
tans used these murders as pretexts for making war on the
Pequots, all three men were unsavory characters whom the
Puritans themselves had previously ostracized. *See* Jennings
189–90, 194, 204–5, 227.

10. Sedgwick is referring to Harriet Vaughan Cheney's *A Peep
    at the Pilgrims.* See Chap. 2, Note 7, above. The incident is
    mentioned in Hubbard, *Narrative* 47; Trumbull 1:82; and in
    a letter from Winthrop to Bradford, July 28, 1637, included
    in *Of Plymouth Plantation*, Appendix 8.

11. *Travels in the Interior Districts of Africa* (1799) by the Scot-
    tish explorer Mungo Park (1771–1806) was one of the most
    popular travel books of the nineteenth century. Sedgwick
    may be referring to Chap. 18, which details Park's capture
    by bandits who strip and plunder him and which ends with
    the consolation he takes in "the extraordinary beauty of a
    small moss": "Can that Being (thought I), who planted, wa-
    tered, and brought to perfection, in this obscure part of the
    world, a thing which appears of so small importance, look
    with unconcern upon the situation and sufferings of crea-
    tures formed after his own image?—surely not!"

Chapter V

1. From "The Departed" by the British poet, Felicia Hemans
   (1793–1835), included in her collection, *The League of the
   Alps, the Siege of Valencia, the Vespers of Palermo, and
   Other Poems* (Boston: Hilliard, Gray, Little, and Wilkins,
   1826). Addressed to those who "fear the grave," the poem
   urges them to take comfort at the thought of joining the
   illustrious hosts who have "gone before."

Chapter VI

1. The last line of a letter from Roger Williams to John Mason
   (leader of the expedition against the Pequots), June 22, 1670
   (Glenn W. La Fantasie, ed., *The Correspondence of Roger*

Williams [Hanover: Brown UP/UP of New England, 1988] 2:609–23). Protesting against attempts by Connecticut colonists to "invade and despoil" his settlement in Providence, Williams reminds Mason of his past services to Connecticut. Among these services, he notes, were his successful endeavors to "breake and hinder the Leauge laboured for by the Pequts agnst the Monhiggins and . . . the English" and to "promote . . . the English Leauge with the Nahiggonsiks and Monhiggins agnst the Pequts" (611). He goes on to condemn "Contentions and Wars . . . for greater Dishes and Bowles of Porridge" (615) and ends by saying that he is ready to exchange this transient world for eternity.

Chapter VII

1. From "Monument Mountain" (1824), 41–50, by William Cullen Bryant (1794–1878), first collected in his 1832 *Poems*. Famous for its description of Berkshire scenery, the poem also recounts the "sad tradition" of an "Indian maiden" who throws herself from a precipice because she cannot "root out" her love for her cousin, "incestuous" according to "the morality of those stern tribes." Sedgwick may be inviting a comparison between the Indian lovers and Magawisca and Everell.
2. Sedgwick is referring to James Fenimore Cooper's *The Last of the Mohicans* (1826).
3. "Whip-poor-will" (Sedgwick's note).
4. The quotation, slightly altered, is from William Wordsworth (1770–1850), *The Excursion* (1814), Book 1, "The Wanderer" (215–16).

Chapter VIII

1. From *A Key into the Language of America*, Chap. 21, "Of Religion, the soule, &c." Despite his commitment to religious toleration, Williams here concurs with Jennet in viewing Indian religion as satanic.

2. Exodus 36.8, 11; the passage consists mostly of measurements.

3.   " '—— —— —— *About the cliffs*
            Lay garlands, ears of maize, and skins of wolf,
            And shaggy bear, the offerings of the tribe
            Here made, to the Great Spirit; for they deemed,
            Like worshippers of the olden time, that God
            Doth walk on the high places and affect
            The earth—o'erlooking mountains.'
                                        ——BRYANT."

(Sedgwick's note; the quotation is from "Monument Mountain," 96–102.)

Chapter IX

1. "My Nanie O," by the Scottish poet, Robert Burns (1759–96) celebrates the simple life of a "country lad."

2. Physiognomy and phrenology were nineteenth-century pseudosciences that claimed to be able to judge character from physical appearance (facial features in the case of physiognomy, the conformation of the skull in the case of phrenology).

3. The concept of *vacuum domicilium* served to legitimate European seizure of Indian land. Jennings traces its formulation back to Winthrop, who was by training a lawyer: "Responding to scrupulous objections against seizing Indian property, Winthrop declared in 1629 that most land in America fell under the legal rubric of *vacuum domicilium* because the Indians had not 'subdued' it and therefore had only a 'natural' and not a 'civil' right to it" (*Invasion* 82).

4. The royalist Lucius Cary, second Viscount of Falkland (c. 1610–43), sought to make peace between royalists and Puritans during the English civil war, first as a member of Parliament (1640–42), then as Secretary of State to Charles I (1642–43).

5. The Congregationalist minister John Wilson (c. 1591–1667) shared the pulpit of the First Church of Boston with John Cotton from 1633–52 and accompanied the Puritan troops as chaplain in the expedition against the Pequots. Wilson

represented a stricter brand of Puritan orthodoxy than Cotton.

6. Edward Johnson (1598–1672) is best known for his history, *The Wonder-working Providence of Sions Saviour in New England* (1654). Written in response to criticisms of the New England Way, it presents New England as the site of the new heaven and new earth prophesied in the book of Revelation. The quotation is from Chap. 20.

7. Everell is (mis)quoting from *As You Like It*, III.iv.7. His dialogue with his companion parodies Rosalind's dialogue with her friend Celia about Orlando, Rosalind's lover. In III.ii, Rosalind, disguised as a man, has proposed to cure Orlando of his love for her, and he has accepted the offer. Here, Rosalind complains to Celia, "His very hair is of the dissembling colour," and then takes it back, saying "his hair is of a good colour." Sedgwick is obviously inviting readers to compare Rosalind with Roslin.

Chapter X

1. *Il Penseroso* (1631?) by John Milton (1608–74) hails "divinest Melancholy" as "pensive Nun" and "Goddes sage and holy." This poem is paired with *L'Allegro*, which invokes the joyful "Goddes fair and free," "The Mountain Nymph, sweet Liberty." Together the poems assert the need for balance between these opposing moods. Sedgwick similarly pairs Esther Downing with Hope Leslie, who is "an allegro to her [Esther's] penseroso" (144).

2. "Emmanuel Downing (1585–1660), lawyer, emigrated to Massachusetts Bay in 1638 and then returned to England at least once before settling in Salem, Massachusetts, in 1654. He and Lucy Winthrop Downing, John Winthrop's sister, had four daughters, Lucy, Anne, Martha, and Dorcas, born between 1625 and 1640." (Note by Mary Kelley to Rutgers University Press edition of *Hope Leslie*.)

3. Sedgwick refers to Anne Hutchinson (see Chap. 2, n. 4, above) and her disciple Mary Dyer (d. 1660).

Chapter XI

1. From the opening paragraph of the *Magnalia Christi Americana* (1702), Book 2, Chap. 4, by Cotton Mather (1663–1728). This famous history of Puritan New England by one of its leading theologians characterizes the various Puritan founders as reembodiments of Old Testament figures. Winthrop is the American Nehemiah.

2. Sedgwick refers to Sir Walter Scott (1771–1832), who typically set the scenes of his novels with summaries of historical events.

3. Sedgwick refers to Thomas Morton (1579?–1647?), who names Winthrop "Joshua Temperwell" in his *New English Canaan* (1637). See Chaps. 23, 25, 28, and 30.

4. Miantunnomoh, also spelled Miantonomi and Miantonomo, was one of the two principal chiefs of the Narragansetts, the most powerful Indian nation in the vicinity of Providence. Though they had allied themselves with the English in the Pequot War, they had aroused Puritan hostility by criticizing the ruthlessness of English warfare. Increasingly isolated after the Pequot War, and concerned about English occupation of Pequot territory promised to the Narragansetts in return for their cooperation, the Narragansetts sought to organize a pan-Indian uprising against the English. While proposing such an alliance to his former enemy, the Mohegan chief Uncas, in 1643, Miantonomo was captured and turned over to the English, who tried and convicted him of murdering another Indian, but allowed Uncas the privilege of executing him with "mercy and moderation" (Bradford 331).

5. "The characteristic conduct of the Narragansett chief is transferred to our pages from Winthrop, who thus describes it. 'When we should go to dinner, there was a table provided for the Indians, to dine by themselves, and Miantunnomoh was left to sit with them. This he was discontented at, and would eat nothing till the governor sent him meat from his table. So at night, and all the time he staid, he sat at the

lower end of the magistrate's table' " (Sedgwick's note; the quotation is from Winthrop's *History* 2:82).

6. The Massachusett chief Chicatabot (also spelled Chickataubut) visited Winthrop in Boston in 1631 and presented him with "a hogshead of Indian corn" (*History* 1:48–49). Frequently mentioned in the *History*, he died of smallpox during the epidemic of 1633.

7. Agur's prayer is recorded in Proverbs 30.1–33. Perhaps relevant here is the verse: "Remove far from me vanity and lies: give me neither poverty nor riches; feed me with food convenient for me" (30.8).

8. Absalom, third son of David, slew his half-brother Amnon for having raped Absalom's sister Tamar. Forced to flee, Absalom was later reconciled with David, but four years after being taken back into the paternal fold, he led a conspiracy against his father and was killed. Winthrop seems to imply that Absalom's rebellion arose from David's "too great indulgence" in forgiving Absalom's earlier crime and that Hope's rebelliousness will bear equally dangerous fruit if not curbed.

9. William Hubbard (c. 1621–1704) is, of course, the Puritan historian whose account of the Pequot War Sedgwick is revising.

Chapter XII

1. "Love" (33–36), from *Alnwick Castle, with Other Poems* (1827) by the Connecticut-born poet, Fitz-Greene Halleck (1790–1867), an acquaintance of Sedgwick's.

2. Sedgwick is quoting the description of "The *Mother* wi' her needle and her sheers" in "The Cotter's Saturday Night" (43–44) by the Scottish poet Robert Burns (1759–96).

3. "Mr. Mathews, (nice observer as he is) as well as many other foreigners, mistakes in adding an *s* to this word for the plural" (Sedgwick's note.) Sedgwick refers to Charles Mathews (1776–1835), a popular English comedian whose "At Home" shows toured the United States and Britain. One of these

shows consisted of a "lecture" mimicking national "peculiarities" he had observed on his trip to America.

4. Samuel Gorton (c. 1592–1677) founded a sect that denied
the doctrine of the Trinity; rejected the ordinances of the
church and the authority of paid ministers, claiming that
each believer could be his or her own priest; and held that
by becoming one with Christ, believers could partake of
God's perfection. Fearing he would spread his heresies, Puritan authorities drove him out of several colonies before he
bought land from Miantonimo and settled with his followers
in Warwick, Rhode Island. The Massachusetts Bay Colony
challenged the sale through two sachems who had become
client-subjects of the colony and in 1643 Gorton and his
followers were arrested, brought to Boston for trial, convicted of blasphemy, and exiled.

5. The quotation is from Hubbard's *A General History of New
England, from the Discovery to MDCLXXX* (1682, rpt.
1848) 402.

6. The antiquarian James Savage (1784–1873) edited Winthrop's *History*, and his annotations influenced Sedgwick's
portrayal of Gorton; see 2:57–59n.

7. Emanuel Swedenborg (1688–1772), a Swedish scientist
turned mystic who wrote many volumes of visionary works,
attracted considerable interest among American intellectuals
in the 1820s. A Swedenborgian church had been founded in
Boston in 1821. In her characterization of Gorton here,
Sedgwick is quoting from both Savage's note and Winthrop's text (*History* 2:57–59n., 142–43).

8. "This was the first burial place in Boston; and as early as
the year 1630, consecrated by the interment of Mr. Johnson,
who died of grief for the loss of his wife, the Lady Arabella,
'*the pride of the colony.*' 'He was,' says Winthrop, 'a holy
man and wise, and died in sweet peace.' And another contemporary historian says, that he was so beloved that many
persons requested their bodies might be interred near his"
(Sedgwick's note; see Winthrop's *History* 1:34).

Volume II

Chapter I

1. Shakespeare, *Henry VIII* III.i.30–32. Queen Katharine, the first of Henry VIII's six wives, is here addressing Cardinals Wolsey and Campeius, who have been conspiring to have her marriage annuled.

Chapter II

1. From *New-England. Or a Briefe Enarration of the Ayre, Earth, Water, Fish and Fowles of that Country. With a Description of the Natures, Orders, Habits, and Religion of the Natives* (1625), a promotional tract in verse by the Anglican minister William Morrell, who had spent two years in Plymouth and Massachusetts Bay. The poem portrays the Indians as in need of enlightenment by Christian missionaries and exhorts readers to help build "An *English* Kingdome from this *Indian* dust."
2. Job 39.5, 7: "Who hath sent out the wild ass free? . . . He scorneth the multitude of the city, neither regardeth he the crying of the driver."
3. From Morrell's *New-England*.
4. Maqua was another name for Mohawk (used, for example, by Cooper in *The Last of the Mohicans*).
5. Hubbard 28 (abridged and slightly altered).
6. Hubbard 53 (slightly altered).

Chapter III

1. The speaker is Rosalind in Shakespeare's *As You Like It* II.iv.4–5. Disguised as a man, she is searching for her father in the forest of Arden. Rosalind's determination to resist giving in to tears, because "doublet and hose ought to show itself courageous to petticoat," invites comparison with Rosa/Rosalin's less successful masculine pose. The play is highly relevant to the cross-dressing episodes in *Hope Leslie*.

2. The quotation (slightly altered) comes from a letter of May 1, 1634, written by Thomas Morton to his friend William Jeffery or Jeffries. Jeffery passed it on to Winthrop, who entered it into the record of Morton's trial and incorporated it into his *History* (2:190–91); see also 1:138n.

3. Thomas Morton (1579?–1647?), an Anglican, headed the colony of Merry Mount at Mount Wollaston. The Plymouth pilgrims regarded him as a threat because he welcomed indentured servants into his colony on equal terms, sold guns to the Massachusett Indians (enemies of Plymouth), conducted a prosperous fur trade with them, and erected a Maypole (an English folk tradition with pagan roots, abominated by the Puritans), inviting the Indians to join in dancing around it. Bradford's *Of Plymouth Plantation*, Chap. 19, tells of how troops from Plymouth under Miles Standish attacked the colony and took Morton prisoner. Morton tells his side of the story in *The New English Canaan* (1637), his satiric name for the pilgrims' would-be new Israel.

4. Another quotation from Morton's letter to Jeffery, in Winthrop's *History* 2:191. Sir F. George is Sir Ferdinando Gorges, who had obtained a charter to the Plymouth region in 1620 and who headed the Council for New England that issued the Plymouth colony's patent. The Massachusetts Bay colonists went over the heads of Gorges and his Council to secure their patent directly from Charles I. Gorges disputed the legitimacy of this patent, and Morton and Sir Christopher Gardiner testified in favor of Gorges's claims to the land the Massachusetts Bay colony occupied.

5. George Villiers, first Duke of Buckingham (1592–1628), chief minister of Charles I, led England into an ill-fated war with France in 1627, during which he laid siege to the Isle of Rhé. The siege failed, and the English lost more than a third of their soldiers in the retreat. Walter Leslie's role in the siege remains undocumented, but there was a Count by that name (1606–67) who served in many military campaigns.

6. Houris were beautiful maidens who served the blessed in the Muslim paradise. Because of its Islamic associations, the

word always connotes illicit sexuality to Christian writers. Hence, Gardiner suggests that Rosa would have found a fitting place in Morton's orgiastic colony of Merry Mount.

7. Gardiner is quoting from Shakespeare's *Twelfth Night* I.iv.31–32, another comedy highly relevant to the subplot with Rosa. The lines are addressed by Duke Orsino to Viola, who, like Rosa, is masquerading as a page.

8. In Milton's *Paradise Lost* (1667), Ithuriel is one of the angels sent by God to guard Adam and Eve. Finding Satan "Squat like a Toad, close at the ear of Eve," "Ithuriel with his Spear/ Touch'd lightly; for no falsehood can endure/ Touch of Celestial temper, but returns/ Of force to its own likeness: up he starts/ Discover'd and surpris'd" (4.800, 810–14).

Chapter IV

1. Shakespeare, *Romeo and Juliet* II.ii.102–5. In this famous scene, Juliet has been soliloquizing on the balcony about her love for Romeo when he overhears her and the two proceed to exchange vows. The literary allusion applies in different ways to Hope and Esther.

2. "A fact gravely stated in Governor Winthrop's journal" (Sedgwick's note; see *History* 2:20).

3. Thomas Reid (1710–96), Dugald Stewart (1753–1828), and Thomas Brown (1778–1820) were all Scottish common sense philosophers, the reigning school of thought in Sedgwick's day.

4. Translated from old French into English, the song means:
     And in truth I remind you
     God and love are in agreement
     God loves good sense and respect,
     Love does not hold that in contempt;
     God hates pride and falseness,
     And Love loves loyalty
     God loves honor and courtliness
     And in no way hates true Love;
     God heeds beautiful prayer
     Love does not neglect that.

5. Shakespeare, *Hamlet* I.ii.141–42. Mrs. Grafton is paraphrasing Hamlet's praise for his father's loving treatment of his mother.

6. *Nil desperandum*, no need for despair.

Chapter V

1. Shakespeare, *Midsummer Night's Dream* III.ii.199–201. As a result of a spell cast by the goblin Puck, Lysander, who has eloped with Hermia, falls in love instead with her friend Helena. In the lines quoted, Helena reproaches Hermia with having forgotten their childhood friendship and joined in a conspiracy to humiliate her. The reproach is relevant to Hope and Esther.

Chapter VI

1. Milton, *Comus* 350–51. In this passage the two brothers serving as her protectors are searching for the Lady, who has taken refuge from the harassment of Comus in a shepherd's cottage, not realizing that the shepherd is Comus in disguise. Hope's perils are similar.

2. "One Captain John Chaddock, son of him that was governour of Bermuda," is mentioned several times in Winthrop's *History* (2:149–50, 153). Most relevant here is the following: "[S]o soon as they came on shore, they fell to drinking, &c. and that evening, the captain and his master being at supper and having drank too much, the captain began to speak evil of the country, swearing fearfully, that we were a base heathen people" (2:149–50).

Chapter VII

1. This is the opening sentence of Williams's Chapter 21, "Of Religion, the soule, &c.," in *A Key into the Language of America*.

2. As Mary Kelley points out, "Sedgwick took a slight liberty with the description of Miantunnomoh in John Winthrop's

History of New England." Winthrop nowhere uses the word "sagacious," although he does say of Miantonimo, "for we knew him to be a very subtle man" and "[i]n all his answers he was very deliberate and showed good understanding in the principles of justice and equity, and ingenuity withal." Both quotations are from 2:81 and refer to Miantonimo's behavior on the occasion that culminated in his protest against being seated at a separate table at dinner. For a different historical perspective on Miantonimo and the alleged conspiracy, see Jennings 260–61.

3. The quotation, slightly altered, is from Samson's speech to Dalila in Milton's *Samson Agonistes* (1671) 871–72.

4. Menenius Agrippa is the faithful friend and counsellor of Caius Marcius Coriolanus in Shakespeare's *Coriolanus*. Banished from Rome, Coriolanus bids him farewell in the words Sedgwick quotes: "Thou old and true Menenius,/ Thy tears are salter than a younger man's,/ And venomous to thine eyes" (IV.i.21–23). Sedgwick may also be inviting readers to compare Hope with the principled but proud and inflexible Coriolanus.

5. In keeping with his masquerade as a Puritan, Sir Philip is quoting William Bradford's explanation for an outbreak of "sundry notorious sins," including "drunkeness and uncleanness," sexual "incontinency" between unmarried people, and "that which is worse, even sodomy and buggery." As Bradford puts it, when "streams are stopped or dammed up," instead of being "suffered to run quietly in their own channels," "they flow with more violence"; similarly, "wickedness being here more stopped by strict laws . . . it searches everywhere and at last breaks out where it gets vent" (*Of Plymouth Plantation*, Chap. 32).

6. Sedgwick may be referring subtly to Bradford's charge that Morton's crew invited "the Indian women for their consorts, dancing and frisking together [around the maypole] like so many fairies, or furies, rather; and worse practices" (*Of Plymouth Plantation* Chap. 19).

7. In his *Key into the Language of America*, Roger Williams translates "Manit, mannitówock" as "God, Gods." He fur-

ther explains: "Besides there is a generall Custome amongst them, at the apprehension of any Excellency in Men, Women, Birds, Beasts, Fish, &c. to cry out *Manittóo,* that is, it is a God. . . . and therefore when they talke amongst themselves of the *English* ships, and great buildings, of the plowing of their Fields, and especially of Bookes and Letters, they will end thus: *Manittówock* They are Gods" (Chap. 21).

Chapter VIII

1. Shakespeare, *Romeo and Juliet* IV.ii.46–47. The speaker is Juliet's father, who is ironically unaware that Juliet is about to take a potion meant to put her into a deathlike sleep.
2. Jennings writes of these events: "The Gortonoges stood trial in a court where their prosecutors were also judges and jurors. . . . [Gorton] and his associates received indeterminate sentence to hard labor in chains, and they were scattered to various towns to perform it. This proved to be a tactical error by the magistrates. The Gortonoges could not be kept quiet even under the harsh terms of their punishment, and their story got around. Such a trial, and particularly the denial of rights under English law, produced disturbance among the people, and murmurings arose. . . . Gorton *et al.* were suddenly unchained and exiled . . . with . . . sentence of death for return to Massachusetts" (271–72).
3. Echoing the same biblical passage, Winthrop would make the same argument in 1645, after being tried and acquitted of charges that he had abused his power. True Christian liberty, he claimed, is "exercised in a way of subjection to authority. . . . The woman's own choice makes such a man her husband; yet being so chosen, he is her lord, and she is to be subject to him. . . . Even so, brethren, it will be between you and your magistrates. If you stand for your natural corrupt liberties, and will do what is good in your own eyes, you will not endure the least weight of authority, but will murmur, and oppose, and be always striving to shake off that yoke; but if you will be satisfied to enjoy such civil and lawful liberties, such as Christ allows you, then will you

quietly and cheerfully submit unto that authority which is set over you, in all the administrations of it, for your good" (*History* 2:229–30).

Chapter IX

1. Shakespeare, 1 *Henry IV* II.iv.262–64. The speaker is Prince Hal, who has caught Falstaff in a barefaced lie and exposed him as a coward. Note the parallel with Sir Philip Gardiner.
2. "We believe we have anticipated by three or four years, this title, so well earned and generally bestowed. We cannot pass the hallowed name of Eliot, without pausing earnestly to beseech our youthful readers to study his history, in which they will find exemplified, from youth to extreme old age, the divine precepts of his master. He was the *first protestant* missionary to the Indians; for nearly half a century their instructor, friend, and father; and when, during the war with the terrific Philip of Mount Hope, fear had turned every hand and heart against them, and their utter extinction was regarded by most, as necessary to the salvation of the English colonies, Eliot was still their indefatigable and fearless advocate. The christian philanthropist will delight to follow this good man through his diocess of Indian churches; to see him surrounded by his simple catechumens, dealing out the bread of life to them; to go with him to his 'prophet's chamber' at Natick—that apartment prepared by the love of his Indian disciples, and consecrated by his prayers; and finally, to stand by his bedside when, in extreme old age, like his prototype 'the beloved apostle,' all other affections having melted into a flame of love. 'Alas!' he said, 'I have lost every thing. My understanding leaves me. My memory—my utterance fails me; but I thank God my charity holds out still. I find that grows rather than fails.'

"His name has been appropriately given to a flourishing missionary station, where the principle on which he at all times insisted is acted upon, viz: 'that the Indians must be civilized, as well as, if not in order to their being christianized.' This principle has no opposers in our age, and we cannot but hope that the present enlightened labours of the followers of Eliot, will be rewarded with such success, as shall convert the faint-hearted, the cold, and the skeptical, into ardent promoters of missions to the Indian race" (Sedgwick's note; see also Vol. 1, Chap. 1, n. 5, above).

3. Viscount Horatio Nelson (1758–1805), vice admiral of the English Navy, defeated the French at the decisive battle of Trafalgar, but was mortally wounded three hours before its outcome. Robert Southey's *The Life of Nelson* (1814) notes that Nelson went into battle wearing "as usual, his admiral's frock coat, bearing on the left breast four stars, of the different orders with which he was invested. Ornaments which rendered him so conspicuous a mark for the enemy, were beheld with ominous apprehensions by his officers. It was known that there were riflemen on board the French ships; and it could not be doubted but that his life would be particularly aimed at" (341). Sedgwick later made a "thrilling" pilgrimage to Nelson's ship, the *Victory* (see *Letters from Abroad to Kindred at Home* 1:17–18). The comparison with Nelson elevates Magawisca to heroic stature. Like Magawisca, Nelson had also lost an arm in a previous battle.

4. The second chapter of Daniel tells of the Babylonian king Nebuchadnezzar's troubling dream, which only Daniel succeeds in divining and interpreting. In the dream Nebuchadnezzar sees a "great image," whose head is "of fine gold, his breast and his arms of silver, his belly and his thighs of brass, His legs of iron, and his feet part of iron and part of clay." A stone smites the feet of the image, which then falls to pieces. Daniel interprets the dream as a prophecy that Nebuchadnezzar's kingdom will be succeeded by a series of lesser kingdoms until God destroys them all and establishes his eternal kingdom. Magawisca's judge applies this story to the Pequots, whose "kingdom" has also been destroyed. The quotation that follows is from Jeremiah 46.28. The preceding verses prophesy that God will deliver all of Israel's enemies "into the hand of Nebuchadnezzar."

5. "This reply of Magawisca, we have somewhere seen given as the genuine answer of an Indian, to the solicitation of a

missionary, but are not able now to refer to our authority" (Sedgwick's note). Sedgwick's "authority" was Heckewelder's *Account of the History, Manners, and Customs of the Indian Nations*, 187.

6. In Acts 19.28, 34 when Paul is preaching to the Ephesians, the makers of idols mobilize opposition to him, arguing that he is destroying their business and threatening to destroy the great temple of Diana at Ephesus. The Ephesian mob then chants this slogan in defense of their temple. Magawisca's opponent accuses the onlookers at her trial of being as easily swayed as the Ephesians.

Chapter X

1. Burns, "My Tochers the Jewel" (13–16), a satirical song addressed by a woman to a suitor who is courting her for her dowry ("tocher").

2. Sir Richard Varney, the arch villain of *Kenilworth* (1821) by Sir Walter Scott (1771–1832), is as "honest" as Sir Philip Gardiner. To help his lord, the Earl of Leicester, achieve his ambition of marrying Queen Elizabeth, Varney murders Leicester's wife. Sedgwick "saluted [*Kenilworth*] with as much enthusiasm as a Catholic would a holy relic" when she read it in 1821 (*Life and Letters* 118).

Chapter XI

1. Shakespeare, *Macbeth* II.iii.147–50. Macduff has just informed the princes Malcolm and Donalbain of the murder of their father, King Duncan. Malcolm concludes that he and his brother should flee before the murderer strikes them. The epigraph suggests that the characters in this chapter are choosing to flee for similar reasons.

2. In I Samuel 19–20, King Saul tries to kill David, because he fears he is becoming too popular and may usurp the throne. Saul's son, Jonathan, who loves David, intercedes for him and when this fails, helps David to escape. In the Greek myth, the musician Orpheus descends into the underworld

to reclaim his wife, Eurydice, from death. Granted permission to take her with him back to the world of the living on condition that he not look back, Orpheus forgets his promise and loses Eurydice forever. The two stories are relevant in different ways to the rescue of Magawisca.

3. Cradock seems to be misapplying scripture in the two instances he cites. In 1 Kings 22.8–28 and 2 Chronicles 18, Jehoshaphat, King of Judah, advises Ahab, King of Israel, to consult the prophet Micaiah before deciding whether or not to go into battle. Contrary to Ahab's other prophets, who tell him what he wants to hear, Micaiah warns Ahab that he will not return from the battle alive. Jehoshaphat receives no warning not to assist Ahab. Perhaps relevant here, however, is that Ahab tries to escape his fate by exchanging clothes with Jehoshaphat. Despite the ploy, Ahab is slain and Jehoshaphat survives to enjoy a long and prosperous reign. In 2 Chronicles 35.20–24, Josiah, king of Judah, dies when he refuses to heed the words of the Egyptian king, Necho, telling Josiah "from the mouth of God" to "forbear thee from meddling with God, who is with me, that he destroy thee not."

Chapter XII

1. "The Fatal Sisters" (1761) by the English poet Thomas Gray (1716–71) is a translation based on a Norse saga. Akin to the Greek Fates, the twelve sisters weave the web of destiny, but their thread consists of human entrails, and their role is to weave the destiny of soldiers in battle, choosing whom to "doom" and whom "to spare." Sedgwick quotes lines 51–52.

2. Shakespeare, *Antony and Cleopatra* IV.xv.74–75. The speaker is Cleopatra, who indeed acknowledges that she is no longer a sovereign but a woman commanded by passion.

3. In the mid-seventeenth century the Spanish Caribbean island of Tortuga became a haven for escaped indentured servants, fugitive slaves, sailor deserters, and other malcontents, who maintained themselves by hunting, plundering, and piracy.

The term buccaneers originated from "boucans," a Carib word for the wooden grills they used to barbecue their meat.

4. A figure straight out of medieval romance himself, the villainous knight Sir Philip appropriately cites that repository of romance, Sir Thomas Malory's *Le Morte D'Arthur*. The quotation is from the sixth tale in the cycle, "Gawain, Ywain, and Marhalt," and refers to the episode in which Ettard, the "lady of Sir Gawaine," is put under a spell by the Damesell of the Lake, causing her to fall in love with her detested suitor, Sir Pelleas.

5. Genesis 16 tells the story of Hagar, the Egyptian bondslave of Sarah, by whom Abraham has a son, Ishmael, with Sarah's permission when Sarah is unable to conceive. Sarah ultimately becomes jealous, accuses Hagar of treating her with contempt, and drives her into the desert. Contrary to Rosa's (or Sedgwick's) interpretation, however, Hagar does receive a sign of God's bounty: the promise that her seed will multiply "exceedingly."

6. According to Winthrop's *History*, Chaddock's ship indeed blew up when "two barrels of [gun]powder took fire" after a crew member struck fire with a pistol; "five of the men being in the cabin were destroyed," but three survived "very much scorched" (2:150). Rosa's gesture of throwing her lamp into a barrel of gunpowder also evokes the Gunpowder Plot masterminded by the Catholic conspirator Guy Fawkes, who was caught with slow matches and a lighted dark lantern, preparing to blow up the houses of Parliament.

Chapter XIII

1. Bryant's "An Indian Story" (1824), first collected in his 1832 *Poems*, tells of an Indian bride abducted by a "ravisher," but restored to her home by her husband, who kills her kidnapper. Sedgwick quotes from the last stanza. The tale invites comparison with Faith Leslie's abduction and rescue.

2. "Among the various conjectures respecting the etymology of the word Massachussetts, the following communicated by Neal, appears the most satisfactory. 'The sachem who gov-

erned this part of the country, had his seat on a hill, about two leagues to the southward of Boston. It lies in the shape of an Indian arrow-head, which is called in their language, 'Mos,' or 'Mons.' A hill in their language is, 'Wetusett,' pronounced in their language Wechusett; hence the Great Sachem's seat was called 'Moscutusett,' from whence, with a small variation, the province received the name ' of Massachusetts.'—*History of Boston*.

"This hill is in the town of Quincy, and is now known by the name of 'Sachem's hill' " (Sedgwick's note).
3. Mary Kelley gives the following translation:
> "Being near the shore
> Makes many drown."

Chapter XIV

1. Mary Kelley identifies the author as the Italian poet and librettist Metastasio (1698–1792), and translates the lines as follows:
> "Enough, I understand you
> You have already explained yourself;
> And would say less to me
> Were you to say more."

Chapter XV

1. The French moralist Francois, the sixth Duc de La Rochefoucauld (1613–80) is famous for his cynical *Maximes* (1665), which remorselessly dissect human motives. The quotation is from *Maximes* CDLXXIII, which translates as: "However rare true love may be, it is still less so than true friendship." Hope's friendships with Esther and Magawisca belie that cynical maxim.
2. In 1643 Miantonimo requested permission to wage war against Uncas, who had attacked one of the Narragansett chief's kinsmen and tributaries. Winthrop replied that "we should leave him to take his own course." Uncas succeeded in capturing Miantonimo, however, and when Miantonimo

asked to be "delivered to his friends the English," they took him prisoner instead, accused him of plotting against them, and returned him to Uncas for execution. For further details, see Jennings 266–68; Winthrop 2:129, 129–34; and Bradford 330–32. For a different interpretation of what occurred between Miantonimo and Uncas, see Salisbury 232–33.

3. Thomas Dudley (1576–1653), who arrived on the *Arbella* with Winthrop, served several terms as governor of Massachusetts. Early historians often played him off against Winthrop to make Winthrop look more humane. The incident Sedgwick cites has been dismissed by modern historians as apocryphal. Sedgwick's source was probably Thomas Hutchinson's *The History of the Colony of Massachusetts-Bay* (1764).

4. Esther is paraphrasing 2 Corinthians 11.17: "That which I speak, I speak it not after the Lord, but as it were foolishly, in this confidence of boasting."

5. The quotation (slightly altered) is from Milton's *Lycidas* (1637) 12–13.

6. Sedgwick is paraphrasing Oliver Goldsmith (1728–74), *Retaliation* (1774), which says of Edmund Burke that he "to party gave up, what was meant for mankind" (32).

FOR THE BEST IN PAPERBACKS, LOOK FOR THE

In every corner of the world, on every subject under the sun, Penguin represents quality and variety—the very best in publishing today.

For complete information about books available from Penguin—including Puffins, Penguin Classics, and Arkana—and how to order them, write to us at the appropriate address below. Please note that for copyright reasons the selection of books varies from country to country.

In the United Kingdom: Please write to *Dept. JC, Penguin Books Ltd, FREEPOST, West Drayton, Middlesex UB7 0BR.*

If you have any difficulty in obtaining a title, please send your order with the correct money, plus ten percent for postage and packaging, to *P.O. Box No. 11, West Drayton, Middlesex UB7 0BR*

In the United States: Please write to *Consumer Sales, Penguin USA, P.O. Box 999, Dept. 17109, Bergenfield, New Jersey 07621-0120.* VISA and MasterCard holders call 1-800-253-6476 to order all Penguin titles

In Canada: Please write to *Penguin Books Canada Ltd, 10 Alcorn Avenue, Suite 300, Toronto, Ontario M4V 3B2*

In Australia: Please write to *Penguin Books Australia Ltd, P.O. Box 257, Ringwood, Victoria 3134*

In New Zealand: Please write to *Penguin Books (NZ) Ltd, Private Bag 102902, North Shore Mail Centre, Auckland 10*

In India: Please write to *Penguin Books India Pvt Ltd, 706 Eros Apartments, 56 Nehru Place, New Delhi 110 019*

In the Netherlands: Please write to *Penguin Books Netherlands bv, Postbus 3507, NL-1001 AH Amsterdam*

In Germany: Please write to *Penguin Books Deutschland GmbH, Metzlerstrasse 26, 60594 Frankfurt am Main*

In Spain: Please write to *Penguin Books S. A., Bravo Murillo 19, 1° B, 28015 Madrid*

In Italy: Please write to *Penguin Italia s.r.l., Via Felice Casati 20, I-20124 Milano*

In France: Please write to *Penguin France S. A., 17 rue Lejeune, F-31000 Toulouse*

In Japan: Please write to *Penguin Books Japan, Ishikiribashi Building, 2–5–4, Suido, Bunkyo-ku, Tokyo 112*

In Greece: Please write to *Penguin Hellas Ltd, Dimocritou 3, GR–106 71 Athens*

In South Africa: Please write to *Longman Penguin Southern Africa (Pty) Ltd, Private Bag X08, Bertsham 2013*